Algernon Sidney Johnston

Memoirs of a Nullifier

With a Historical Sketch of Nullification in 1832-33

Algernon Sidney Johnston

Memoirs of a Nullifier
With a Historical Sketch of Nullification in 1832-33

ISBN/EAN: 9783337014551

Printed in Europe, USA, Canada, Australia, Japan

Cover: Foto ©Raphael Reischuk / pixelio.de

More available books at **www.hansebooks.com**

AUTOBIOGRAPHICAL

RECOLLECTIONS.

BY THE LATE

CHARLES ROBERT LESLIE, R. A.

EDITED,

WITH A PREFATORY ESSAY ON LESLIE AS AN ARTIST,
AND SELECTIONS FROM HIS CORRESPONDENCE,

By .TOM TAYLOR, Esq.,
EDITOR OF THE "AUTOBIOGRAPHY OF HAYDON."

WITH PORTRAIT.

BOSTON:
TICKNOR AND FIELDS.
M DCCC LX.

Albemarle Street, London, *April* 30, 1860.

Messrs. TICKNOR AND FIELDS :

DEAR SIRS, — Acting on behalf of the representatives of the late
Mr. LESLIE, R. A., I have great pleasure in placing in your hands
the early sheets of that eminent Artist's "Memoirs and Correspondence" for exclusive publication in the United States; believing that
you, as personal friends of the late Mr. LESLIE, will be most disposed to promote the interests of the work and of the family.

I remain, Dear Sirs,

Yours very faithfully,

JOHN MURRAY.

RIVERSIDE, CAMBRIDGE:

STEREOTYPED AND PRINTED BY

H. O. HOUGHTON AND COMPANY.

EDITOR'S PREFACE.

It is owing to the innate modesty of the late Mr. Leslie's character, that in his Autobiographical Recollections the part occupied by himself and his pictures is small in comparison with that devoted to his contemporaries and friends. So great is my respect for Mr. Leslie, that I have hesitated long before giving to the world any more about him than he had thought fit himself to prepare for publication.

But when I took into account his claims to consideration as a painter, I felt strongly that readers must wish to know more about the man than he had himself told them — more about the circumstances and influences under which his pictures were produced; the present state and locality of these pictures; their subjects; the way in which those subjects are treated, and the general characteristics of his style.

I have therefore attempted, in an Introductory Essay, to classify and describe such of Leslie's more important works as I have been able to examine personally, and to give a general appreciation of his artistic qualities, and his position in the English school.

I have, further, selected from the correspondence placed

at my disposal, the parts bearing on the painter's works, and on his life as connected with his works. Without such an addition to the Autobiographical Recollections which Leslie had himself made ready for posthumous publication, this volume would not — as it seems to me — have contained the information required to give it its proper place among the artistic biographies of the time — such lives as have been published, or are preparing, of Wilkie and Constable, Etty, Haydon, and Turner.

In using the matter entrusted to me, I have been guided by the strongest regard and respect for the painter, and for the family that is left to lament the irreparable loss of such a husband, brother, and father. I have endeavoured to bear in mind, always, the modesty, tolerance, and good taste which ruled throughout Leslie's life and labours; and to respect the time and patience of my readers. Affectionate admiration for my subject may, however, have in some cases misled me as to what was worth printing about him — having regard, at least, to the wider public. I have little fear that the many friends of Leslie, and the large circle of them who, like myself, have loved and bene-fited by his works, will think I have extracted too much from his letters, or that I have rated the man or his pictures too highly.

His son, Mr. George Leslie, writes thus to me, of the manner in which the Autobiographical Recollec-tions were composed : —

" The manner in which my father's autobiography was writ-ten was this. He was in the habit of writing down accounts of anything of importance that occurred to him all his life, and it is from these notes and from letters which he collected, that the autobiography you have was composed.

"We have reason to believe that he commenced it about ten years ago, writing in it from time to time. The reason it ends abruptly was not on account of failing health, but because all the time he could spare from his painting was, during the last year of his life, occupied by him in writing the life of Sir Joshua Reynolds, at which he worked hard even a month before his death."

TOM TAYLOR.

AUTHOR'S PREFACE.

My object has been to preserve in these pages some recollections of those chiefly whom I could praise; and of them, not the faults and foibles that are more or less common to all men, but the merits that are rare, and on which alone their claims to distinction rest. I mention this that I may not be charged with dealing too much in panegyric.

C. R. LESLIE.

CONTENTS.

———◆———

INTRODUCTION.

ON LESLIE'S PICTURES.

IT has been my lot to be entrusted with the arrangement for the press of two artistic autobiographies — that of Haydon, and that of Leslie. It is difficult to imagine a completer contrast than is formed by the characters, lives, and works of these two painters. Haydon presents to us a nature all self-confidence, passion, and combativeness. He was exclusive in his theories; reckless in his defiance of difficulties; unscrupulous in the means he took to relieve them; untiring in his appeals to patrons, and public men, and the public. Regarding himself as a martyr to High-Art, he claimed to the full all the immunities and indulgences that the most lenient and sympathetic judgment could attach to that position. Alternately elated with the most buoyant hope and depressed by the deepest despair — fighting, struggling, appealing, asserting himself his whole life through, he closed a stormy and sorrowful career by suicide. But through all this tempestuous life, he loved his art passionately, and was truly and deeply attached to his wife and his children. His pictures seem to me to reflect at once his lofty aims and his practical short-comings. Their unquestionable power and vigour are marred by ever recurring evidences of haste, slovenliness, coarseness, and lack of taste.

In Leslie, on the other hand, we see the man of cautious, trustful, respectful nature from the first. Slow in the formation of his judgment, disposed to defer to others in his art and out of it, but strong in principle, and apt to hold stubbornly to convictions once grasped; not given to court notoriety or publicity, and rather shrinking from than provoking conflict; asking only leave to pursue the even tenor of his way in the practice of the unambitious art he loved, among the quiet friends he valued; equable, affectionate, self-respecting to the point of reserve and reticence; valuing good taste and moderation as much in art as in manners; averse to exclusive theories or loud-sounding self-assertion in all forms; closing a happy, peaceful, successful, and honored life, by the calm and courageous death of a Christian, and leaving behind him pictures stamped in every line with good taste, chastened humour, and graceful sentiment — pictures which it makes us happier, gentler, and better to look upon — pictures which help us to love good books more, and to regard our fellow-creatures with kindlier eyes.

The lessons of two such lives ought not to be written in vain. For power, passion, and variety; for curious revelation of character, eloquent criticism, and vivid sketching of men and manners, the little Leslie has left written is altogether unworthy of comparison with those bulky records of himself from which I selected the materials for the autobiography of Haydon. But scanty, and comparatively colourless, as Leslie's remains may be, they are of value in throwing light on the character, as well as on the works, of the painter — that part of him which alone has an interest for us.

Before entering on the subject of Leslie's pictures

in detail, I think it essential to fair appreciation of the painter and the man, to give the reader such knowledge as I can of his method of working, and of his daily habits.

" His painting-room," says his son George, " differed from those of most artists in one point. He never hung up any of his own works or studies on the walls, but had a great many fine examples of other painters — chiefly copies by himself from the old masters. He considered that an artist who fed his eye with his own works was sure to get into a mannered style of painting. He painted in the simplest manner, always trying to get his work like in tone and colour to the object he painted from as *soon* as possible. He had a particular objection to the practice of preparing his work in one colour, to be afterwards altered to another by glazing. He used to say, that unless you possessed a most extraordinary knowledge of the chemical, as well as modifying, qualities of colours, it was always very uncertain whether you would obtain by that means the exact tint you wanted.

" He was very quick in working, especially in painting heads ; I don't think he ever kept a model more than two hours at a time, and generally finished a head the second day, though he frequently rubbed his work out, if it was not satisfactory to him, and painted it in afresh. I have often sat to him, and he had always finished before I was tired.

" He very seldom praised his own work ; but I have often seen him laughing at some expression that pleased him in his picture.

" In giving instruction to young artists he used to say very little, but he would take the palette and brushes himself, and show them a great deal. He never, however, took this trouble with any student for whom he felt there was no hope. He was kind to all young artists, and never spoke to them in the way of criticism without some qualifying expression, such as, ' I may be wrong,' or ' Perhaps you are right.'

" His palette was always kept clean, and he put more colour on it than he thought he should use, as he said he hated a *starved* palette. On the same principle he provided himself with a most liberal supply of brushes, in the choice of which he was a little different from most artists I have seen work. He used a great many more sable brushes than any other, and was especially fond of very small ones, with which he put the delicate touches on his heads.

" He worked very steadily and cheerfully, keeping up a sort of whistling at times, which I think he was unconscious of, as he was always absorbed in thinking about what he was painting. I remember him once walking about looking for his palette-knife, which he was holding in his hand all the time.

" He had a very pretty habit of going into the garden before breakfast and picking either a honeysuckle or a rose — his favourite flowers — and putting them in a glass on the mantel-shelf in his painting-room. I hardly ever saw his room in the summer without these flowers, and we have a little sketch of a rose, which he picked and brought into the house so gently that he did not disturb a beautiful little moth on it.

" He took a great interest in astronomy. His knowledge of this science was very slight, but the pleasure he had in the various appearances in the heavens was unbounded, so much so, that he used to say an eclipse seemed to take place on purpose for his pleasure. He once said to me that he thought it very likely that part of our happiness in the next life would be derived from finding out the wonders of the creation which are hidden to us here.

" He entertained the greatest veneration for all celebrated scientific men, and once had a correspondence with Professor Faraday on the blue colour of the sky. The Professor's kind replies delighted my father beyond measure."

The following was the usual distribution of his day : —

" He would rise," writes his son, " about eight o'clock in the winter, and about seven in the summer, when he would walk in the garden before breakfast. He had breakfast at nine, and enjoyed the newspaper very much, taking great interest in politics, or any topic that occupied the public attention. He always read a chapter in the Bible to us all afterwards, and then, about half-past nine or ten, he would commence work, sometimes being read to at the same time. He did not object to the presence of any of his family in his room, but sometimes, when very busy, he would turn us out, especially the younger ones, whom he called 'trudies,' his corruption of intruders. He was never irritated by anything whilst at work, but seemed always calm and happy. He was rather absent in his mind about trivial things. He would sometimes strike a carpet-pin, mistaking it for a lucifer match, and was very apt to forget people's names, unless connected in some way with his art. But if any one possessed a fine picture, however commonplace and uninteresting that person might otherwise be, he always remembered his name, and was always ready to go and see him.

" He lunched at one, and would generally leave off work about four o'clock, when he would go out, but seldom without some object, as to see pictures at the auction-rooms, or to call on people who possessed pictures.

" He dined generally at six o'clock, and, after a nap, would either play at chess, which he was very fond of, or else would read to us from Shakespeare or ' Don Quixote,' and sometimes passages from 'Tristram Shandy.' He was very fond of having friends to see him in the evening, though unless his company possessed some knowledge of the art he took but little pleasure in them."

The Petworth Collection is richest in Leslie's pictures of all our private galleries — having regard to the merit, if not the number, of the pictures it contains. After Petworth must be ranked the galleries of Mr. John Naylor at Leighton Hall, Welshpool, Mr. Edwin Bullock and Mr. Joseph Gillott at Birmingham, Mr. Thomas Miller at Preston, and Mrs. Gibbons in the Regent's Park, London. Our National Gallery, especially the Sheepshanks collection, is, happily, richer than even the richest of these. *

---

* The Duke of Bedford, the Earl of Essex, Mr. Harris, Mr. Bates, Mr. Bicknell, Mr. Thomas Baring, Mr. Heugh, Mr. Newsham, Mr. W. C. Sole, and other collectors in this country, possess important pictures of this master. There

It is pleasant to me to think that so many of Leslie's pictures should have found a home among the mills of Lancashire and the smoking forges and grimy workshops of Birmingham. They are eminently calculated to counteract the ignobler influences of industrial occupation by their inborn refinement, their liberal element of loveliness, their sweet sentiment of nature, their literary associations, and their genial humour. I can speak from personal observation to the real appreciation of these pictures in such places, not on the part of their possessors only, but among the many, both masters and workmen, to whom these galleries are so liberally opened. Leslie testifies in one of his letters to the extraordinary change which he had lived to see in the source and spread of patronage for the painter. The nobleman is no longer the chief purchaser of contemporary pictures. It is mainly to our great manufacturing and trading towns that the painter has to look for the sale of his works. The class enriched by manufactures and commerce is now doing for art in England what the same class did in earlier times in Florence, Genoa, and Venice, for the art of Italy; in Bruges, Antwerp, and Amsterdam for that of the Low Countries and Holland. The change may have its evil as well as its good. There may be some risk that it will multiply the manufacture and increase the homeliness of pictures, to say nothing of less direct and obvious ill-consequences.

But against such risks is to be set the likelihood that purchasers of this class will, in the main, insist upon something like fidelity to nature, and truthfulness of expression and sentiment. They are rarely beset by prejudice in favour of old schools or time-honoured conventionalities; *ceteris paribus*, they are likely to prefer pic-

are others in America, in the collections of Col. Lenox of New York, and Mr. Joseph Miller of Virginia, U. S.

tures which are the growth of the time, and appeal to the time, to those which belong to the past, and speak to the past — or, in other words — living to dead art.

In Mr. Naylor's collection the painter may be studied in his earliest and latest manners, — in the 'Sir Roger de Coverley going to Church' (1819), (the original picture painted for Mr. Dunlop), and the 'May Day in the time of Queen Elizabeth' (1821); and in one of the last works of his pencil, 'The Interview of Jeanie Deans and Queen Caroline' (1859).

The two former pictures demand notice first as works of a time when Leslie was most himself; that is, when he had felt the influence of neither of two painters who materially affected his later practice — Newton on the one hand, and Constable on the other.

Both these pictures are simply painted, with a due admixture of solid and glazing colour; and neither shows the least sign of impaired tone or failing surface. They are as bright and sunny in effect, and as free from crack or decay, as when first painted.

The original 'Sir Roger' is finer in tone than the repetition. Parts of it indicate a close study of Hogarth, especially the old yeoman who stands to receive the Squire's greeting, with his fresh, pretty daughter on his arm. In the latter I recognise the lady who, some four or five years after the picture was painted, became the painter's wife. Sir Roger, in his full suit of crimson velvet, on his way up the pathway to the little church, pats on the head the widow's children, who look up to him with round, wondering eyes. Their mother is a sweet and comely rustic matron. The head of Sir Roger, Leslie tells us in his Life of Constable, was painted from an old Royal Academician, Mr. Bigg,* likelier to go down to posterity in this picture

---

* "I thought him," he says, "in appearance and manners, a perfect speci-

of Leslie's than in any of his own works. The Spectator, who accompanies Sir Roger, is commonplace enough. But he is, after all, but a colourless personage in Addison's own hands. The rustics who line the pathway are all true to nature. Besides the group of the old man and daughter already described, there is a full-blown young woman, sticking a flower into her boddice, and a moon-faced labourer, in a smock frock, looking over her shoulder, both quite worthy of Hogarth. Even in this picture — painted in 1819, when the painter was only twenty-four, — there is no observable deficiency either in drawing, colouring, or composition, or in linear or aërial perspective.

I should say at least as much for the ' May-Day,' in which, besides all these merits ·in the figures, there is shown a power of effective landscape-painting, of which Leslie has left us few examples. The scene may be supposed to be in Kent. The foreground is a knoll, from which the eye ranges over a wide stretch of level and richly cultivated woodland, with a distant manor-house and church. Overhead is a bright spring sky, with wreaths of sunlit cloud. The family and guests of the manor-house furnish the foreground groups, the principal of which is made up of a fantastically dressed gentleman of the court in crimson velvet, and the rustic beauty of the manor to whom he is paying euphuistic court. She timidly accepts his offered hand for the dance, hardly understanding the meaning of his quaint and far-fetched phrases. She wears a tawny robe, over a blue petticoat. To the right of the foreground, a stately Elizabethan dame, in farthingale of scarlet and gold, and ample ruff, looks on at the sports, while her jester behind her in red, yellow, and green motley, slyly

men of an old-fashioned English gentleman. He was one of the most amiable men who ever existed."

draws an ass in a lion's skin on the buckler of one of the blue-coated serving-men, who complete the right-hand group. A little further off, to the left, are gathered, in reclining groups on the grass, or standing under the trees, the rest of the gentry, who have assembled to watch the shooting at the butts and the May games, in full swing on the green below. You see part of the line of the merry morris-dance, where the meadow falls beyond the foreground. These dancers are drawn and grouped with a spirit and freedom not unworthy of Rubens. Near them stands the old sable-clad schoolmaster — rod in hand, and spectacles on nose — who watches the dancers himself, reverently and fearfully watched the whole time by a group of his small scholars, who clearly are not satisfied that the rod is there by mere inadvertence of habit. On the level sward in the distance sits the May Queen under her arbour, while before her sweeps the merry rout of masquers round the May-pole — Robin Hood and Maid Marian, Much and Scathelock, Little John and Friar Tuck, with the fool, the dragon and the hobby-horse, surrounded by a ring of applauding village spectators. As we look, we seem to feel the fresh soft spring breeze among the trees; to hear the clashing peal from the steeple, mingled with the pipe and tabor, and the sound of joyous carouse, over beef and ale, from the booth beyond.

I know no blither, brighter, more exhilarating picture. There is masterly skill, and truth above all, in its distribution of light and shadow, always so difficult in a day-light, open-air picture, with many figures. The well-known engraving by Watt does justice to it.

Next in order of time, to these pictures, come those in the gallery at Petworth. First of these stands 'Sancho and the Duchess.' Of all Leslie's pictures this is probably the most popular, and in none are his peculiar merits more gracefully and happily displayed. The incident is fully described in the passage * from Shelton's translation of Don Quixote, which accompanied the picture in the Academy catalogue for 1824.

In the expressions of the actors, the painter has caught the very spirit of the scene. Sancho half-shrewd, half-obtuse, takes the Duchess into his confidence, with a finger laid along his nose; his way of sitting shows that he is on a style of seat he is unused to. Chantrey sat to Leslie for the expression of the Sancho, and his hearty sense of humour qualified him to embody the character well. The Duchess's enjoyment breaks through the habitual restraint of her high breeding, and the grave courtesy of her Spanish manners, in the sweetest half-smile — a triumph of subtle expression. The sour and literal Doña Rodriguez is evidently not forgetful how Sancho, on his arrival, had desired her to have a care of Dapple. The mirth of the whispering waiting-maids culminates in the broad sunshiny grin of the mulatto-woman. Nor has Leslie ever been happier in the composition of any picture.

All the accessories are painted with fine finish, the nicest sense of propriety, and careful attention to effects of direct and reflected light. Petworth was a treasure-house to Leslie of old-world wealth in furniture, jewellery, china, and toilet ornaments; and during his visits there he made careful and numerous studies of such objects. Here he saw and studied such things in their places, which may help to account for the naturalness and propriety with which they are always introduced by him.

The three versions † of this subject are full of varia-

* See correspondence of that year.

† I might have said *four*, for I have just learnt that there is a fourth Sancho, which had found its way to the United States, and is now in this country, in the gallery of Mr. Farnworth. Leslie painted a good deal upon it after its ar-

tions in detail. Leslie never repeated a picture exactly. In the Petworth picture the principal light falls upon the lovely face and white satin robe of the Duchess, and is carried out by the lightish green china vase to the left. In the Vernon repetition, the principal light is focussed by the white and gold pilasters, conducted thence by the Duchess's head and shoulders, and the duenna's white apron, — which is wanting in the Petworth original, — and carried out to the left by the open music-book and the back of the chair; while on the right it is continued in both by the shoulder of the mulatto, the head-dress and collar of one of the waiting women, and Sancho's shining bald pate. The Petworth Sancho has blue breeches: the Vernon Sancho is dressed entirely in black and drab. In the original picture the Duchess's inner robe is a pure silvery satin, deliciously painted; the outer robe a delicate purplish grey; in the Vernon picture her inner dress is a light golden yellow: her saccque a darker purple lined with green. The wall to the right, in the earlier version, is covered with green tapestry. This tapestry is red, with a blue border in the later one. There is no picture of the Duke on the wall behind the Duchess in the Petworth original, as there is in the Vernon repetition. The dress of the waiting damsel in the foreground of the earlier version is a warm salmon colour; it is russet green in the other; and the flower on the toilet-table is red in the former, white in the latter picture. In the quality of its colour the Petworth picture is, to my mind, immeasurably finer than either the version of the subject painted for Mr. Rogers, or that painted for Mr. Vernon.

The lines of the composition are the same in all three pictures; and the general distribution of the light and

rival here from North America; but not having seen this picture I can say nothing of its variations from the others.

shade is identical, though the objects which make up
the balance of colour are varied in each, with great
pains, and thorough knowledge.

The Rogers picture brought eleven hundred and fifty
guineas at the sale of the poet's gallery. Mr. Leslie
was present. A country dealer seated beside him, who
had been absent from the room when the picture was
knocked down, seeing that Mr. Leslie had noted the
prices in his catalogue, asked to look at it. " Good
gracious me! Eleven hundred and fifty guineas for
Leslie's picture! Did you ever hear of such a price,
sir?" "Monstrous, is it not?" said Leslie, who told
the story to his family with great glee on his return
home.

The Petworth picture is singularly rich and harmonious in effect, and transparent throughout in its painting. It is, I think, altogether, for expression, composition, and colour, the finest example of the painter, and
exhibits him in the very prime of his powers, and while
under the influence of Newton as a colourist and workman. But the surface has cracked slightly, owing to
the incautious use of glazing colours — asphaltum,
above all, that most fatal.to durability of all pig-
ments. The repetitions, though less glowing, are both
in perfect preservation, and are solidly and simply
painted, with a very cautious use of glazing. They
both belong to the period when Constable's influence
had superseded Newton's, and when Leslie was satisfied that his pictures should look white and chalky
while fresh, in the faith that they would mellow with
time. His practice exemplifies the only case in which
the colour of pictures does really change for the better.
Leslie's later works have mellowed in a very noticeable
degree. I can myself perceive that even his latest and
weakest pictures — the ' Jeanie Deans ' for example —

have improved wonderfully in the short period which has elapsed since they were painted.

After the ' Sancho,' the most interesting picture at Petworth is the ' Catherine and Petruchio.' This is the first version of the subject, of which the Sheepshanks' picture is a repetition with variations. For example, the remains of the meal on the table to the right of the spectator are quite different in the two, though touched in both with a precision worthy of Teniers. In this case also the colour of the Petworth picture is superior in glow and power, and I did not detect in it any sign of cracking. In their disposition of colours, the two pictures are very much alike; but we have only to compare the satin gown, which is the object of Petruchio's rage, in the one and in the other, to recognise how much more powerful Leslie was in his management of colour in 1832, than at the later date of the Sheepshanks' picture.

The ' Introduction of Gulliver to the Queen of Brobdingnag,' (1835) appears to me a mistake in subject, and a very inferior work of the painter's in all technical respects. Instead of the Brobdingnagians looking like giants, Gulliver looks like a pigmy. The colour, tried by Leslie's own standard, is violent without being rich, and for the first and last time, as far as I know, in Leslie's pictures, appears to me unrefined and inharmonious.* The only passage of humour worthy of the painter is the face of the old lady, who is curiously examining the strange little creature through her eye-glass, and the look of the farmer's little girl who is crying for the loss of her plaything. The other Petworth pictures — ' Lady Carlisle carrying the pardon to her Father in the Tower, and ' Charles II. at Tillietudlem ' — must be classed

---

* Another picture very closely resembling this in the quality of its colour, is the ' Columbus,' now in the Collection of Joseph Gillott, Esq.

in the second rank of the painter's works. The first subject is hardly a paintable one. It is impossible to convey, by a momentary expression, the conflict in the Duke's mind between the temptation of liberty, the stubbornness of parental authority outraged by his daughter's marriage against his will, and the haughty consciousness of innocence, which kept him so long a prisoner when the least submission or effort might have opened his dungeon door. Nor is there anything very available for the painter in the Duke's "three magi," — Harriot, Warner, and Hughes; nor does one see very clearly what part Raleigh is taking in the action of the picture. Perhaps the point of effect, after all, is in the contrast of the eager, fluttering young woman, and the serene abstraction of the two learned prisoners, and their three aged companions in study, thus startlingly broken in upon. The stately old lady of Tillietudlem gives a better opportunity to the painter, and he has indicated her delighted pride in the King's salute, in his happiest manner. There is Lesliean humour too, in the introduction of Cuddie Headrigg as an attendant stripling, gazing, open-mouthed, upon the royal visitor.

To those who feel an affection for Leslie, Petworth is almost as interesting for its associations with the painter's life and works as for his pictures to be seen there. It was here that he was able to study the forms and colour of rococo furniture — of tapestried chairs, China jars and monsters, broad Venetian mirrors, gorgeous brocade and damask hangings, and massive silver and silver-gilt plate, still in daily use. You may see at Petworth, where Leslie is still affectionately remembered by the old servants, the screen and chairs which he has painted in the ' Rape of the Lock ;' the old globe, introduced in the ' Lady Carlisle ;' the carved mirror and jewelled casket of the Duchess's toilet-table ; Sophia

Western's China jars, and console; the window, with
its look out on the swelling slopes of the park, where
sweet Lady Jane Grey sits absorbed in Plato, while the
hounds and horns are making merry music in the sunshine without. Here is the very Gainsborough which
Constable tells Leslie he could not " even think of without tears in his eyes," and the Bassan which Leslie was
allowed to have up in his bed-room; Vandyke's Lady
Anne Carr, which showed him the height to which high-
bred grace and loveliness could be carried in portraiture; Titian's Catherine Cornaro, to reveal the still deeper
magic of diffused Venetian splendour. Here too, among
some of Turner's finest landscapes, and Romney's most
bewitching repetitions of Lady Hamilton's haunting
face, the visitor will find the ' Jacob's Dream,' the masterpiece of Leslie's early friend Allston, a correct but cold
Academic production, with a grace that seems to belong
half to Westall, half to Raffaelle; and the ' Contemplation,' of the same painter, a female figure of a conventional cast of beauty, in a somewhat affected attitude,
backed by a mannered landscape.

Don Quixote was a favorite source of subjects to
Leslie. Besides his thrice repeated ' Sancho in the
apartment of the Duchess,' we owe to the same book
many of the painter's best pictures. As first of these
in date after the ' Sancho' should be mentioned, ' Don
Quixote while doing penance in the Sierra Morena,
deceived by the disguised Dorothea and the Barber.'
The picture belongs to the Earl of Essex, for whom it
was painted, and has been well engraved.

The Knight of the Rueful Countenance, "all naked
to his shirt, lean and yellow," courteously promises to
redress the wrongs of the " fair princess Micomecona,
Queen of the Great Kingdom of Micomeca in Ethiopia." Dorothea kneels before the knight in her gor-

geous attire — " a whole gown of very rich stuff, and a
short mantle of another green stuff, and a collar, and
many other rich jewels," — while her train is borne by
the masquerading Barber, who kneels before the mules,
with much-ado keeping on the beard that hangs down
to his girdle, " half red and half white, as being made of
the tail of a pied ox." Sancho whispers the mysterious
lady's quality in his master's ear, while the Don's armour hangs like a trophy on the cork-tree to the right.

The knight is an admirable conception, dignified,
courteous, and gentle in his craziness; and quite indifferent to his scanty costume, in his anxiety to relieve the
injured princess. Leslie was the very man to appreciate the noble side of Don Quixote's character; and
even if his own refinement had not revealed this side
to him, he had ample opportunity of learning it from
Coleridge's exposition of the profound conception of
Cervantes. This picture is another good example of
the painter's best time as a colourist; but it is not superior in this respect to the little sketch of the subject in
the National Collection, which is quite Venetian in its
glow of harmonious colour.

I know only from the engraving the head of Don
Quixote painted in 1827. Perhaps Ogilvie sat for it —
an old friend of Irving's and Leslie's. He was certainly
one of his models for the knight. Another was an old
Frenchman — a protégé of Constable's — called Fon-
taine. But I think I trace Leslie's own features in
the Don Quixote of Mr. Bates's picture, and I am told
by his son that he was much in the habit of studying
expressions from his own face. He painted a head of
Sancho too, in 1827. But the admirable ' Sancho ' in
the Sheepshanks' Collection is of the date of 1839.
This is the engraved head. Sancho sits at his Tan-
talus-table, in the sumptuous palace of his capital of

Barataria, the laced bib under his chin. You see the hand of the physician Don Pedro Regio de Aquero, holding the whalebone rod at whose touch the dishes vanish from before the hungry Governor. We may suppose the partridges to have been borne away by tap of rod, followed by the boiled conies and the veal — and last but worst — the olla podrida. Sancho's choler is just rising to that point at which, after threats to do for the physician, he bids them let him eat, or else take his government again: for " an office that will not afford a man his victuals, is not worth two beans." Leslie painted the scene in full for Lady Chantrey, in 1855. I will not venture to speak of the merits of that picture from my half-effaced recollection of it in that year's Exhibition, and it was not within my reach while preparing these remarks. But the Sheepshanks' ' Sancho ' all can see, at cost of a visit to South Kensington. More truthful humour was never put on canvas of the same dimensions by any painter at any period. The hot, hungry impatience, and indignant questioning expression of the face are irresistible. It is only a pity that, to enjoy the picture thoroughly, one must know one's Don Quixote well. As a piece of sound, solid painting, this head ranks high among Leslie's minor works. Chantrey may have aided Leslie as a model for the expression. But the head was painted, his son George tells me, from the family fly-driver. The Dulcinea which hangs near it might as well be called by any other name. It is neither the Dulcinea indicated in Cervantes, nor a Spanish peasant-girl at all. Probably the painter never gave it the name of Dulcinea.

The picture painted for Mr. Bates in 1849 represents the Duke's chaplain leaving the table in disgust at his lord's encouragement of Don Quixote's delusions. The canvas is of the largest dimensions ever ventured on by

Leslie. In a rich hall of noble decorated architecture is spread a stately table, covered with silver plate, fruit, and wine in chased flagons. Don Quixote, in the centre, in his straight hose and chamois doublet, draped in "the fair mantle of finest scarlet," which the two beautiful damsels had cast upon his shoulders on entering the castle, drawn up to his full height, and "trembling from head to foot like a man filled with quicksilver," is delivering that impassioned and grave rebuke to the vulgar Canon — " Is it, happily, a vain plot or time ill spent, to range through the world not seeking its dainties but the bitterness of it, whereby good men aspire to the seat of immortality? . . . . Some go by the spacious field of proud ambition; others by the way of servile and base flattery; a third sort by deceitful hypocrisy; and few by that of true religion. But I, by my star's inclination, go in the narrow path of knight-errantry; for whose exercise I despise wealth, but not honour; I have satisfied grievances, rectified wrongs, chastised insolencies, overcome giants, trampled over spirits." By the hidalgo's side stands Sancho, just risen to vindicate himself and his master. The Duke, in black velvet doublet and purple hose, is enjoying the wrath of the indignant churchman, hiding his laughter behind his hand. The face of the gentle Duchess, who looks up at the angry confessor from among her attendant damsels, is irradiated with one of those latent half-smiles, by the charm of which Leslie has enabled us almost to excuse in her the thoughtlessness that could find matter for mirth and practical joking in the wreck of Don Quixote's noble nature. The puzzled but well-disciplined attendants stand round, doing their best to suppress all expression in their looks. In the fore-ground the indignant ecclesiastic is sweeping out of the room with protesting hands outstretched, and an angry flutter of his ample black robes, his fat, vulgarly-imperious face swollen and inflamed with rage — " Your Excellency is as mad as any of these sinners ; and see if they must not needs be mad, when wise men canonise their madness. Your Excellency may do well to stay with them, for whilst they be here I'll get me home, and save a labour of correcting what I cannot amend."

I am inclined to think this the finest picture, both in point of expression and technical qualities, painted in the latter half of Leslie's career. Its tone is luminous and rich, without blackness. The architectural features are peculiarly graceful and stately. The figure of the chaplain is admirably conceived and perfectly natural ; in the angry insolence of the attitude and countenance you see the overbearing indignation of the narrow-minded man, accustomed to lay down the law and to be listened to — and now bearded by a madman! Don Quixote is thoroughly earnest and dignified ; Sancho inimitably quaint and sturdy. The plate and dessert on the table are painted with the greatest relish, and a precision worthy of Teniers. Leslie had· a passion for fine old silver, and preferred its pictorial effect to that of gold plate. He made the most careful water-colour studies of every thing on the table, down to the figs, grapes, and melons, and borrowed the plate for painting from Storr and Mortimer's, I believe. Mr. E. M. Ward, the Royal Academician, stood for the figure of the attendant, near the entrance in the back-ground, and his brother for the Duke. He had Spanish models for some of the other heads. The Duchess, in her dove-coloured robe and ruff, is only second, for high-bred charm, to the Duchess of the Petworth picture.*

---

* I gather from the extracts in the Royal Academy Catalogues, that Leslie used Shelton's — the raciest and oldest — translation of the masterpiece of Cervantes, made in the reign of Charles the Second.

There is a little picture in the collection of Mr. Joseph Gillott, at Birmingham, of the Duke and Duchess reading 'Don Quixote.' It has a sober power in its colour, and a quiet gracefulness in its composition that make it very noticeable in spite of its small size.

After Addison and Cervantes, Leslie resorted for subjects to Shakespeare, Molière, Swift, Pope, Sterne, Fielding, Goldsmith, and Smollett. Besides his illustrations of books, he painted portraits, a few subjects from English and Spanish history, some from the New Testament, and a very few from his own invention. I propose to notice briefly the principal works in each of these classes. As he began and ended with Shakespeare, — painting 'Murder' from 'Macbeth,' as his first picture, in 1813, and 'Hotspur and Lady Percy,' as his last, in 1859 — and as he took more of his important compositions from our great dramatic poet than from any other single source, I notice the Shakespeare subjects first:

The 'Merry Wives of Windsor,' for reasons one can easily understand, was a special favorite with Leslie. Its life-like, genial pictures of English country manners in the days of Elizabeth, and its copious introduction of marked types of humorous character, gratified the painter's peculiar tastes, and suggested capital subjects for his pencil. The play is eminently English in feeling, and Leslie was "ipsis Anglis Anglior." He loved and knew the quiet meadows and shady elms of Windsor, and all the green borders of the Thames from Hampton to Maidenhead. I have no doubt he believed, with perfect faith, in the inmates and visitors at Ford's and Page's. They were to him actual men and women, and not clothes-pegs. He painted the scene of 'Slender's Courtship' three times, besides the early picture of the garden scene, with Anne inviting her bashful

admirer in to dinner. I have seen none of these pictures, and only know their composition from the plates.
The former has been well engraved for the American
Art Union, from which I infer that one of the three versions of the subject is now in America.

The scene is an oak-panneled parlour in Page's house.
Anne stands in the bay window, with the summer light
glowing in her pretty face and on her rounded figure, as
she plucks a flower to pieces to give herself a countenance. Slender stands afar off, hat in hand and looking
half sheepish, half scared, and wholly silly; while Shallow, in his velvet coif, with an emphatic crutch-handled
stick to give point to his periods, spurs him on to his
wooing. Judging from the engraving, the picture must be
a peculiarly sunny one, suggesting pleasant country life
in low-roofed old oak-panneled rooms, with buck's heads
over the doors, moral saws carved over the heavy man-
tel-pieces, iron dogs on the hearths, a pleasant breath
of lavender and honeysuckle from the garden without,
and glimpses of the castle and the park oaks, through
the broad, stone-shafted, deep-bayed lattice windows.
I have little doubt all these interiors were painted from
real houses. They have a look of such genuine truth.
It is in the chief room of such a house that he has twice
painted Page's dinner-party — with the pippins and
cheese on the side-table — first in 1831, and afterwards
in 1838. The second picture is at South Kensington.
He has been happier, I think, in later Falstaffs. The
fat knight, in chamois doublet and long boots — a bottom of sherris-sack in his glass — is passing compliments with Mrs. Ford and Mrs. Page, who stand arm-
in-arm a little behind him — two plump, comely, sly-
looking matrons, in whose faces the painter has cleverly
indicated their mutual understanding and quiet resolve
to have their will of the greasy old cozener. Page, with

his broad back to the spectators, swings back in his
chair, offering a cool tankard to poor Slender, who, with
Simple in attendance behind him, fidgets uncomfort-
ably on the edge of his stool, his embarrassing beaver
and gloves beside him, not daring to lift his eyes to
demure Mistress Anne, sitting coyly apart on her own
side of the table. Ford is draining his glass higher up
the board, beyond the group formed by Bardolph and
Pistol, who are noisily claiming Sir John's ear. Shallow, at the opposite end of the table to Page, is directing
Sir Hugh Evans's attention to the progress of Slender's
sheepish wooing. Through the broad window behind
the justice the creepers and trees of the garden make a
pleasant rest for the eye. The side-table, on the right
of the fore-ground, is spread with the immortal pippins
and cheese, painted with that truth and relish which
Leslie always puts into the accessories of his pictures,
but not so daguerreotypically wrought as to divide and
distract attention from more important matters. Over
the broad fire-place is one of those gnomic inscriptions,
once common in English country-houses, and the logs
are smouldering — summer as it is — against the fire-
dogs on the open hearth. The picture is a fine example
of the painter's middle manner, without any dangerous
use of asphaltum, (of which the visitor may see the
charm and danger exemplified in Newton's ' Bassanio '
in the same room,) and equally free from such excess of
chalky-white as is apparent in the ' Who can this be ? '
just over it. Attention should also be directed to the
masterly perspective of the picture, both linear and
aërial. This is evidently a chamber to be walked about
in, with room and verge for the fair long table, the guests
and servants.

A later ' Falstaff ' may be compared with this, in Mr.
Harris's picture of the fat knight personating the king

before Prince Hal, Poins, Dame Quickly, and the other
actors in the scene at the Boar's Head, from ' Henry the
Fourth.' This picture was painted in 1851, and, though
it is surpassed in technical qualities by the Sheepshanks
picture, I prefer its Falstaff, for conception and character, to the earlier one. No doubt Leslie felt and meant
to indicate the superior humour and raciness of Shakespeare's great creation in its original form. Here Falstaff has just assumed his cushion-crown and his foot-
stool-state, and is lecturing the Prince who stands before him with a well-expressed air of mock respect.
Francis, the lank drawer, setting down a pottle of sack,
glances up with the expression of one who humbly
asks leave to enjoy the fun, while his mistress, Dame
Quickly, in full giggle, seems to say, ' Oh, the Father!
How he keeps his countenance.' Poins looks criticiz-
ingly on, leaning on one of the joint-stools, which we
may suppose he has an itch to vault over, half-jealous of
the way the knight is making as his young master's tav-
ern-joker in ordinary. But even in this orgie Leslie has
contrived to give us a refreshing glimpse of pure and
lovely nature, in the flowers strewed over the floor,
which he has painted with most affectionate delicacy
and faithfulness. Whole sheets of studies in oil for
these flowers were among the relics of the painter sold
at Foster's a few weeks ago. They must have cost him
many a day's labour. But this he never spared — painting and repainting even the minutest accessories, till he
had brought every detail in his picture up to his own
high standard. Nor was his labour done when he had
painted such things from nature. There was as much
thoughtful work afterwards in subordinating and gener-
alizing these studies, to suit their place, purpose, and
relative importance in his composition. In this point,
as in so many others, Leslie's example is of especial

value in these days of over-emphasized and unbalanced
elaboration. His picture from 'The Taming of the
Shrew' I have already noticed. From the 'Winter's
Tale' he painted two subjects — the 'Autolycus,' a picture projected and partly painted before 1823, but not
exhibited till 1836 ; and the 'Perdita,' exhibited the following year. Both are now in the Sheepshanks collection, and deserve to rank among the best works of this
period. The former represents the scene where Autolycus is puffing his pedlar's wares among the shepherds
and shepherdesses outside the old shepherd's cote. The
knave, with his box of trinkets and trumpery about his
neck, is just twanging off the title of his wonderful
ballad " of a fish that appeared upon the coast, on
Wednesday the four-score of April, fifty thousand
fathom above water, and sung the ballad against the
hard hearts of maids." Mopsa and Dorcas are scanning
the pedlar's toys with greedy eyes, while another shepherdess listens entranced to the tale, " very pitiful and
as true," and the clown, eager for ballads, bids the rogue
" lay it by." The sky is a bright and breezy blue, with
white clouds. Beyond is a stretch of level mead, with
the far-off sheep feeding, and to the right of the group
is the mountain ash, with its red berries, which Leslie
introduced by the advice of Constable.

In this picture, at least, the influence of the last
named painter upon Leslie is seen under its pleasantest
form — in the delightful character of summery open-
air freshness and breeziness, which indeed it needed no
secondary influence to make Leslie feel, but in the representation of which Constable's counsel and example
powerfully helped him. For my own part, I feel this to
be, on the whole, the most cheery and 'happy' work of
the painter. It is free from chalkiness, and its colour is
bright and harmonious. I should have been thankful

'for the absence of the vermilion cap which Autolycus wears; but to Leslie no picture was complete without its vermilion element, though I think he has seldom managed it with the felicity which gives the colour such value in the De Hooghes and Terburgs, from whose practice he adopted it. Irving particularly admired the expression and character of Autolycus, and, as I think all who study the picture, must admit, with good reason. In the ' Perdita ' by its side, the painter has not fallen behind the exquisite sentiment of Shakespeare's scene, in which the royal shepherdess distributes the flowers to her guests. Perdita herself, is one of the sweetest and most graceful creatures ever embodied upon canvas; and the painter has never, as far as I know, exceeded this most graceful conception for loveliness and unaffected charm. Exception may be taken to the colour and texture of the scarf over her shoulders, which looks more like oiled silk than any other material. Nor can I admire the disguised Polixenes and Camillo; nor does the Florizel seem to me worthy of such a Perdita. Leslie painted a Hermione from the same play for Mr. Brunel, but I cannot speak of this picture from recent examination.

' Henry the Eighth ' was another of Leslie's favourites among the historical plays. He has painted no fewer than five pictures from it — two repetitions of Catherine's dying scene, where through Capucius she commends her daughter and her women to the king: and two of the same sick and dethroned queen in her palace at 'Bridewell, where she addresses one of her women —

> " Take thy lute, wench; my soul grows sad with troubles,
> Sing and disperse them if thou canst."

The former date in 1850. Of the latter the first was

Leslie's diploma picture in 1826 : the second was painted in 1842. There is in all a pathos befitting their incidents. I cannot help thinking the smaller repetition of the former subject, in the collection of John Naylor, Esq., finer in chiaroscuro and colour than the original picture painted for Mr. Brunel. Another picture from the same play represents the moment, from the fourth scene of the first act, when Henry at the masque in York Place pulls off his vizard and makes himself known to the Lord Cardinal. A warm glow of lamplight is diffused over the picture. The king — the central figure in the group of masquers and ladies, in a tunic of gold and scarlet, leading fair Anne Boleyn in his hand — reveals himself to Wolsey with a laughing face and a jovial rollicking swing of his brawny body — not yet that mountain of flesh which Holbein painted. Wolsey comes forward from his seat on the dais under the canopy of state, to " make his royal choice " — a wily, smooth, politic priest, with a subtle blending of inward imperiousness and outward respect in his bearing. But the picture does not rise, either in expression or execution, beyond the second rank among the painter's works.

If Leslie ever painted a sweeter head than the Perdita, it is certainly the ' Beatrice,' running like a lapwing, her mantilla thrown over her shining brown hair, through the sun and shade of the pleached garden alley, to listen to the gossip of Hero and Ursula. No wonder he was often called on for repetitions of this bewitching picture. The original is in the gallery of Mr. Gibbons, and I have often wondered how it has so long escaped the graver. This is Beatrice in her arch natural loveliness of feature and mien — not Benedick's biting, gibing, persecutrix. In its sober yet sunny harmony of colour the slightly-painted garden background forms a setting worthy of the sweet face and lovely stooping figure.

'Twelfth Night' supplied him with a twice-painted subject — Sir Toby Belch encouraging Sir Andrew Aguecheek to accost Olivia's roguish maid Maria. The original picture was painted in 1842 for Mr. Thomas Baring: the repetition in 1850 for Mr. Edwin Bullock. It is hard to say which is the better picture, and this is true of several of Leslie's repetitions. In both, the Sir Toby is admirable — a better embodiment of Shakespeare's conception, I am inclined to think, than Leslie's Falstaff. Probably the latter defies the painter for the same reason that he defies the actor; the character has too many shades, too subtly blended, for complete realization either on the boards or on canvas. It is worth noting how nicely Leslie has discriminated Sir Andrew Aguecheek and Slender, two characters which on the surface seem so like each other. The feeble conceit and pretension of the shallow Illyrian knight are rendered with a thorough appreciation, which imparts an expression to his face and figure quite different from that of the sheepish, but comparatively simple-minded Windsor franklin. The Maria is an arch little shrew; very different in dress and feature in the two pictures, but in both true to the character drawn by Shakespeare. In point of transparency and richness of colour, especially in the background — an oak panelled room, with a palma-like portrait on the wall half hidden by a crimson curtain — the latter picture is the better of the two, but it shows rather a greater tendency to that blackness which was always one of Leslie's besetting sins, as he was quite conscious. He twice painted the subject of Olivia showing her face to Viola, from the same play, and a sketch for a third version of this incident was on his easel at the time of his fatal attack. Mrs. German Reed, when Miss Priscilla Horton, sat to him in Covent Garden green-room in her costume of

Fortunio, as a model for the Viola. But I have not seen the pictures. The sketch sold after his death was very sunny and brilliant in effect.

From Milton Leslie painted but one subject — the Lady in Comus with the Enchanter presenting to her the Circean Cup. His fresco from this incident in the summer-house in Buckingham Palace garden, though cold and dry in colour, and poor in the nude portions of the composition, is successful, as might have been expected, in the Lady, its central figure, which is purely conceived, chaste in expression, and graceful in action.

Tristram Shandy was one of Leslie's favourite books, and has furnished the subject of one of his best pictures — Uncle Toby in the sentry-box, innocently undergoing the fire of Widow Wadman (1851). Three versions of this subject are in the National Collection, bequeathed respectively by Mr. Sheepshanks, Mr. Vernon, and Mr. Jacob Bell, and the plate by Lumb Stocks is one of the most popular engravings after Leslie. As usual, the three pictures vary in detail. In the Vernon picture, for example — the second painted — Uncle Toby wears a red waistcoat, and the widow has no apron, while her lawn kerchief is thicker and more closely pinned than in the earliest and latest versions, in both of which Uncle Toby wears a buff waistcoat, and the widow a lawn apron as well as kerchief. On the whole, the Sheepshanks picture must be pronounced, I think, the most vigorous in colour and the most perfect in expression ; but Uncle Toby's hands are too delicate for the rest of his figure, and inferior to those in either of the later pictures. ' Inimitable Jack Bannister,' one of the pleasantest of actors, most genial of companions and kindest of men, and a genuine lover of Art into the bargain, sat for the Uncle Toby ; and it would be hard to find a better model for him. This picture is perhaps the best illustration of Leslie's perfect taste. Any painter with a stain of impurity in his imagination would have risked offence in touching such a subject. There is more prurience in Sterne's pen than in Leslie's pencil. In his hands the widow becomes so loveable a person, that we overlook the fierceness of the amorous siege she is laying to Uncle Toby's heart; while Uncle Toby himself is so thoroughly the gentleman, — so unmistakeably innocent and unsuspecting, and single-hearted, — that the humour of the situation seems filtered of all its grossness. I like less Leslie's other picture from Tristram Shandy, of Tristram discovering his unfortunate " remarks " twisted up into papillotes in the hair of the chaise-vamper's wife (1833). He seems to me to have missed his usual grace in the figure of the French-woman, and the colouring appears to my eye heavy and disagreeable. Constable, Leslie tells us in one of his letters, arranged the chiaroscuro of this composition for him.

The only picture which Leslie painted from Gold-smith, — whom one would have supposed likely to be one of his favourite authors, — is the 'Fudge' scene from the 'Vicar of Wakefield' (1843), now in the collection of Mr. Miller at Preston. I regret that I am unable to speak of this picture from recent examination.

Fielding has furnished him with the subject of one of his prettiest small pictures — Tom Jones showing Sophia Western her own face in the glass as the best security for his own future good behaviour. The picture was painted in 1849, and repeated in 1850 for Mr. John Harris. I only know the latter; but I find it difficult to believe that the original Sophia Western could have been lovelier than she is in the repetition. Besides the exquisite ladylike grace of the Sophia, the picture

is remarkable for the great skill with which the painter
has managed the light from the windows between which
hangs the mirror reflecting Sophia's sweet face.   This
is one of many examples of the profit to which Leslie
had put his studies of De Hooghe.   Another is to be
found in Mr. Bicknell's picture, 'The Heiress,' — a
young lady just come into a large fortune, and embar-
rassed by the multiplicity of the correspondence, and
the excessive kindness of the friends her money has
brought upon her.   Here the light falls through tall red-
curtained windows, throwing a mellow glow over the
furniture of the handsome room, in which the graceful
young heiress is receiving her guests and dictating to
her amanuensis.   The effect was probably suggested by
a well-known evening piece of De Hooghe's in the collection of the Duke of Wellington.

Molière was another of the great humourists often
laid under contribution by Leslie.   He painted three
times over the scene of M. Jourdain's discomfiture in his
newly acquired art of fencing under the vigorous, inar-
tistic thrusts of his servant-girl, to the immense delight
of his shrewish wife, who stands by.   The Sheepshanks
version of the subject (1841) is slight and sketchy, but
full of spirit in the action, and of truthful indication in
the light and shadow.   The repetition in Mr. Gillott's
collection appears to me richer in colour and more solidly painted.   The Jourdain in both is perfect as a conception of character, and it would be impossible to
convey better the suddenness and irresistible fury of
Nicole's attack.   She has not even thought it worth
while to lay aside her besom.   The scene where Trissotin reads his sonnet to the blue-stockings of the Hôtel
Rambouillet (painted for Mr. Sheepshanks in 1845) is a
picture of far higher technical merit.   Though as a
whole it is disagreeably chalky in texture, there is great

power over the resources of the art shown in the way
the light from the lustres is distributed over the scarlet
hangings, and reflected in the tall mirror. Hogarth himself would not have surpassed the action and expression
of the reading pedant, and the die-away ecstacies of his
lady-audience, whose affectation is relieved by the sweet
face of Henriette, one of the most graceful of Leslie's
many exquisite conceptions of female beauty.

Another subject from Molière in the Sheepshanks collection is that scene of the ' Malade Imaginaire,' where
the unhappy Argan is abandoned by his indignant physician to all the terrors of his own unaided constitution.
I have little doubt that Leslie painted the expression of
the pleading hypochondriac from his own face. The
Toinette is peculiarly successful. The picture was
painted in 1843, but is not one of the pleasantest of its
period in colour or execution.

From the ' Rape of the Lock' Leslie took one of his
largest and most elaborate compositions. The first picture was painted for Mr. Gibbons in 1854. It was
repeated for Mr. Bullock two years later, with many
variations in detail. The scene represents the moment
when Belinda mourns over the discovery of the ravished
lock. She is weeping in the foreground surrounded by
a sympathetic group of ladies. The Amazonian Tha-
lestris, in *tricorne* and riding habit, indignant at the
Peer's boldness, grasps her whip with an evident longing to use it over the insolent beau's shoulders. In
the background Sir Plume is occupied on his unavailing
mission, and the Peer displays the captured lock in
triumph. The scene in which the action passes was
painted from one of the rooms in Hampton Court Palace, and most of the details of the furniture were from
Petworth studies. Mr. Millais stood for the Peer, and I
trace the features of two of the painter's daughters in

the group round the aggrieved Belinda. When he repeated the subject for Mr. Bullock, he introduced portraits of that gentleman's daughter, in place of his own.
As a composition this is among the best works of Leslie's pencil, though there is an unpleasant predominance
of that chalkiness in colour which grew upon him during the last ten years of his practice. The peer is the
weakest figure in the composition. Strange to say, he
does *not* look like a gentleman of the time of Pope,
but like a modern gentleman masquerading. The Sir
Plume is as genuine as the Lord Petre is unreal. The
tall and commanding lady in the crimson sacque, whose
back is turned to the spectator in the foreground, is a
masterly example of drawing and colour, and the picture is deserving of close study by young artists for the
great art shown in its easy, natural, and yet most pro-
foundly calculated composition. It is a capital example, too, of Leslie's admirable management of light and
shadow.

· But, on the whole, I cannot but prefer to it, — for
power in the rendering of character and for nice discrimination of humorous expresssion, — the ' Reading of
the Will,' from Roderick Random (1846), also in Mr.
Gibbons' collection. Here, though all the figures, with
the exception of Lieutenant Bowling and little Roderick, are in deep mourning, so masterly has been the
painter's management of colour and light and shadow,
that there is no heaviness or monotony in the general
effect of the picture. Lieut. Bowling was painted, I
believe, from an old harbour-master at Broadstairs, and
is a capital conception. One of Mr. Stanfield's sons
sat for the Roderick, and one of the painter's daughters
for the fainting legacy-hunter, who is upset by the discovery that her name is not among the squire's legatees.
This is, I think, the picture in which Leslie most chal-

lenges comparison with Hogarth, both as a painter and
as the teller of a story ; and his work bears the difficult
test bravely. In point of composition the picture is as
deserving of study as the ' Rape of the Lock,' which
hangs opposite to it.

It is not my intention to say much of Leslie as a
portrait-painter, though his head of Archbishop Howley,
and his full length of Lord Cottenham, in his Chancellor's robes, show that he might have taken a high rank
in this branch of his art, had he followed it. He rarely,
however, painted life-size portraits, and in the absence
of such evidence of his power as only portraits on the
scale of nature can supply, it may be well not to insist
on his claims in this particular department of art. We
may be certain he never would have failed in his rendering of character. I have not seen his picture of ' Lady
Jane Grey refusing the Crown,' but the engraving sug-
gests an effect of colour which shows the influence of
another of his favourite masters, Paul Veronese. I remember the delight which I experienced before his little
picture of the same gentle lady found by Roger Ascham
sitting over Plato in the oriel, while the chase sweeps
on without. But I have not seen the picture (which
is in Mr. Miller's fine collection at Preston) since it was
exhibited in 1848. I can recall its silvery summer light,
the serene sweet face and slender figure, and the glimpse
of the green park, with its swelling uplands and stately
trees — a reminiscence of Petworth. There is another
pathetic little historical picture at Kensington, of the
Infant Princes at their prayers, in their dark Tower bed-
chamber, on the night of their murder. The subject is
taken from an affecting scene in Heywood's tragedy of
' Edward the Fourth,' and was twice painted by Leslie. Of his Court pictures — the ' Coronation,' and the
' Christening of the Princess Royal ' — I will only say

that he appears to have encountered the difficulties of
the subjects boldly, and to have vanquished as many
of them as a painter of such scenes in this age can be
expected to do.   To make courtly ceremonials effective
incidents for the pencil, there needs, at once, in the
painter a kindred power to that of Veronese and Titian,
and in the subject something of that splendour of pag-
eantry and glory of costume which embellished mediæ-
val life.   In our day it is hardly possible to keep down
the most fatal suggestions of the upholsterer and the
milliner.   But, even if the difficulty had been less, Leslie was not a decorative painter.   He was unaccustomed
to the scale demanded by such subjects, and had nothing of the splendour of colouring which can invest with
a charm even the fittings of Banting and Gillow, or the
inventions of the Court *modiste* and *plumassier*.   Leslie
succeeded admirably in the portrait portion of these difficult pictures.   The group of attendant ladies in the
coronation picture, especially, is painted with an intense
sentiment of that grace and beauty which the subject
supplied, and the painter was peculiarly qualified to
reproduce.   Again, the passages in either picture which
most appeal to the heart, are painted with true feeling;
as, for example, the Maiden Queen, kneeling with bared
and bowed head at the altar under the heavy burden
of her coronation robes, while the sunbeams shed their
glory upon her, like the blessing of heaven made visible; or the crowned young mother's look, as she turns
to her first-born with that yearning which makes all
women kin.

I have spoken elsewhere of Leslie's pictures from
sacred subjects, and from those domestic incidents, such
as furnish the subjects of ' The Shell,' and ' The First
Lesson,' in the treatment of which the painter was so
peculiarly happy.

My narrowing space warns me to draw this introduction to a close, but before I retire to let Leslie speak for himself, I am tempted to close these desultory notices of particular pictures by some general remarks on the qualities of the painter, and on his place among the artists of this country and time.

GENERAL CHARACTERISTICS OF LESLIE AS AN ARTIST.

IN passing from the consideration of particular pictures of Leslie's to his general characteristics as a painter, I feel distrustful of my own judgment. Memory of the delight which his exhibited pictures have afforded me year after year makes me shrink from the attempt to analyze the sources of my gratification. I feel too grateful to the man who has given his generation so much refined and innocent pleasure, to be disposed to scan the " why " and the " how " of his working, or to be sure how much of what I write is present judgment, how much recollected enjoyment. In *almost* all that Leslie attempted he appears to me to have succeeded in a rare degree. Few painters have better known the range of their own powers, or more honestly followed the guidance of their real tastes and feelings. But most, even of his warmest admirers, will probably agree with me in the opinion, that he has satisfied us least in the few subjects he has painted from Holy Writ. Not that he wanted reverence, or earnestness, or elevation of sentiment, for such themes. But in the treatment of them we have been accustomed to look either for such epic largeness and simplicity of handling as they have received from the greatest Italians, or for that vivid nat-

uralism and local colour with which Wilkie dreamed of
investing the incidents of Biblical life, and which Vernet in France, and Mr. H. Holman Hunt and others at
home, have actually applied to it. Leslie, by his practice as a painter of cabinet pictures, was unfitted for the
one mode of treatment, while his ignorance of Eastern
life and nature, if nothing else, debarred him from the
other. But even among these subjects there are homely
and domestic incidents which Leslie was quite fitted
to make both lovely and impressive, as I think he has
proved by his Martha and Mary, painted originally in
1847. · A third repetition of this subject was among
the pictures left unfinished at his death.

But Leslie had no vocation for what may be called
epic painting, or, indeed, for any form of painting calculated by scale and style to speak to numbers. He
seems, from passages in his writings, to have undervalued all that class of work which he considered as merely
subsidiary to architecture, but which ought rather to be
estimated as originally Bible record, legend, or history,
put into pictures for the sake of those who had no
books, and afterwards in the stateliest form of decoration. He had no ambition to adorn public halls, or to
cover the walls of churches. He no doubt thought that
the time for giving instruction or information through
pictures has passed away, while stately decoration is in-
appropriate to our social life and usages — in this country, at least — and that painting now-a-days cannot use-
fully aspire to any higher functions than those of pleasing and refining. And of all the ways in which the
painter can impart pleasure or promote culture, there
was evidently none which Leslie valued so highly as
his power to enhance our relish for good books, and to
enlarge our enjoyment of out-door nature. He wrought
in the one field himself: he thoroughly and generously

appreciated those who laboured honestly and lovingly in the other. His own art was eminently literary. But he not the less passionately admired Constable's pictures for their single-hearted reproduction of the skies and streams, the downs and meadows, about Dedham and East Bergholt.

Both in his appreciation of art and literature, Leslie was eminently catholic, and in the main sound of judgment. His lectures testify to the comprehensiveness of his artistic canons, while how keenly and genuinely he loved books is evident in his choice of subjects from first to last. When we recall his pictures, it is in connection with Shakespeare, Cervantes, and Le Sage, Molière, Addison, Sterne, Fielding, and Smollett. These were the books his father loved, and on such strong and nutritious literary food young Leslie was reared. He first attracted notice by his ' Sir Roger de Coverley going to Church' (1819). 'Sir Roger de Coverley in Church' (1857),* was the last picture from his hand which retained any strong impress of that which most charmed us in him. He has left few works in which subject, as well as embodiment, is of his own imagining. His ' Mayday,' the ' Mother and Child,' the ' Who can this be ? ' and ' Who can this be from ? ' are the best examples of such pictures. But as an illustrator and pictorial embodier of other men's conceptions, he ranks among the first — if not as the very first — of English painters. So entirely true and subtle is his rendering of character and expression, so fine his appreciation of his author's sentiment, so hearty his relish for the subject in hand, that his pictures seem to me quite to escape the charge so justly brought against most pictures taken from books, that they weaken instead of strengthen our conception and enjoyment of the scene

* In the Collection of Mrs. Miller, at Preston.

d

represented. What painter has entered so completely as Leslie into the mind of Shakespeare and Cervantes, of Molière and Addison? His Sancho seems to me absolutely to satisfy one's conception of the burly squire. I should say the same of his Autolycus and Perdita; his Beatrice and his Catherine; his Uncle Toby and the Widow Wadman; his Trissotin and Monsieur Jourdain; and all those saucy, sprightly *suivantes* of Molière's comedies — the Nicoles and Toinettes, and Mariannes. In his choice of subjects from his favourite authors, I fancy one may trace the same hearty and intimate appreciation. He does not pick out his incidents, only or mainly, because they admit of picturesque costume, effective grouping, or stirring and varied action, but because they reflect the inner and more subtle sentiment of the play or novel, or poem which furnishes them. It has always seemed to me that our liking and appreciation of the Duchess in Don Quixote must be permanently heightened after we have learned to enjoy her high-bred humour and courteous grace from Leslie's picture of her; after we have caught that radiant but restrained half smile, so exquisitely contrasted with the broad and boisterous merriment of the attendants — the mulatto girl above all — and the bilious contempt on the starched, vinegar face of the Duenna. So, I think, we must all acknowledge an enhanced sense of the humour of Uncle Toby's dangerous tête-à-tête with the Widow Wadman in the sentry-box, after studying the two in Leslie's picture of that critical situation.

In selecting the most salient merits of this painter, I am only echoing the general verdict when I pitch first upon his power of rendering character, particularly of the humorous kind. But this power was thoroughly under the guidance of that chastening good taste which can treat even coarse subjects without vulgarity, and make otherwise odious incidents tolerable by redeeming glimpses of humanity and good feeling. In his " Reading of the Will," from Roderick Random (1846), I would note, in illustration of the latter characteristic, the real grief of the little girl at the window — the one personage in that assembly of sharking fortune-hunters who is thinking of the dead with regret. She is unnoticed by the rest of the characters, and might easily escape observation, so unobtrusively is she introduced. But once seen, she leavens the whole scene with that salt of human kindness, which without her would be wanting, even in presence of the bluff honesty of Lieutenant Bowling, and the innocent unconcern of little Roderick. There are few of the painter's pictures in which he does not contrive to introduce some such touch, to make us love him, and feel kindly towards our kind.

Another charm in Leslie's work is the inborn and genuine — if often homely — beauty and grace of his women. Speaking from my own feeling, I should find it difficult to parallel, for this quality, his Perdita in the Sheepshanks picture, or his Beatrice in the Gibbons collection. But all his women, even the humblest, have as much beauty as is compatible with their class, character, and occupation. This beauty never degenerates into the meretricious or the tawdry. It is eminently the real and work-day charm of human flesh and blood, whether it be refined and high-bred as in the Duchess or the ladies of the " Rape of the Lock; " or simple and *naïve* as in the Perdita ; or rustic and blowsy as in the Mopsa and Dorcas ; or ripe, melting, and provocative as in the Widow Wadman. Closely akin to this sentiment of genuine womanly loveliness, is Leslie's intense feeling for the domesticities. No mother, I should think, can see that little picture of his,* in which a lovely young

* In the Collection of Mrs. Gibbons, Regent's Park.

woman nestles her face in the chubby neck of the crow-
ing baby on her knee, without a thrill of maternal love
at her heart. But whatever he has done in this way is
free from all mawkishness. There is no trading in the
" deep domestic," as a good saleable article for the market. In this, as in all he did, good taste has chastened
and checked Leslie's pencil. His lectures show how
highly he valued this guiding and restraining faculty,
and his pictures throughout supply the best illustrations I know of the faculty in operation.

How genuine all these qualities were in Leslie is best
shown by his life and by his character, as indicated in
his conversation and his writing. How could *he* be
other than truthful, lovely, charitable, and tasteful in
his pictures, who in his home as in society, in his
teaching as in his conduct, was habitually sincere, affectionate, equable, thoughtful of others, tolerant, loving to
dwell rather on the good than on the bad about him?
It would be well if there were more lives that should
show so exact a parallel of good attributes in the workman and his works.

In going through Leslie's recollections and correspondence, I have found myself often drawn to a comparison of him as a painter with his friend Washington
Irving as a writer. I trace a good many points of resemblance between them, as in the hearty love of both
for the nearer past of English life and manners; their
unaffected sensibility to the graceful and refined in woman, and to the domestic affections; their genial relish
for the humourous in character, with a not unkindred
appreciation of the pathetic; their genuine Anglicism
of sentiment and spirit — Americans as both were by
blood : and lastly, their ever-present good taste in treating every subject they took in hand. It may seem not
a very high place in art to claim for Leslie, which sets

him on a level with Washington Irving in literature.
But Leslie loved Irving so well and admired his work
so heartily, that I am sure Leslie would not complain
of the parallel.

I am very imperfectly qualified to pronounce on the
technical merits and demerits of Leslie as a painter. I
venture what I say on this point subject to the correction of better informed judges. It is evident from his
works, as well as from what his letters tell us about
them, that he wrought his way in his art slowly and la-
boriously. His taste, he tells us, was long in forming.
He honestly confesses there was a time when he thought
West equal to Raffaelle, and when he was insensible to
the glory of Venetian colour; and though by diligent
cultivation he tutored his mind and eye to juster appreciation, it seems to me clear from his works that he had
not by nature the gift of colour, and never quite made
up for this want by self-culture. The colour of his earlier works is mellower and richer than that of his later
ones. Failing sight may have had something to do
with this, as well as the influence of Constable; but it
may, also, be partly due to a natural relaxation of effort
after alien perfections in one who had succeeded in win-
ning public favor by the qualities which were natural
to him. From about 1819 to 1838 — judging from the
pictures I have had opportunities of examining — Leslie seems to me to have been at his best as a colourist.
His pictures painted after 1838, exhibit an increasing
tendency to opacity and chalkiness, though he ever and
anon escapes from these besetting sins, and, as in his
Beatrice (1850), paints a head as perfect in the softness
of its texture, and the pearliness of its tone, as the most
exacting critic could require.

But making every allowance for such occasional
felicities, I fear it must be admitted that Leslie was not

d*

a great colourist, at least if one considers the quality of his tints in themselves, rather than the choice and arrangement of them in combination. This was not for want of honest effort, for no man ever laboured more strenuously, by observation and practice, to reproduce the true effects of light, or knew better what these ought to be, or more enjoyed them in the works of other masters. De Hooghe, Maas, and the Flemish school generally, were his especial favourites for their mastery in this respect, above all others.

And if Leslie's pictures lack the peculiar charm of colour, so they are not marked by any special dexterity of manipulation. There is none of what Hazlitt called "the sword play" of the pencil about them. But against their technical defects we must, I think, set off a rare feeling for so much of atmospheric effect as is independent of positive colour. Leslie's pictures are full of air; we can breathe in them and walk about among his groups, and retire into his distances.

Of composition he seems to me a master; quite as happy in the disposition of his personages, and in their combination with the still life of his scene, as in the rendering of character by face and action. As a draughtsman, too, his merit is, unquestionably, of a very high order.

Very few painters have made so good a use of the model — getting reality and life from the living sitter, without any sacrifice of the ideal intention of the painter. His pictures, thanks to the thoroughness with which the conception is thought out, are quite free from all suggestion of the masquerade warehouse, or the old furniture shop. He is a thorough master of perspective, and has seldom been exceeded in the taste with which he selects his accessories, and the well considered degree of finish with which he paints them. In this, as in his

conceptions of incident and character, guiding good taste
is everywhere apparent.

In the gradation of their finish, above all, Leslie's
pictures should supply valuable lessons to the young
painter of the present day. They will help to correct
that prevailing tendency to elaborate *everything* to the
utmost of the painter's power, in disregard of the law
that such equality of elaboration may be fitted for *studies* of parts, but can never be compatible with the conditions of a *picture* regarded as a whole.

Leslie's choice of materials and his mode of work, as
finally settled, were of that honest kind which postpones
immediate effect to permanence, and resists with rare
firmness the temptations of the exhibition room. There
is no fear of his pictures falling into ruin from his resort
to ill considered or reckless means of immediate effect.
His method of painting, as it appears from the description of it already given, was eminently solid, simple, and
straightforward.

Leslie's pictures must, I apprehend, be classed among
those works of which the expressional qualities will always in popular estimation overbear the technical ones,
and in a great measure render all but artists indifferent
to the latter. Had he but united the power of colour
and the chiaroscuro of the Flemish school to his own fine
humour, refinement, and appreciation of the resources
of art, Leslie would have taken a place which still remains for his successors to fill up in the hierarchy of
painting.

In the technical qualities, however, most essential to
the rendering of expression, Leslie's art, for most of us,
leaves little to desire.

I feel confident that when the pictorial art of our
time comes to be compared with that which preceded
and that which will follow it, Leslie's name must stand

honoured, for the prevailing presence in his works of
good taste, truth, character, humour, grace, and kindliness, and for the entire absence of that vulgarity, bra-
vado, self-seeking, trick, and excess, which are by no
means inseparable from great attainments in painting,
and which the conditions of modern art are but too apt
to engender and to foster.

If I have succeeded in my earnest attempt to supply
that information about the painter's works, and that estimate of their qualities, which his native modesty has
restrained him from incorporating with his own autobiographical recollections, I shall feel that I have paid off a
little of the great debt of enjoyment I owe to this
charming painter, and most excellent man.

LESLIE AS A WRITER ON ART.

AMONG writers on art, I should give Leslie a high
place, for the sound sense which guides his judgment,
the taste which governs his criticism, and the freedom
from one-sidedness shown in his " Handbook for Young
Painters," as he modestly called the work into which he
re-cast the lectures delivered by him as Professor of
Painting in the Royal Academy.   There is a great deal
in this treatise that many old painters may profitably
study and take to heart.   The book is anything but ambitious in its scope or in its style of handling the subject.   There is no attempt at systematising, and no pretension to exhaustion of its theme.   It is rather a collection of well-weighed observations on the heads of
its several sections, which deal, in succession, with the
imitation of nature and style ; the imitation of art ; the

distinction between laws and rules; classification; self-teaching; genius, imagination, and taste; the ideal and beauty of form; drawing; invention and expression; composition; colour and chiaroscuro, the cartoons of Raphael; the Flemish and Dutch painters of the seventeenth century; landscape and portraits.

It seems to me that there has been hardly any book written on the theory of painting which enunciates a larger proportion of sound principles, for its bulk, or one more likely to guide the student safely, so far as it attempts to guide him.

Were I to select for exception conclusions or opinions from this treatise, they would be those which the author puts forward as to decorative painting, in connection with architecture, on which subject Leslie wrote in ignorance of the finest examples in this kind, which Italy alone supplies. I think, too, that Leslie undervalued both the historical importance and the expressional qualities of early art; and that this under-estimate has misled the author in his criticism of the principles that should guide the selection of pictures for our National Gallery.

Among examples of artist biography, Leslie's " Life of Constable " deserves, I think, to rank as a model. Affection for his subject may have had as much to do in guiding Leslie through this task, as any theory of editorial duties. But to whatever cause we are to ascribe the result, I know of no more striking example of perfect good taste than Leslie's part in this book. It seems to me difficult to praise too highly the subordination, all through, of the editor to his subject; his industry in research; his arrangement; the skill with which he has left the subject of the biography to tell his own story in letters judiciously chosen and carefully linked by brief explanatory statements; the simple earnestness with which the editor has conveyed his admiration and affection for the subject of his memoir, till he creates a kindred feeling in those who read what he has written. It may be the consciousness of my own difficulties and shortcomings in attempts of the same kind, that makes me so sensible of Leslie's editorial merits.

The good taste and good feeling so conspicuous in his " Life of Constable," are equally apparent, I think, in the Autobiography, from which I have but too long detained the reader.

AUTOBIOGRAPHY

OF

CHARLES ROBERT LESLIE.

CHAPTER I.

Voyage to America — Engagement at sea — French ship vanquished — Youthful bravery — The Newfoundland dog — Residence at Lisbon — Departure from Lisbon — Arrival at Philadelphia.

In looking back on the opportunities my profession has given me of knowing many persons whose names will outlive the present age, I cannot doubt that much which has interested me will be read with interest by others. Without the hope that I can do justice, in my relation, to what I have seen and heard, I am yet tempted to commit to paper those of my recollections on which I dwell with the most interest, and to connect with them some account of my life.

My father, Robert Leslie, and my mother, Lydia Baker, were Americans, natives of Cecil county in the state of Maryland. Their forefathers had settled in that neighbourhood early in the last century as farmers; my father's ancestors being from Scotland, and my mother's from England.

My father was a man of extraordinary ingenuity in mechanics. He settled in Philadelphia in the year 1786, as a clock and watchmaker, having previously pursued that business at Elktown. He was a member of the Philosophical Society, and was known and respected by some of the most eminent scientific men in America, among whom I well recollect Latrobe, the architect of the Capitol at Washington. His business having become prosperous, he determined to extend it by taking a partner in Phila-

1

delphia, and by going himself to London to purchase the clocks
and watches wanted for the establishment. This he did about
the year 1793. He was accompanied by his family, which consisted of my mother and three young children (girls), and his
sister, Margaret Leslie.

I was born in London on the 19th October, 1794, and my first
recollections are of our living in a house in Portman Place, Edgeware Road, two doors from that which I occupied after an interval of thirty years. My brother, the youngest of my father's
children, and about two years younger than myself, was also
born in London. On the death of my father's partner, Mr.
Price, he returned to America with his family.

Our voyage was a remarkable one; and, as my father kept a
journal, and as I have been favoured, within these few years,
with a sight of another kept by one of our fellow passengers, Mr.
Lawrence Greatrakes, I am enabled to give some account of the
principal events of it.

We sailed, on the 18th September, 1799, from Gravesend, in
the ship *Washington*, 875 tons burthen, carrying sixteen 24-
pounders (carronades), six long twelves, and two 6-pounders.
She was an English-built East Indiaman, but when we sailed in
her she was in the American merchant service, and armed in
consequence of the war between the United States and France.
She had a complement of sixty-two men and boys, and was
commanded by Captain James Williamson, a Scotchman. Mr.
Greatrakes remarks, that " Perhaps few instances ever occurred
of a vessel' suffering greater difficulties, and not being lost, in
endeavouring to beat out of the Channel." And my father says:
" We were only just clear of the land when we had been thirty-
four days on board.

" On the 23rd October we passed through an English fleet
from the Mediterranean, and were brought to by the largest of
the ships — the *Majestic*, 74. The gun she fired as a signal had,
by the carelessness of the gunner, a ball in it, which came on
board of us, and, passing very near the heads of two of our passengers, sunk into a spar on the deck.

" On Thursday, the 24th," continues my father, " we were
called up by the mate and gunner, who informed us that there

was a French ship in sight, and that we must prepare for an
engagement. As soon as I got on deck, the captain requested
me to get Mrs. Leslie and the children up and dressed, as he
wished to have them ready to go below at a minute's warning.
We were steering west, with the wind right aft, and the Frenchman following us at the distance of about four miles. It was, no
doubt, a ship we had seen the evening before, dogging the fleet
we had passed through, probably in the hope of cutting one or
two of them off. He did not seem to be gaining on us, so that, at
eight, we had breakfast as usual, soon after which we found that
our enemy could keep up with us with less sail than we had, by
which it was evident he could overtake us if he pleased. Our
captain determined, therefore, to slacken sail, and have our fate
decided while we had the day before us."

Mr. Greatrakes says: "The orders to clear for action were
productive of some droll scenes. Great was the confusion produced among the passengers — some half-asleep, some only half-
dressed, running every way but the right one, and carrying their
moveables everywhere but where they should; bemoaning their
unhappy lot in coming to sea in time of war; rolling up their
bedding, and tumbling their trunks down the orlop deck stairs;
and some of them tumbling themselves after them; inquiring of
every one whom they judged in the least likely to know, whether
it would be a hard fight; whether the French would take all the
passengers' property; whether they should be put into prison;
whether they should ever get home; &c., &c."

To return to my father's journal: "At half-past nine we had
everything in readiness, and every man to his station: the guns
all primed, the matches lit, and all the women and children
ordered down into the hold. . . . At a quarter before ten
the Frenchman fired one gun, though at too great a distance to
reach us. In five minutes more they were near enough, when
our captain fired our first gun with his own hand, it being one
that stood on the quarter-deck; the men gave three cheers, and
the action commenced very briskly on both sides, the two ships
being near enough to use muskets and have a distinct view of
each other. The French ship appeared new, and in every
respect like a frigate, except in size. Their musket-balls for a

few minutes were sent so rapidly against the side of our ship, that the noise to us was like a hail-storm against a window, and yet we had not a man killed by them. One grazed our steward's neck, and another went through the fleshy part of a man's arm. No muskets were fired from our ship, except by some of the passengers, as our men were all required to work our heavy guns; in which we were, in one respect, very unfortunate, as almost every one of the 24-pounders that was fired tumbled over. I counted at one time five of them lying on their sides on the gun-deck. The carriages were made on a new patent plan, but so high and narrow that they could not bear the recoil. One of them in falling broke the leg of our carpenter. The two ships were but for a few minutes near enough to use muskets; after which some of the passengers who had been engaged with them went to assist in making wads and handing cartridges, and the rest went below. The action was now continued with the cannon on both sides; ours were pointed at the hull of the enemy, and we saw the effects of them in several places. They generally aimed at our rigging with double-headed shot, grape-shot, large spike nails, bars of iron from six to twelve inches long, and some of them an inch square, which did much damage to our sails and ropes. At eleven o'clock the privateer steered off, to our great joy, as almost all our cartridges were gone, most of our 24-pounders dismounted, and our crew much fatigued. We had lost, however, but one man, who was hit by a grape-shot through the head, and died instantly.

"It was the opinion of our captain, that the enemy had gone only to repair some of her damages, and meant to attack us again. After some grog, therefore, all hands went to work making cartridges, wads, &c., and getting the guns in their places; and rather before all was ready, we saw the Frenchman bearing down on us a second time, though not so fast but that we were enabled to be quite prepared before he came near.

"They began to fire at a great distance; but our captain ordered his men not to fire till they were close to us, and then as fast as possible with the 24-pounders. At a quarter past one we commenced the second action, with more vigour on our part than the first. The men were so eager to despatch the business, that they charged the guns with a 24-pound ball and two double-headed shot. The French, as before, aimed at our rigging, and we at their hull, which our 24-pounders damaged very much; four of them were seen to go through her on one side below the wale, and another stove in the whole of her gangway. At a few minutes before two o'clock she sheered off, and did not return, leaving us with our rigging terribly damaged: our main-mast shot through in four places, the mizen top-sail yard in one, and the cross jack-yard cut in two in the middle; one ball through the fore-top mast, and nearly half the shrouds and stays of the ship cut away. Most of the braces were gone; and the mizen stay-sail, the smallest we had up, had thirty holes in it, the main-sail sixty-two, and the others in the same proportion: yet in the last action not a man was either killed or wounded.

"At three o'clock the French ship was so far off that we had no expectation of her return; when the captain told me I might get my family up from where they had been confined for more than five hours, with very little air, and the light of only one lanthorn. At four the privateer was nearly out of sight, and we sat down to dine on a large boiled ham, which the cook had got done for us, notwithstanding all the bustle. The men had at the same time their usual fare, to which the captain added two cheeses and an extra allowance of grog. Thus ended the busy part of the day; and, although we had beaten off our enemy, the evening prospect was but a gloomy one. Our deck was as black as the sides of the ship with the quantity of powder that had been burnt on it, and was covered with ropes, blocks, pieces of masts, yards, &c., balls, shot, and spike-nails.* We had only four rags of sails up, and were not able to manage them for want of braces. Night coming on, put it out of our power to do any-thing but let the ship drift before the wind, which was east.

"The evening was closed by bringing up on deck the man that had been killed, sewn up in canvas, with a cannon-ball at his feet. He was laid on the deck; the company stood round while one of the passengers read prayers over him, and he was then lowered gently into the sea. The name of this young man was

* I remember hearing my father say, that he found the iron of an old patten sticking in the side of the ship

Samuel Reed; he was a good sailor, and had been with Trux
ton when he took a French frigate, and afterwards in the ship
Planta when she beat off a French privateer in the Channel
in the early part of the summer."

Mr. Greatrakes says: "During the action a circumstance occurred that showed the character of our captain. A wad from
one of the Frenchman's 32-pound carronades struck the starboard quarter-rail and flew back, spinning round with great veloc-
ity. He instantly attempted to jump on it and stop it, almost
pushing me down to get it. Then tearing and cutting it to
pieces, he charged the larboard 6-pounder several times, and,
stuffing the fragments of the wad into it, fired it back again
at the Frenchman, swearing bitterly at the whole nation all the
time.*

"Two boys, from thirteen to fifteen years of age, got a stroke
or two from the first officer for dancing hornpipes on the main-
deck during the heaviest part of both ships' fire. Another boy,
in carrying forward a 24-pound cartridge, had it shot away from
his hands. 'There,' said he, with an oath directed to the Frenchman, 'you ——, now I must go back for another.' In the early
part of the action our colours were shot down, when our third
mate, Mr. Thomas (an Irishman) and our little steward emu-
lously contended for the honour of first mounting the poop, to
nail them to the mizen-mast, in the midst of a most heavy fire
of musketry. Thomas succeeded in getting the fallen colours
and nailing them up, though they were shot through several
times while he was doing it, and two geese were killed in the
coop on which he stood. A young American gentleman, named
Wallraven, distinguished himself by his gallantry, and was pub-
licly thanked by the captain after the action."

Of such of the occurrences of this eventful day as were most
calculated to make an impression on the mind of a child of five

* Young as I was, I can recall to mind the figure of Captain Williamson.
He was a well-formed, strong-made man, of a good height, but not tall. On
this occasion he wore a kind of naval uniform, a hanger at his side, and a belt
round his waist, in which were stuck a pair of pistols. From what will be
related, he seemed (like Dr. Johnson), to consider one Englishman a match for
four Frenchmen; and with Englishmen he no doubt classed Americans, as well
as Scotchmen.

years of age, I have a tolerable recollection. I had often before looked with awe down the hatches into the gloomy region in which we were confined during the battle, and had seen indistinctly the upright post with notches in it for the feet, by which we children were carried down. My wonder and admiration were now excited by the steward, who seemed to me almost to fly up and down this post by the help of the hand-rope, his frequent visits having no other object than to see that we were as comfortable as circumstances permitted, to tell us all the best news from the decks, and to bring us reinforcements of ginger-bread, oranges, and wine.

All my notions of war were associated with the then popular piece of music, the "Battle of Prague," which I had heard my eldest sister play on the piano; and, accordingly, when I heard the groans of the poor man whose leg was crushed, and who was brought somewhere near us, I exclaimed, "There are the *cries of the wounded.*" The burial of the man who was killed made a deep impression on me, for I saw his messmates carry him to the bow of the ship, and I could distinctly trace the human form through the white canvas in which it was tightly sewn up; and this — to me, the first — image of death, has never been effaced from my recollection.

Often as children are frightened without cause, they are as often in moments of real danger less alarmed than their elders; and I, though constitutionally timid, have no recollection of being terrified by what was going on, perhaps because I believed the hold to be a place of perfect safety. I remember that my brother and I amused ourselves for a great part of the time with playing at hide and seek among the water-casks, with some of the other children of the passengers. My brother, indeed, who was more heroic than I, wanted a little pistol, that he might go on deck and shoot the "naughty Frenchmen." My two elder sisters were of an age to understand and feel alarmed for our situation, and my youngest sister was dangerously ill with an attack of pleurisy, and in that state taken out of bed and carried below. What must my poor mother have suffered!

The captain had a very fine Newfoundland dog, named Nero, who was always greatly excited by the firing of guns. During the engagement, he was so much in the way of the sailors, running from one end of the ship to the other, jumping on the guns and barking, that either by chance or design he was thrown down a hatchway, and his leg 'broken by the fall. The poor animal became so restless, and his howls were so distressing, that my father, having fastened a rope to his collar, carried him to a part of the hold as far as possible from that which we occupied, and while endeavouring to find some means of securing him, he found one of the passengers sitting alone and quite in the dark. My father asked him to hold the dog, but receiving no answer, he placed the rope in his hand, but it was cold and trembling, and incapable of retaining it.

The broken leg was probably not the worst hurt poor Nero received by his fall, for he died a few days afterwards, greatly regretted by his master, who gratified him, in his last moments, by firing a pistol over him; a favour Nero acknowledged by slightly moving his tail, and making a faint attempt to bark.

Some of these particulars have probably remained with me from hearing my father and others of the family mention them after our arrival in America, rather than from my own recollection.

Mr.. Greatrakes relates that — "As our damages were too great to be repaired at sea, and the wind was unfavourable either for England or Ireland, the captain determined to go to Lisbon to refit, from whence we were about 500 miles distant.

"On the 26th, another privateer, a brig, appeared in sight with all sails set to overtake us; probably supposing, from our shattered condition, she would find us an easy prey. She came up with us towards evening, and our captain determined to sink her, which his weight of metal enabled him to do. Luckily for her, however, a shot fired prematurely reached her, and she took *French leave* as quickly as possible.

"On the 30th we took a Lisbon pilot, who came on board with a cocked hat and a high plume of red feathers, laced ruffles to his shirt, and a sword by his side.*

* The house in which we passed our " Winter in Lisbon," had been built purposely for the accommodation of lodgers. It was four stories high. On each story were two complete and distinct suites of rooms; each suite com-

"The repairs of the ship detained us at Lisbon five months
and two days, though the carpenter had engaged to send us to

prising a very large parlour or drawing-room, four chambers, and a kitchen.
Our family occupied a set of apartments on the second story or first-floor.
The adjoining set was rented by a Portuguese *fidalgo* who held a small place
under the government, and with his wife, sister, and children, led a life of pretension and poverty, show and dirt. All the rooms, except the kitchens, were
built entirely without fire-places, or any means of heating them except by the
occasional introduction of a brazier of charcoal, in which case it was of course
imperative to sit with a door or window open. And even then, the fumes produced such headaches that we thought it better to endure the cold. In the
south of Europe, the lamentable scarcity of fuel is a serious drawback to any
pleasure that may be derived from passing a winter in those countries. The
houses are built as if for perpetual summer. Though during the whole winter
there was no snow that lay on the ground, and no ice thicker than a shilling,
we had several weeks of almost incessant rain, accompanied by cold, driving
winds; and afterwards occasional rain-storms of three or four days. And such
rains! a whole cloud seemed to descend at once. The streets (fortunately for
them) were so flooded that at times they looked as if cataracts were rushing
down between the two rows of houses. But it washed them clean. Our door-
windows fitted so badly, that the rain poured in at them through all sorts of
crevices and open places; so that, at each of the three, large tubs had to be
placed to catch the water that would otherwise have deluged the floor. After
the first rain, however, my father contrived means to stop up these cracks, so
as to render the in-pouring less violent. But the dampness that pervaded the
house, and all other houses in this fireless country, was without remedy. The
shoes that we took off at night were frequently in the morning found covered with
blue mould. So also were the surbases, and the frames of the chairs and tables.
Our clothes became mouldy in the bureaus and presses; the covers and edges
of our books were frequently coated with mould in a single night. To guard
against the effects of this humid atmosphere, which there was no fire to counteract, we had recourse to many strange expedients. Every morning, on rising,
we dressed ourselves as if we were going to spend the day in the street; putting on as many under garments as we could, and finishing with our pelisses or
outside coats, and fur tippets. We wore our bonnets all day long; and my
sisters and myself rejoiced in cottage beavers, tied in closely to our faces. My
father (always in his great coat) likewise kept on his hat, and the two boys
were made to keep on theirs. Several days were really so cold, as well as
damp, that after breakfast we all went regularly to bed; remaining there the
whole day, except at meal-times. This we found a tolerably good plan, and *I*
liked it very well, as I could then give myself up entirely to reading. One of
the amusements of the juvenile part of the family, when our parents were not
present (with shame I speak of it), was to peep through the keyhole, with a
desire to be enlightened as to the manners and customs of the Portuguese people who occupied the adjoining suite of apartments; a door, always locked,
being between their drawing-room and ours. We would not have acted so dis-
honourably towards persons of our own country, or even to British neighbours;
but we regarded the Portuguese as "no rule." We soon ascertained that

sea in six weeks, or two months at the farthest. The expense
was £12,000 sterling, with a deduction of £2000 for old materials.

their general habiliments were old and slovenly, but that whenever a fine day
tempted the lady-wife to walk out, she covered her dirty dark calico dress with
an elegant blue satin cloak trimmed with ermine; and had a barber to come
and dress her hair, and decorate it with embroidered ribbons; bonnets not yet
being introduced into Portugal. Keeping no regular servant, she, for these
occasions, hired, by the hour, two maids to walk after her. When any of her
female friends came to visit our neighbour, *they* also brought their maids with
them; and while the mistresses were conversing on the sofa, the maids sat flat
on the floor in front of them, and kept up a whispering talk with each other.
Among other items of keyhole knowledge, we discovered that every day, about
dinner-time, our neighbours had a table set out in their parlour with clean
damask cloth and napkins, pieces of bread, silver forks, spoons, castors, &c.;
handsome wine-glasses, and goblets, and all the paraphernalia of a very genteel
dinner equipage. The table stood thus during an hour or more; so that if visitors came in, they might suppose that the family were preparing to sit down
in style *comme il faut.* But to this table they never *did* sit down; for when the
time of exhibition had elapsed, all the fine things were taken off and carefully
put away for a similar show the next day, and the next. Meanwhile (as we
found by reconnoitring through the kitchen keyhole) the Portuguese family all
assembled in the place where their food was cooked; seated themselves on the
floor round a large earthen pan filled with some sort of stew; and each dipped
in a pewter spoon and fed out of that same pan. Our house was supplied with
milk in the usual Portuguese fashion; the fashion at least of that time. A
dirty old man with a red woollen cap on his head, and round his ragged jacket
a red woollen sash, to which hung several tin cups of various measures, drove
before him a cow, two she-asses, and three or four goats, stopping to milk
them at the doors of his customers, who thus had their choice of cow's milk,
ass's milk, or goat's milk. The two last milks are considered good for invalids;
English people of that unfortunate class being then in the habit of resorting to
Lisbon for the improvement of their health. They have grown wiser since the
whole European continent has been opened to them. Our milkman, like all
other Portuguese, took snuff *à l'outrance;* always stopping to regale himself
with a pinch more than once during the process of milking into the tin mug,
and then resuming with his snuffy fingers. A remonstrance from the person
who stood at the door to take the milk so offended his Portuguese dignity, that
he immediately drove off his beasts in high dudgeon, and there was no milk
that day. Next morning, when he was caught with some difficulty as he
passed grandly by, it required considerable coaxing and apologising, and many
promises of future good behaviour, to prevail on him to stop, and supply milk
as usual. The fashion of knee-breeches, cocked hats, and hair tied and powdered, was retained by the Portuguese long after that style became obsolete in
all other parts of the world. With their long and ample cloaks, there was no
need of wasting money on good clothes to wear underneath; and linen was
rarely discerned about their necks, for very good reasons. A large house was
building next door to ours. Immediately in front, the street was chiefly occu-

"While we were at Lisbon we heard from the American consul at Corunna, of the privateer we had been engaged with.

pied by a wide deep slough or mud-hole, where the paving-stones had sunk or
died away; and the councilmen, or aldermen, or selectmen (if there are any
such persons in Lisbon) had taken no account of it. When the weather was
uncommonly bad, the carts that brought stone for the building generally stuck
fast in this capacious hole. The Lisbon carts were of very primitive structure.
They had no close sides; neither had they iron stanchions like those of drays
to keep things from falling; there were only a few crooked sticks, stuck in
here and there along the edges. Though wood is so scarce in Portugal, there
was a great waste of it in the wheels, which had no spokes, but were solid and
massy, like grindstones; and the axle-tree revolved with them, groaning, or
rather, shrieking dismally all the time. These carts were drawn by a pair of
oxen, which it always required two men to urge along. The dress of these
carmen began by cocked hats, and powdered hair tastefully queued with blue
or pink ribbons; cotton velvet jackets with tarnished, tinsel-looking ornaments; faded breeches open at the knees; and their bare Portuguese legs
ended, as usual, in old shoes with large showy buckles. Each driver carried
a goad, and when the cart-load of stone got into the slough, while one man
goaded the oxen, shouting violently something that sounded like "*shah!*" the
other went to their heads, and endeavoured to frighten the poor beasts out of
the mud-hole by making ferocious faces at them, and *shahing* also in a loud
voice, and brandishing his stick threateningly. The workmen came out of the
house to assist in this enterprise of extricating the cart; and they always had
to do at the end what they should have done at the beginning, — unload it of
the slabs of stone; after which, the oxen and the empty cart were generally
shahed out of the hole in less than half-an-hour. Among the sights of Lisbon
streets, those that have a taste for such things may be treated daily with the
gratuitous view of a pig-killing. If a man is driving a pig, and the animal
seems to have more than his usual disinclination to "go a-head," the driver, to
cut short all further argument, stops in the open street, takes out his knife, and
deliberately kills the pig. Then, getting some dry furze from the nearest shop,
he makes a fire in the street, singes and scrapes the animal, removes the
inside, and carries the carcase home on his shoulder, all ready for selling or
cooking. The Portuguese pork is the finest in the world: being fattened on
chestnuts and *sweet* acorns. This food gives a peculiar sweetness and delicacy
to the meat, the fat of which is as mild as cream. The beef is far from good;
and there is a law against killing calves; it being thought better they should
live and grow up into larger and more profitable animals. Nevertheless, mysterious men came sometimes to our house, and with many and solemn injunc-
tions to secrecy, produced from under their cloaks a piece of veal, for which
they asked an enormous price as an indemnification to their consciences for
having violated the law. Kids are much eaten in Portugal; but it is not altogether safe to venture on one, unless you are quite sure that it is not a cat. I
am still uneasy with a misgiving, that, at a table not our own, I *did* eat a slice of
grimalkin kid; and I can never be quite certain that I did not. I must say,
however, that whether of the feline species or not, it looked and tasted well.
Among the country people that came into market, were the wine-sellers,

She was called *La Bellone*, of Bordeaux, a beautiful new ship, mounting twenty-six brass twelves and four thirty-two pound carronades. She was a very swift sailer, and had, when she left port, 275 men; but when she engaged us her complement was 240, having put the others on board a British prize. We killed thirty-seven and wounded fifty-eight, and when she got to Corunna, she had four and a half feet water in the hold." These particulars are confirmed by my father's journal, with the exception of the number of men killed, which he states at thirty.*

"On the 31st of March," says Mr. Greatrakes, "we left Lisbon, and the same day we carried away our new fore top-mast in a gale, and the next morning though the wind had subsided suddenly, it left such a deep trenching sea that the ship rolled in the most dreadful manner, and about 11 o'clock our new main top-mast was rolled over-board, with a man and a boy on it. The man was killed, but the boy saved himself by catching in the shrouds, though he was severely wounded.

"On the 3rd April, while all hands were busily employed in clearing the wreck of the two masts, at five, p. m., we saw a sail to windward, appearing like a ship of war. We could not make sail from her, if we would, and our captain now pronounced her a frigate, and declared his intention of fighting her, should she prove to be an enemy. We cleared for action, and at six we could see her hull, but no colours; at half-past six we were ready, and could now discern her hoisting colours, but it was too dark to see what they were. At seven she shot across our bows, within pistol-shot, matches lighted, and every gun with lanthorns, as were ours. At this moment a perfect silence reigned in both ships; not a whisper was to be heard in our own. We were incapable of preventing her from lying on us in any situation she might choose, and her taking this very formidable one of crossing our bows alarmed us much, as she might in passing, being higher than ourselves, have raked us

each carrying on his back a borachio or goat-skin, distended with new wine, the forelegs being brought round the neck of the man and tied together in front. Such were the wine-skins that Don Quixote attacked with his sword, mistaking them for an army of soldiers. — " *Recollections of Lisbon*," by *Miss Leslie.*

* The remainder of my father's journal has unfortunately been lost.

dreadfully. We now concluded she was an enemy, and respiration seemed almost to cease among us for a few seconds, expecting her fire. She, however, swiftly crossed our bows from starboard to larboard, and wearing round, as if animated by an instinctive spirit, laid herself alongside of us at about twenty yards' distance. In this manœuvre was fully exhibited the great skill and discipline of British seamen, and all was done in profound silence. She hailed us in English, a language at this moment peculiarly musical to our ears, and she proved to be the *Sea Horse*, a 38-gun frigate, most gallantly manned and homeward-bound from a cruise.*

"On the 11th May we arrived at Philadelphia, forty-two days from Lisbon, and seven months and twenty-six days from London."

My father now found himself obliged to engage in a lawsuit with the executors of his deceased partner, who had greatly mismanaged the business. The lawsuit turned out tedious and expensive, and before it was decided my father, whose health had been long declining, died, after a confinement to his room of one week.

This was in 1804. I was too young to feel how much we all lost in him. He was a most kind parent, and I cannot now recollect that I ever had an angry word from him, though I can remember many indulgences and gratifications which he afforded to my sisters, my brother, and myself, at an expense of time and trouble, of which we were then little aware. The retrospect convinces me that his chief happiness consisted in making his children happy, as well as his wife, between whom and himself I can remember nothing but entire harmony and affection. The only recollections of my father that are painful, are of his ill-health. I cannot recall to mind a single day in which he seemed quite well; and his disorders must have been greatly aggravated by his pecuniary embarrassments during the last years of his life.

Among his most intimate friends, I remember the leading phy-

---

* It may seem incredible that the captain of our ship should have thought of fighting a frigate, disabled as he was; but he assuredly did so, for I distinctly remember, when we came up from the hold, seeing our sailors all ranged at their guns with lighted matches, and I can, therefore, vouch for the veracity of Mr. Greatrakes.

sicians of Philadelphia — Doctors Rush, Barton, Whistar, Physick, and Mease.   He had also known Franklin, and among his
daily associates were Charles Wilson Peale, and Oliver Evans,
two men of great ingenuity — the first in many ways, the last as
an engineer.   That a man, without any advantages of education,
should have lived constantly in such society, proves that he possessed no ordinary mind.   His reading was, probably, not extensive ; but I remember that, after Shakespeare, his favourite authors were Addison, Pope, Fielding, Sterne, and Goldsmith.   He
made a small collection of engravings in England, and " Hogarth's
Apprentices " were among the number.

CHAPTER II.

AT my father's death there was so little property left that my mother was obliged to open a boarding-house, and my eldest sister to teach drawing to support the family. My brother and I had been sent to school at the University of Pennsylvania, which then occupied a splendid house in Ninth-street, built by the citizens of Philadelphia to present to General Washington, but which the removal of the seat of government from that city prevented his occupying.

It would not have been in the power of my mother to continue sending us to this school, but for the kindness of Dr. Rogers, the English professor, a Baptist minister, who abated considerably in his charge for our tuition, and Mr. Robert Petterson, the professor of mathematics, who, having known my father intimately, made no charge whatever. I am sorry to say, however, I did not appreciate this liberality as I ought to have done, but neglected the study of mathematics as much as I possibly could.

My summers and autumns were at this period regularly spent in visits to my great uncles, Philip Ward and George Hall, with my eldest sister, Eliza, and my kind aunt, Margaret Leslie (my father's sister). These uncles lived in Chester county, and were farmers. The scenery about Mr. Ward's house was very beautiful, the Brandywine creek ran near it, and one of its tributary streams turned a flour-mill and a saw-mill belonging to my uncle. I shall never forget the kindness I received from my worthy relatives, while under their roofs. Their habits were simple and

rustic. My uncle Hall performed all the work of his little farm
himself; but then, he belonged to a volunteer corps of cavalry;
indeed, he had served in the revolutionary war, and his horseman's boots, cap, sword, and his blue coat with red facings, which
I saw hanging up in his bed-room, though they never happened
to be worn during our visits, gave him great importance in my
eyes. At Mr. Ward's, one of his sons was the working miller,
and the other the farmer, and here I became familiar with all the
operations of both mill and farm. I accompanied my cousin
Tommy Ward in the fields when he was ploughing or sowing,
and in the barn when he was thrashing or winnowing the corn,
and I well remember a grand husking party (or " frolic," as it
was called), when the neighbours for miles round came to assist
in stripping the Indian corn of its outer covering, and afterwards
sat down to a most substantial supper. To the imagery treasured
in my recollection of these simple scenes, I believe I owe much
of the exquisite enjoyment I receive from reading the poetry of
Burns. His " Hallowe'en," his " Twa Dogs," and other poems,
in which the labours and enjoyments of the cottage are described,
always transport me to the log-houses of my kind-hearted uncles
and aunts in Chester county.

From my infancy I had been fond of drawing, and when old
enough to think of a profession, I wished to be a painter. But
my mother had no means of giving me a painter's education,
though I believe she thought at one time of placing me with an
engraver. This notion was however abandoned, and in the year
1808 I was bound apprentice to Messrs. Bradford and Inskeep,
Booksellers. Samuel T. Bradford, the senior partner, was at that
time the most enterprising publisher in Philadelphia. While I
was under his care he treated me with the kindness of a father,
but was strict in exacting from me attention to business. If he
found me drawing when I should have been otherwise engaged,
he shook his head and seemed so much displeased, that the most
distant hope of his ever assisting me to become a painter never
entered my mind. The circumstance which changed his opinion
and fixed my destiny grew out of the arrival in America of the
celebrated actor, George Frederick Cooke. The excitement produced among play-going people on his first appearance in Phila-

delphia was most extraordinary. — He was to play *Richard* on a Monday night, and on the Sunday evening the steps of the theatre were covered with groups of porters, and other men of the lower orders, prepared to spend the night there, that they might have the first chance of taking places in the boxes. I saw some of them take their hats off and put on nightcaps. At ten o'clock the next morning the door was opened to them, and at that time the street in front of the theatre was impassable. When the rush took place, I saw a man spring up and catch hold of the iron which supported a lamp on one side of the door, by which he raised himself so as to run over the heads of the crowd into the theatre. Some of these fellows were hired by gentlemen to secure places, and others took boxes on speculation, sure of selling them at double or treble the regular prices. When the time came for opening the doors in the evening, the crowd was so tumultuous that it was evident there was little certainty that the holders of box-tickets would obtain their places, and for ladies the attempt would be dangerous. A placard was therefore displayed, stating, that all persons who had tickets would be admitted at the stage door before the front doors were opened. This notice soon drew such a crowd to the back of the theatre, that when Cooke arrived he could not get in. He was on foot, with Dunlap, one of the New York managers, and he was obliged to make himself known before he could be got through the press. "I am like the man going to be hanged," he said, "who told the crowd they would have no fun unless they made way for him."

I should have had little chance of seeing him that night but for a friend in the theatre, Tom Reinagle, a lad of my own age, and one of the assistant scene painters. He obtained me a place in the flies, as a kind of gallery just over the stage is called, and from that eminence I first saw George Frederick Cooke, the best *Richard* since Garrick, and who has not been surpassed even by Edmund Kean. Cooke had seen Garrick, and no doubt this was much to his advantage.

The other characters in which I saw him were *Lear, Shylock, Falstaff, Iago, Sir Giles Overreach, Sir Pertinax Mac Sycophant,* and *Sir Archy Mac Sarcasm;* and I have a perfect recollection of him in all. I thought Edmund Kean inferior

2

to him in *Lear*, but in *Sir Giles Overreach* superior, particularly in the last scene. I was told by Bannister that Cooke's
Falstaff was much below Henderson's, but it certainly was
above any other *Falstaff* I ever saw; and his *Mac Sycophant*
and *Mac Sarcasm* were perfection. I think of him always with
particular interest, not only as one of the *very* few really great
tragic actors I have seen, but as the cause of my coming to
England.

I dined once in company with him at the fish-house on the
banks of the Schuylkill, with a club of gentlemen who, in the
summer months, resorted there to fish. Cooke's manners, when
sober, were perfect, and I came away before he got drunk.

I had served three years of my time at the bookselling business when a likeness which I made of Cooke attracted the attention of some of my friends, and Mr. Bradford became of opinion
that I might succeed as an artist. From that moment he encouraged my attempts at drawing, as much as he had before
discouraged them. Mr. Clibborn, an Irish gentleman, and a
friend of Mr. Bradford, who had often honoured me with his
notice while I was behind the counter, carried the sketch of
Cooke to the Exchange Coffee House at the hour when it was
most frequented by the merchants; the attempt was thought
surprising for a boy, and in a few hours my fame was spread
among the wealthiest men in the city. Mr. Bradford therefore
found no difficulty in raising a fund by subscription, to which
he contributed liberally himself, sufficient to enable me to study
painting two years in Europe.

As to the little likeness of Cooke, there was nothing very
wonderful in it. I had studied over and over again the pictures in Peale's Museum, having had access to it at all times,
in consequence of the intimacy between my father and the very
ingenious proprietor. I was not acquainted with Mr. Sully, the
best painter in Philadelphia, but I never passed his door without running up into his show-room (which was at all times
accessible), and spending as much time there as I had to spare.
The windows of the print-shops were also so many academies
to me, and often detained me so long when I was sent on
errands, that I was obliged, on leaving them, to run as fast as

possible to make up for lost time. When all this is considered, and also that I took an uncommon interest (even for a boy) in everything relating to the stage, and that I shared fully in the excitement produced by the arrival of such an actor as Cooke in America, it would, I think, have been more surprising had I failed in the attempt to make a likeness of him from recollection, than that I should, to a certain degree, have succeeded.

Luckily, however, for me, my drawing was thought wonderful; and my liberal friend, Mr. Bradford, determined to send me to England, under the care of his partner and brother-in-law, Mr. Inskeep, who was about to sail for London on business.

Before I left Philadelphia, Mr. Sully, with whom I had become acquainted, gave me the first lesson I received in oil-painting. He began a copy of a picture in my presence, and then put his palette and brushes into my hand, telling me to proceed in the same way with a copy of my own. The next day he carried his work further, and I again followed him, and so on, until the copies were both finished; thus explaining to me at once the processes of scumbling, glazing, &c.

Sully gave me letters to Mr. West, Sir William Beechey, Mr. Charles King, and other artists; and thus provided, I sailed from New York on the 11th of November, 1811, and, after a short and pleasant passage, arrived at Liverpool on the 3rd of December. Notwithstanding the gloomy season of the year, I entered London with such feelings as we can experience, perhaps, but once in our lives. It was my birth-place, and my earliest recollections belonged to it. I had a kind of dreamy remembrance of the magnificence of St. Paul's, and the splendour of the Lord Mayor's show. The novels of Miss Burney, and the "Picture of London," had made me acquainted with its chief objects of interest, and I had often amused myself with tracing its localities on the maps. Familiar with the engraved works of Hogarth, the very purlieus of St. Giles's, from whence his backgrounds are so frequently taken, possessed to my imagination the charm of classic ground.

For the last three years I had enjoyed opportunities of seeing all the most interesting books as they arrived from England in the bloom of novelty. The talk of the literary men who frequented Mr. Bradford's shop, was often of London and its wonders. I knew the names and styles of the principal English artists from the many engravings I had opportunities of seeing. Passionately fond of the theatre, I knew that Kemble, Mrs. Siddons, Mrs. Jordan, Bannister, Dowton, and Munden were still on the stage; and I had heard of Liston, Matthews, and Emery, who were then in the meridian of their glory. I had seen one of the finest of West's pictures (his "Lear in the Storm"), and I was to see and know the great artist himself. All this to a boy of sixteen, and of such tastes as I have described, could not but afford anticipations of the most intoxicating delight. Nor did the reality fall short of the anticipation.

For a few days I was at the London Coffee House, on Ludgate Hill, with Mr. Inskeep and other Americans. I delivered my letters to Mr. West, and was kindly received by him. I visited the galleries of artists, the theatres, and the other principal objects of attraction to strangers, and

> " Such sober certainty of waking bliss
> I never knew 'till now."

But these enjoyments were soon interrupted by a severe illness, which confined me to my room in the hotel. I was solitary, and began to find that even in London it was possible to be unhappy. I did not, however, feel this in its full force until I was settled in lodgings, consisting of two desolate-looking rooms up two pair of stairs, in Warren Street, Fitzroy Square. My new acquaintances, Allston, King, and Morse were very kind, but still they were *new acquaintances*. I thought of the happy circle round my mother's fireside, and there were moments in which, but for my obligations to Mr. Bradford and my other kind patrons, I could have been content to forfeit all the advantages I expected from my visit to England, and return immediately to America. The two years I was to remain in London seemed, in prospect, an age.

Mr. Morse, who was but a year or two older than myself, and who had been in London but six months when I arrived, felt very much as I did, and we agreed to take apartments together.

For some time we painted in the same room, he at one window
and I at the other. We drew at the Royal Academy in the
evening, and worked at home in the day. Our Mentors were
Allston and King; nor could we have been better provided:
Allston, a most amiable and polished gentleman, and a painter
of the purest taste; and King, warm-hearted, sincere, sensible,
prudent, and the strictest of economists. These gentlemen were
our seniors; our most intimate associates of our own age were
some young Bostonians, students of medicine, who were walking
the hospitals, and attending the lectures of Cline, Cooper, and
Abernethy. With them we often encountered the tremendous
crowds that besieged the doors of Covent Garden Theatre when
John Kemble and Mrs. Siddons played. It was the last season
in which the public were to be gratified with the performance
of the greatest actress that ever trod the stage, and we practised
the closest economy that we might afford the expense of seeing
her often. In the acting of Mrs. Siddons and John Kemble, I
remember particularly (perhaps because it was somewhat unexpected) the grace with which they could descend from the state-
liness of tragedy to the easy manner of familiar life. The scene
in which Mrs. Siddons, as *Volumnia*, sat sewing with *Virgilia*,
and the subsequent scene with *Valeria*, and in *Hamlet*, the manner in which John Kemble gave the conversations with the
players, were beautiful instances of this. These passages are
not comic; but both brother and sister, in giving them, indicated
the perfection of genteel comedy. Perhaps it is the highest
praise of such acting to say, that it was truly Shakespearian,
and made one feel, still more than in reading the plays, the value
of such scenes. In the "Winter's Tale," also, the by-play of
Leontes with the child *Mamillius*, while he is jealously watching
Hermione and *Polixenes*, was marked by John Kemble with the
same fine tact; and the manner in which Mrs. Siddons, as *Lady
Macbeth*, dismissed the guests from the banquet scene, has often
been noticed among the minor beauties of her acting. After
her retirement from the stage she was fond of adverting to her
theatrical career, and in a conversation on this subject she said
to my friend Newton, "*I was an honest actress*, and at all times
in all things endeavoured to do my best."

I thought the *Falconbridge* of Charles Kemble as perfect as
the *Coriolanus* of his brother John. Nature, as well as art,
had admirably adapted the brothers for these two characters.
Charles, then young, possessed a heroic face and figure, and
the spirit he threw into the reputed son of Cœur de Lion, as
he played the character, was too natural not to be his own;
while the impatience of plebeian dictation as certainly belonged
to John Kemble as his noble Roman countenance: indeed, I can
imagine no other *Coriolanus* or *Brutus*. The cast of parts at
that period was glorious. In the " Winter's Tale " we had John,
and Charles Kemble, and Mrs. Siddons; with Fawcett in *Autolycus*, Liston in the *Clown*, Blanchard in the old *Shepherd*,
and Mrs. Harry Johnstone (a beautiful creature), in *Perdita*.
It says much for the company of Drury Lane that they could
attempt to compete with that of Covent Garden. The former
had Bannister, Munden, and Dowton, and attracted full houses
at the Lyceum Theatre, where they played while Drury Lane
was rebuilding.

My first instructors in painting were Mr. West and Mr. Allston. They permitted me at all times to see the works they
were engaged on, and were ever ready to give me advice and
assistance in the pictures I attempted, which were then chiefly
portraits of the size of life. It was Allston who first awakened
what little sensibility I may possess to the beauties of colour.
He first directed my attention to the Venetian school, particularly to the works of Paul Veronese, and taught me to see,
through the accumulated dirt of ages, the exquisite charm that
lay beneath. Yet, for a long time, I took the merit of the Venetians on trust, and, if left to myself, should have preferred works
which I now feel to be comparatively worthless. I remember
when the picture of " The Ages," by Titian, was first pointed
out to me by Allston as an exquisite work, I thought he was
laughing at me. It is but fair to myself, however, to say, that
from the first I was delighted with the Raffaelles in the same
collection (the Bridgwater).

Mr. West gave me a note to Fuseli, whose authority was at
that time sufficient to admit me to draw in the Royal Academy as a probationer. I also became a student of the Townley

Marbles in the British Museum, and through the introduction of Mr. West I had access to the Elgin Marbles, then deposited in a temporary building in the garden of Burlington House. Morse and I studied there from six till eight o'clock in the summer mornings, and I copied several pictures at Mr. West's house, where I had the constant benefit of the advice of the venerable and truly amiable President.

I think it was during the second year of my residence in London that Allston's health became seriously affected; and, as change of air was recommended, he determined to visit Bristol, where he had an uncle living, who hearing of his state had advised him to try the air of Clifton. Mr. and Mrs. Allston left London, accompanied by Morse and myself; but when we reached Salt Hill, Allston became too ill to proceed, and it was determined that Morse should return to town and acquaint Coleridge with the circumstance. He was affectionately attached to Allston, and came to Salt Hill the same afternoon, accompanied by his friend Dr. Tathill. He stayed at the Inn for the few days that Allston was confined there. The house was so full that the poet was obliged to share a double-bedded room with me. We were kept up late in consequence of the critical condition of Allston, and, when we retired, Coleridge seeing a copy of "Knickerbocker's History of New York" (which I had brought with me) laying on the table, took it up and began reading. I went to bed, and I think he must have sate up the greater part of the night, for the next day I found he had nearly got through Knickerbocker. This was many years before it was published in England, and the work was of course entirely new to him. He was delighted with it.

I had seen Coleridge before, but it was on this occasion that my acquaintance commenced with this most extraordinary man, of whom it might be said, as truly as of Burke, that "his stream of mind was perpetual." His eloquence threw a new and beautiful light on most subjects, and when he was beyond my comprehension, the melody of his voice, and the impressiveness of his manner held me a willing listener, and I was flattered at being supposed capable of understanding him. Indeed, men far advanced beyond myself in education might have felt as children in his presence.

Luckily for me he could not help talking, be he where or with whom he might, and I shall ever regret that I did not take notes, imperfect as they must have been, of what he said. I can only now remember, that besides speaking much of Allston, whom he loved dearly, he gave an admirable analysis of the character of Don Quixote. He said, " there are two kinds of madness; in the one, the object pursued is a sane one, the madness discovering itself only in the means by which it is to be gained. In the other, an insane intention is aimed at or compassed by means that the soundest mind would employ, as in cases of murder, suicide, etc. The madness of Don Quixote is of the first class, his intention being always to do good, and his delusion only as to the mode of accomplishing his object."

It was said of Coleridge by one who knew him intimately, and was indeed one of his most active friends, that " he was a good man, but whenever anything presented itself to him in the shape of a moral duty he was utterly incapable of performing it." He had, no doubt, great faults and weaknesses, but this was unquestionably a sweeping exaggeration, uttered perhaps in a moment of irritation. At Salt Hill, and on some other occasions, I witnessed his performance of the duties of friendship in a manner which 'few men of his constitutional indolence could have roused themselves to equal.

I accompanied Mr. and Mrs. Allston to Clifton, where I spent a fortnight with them, and had the pleasure to leave our patient convalescent under the care of Mr. King, to whom Coleridge had procured him a letter from Southey. To this eminent surgeon (under Providence) Allston believed he owed his life. During the gradual cure of his painful disorder, he was, however, subject to a great deal of annoyance from his uncle, Mr. Vanderhorst, of a nature to be severely felt in his weak and nervous state; and never, perhaps, did one kind-hearted man torment another more.

Among one or two other prejudices, Mr. Vanderhorst cherished an inveterate animosity against doctors. " Don't let one of those rascals enter your door," was the burthen of his first visit to his suffering nephew. " Follow my advice, live well, and trust to the air of Clifton. You see how well I am," — he had only the gout, — " and how healthy all my family are, and this is because we never let a doctor come near us." At the very moment in which this advice was inflicted on the patient, we were expecting the arrival of Mr. King. Mr. Vanderhorst luckily left before the doctor came; but as the latter visited Allston regularly twice a day, and Mr. Vanderhorst or one of his family called often, our apprehensions of a collision, or at least a discovery of what was going on, were unceasing. In the mean time Allston's gradual recovery was evident, and Mr. Vanderhorst took the whole credit of it to himself.

While I was at Clifton, Coleridge very unexpectedly arrived and engaged to give a course of lectures on Milton and Shakespeare. I heard three of them, and here again the regret arises that I took no notes. In a letter I wrote at the time, and which has since been returned to me, I find the following passage: — " His object, he says, is not to show, what everybody acknowledges, that Shakespeare and Milton were men of great genius, but to efface the impression, that because their genius was great, they must *necessarily* have great faults, and to prove that their judgment was equal to their genius; — in other words, that neither of them was *an inspired idiot*." " He has given me," I added, " a much more distinct and satisfactory view of the nature and ends of poetry, and of painting, than I ever had before."

I was now admitted a student in the Antique Academy of which Fuseli was the keeper. I had been impressed with the greatest respect for his genius, both as a painter and a writer, before I left America. The engraving from his " Hamlet and the Ghost " had scared me from the window of a print shop in Philadelphia, and I still contemplate that matchless spectre with something of the same awe which it then inspired. I hoped for much advantage from studying under such a master, but he said little in the Academy. He generally came into the room once in the course of every evening, and rarely without a book in his hand. He would take any vacant place among the students, and sit reading nearly the whole time he stayed with us. I believe he was right. For those students who are born with powers that will make them eminent, it is sufficient to place fine works of art before them. They do not want instruction, and those that do are not worth it. Art may be *learnt*, but can't be *taught*. Under Fuseli's wise neglect, Wilkie, Mulready, Etty, Landseer, and Haydon distinguished themselves, and were the better for not being made all alike by teaching, if indeed that could have been done.

I obtained two silver medals in the Academy, and, Mr. West being indisposed, I received them on both occasions from the hand of Fuseli. The first was for a drawing from the Laocoon ; Fuseli had ordered that we should draw the principal figure only : but as, from the number of competitors, I could obtain no other seat than one from which part of the father was hidden by one of the boys, I asked him if I might introduce that boy. He objected. I urged that I could not draw the limb that was hidden, except from imagination, and again I begged him to let me put in the boy. He replied, " if you draw one you must draw both, and I won't have an ape and two monkeys," — alluding to the caricature of the group, by Titian.

The other drawing for which I received a medal was from the life, and the figure was set by Flaxman. I value my medals, therefore, the more as being associated with my recollections of these two great artists.

One evening, in the Life Academy, while Westmacott was visitor,*Fuseli came in, and I heard part of an argument between them on the merits of the Elgin Marbles. Fuseli had never fully shared in the enthusiasm with which Mr. West and other artists hailed their arrival in England. It was the fashion with some of them (not with Mr. West, I think,) to praise the Elgin Marbles as superior even to the Apollo. To some remark of Westmacott, in praise of the Theseus, Fuseli replied :

" The Apollo is a god, the man in the Mews is a demi-god,* and the Theseus is a man."

" You will admit," said Westmacott, " that he is a hero ? "

" No," replied Fuseli, " he is only a strong man."

Edwin Landseer, who entered the Academy very early, and was a pretty little curly-headed boy, attracted Fuseli's attention by his talents and gentle manners. Fuseli would look round for him, and say, " Where is my little *dog boy* ? "

---

* A cast from the collossal figure of the Monte Cavallo, then exhibited in the King's Mews.

Allan Cunningham has said truly that Fuseli was liked by the students, notwithstanding the occasional violence of his temper. I have no recollection, however, of his being near-sighted, as this biographer asserts. On the contrary, my impression is, that his sight was remarkably good at any distance. He was ambi-dextrous, and generally corrected our drawings with his left hand. Harlowe's small portrait of him is the most like : but it would have required a Reynolds to do justice to the intelligence of his fine head. His keen eye, of the most transparent blue, I shall never forget.

None of his peculiarities, either as a man or a painter, prevented his being a great favourite among ladies. He was fond of female society, and at the theatre, particularly, as I was told by a lady who knew him intimately, he was a truly delightful companion. He was most fond of those nights when the plays of Shakespeare formed the entertainment, and on such occasions his deep knowledge and enthusiastic admiration of the poet, as well as his own wit, rendered the intervals between the acts as agreeable to his companions as the time occupied in the performance. As the influence of women softened his temper and called forth all his powers of pleasing, it is not surprising that Mary Wolstonecraft fell in love with him when he was fifty, or that more than one lady felt for him something akin to love in the very last years of his life.

The first large picture I attempted was of Saul and the Witch of Endor. West greatly assisted me in the composition, calling frequently at my room while I was about it. When the picture was done I sent it to the British Gallery for exhibition ; but, as it was not varnished, it appeared unfinished, and was turned out. Mr. West desired me to carry it to his house, where I varnished it in his large room, and there, by his kind influence, it was soon purchased by Sir John Leicester,* who gave me a hundred guineas for it.

Allston was now in London again. His own health was re-established, but that of his excellent wife was much impaired. They had taken a house and furnished it, having till now lived in lodgings, and had but just removed when her illness suddenly

* Afterwards Lord de Tabley.

increased, and she died in two or three days. In fact, after taking possession of her new home, she never recrossed the threshold alive. She was a sister of Dr. Channing, of whom I often heard her speak before he was known in England. She was never tired of talking of "that little saint, William," as she called him. The very clay of which the Channings were formed seemed to have religion in its composition. Mrs. Allston told me that her brother, when· a child, used to turn a chair into a pulpit and preach little sermons to the other children of the family. I saw Channing often during his short stay in London — and to see was to love him. At his request, I accompanied him to the burying-ground of St. Pancras Chapel, to show him his sister's grave. After the death of his wife, Allston quitted his house and hired apartments at No. 8, Buckingham Place, Fitzroy Square, where Morse and myself lodged.

In September, 1817, I went with Allston and William Collins to Paris. We all made studies in the Louvre, and visited the houses of the principal artists, though Gérard was the only one with whom we had an interview, and he, though he received us very politely, did not show us any of his pictures. Of the modern French pictures we did see we were most pleased with those of Guérin. His " Dido and Æneas " was just then completed, and a picture of La Roche Jacquelin heading a charge of Vendeans. I was asked by a French lady how I liked the great works of David — the " Romans and Sabines " and the " Leonidas." I said I did not think them natural.

" Not natural!" she exclaimed. " I assure you he never paints any object whatever without having nature before him." I could have told her, had it been worth while to pursue the argument, that many an artist paints with nature before him without painting naturally. Many a one paints from nature in the sense in which the Irishman, who was mistaken for a Scotchman, said he was "*from* Scotland — *a great way from Scotland,* thanks be to God for that same ! "

We found that Wilkie's reputation was, at that time, very high in France. " I like your *Vilkes*, but I don't like your *Vest,*" said a Frenchman to me.

Being employed to paint some portraits of Americans in Paris,

I remained there three months, and then returned to London, in company with Stuart Newton, whom I met in Paris for the first time. He was on his way from Italy to England, and he and I made an excursion through Brussels and Antwerp, where I had the pleasure of dining at the house of my friend, Mr. Clibborn, whose exertions for me in Philadelphia had, in a great measure, led to my becoming a painter.

Washington Irving was in England, but at Liverpool, occupied with business; the mercantile house to which he belonged being at that time in a state of embarrassment which led to a bankruptcy. When this took place, Irving, after a short excursion to Scotland, where he became known to Sir Walter Scott, came to London with the intention of exerting himself as an author, though with no expectation of becoming popular in England. The " Sketch Book" was written solely with a view to publication in America, where " Salmagundi," and " Knickerbocker" had gained him a high reputation.

Morse had returned to America, and Allston soon after followed him. The best picture the latter left in England was his "Jacob's Dream," at Petworth. It was bought by Lord Egremont, who invited the artist to Petworth, and would, no doubt, have employed him on other works, if he had remained in this country. The friends with whom I now spent most of my leisure were Irving and Newton.

I had frequent opportunities of seeing and hearing Coleridge. He delivered a course of lectures on Shakespeare, to which he gave me tickets, but I was sorry to see his London audiences much smaller than those at Bristol. The following note from him marks the date of these lectures.

" Highgate.

" MY DEAR LESLIE,

" Mr. Colburn has entreated my influence with you to have intrusted to him for a week or ten days your last drawing of my phiz to have it engraved for his Magazine. I replied that I had no objection, and thought it probable that you would have none, and have in consequence given him this note.

" You see, alas ! by my scanty audiences that there cannot be

the least objection to your taking with you half a dozen friends
to my lectures, who are like ourselves, with more in our brains
than in our pockets. Why, my dear *Leslie*, do you so wholly
desert us at Highgate? Are we not always *delighted* to see you?
Now, too, more than ever; since, in addition to yourself, you are
all we have of Allston.

                                              "S. T. COLERIDGE."
" 1st *March*, 1819."

On looking back to the time when this note was written, I
grieve to think that I should have allowed my natural indolence,
the distance, and occupations, often trifling in comparison with
the privilege of enjoying Coleridge's society, to give ground for
the charge in the latter part of it.

It is not the lot of any one, twice in his life, to meet with so
extraordinary a man. I now read over and over again what his
nephew has recorded of his conversation, and I can vouch for the
exactness with which his manner is preserved in those precious
little volumes. The remarks there given, on " Othello " and
" Hamlet," formed parts of his lectures on Shakespeare : —
" The clue to the inconsistencies of *Hamlet* might be found,"
he said, " in the undue predominance of the inner over the outer
man."

Coleridge did not consider that the *passion* of jealousy was the
subject of the tragedy of " Othello," but that Shakespeare had
displayed it fully and truly in the " Winter's Tale." " *Othello* is
anything but jealous in his nature, and made so only by the
machinations of *Iago*, while *Leontes* requires no prompter but his
own suspicious mind." He observed, that the difficulty was great
in imagining an expression adequate to the feelings of *Othello*
when he first sees *Iago* after having discovered his villany, and
he thought it a master stroke of Shakespeare to surmount it as
he has done :   .

> " I look down towards his feet; but that's a fable.
> If that thou be'st a devil I cannot kill thee."

He pointed out the great dramatic beauty of the opening scenes
of " Hamlet," and the admirable skill with which the ghost is
introduced. Although *Marcellus* and *Bernardo* are expecting its

appearance, and *Horatio* has joined their watch with the same expectation, and they are even talking about it, its entrance is startling, and every succeeding appearance alike thrilling. In reading passages from the first scenes of this play, Coleridge noticed Shakespeare's respect even for the *superstitions* connected with the mysteries of Christianity, a beautiful instance of which occurs in the lines,

> " It faded on the crowing of the cock.
> Some say, that ever 'gainst that season comes,
> Wherein our Saviour's birth is celebrated,
> This bird of dawning singeth all night long:
> And then, they say, no spirit dares stir abroad;
> The nights are wholesome; then no planets strike,
> No fairy takes, nor witch hath power to charm;
> So hallow'd and so gracious is the time."

He said the reply of *Horatio* was, he believed, exactly that which Shakespeare himself would have made :

> " So have I heard, and do in part believe it."

He could never read, he said, any of those scenes in which children are introduced, " without laying the book down and *loving Shakespeare over again*." He said the anachronisms noticed by Shakespeare's critics would not, perhaps, have given the poet himself any great uneasiness had they been pointed out to him, as possibly they were ; and this may have given rise to that curious intentional anachronism in the third act of " Lear," where the fool, after fourteen lines of a burlesque prediction, says :

> " This prophecy Merlin shall make, for *I live before his time*."

I wish I could recollect what Coleridge said of the character of *Falstaff*. I only remember, with certainty, his opinion that Shakespeare, in the " Merry Wives of Windsor," had departed from the original conception of the character, and that the *Falstaff* in that play, though very amusing, was much below the *Falstaff* of the two parts of " Henry the Fourth." I am not sure whether it was Coleridge who remarked, that in the scene in the First Part of " Henry the Fourth," in which *Falstaff* brags of his feats at Gadshill, he begins with the intention of imposing on the *Prince* and *Poins*, but quickly perceiving that they do not believe him, he goes on buffooning, and adds to the men in buckram until they amount to eleven, merely to make the *Prince* laugh.

A most interesting portion of Coleridge's lectures consisted in his pointing out the truth and refinement of Shakespeare's women, beyond those of all other dramatists ; and how purified his imagination was from everything gross, in comparison with those of his contemporaries.

Coleridge's lectures were, unfortunately, extemporaneous. He now and then took up scraps of paper on which he had noted the leading points of his subject, and he had books about him for quotation. On turning to one of these (a work of his own *), he said, " As this is a secret which I confided to the public a year or two ago, and which, to do the public justice, has been very faithfully kept, I may be permitted to read you a passage from it."

His voice was deep and musical, and his words followed each other in an unbroken flow, yet free from monotony. There was indeed a peculiar charm in his utterance. His pronunciation was remarkably correct : in some respects pedantically so. He gave the full sound of the *l* in *talk*, and *should* and *would*.

Sir James Mackintosh attended the whole course of these lectures, and listened with the greatest interest. This was heaping coals of fire on the head of Coleridge, who had lampooned him with great severity for his political apostacy, as it was considered. I remember many years afterwards, when I had frequent opportunities of seeing Sir James, hearing him say that the best thing ever said of ghosts was by Coleridge, who, when asked by a lady if he believed in them, replied, " No, Madam, I have seen too many to believe in them."

It was in company with Coleridge that I first heard the nightingale, that is, to know that I heard it. It was in a lane near Highgate where there were a number singing, and he easily distinguished and pointed out to me their full rich notes among those of other birds, for it was in the day time. He even told how many were there. He took me to an eminence in the neighborhood, commanding a view of Caen wood, and said the assemblage

* Probably the " Biographia Literaria," published in 1817.

of objects, as seen from that point, reminded him of the passage in Milton, beginning —

" Strait mine éye hath caught new pleasures,
Whilst the landskip round it measures ; "

— and running through the following eighteen or twenty lines.

Among the fragments of his conversation that I remember, are the following : —

" How natural is the exaggeration in the account the woman of Samaria carries to her friends of our Saviour. ' Come, see a man which told me *all things that ever I did ;*' when, in reality, our Lord had only told her that she had had five husbands, and that he, whom she now had, was not her husband."

He said he did not doubt but that in the 12th chapter of St. Matthew, the 40th verse was a gloss :

" For as Jonas was three days and three nights in the whale's belly : so shall the Son of Man be three days and three nights in the heart of the earth."

Now, as our Saviour was crucified on Friday, and rose again on Sunday morning, he was but one entire day and two nights in the tomb; besides which the following verse shows sufficiently what was intended by the refusal to give any other sign than the sign of the prophet Jonas.

" The men of Nineveh shall rise up in judgment with this generation and condemn it, because they repented at the preaching of Jonas, and behold, a greater than Jonas is here."

Speaking of the utilitarians, Coleridge said, " The *penny saved penny got* utilitarians forget, or do not comprehend, *high moral utility,* — the utility of poetry and of painting, and of all that exalts and refines our nature." He thought Lord Byron's misanthropy was affected, or partly so, and that it would wear off as he grew older. He said that Byron's perpetual quarrel with the world was as absurd as if the spoke of a wheel should quarrel with the movement of which it must of necessity partake.

But Lord Byron had not then proved, as he afterwards did, that with all his surprising and varied powers, possessing an eye for material beauty, and extraordinary eloquence in describing it, he wanted the first requisite of a great poet, *a true perception of moral beauty.*

Coleridge dearly loved Allston, and of Mrs. Allston he said (and I who knew her intimately, can bear witness how truly), "She is an Israelite indeed, in whom is no guile."

I once found Coleridge driving the balls on a bagatelle board for a kitten to run after them. He noticed that, as soon as the little thing turned its back to the balls it seemed to forget all about them, and played with its tail. "I am amused," he said, "with their little short memories."

Coleridge's want of success in all worldly matters may be attributed to the mastery possessed over him by his own wonderful mind. Common men as often succeed by the qualities they want, as great men fail by those they have. Coleridge could not direct his extraordinary powers to the immediately useful occupations of life, or to those exercises of them likely to procure him bread, unless he was perpetually urged on by some kind friend. The tragedy of "Remorse" was written whilst he lived with Mr. Morgan, and I believe would never have been completed but for the importunities of Mrs. Morgan. A few days after the appearance of his piece, he was sitting in the coffee-room of a hotel, and heard his name coupled with a coroner's inquest, by a gentleman who was reading a newspaper to a friend. He asked to see the paper, which was handed to him with the remark that "It was very extraordinary that Coleridge, the poet, should have hanged himself just after the success of his play ; but he was always a strange mad fellow." "Indeed, sir," said Coleridge, "it is a *most extraordinary* thing that he should have hanged himself, be the subject of an inquest, and yet that he should at this moment be speaking to you." The astonished stranger hoped he had "said nothing to hurt his feelings," and was made easy on that point. The newspaper related that a gentleman in black had been cut down from a tree in Hyde Park, without money or papers in his pockets, his shirt being marked " S. T. Coleridge ; " and Coleridge was at no loss to understand how this might have happened, since he seldom travelled without losing a shirt or two.

When Allston was suffering extreme depression of spirits, immediately after the loss of his wife, he was haunted, during sleepless nights, by horrid thoughts ; and he told me that diabolical imprecations forced themselves into his mind. The distress of this to a man so sincerely religious as Allston, may be imagined. He wished to consult Coleridge, but could not summon resolution. He desired, therefore, that I would do it; and I went to Highgate, where Coleridge was at that time living with Mr. Gillman. I found him walking in the garden, his hat in his hand (as it generally was in the open air), for he told me that, having been one of the Blue-coat boys, among whom it is the fashion to go bare-headed, he had acquired a dislike to any covering of the head. I explained the cause of my visit, and he said, "Allston should say to himself, ' *Nothing is me but my will.* These thoughts, therefore, that force themselves on my mind are no part of *me*, and there can be no guilt in them.' If he will make a strong effort to become indifferent to their recurrence they will either cease, or cease to trouble him."   He said much more, but this was the substance, and after it was repeated to Allston, I did not hear him again complain of the same kind of disturbance.

At Mr. Morgan's house in Berners Street, I first saw Charles Lamb, who was intimate in a literary coterie composed of persons with principles very opposite to those of Coleridge. Somebody, wishing to give the latter a favourable impression of these people, spoke of Lamb's friendship for them; and Coleridge replied, " Charles Lamb's character is a *sacred* one with me ; no associations that he may form can hurt the purity of his mind, but it is not, therefore, necessary that I should see all men with his eyes."   There can be no doubt that it was of Lamb he spoke in the following passage from the " Table Talk : " — " Nothing ever left a stain on that gentle creature's mind, which looked upon the degraded men and things around him like moonshine on a dunghill, which shines and takes no pollution. All things are shadows to him, except those which move his affections."   No one ever more fully pictured his own mind in his writings than Lamb has done in his delightful Essays ; and every reader of them, I think, must acknowledge that Coleridge, in what he said, only did his friend justice. But Lamb, from the dread of appearing affected, sometimes injured himself by his behaviour before persons who were slightly acquainted with him. With the finest and tenderest feelings ever possessed by man, he seemed carefully to avoid any display of sentimentality in his talk. The fol-

lowing trifling anecdote is merely given as an illustration of his
playfulness. I dined with him one day at Mr. Gillman's. Returning to town in the stage-coach, which was filled with Mr. Gillman's guests, we stopped for a minute or two at Kentish Town.
A woman asked the coachman, "are you full inside?" Upon
which Lamb put his head through the window and said, "I am
quite full inside; that last piece of pudding at Mr. Gillman's did
the business for me."

Much as I then admired the traits of his mind and feelings
shown in his charming Essays, little did I comprehend the entire
worth of his character. I had often met his sister Mary, a quiet
old lady, who was like him in face, but stouter in figure. I knew
that, at times, her mind had been unhinged from an early period,
but I never heard of the dreadful act with which her insanity
began until long after the time of which I am writing; and I
was unacquainted, therefore, with the unparalleled excellence of
her brother, the strength of his love, the greatness of his courage,
and that noble system of economy in which he persevered to the
end of his days, so difficult to a man who had so thorough a relish for all the elegances and luxuries of life; indeed impossible,
had he not had a still higher relish for the luxury of goodness.
The letters published, after his death and that of his sister, by
Mr. Talfourd, make up a volume of more interest to me than
any book of human composition.

I have noticed that Lamb sometimes did himself injustice by
his odd sayings and actions, and he now and then did the same
by his writings. His "Confessions of a Drunkard" greatly ex-
aggerate any habits of excess he may ever have indulged. The
regularity of his attendance at the India House, and the liberal
manner in which he was rewarded for that attendance, prove that
he never could have been a drunkard. Well, indeed, would it
be for the world if such extraordinary virtues as he possessed
were often found in company with so very few faults.

Sir George Beaumont left £100 to Mrs. Coleridge, but nothing
to her husband, who was then, as always, very poor. Lamb was
indignant at this, and said it seemed to mark Coleridge with a
stigma. "If," he added, "Coleridge was a scamp, Sir George
should not have continued, as he did, to invite him to dinner."

CHAPTER III.

I SHOULD have mentioned that, in the year 1818, I was invited into Devonshire by my kind friends, Mr. and Mrs. Dunlop, who had taken a house at Dawlish for the season. I spent a fortnight very delightfully with them, and then visited Plymouth, and the pretty village of Plympton, where I made a sketch of the house in which Sir Joshua Reynolds was born.

After my return to London I painted, for Mr. Dunlop, " Sir Roger de Coverley going to Church, accompanied by ' The Spectator.' " This picture attracted more notice in the Exhibition than anything I had hitherto painted, and the Marquis of Lansdowne employed me to repeat the subject for him.

In the spring of 1819, Mr. West was confined to his house by illness. I was with him a few days before the close of the Exhibition, and on his expressing a wish that he could see it, I asked him if it was not possible. He answered " that he was too feeble to go on a public day, and that his only chance of visiting it was on the day after it closed ; but that, if the Prince Regent went, he, as President, must attend upon His Royal Highness — a ceremony for which he was too unwell."

" But surely," said I, " the Prince, knowing how ill you are, would excuse you from the fatigue of attendance."

" No," he replied ; " if the Prince goes, I cannot ; " and then, after a pause, he added, " Mr. Leslie, it is now many years since I have had cause to know the wisdom of David's advice, ' put not your trust in princes.' "

George the Third had been cordially West's friend, as long as he possessed his senses ; but as soon as his derangement trans-

ferred his powers to others, the pension Mr. West had received
from him was stopped, and he was given to understand that those
works he was engaged on for the King, would not be paid for.
He was unable to see the Exhibition of 1819, whether in consequence of ill-health, or of its being visited by the Prince, I now
forget; and before the Exhibition of 1820, this eminent artist,
and amiable, generous man, was no more.

Constable told me that on calling at his house the day after his
death, West's old and faithful servant, Robert Brenning, remarked
to him, "Ah, sir! where will they go now?" meaning the
younger artists. And well might the old man say so; for although I know of no eminent painter in London, who is not willing to communicate instruction to any of his brethren who need
it, yet at that time there was not, nor indeed has there been since,
any one so accessible as Mr. West, and, I may add, so well qualified to give advice on every branch of the art. He had generally a levee of artists at his house every morning before he began
work.* Nor did a shabby coat or an old hat ever occasion his
door to be shut in the face of the wearer. Constable said truly
of West that, " in his own room, and with a picture before him,
his instructions were invaluable; but, as a public lecturer, he
failed." This arose, partly, perhaps from diffidence. On the only
occasion on which I heard him address an assembly, the venerable old man, when he began to speak, blushed like a young girl.
In this lecture, he explained to us his theory of the arrangement
of colours, which he said was founded on the rainbow. The
principal masses of warm colour, as orange, yellow, and red, by
this principle, he placed on that side of the picture where the
light enters, and the green, blue, and purple on the opposite side,
where also he placed his chief mass of white. He said he could
only trace the observance of this rule, as a principle, in the later
works of Raffaelle, and that it was from studying the cartoons he
had discovered it. He admitted that in Titian's " Peter Martyr,"
the arrangement of colour is on a plan exactly contrary, but
added, " Titian's eye was so fine that he could produce harmony
by any arrangement."

* This, I am told, was also the case with Sir Joshua Reynolds, who was
equally ready to advise and assist young painters.

I remember his remarking to me how different, at different times, and under different circumstances, the same picture may appear to us, and how greatly we are often influenced in the impression we receive from one picture, by the effect produced on us by another which we have just seen. As an illustration of this, he told me that, having to superintend an alteration of the arrangement of some of the pictures in the Royal collection (of which he had the care), and knowing that a Vandyke, which Sir Joshua Reynolds greatly admired, would be taken down, he called on him on his way, and Sir Joshua very gladly accompanied him to Buckingham House. They found the Vandyke standing on the floor. Sir Joshua eagerly ran up to it, and after examining it very closely, turned to Mr. West with an air of disappointment, and said, "After all it is a copy." To this West made no immediate reply, but they looked at some of the other pictures in the room; and then returning to the Vandyke, Reynolds said, " I don't know what to think of it; it is much more beautiful than it appeared to me at first. It can hardly be a copy." Mr. West replied, " I have no doubt of its originality, and I can explain the cause of your disappointment on first seeing it. When I called on you, you were engaged on one of your own dashing backgrounds, preparing it with the brightest colours for glazing. Your eye had perhaps been for an hour on your own work, and anything would look tame and dull after it. The Vandyke appeared to you, at first sight, to want brightness, and to be weak and timid in execution; but when you had looked at the other pictures in the room and returned to it, the taste, truth, and delicacy with which it is painted, became apparent to you."

In talking with Mr. West on dress, he mentioned the great importance that attached to an expensive wig within his own recollection. He remembered an argument on the merits of O'Brian,* an actor of genteel comedy in the early part of the reign of George the Third, in which a gentleman of the old school maintained, contrary to the opinion of the company, that he was not

* The same whose marriage with Lady Susan Fox, eldest daughter of the first Lord Ilchester, excited such a sensation in the fashionable world of the last century. (See Walpole's letter to the Earl of Hertford of April 12, 1764.) — ED.

successful in characters of high life. "Mr. O'Brian," said he, "does not play the fine gentleman; nor can any man play the fine gentleman without a fifty guinea wig on his head."

Galt, in his "Life of West," says, "When the West family emigrated, John, the father of Benjamin, was left to complete his education at the great school of the Quakers, at Uxbridge, and did not join his relations in America till the year 1714." Whether or not John West went to America immediately on leaving school, I have heard, on good authority, that he was married before he left England, and that his wife, not being in a condition to undertake the voyage, remained at home, another reason for this being his uncertainty whether he should settle in America. She gave birth to a son, and died. The child was taken care of by relations, who, when the father desired it should be sent to him, begged to keep it. To this he assented; and marrying again, the painter was the youngest of the ten children of his American wife. When Benjamin left home to seek his fortune in Europe, he was engaged to the lady he afterwards married, Elizabeth Shewell. In 1765 his venerable father accompanied her to England, and then, for the first time in his life, was introduced to his eldest son, who was fifty years of age. He was a watchmaker, and lived at Reading.

There is a stippled engraving * of West's family, which I remember to have seen in the window of a print shop in Philadelphia when I was so young as not even to have heard of the painter. The natural and simple treatment of the subject made a great impression on me even then, and to this hour it has not ceased to interest me more than any other composition by West, great or small. I look on it indeed as the most original of all his works; and cannot but regret that, instead of being ambitious to produce, too rapidly for excellence, many pictures of large dimensions, he had not looked more about him in real life for subjects like this, in which he seems to have been eminently qualified to excel. His works of higher pretension, compared with it, prove the truth of Johnson's remark, "That which is *greatest* is not always best." The picture, which now belongs to Raphael West (the boy standing by his mother's side), is no larger than the

* This engraving used to hang in Leslie's drawing-room. — ED.

print, and of no great excellence in colour. West himself seems
to have been pleased with the group, as a happy treatment of
the often-painted subject, " The Ages of Man." To my mind,
it is incomparably the best. He repeated it with great variations,
substituting loose draperies for the modern dresses, and it immediately became common-place; an additional proof to those
furnished by the histories of most artists of the danger of endeavouring to improve on incidents taken from real life. In the
first picture, everything is individual and characteristic, everything *essential.* The hats on the heads of John West and his
eldest son, in the presence of a lady, mark the sect who never
uncover their heads in token of respect but when they kneel to
God. These relatives are paying their first visit to Mrs. West
on the birth of her second child. They are sitting, as is the
custom of quakers, for a few minutes in silent meditation, which
will soon be ended by the old man's taking off his hat and offering up a prayer for the mother and infant. Wilkie greatly admired this composition before he knew the entire meaning of the
subject. He was struck with its extreme simplicity, and the un-
ostentatious breadth of its masses of light and dark.

Mr. West told me that on asking his father how he was struck
with the appearance of London after his long absence, he replied, " The streets and houses look very much as they did; but
can thee tell me what has become of all the Englishmen? When
I left England, the men were a portly, comely race, with broad
skirts and large flowing wigs; rather slow in their movements,
and grave and dignified in their deportment: but now they are
docked and cropped, and skipping about in scanty clothes like so
many monkeys." The impression made on the old man shows
how greatly French fashions and manners had gained ground in
England during the half century he had passed in America.

In Hogarth's works there are many hints of this. The bride-
groom in the first picture of the " Marriage à la Mode," is evidently dressed on the model of a Paris beau; the boy beating a
drum in " The enraged Musician," has been metamorphosed, as
far as dress could do it, into a little Frenchman; the two gallants
in the boxes in " The laughing Audience," are as French as
possible, while the pit is filled with plain English folk who are not

too fine to take an interest in the performance ; and in . " Taste in
High Life," the antiquated beau, dressed in the extreme of the
Parisian fashion, has succeeded in making himself look very like
a monkey. Goldsmith represents the landlord of " The Three
Pigeons " as telling Tony Lumpkin that Hastings and Marlowe
" may be Londoners, for they look woundily like Frenchmen."

This fashion was checked by the French Revolution, and put
an end to, for a time, by the war that followed it ; but there can
be no doubt that, though often interrupted by political events, it is
(among the aristocracy of England) as old as the time of William
of Normandy, and the natural result of the Conquest.*

In April, 1820, Irving took me to breakfast with Sir Walter
Scott, who was then in London, and at the house of his friend,
Mrs. Dumergue, in Piccadilly. I had never before seen the great
novelist. He was in the full enjoyment of his high and increasing reputation, and he appeared to great advantage. A large
party of ladies and gentlemen were assembled at the breakfast
table, among whom was one of·the sons of Johnson's Boswell.

Nothing could be more agreeable than my daily intercourse at
this period with Irving and Newton. We visited in the same
families, chiefly Americans resident in London, and generally
dined together at the York Chop House, in Wardour Street.
Irving's brother, Peter, an amiable man, and not without a dash
of Washington's humour, was always of our party. Delightful
were our excursions to Richmond or Greenwich, or to some
suburban fair, on the top of a coach. The harmony that sub-
sisted among us was uninterrupted ; but Irving grew into fame as
an author, and being, all at once, made a great lion of by fashionable people, he was much withdrawn from us. Newton, too, who
was naturally formed for society, was soon much noticed for his
agreeable qualities, as well as for his eminence in art, and our
intercourse was a good deal interrupted in consequence.

Irving writing to me from Paris in 1824, said, " I often look
back with fondness and regret on the times when we lived together in London, in a delightful community of thought and feeling ; struggling our way onward in the world, but cheering and

* I should be inclined to trace it to a more recent source of influence — the
imitation of French fashions among the courtiers of the Restoration. — ED.

encouraging each other. I find nothing to supply the place of that heartfelt fellowship."

I had been for some time what is called *acquainted* with Constable, but it was only by degrees and in the course of years that I became really acquainted either with his worth as a man, or his true value as an artist. My taste was very faulty and long in forming; and of landscape, which I had never studied, I really knew nothing, or worse than nothing, for I admired, as poetical, styles which I now see to be mannered, conventional, or extravagant. But the more I knew of Constable, the more I regretted that I had not known him at the commencement of my studies.

As I have published all I recollect of him that seems to me best worth preserving, I have nothing to add except some memoranda made at a later period than that of which I am now writing.

Towards the close of the summer of 1821, I made a delightful excursion with Washington Irving to Birmingham, and thence into Derbyshire. We mounted the top of one of the Oxford coaches at three o'clock in the afternoon, intending only to go as far as Henley that night; but the evening was so fine, and the fields, filled with labourers gathering in the corn by the light of a full moon, presented so animated an appearance, that although we had not dined we determined to proceed to Oxford, which we reached about eleven o'clock, and then sat down to a hot supper.

The next day it rained unceasingly, and we were confined to the inn, like the nervous traveller whom Irving has described as spending a day in endeavouring to penetrate the mystery of " the stout gentleman." This wet Sunday at Oxford did, in fact, suggest to him that capital story, if story it can be called. The next morning, as we mounted the coach, I said something about a *stout gentleman* who had come from London with us the day before, and Irving remarked that " The Stout Gentleman," would not be a bad title for a tale. As soon as the coach stopped he began writing with his pencil, and went on at every like opportunity. We visited Stratford on Avon, strolled about Charlecot Park and other places in the neighbourhood, and while I was sketching, Irving, mounted on a stile, or seated on a stone, was busily engaged with " The Stout Gentleman." He wrote with the greatest

rapidity, often laughing to himself, and from time to time reading
the manuscript to me. We loitered some days in this classic
neighbourhood, visiting Warwick and Kenilworth; and by the
time we arrived at Birmingham, the outline of "The Stout
Gentleman" was completed. The amusing account of "The
Modern Knights Errant," he added at Birmingham, and the
inimitable picture of the inn yard on a rainy day was taken from
an inn where we were afterwards quartered at Derby.

It had been the custom for visitors to Shakespeare's house to
scribble their names, and sometimes scraps of bad poetry, on its
walls. Irving, on a former visit to Stratford, had given a large
blank book to the woman who had the care of the house, to save
the walls from further desecration. We found in it the name of
Sir Walter Scott, who had been there with a party not long
before, and were amused with the following anonymous parody
on the inscription which Shakespeare wrote for his own tomb:

> " Good friend, for Shakespeare's sake, forbear
> Thy wit or lore to scribble here;
> Blessed are they that rightly con him,
> And curs'd be they that comment on him."

In November, 1821, I was elected an associate of the Royal
Academy. I was, on every account, much elated with this event,
one of the great advantages resulting from which was the opportunities it afforded me of frequent intercourse with the best
artists; with Wilkie, Stothard, Flaxman, Chantrey, Lawrence,
Turner, Chalon, and Smirke, upon whom, though he had then
retired from the world, I was now entitled to call. I found him
a most sensible and agreeable man. I remember, when I was a
student of the Academy, hearing Sam Strowger tell of a dialogue
that had just passed between Fuseli and himself, as follows : —

" Sam, I am invited to dine out; have you any objection to my
going ? "

" That's according where it is, Mr. Fuseli."

" At Mr. Smirke's, Sam."

" Oh no, sir. Mr. Smirke is a very nice gentleman; and I
only wish I was qualified to go with you, sir."

Strowger will long be remembered at the Academy, not only

as a character, but as the most intelligent and faithful of servants to the Institution. When he brought me my Associate's diploma, he said, " I wish you health to enjoy it, sir, and I hope I shall soon bring you another; but all in good time ; we must not be in too great a hurry to get rid of old masters and get new ones ; " and then, fearing he had depressed me, he added in a lower tone, " but there are some of them, sir, can't last long."

It is the etiquette for a newly-elected member to call immediately on all the Academicians, and I did not omit paying my respects to Northcote among the rest, although I knew he was not on good terms with the Academy. I was shown up stairs into a large front room filled with pictures, many of the larger ones resting against each other, and all of them dim with dust. I had not waited long, when a door opened which communicated with his painting-room, and the old gentleman appeared, but did not advance beyond it. His diminutive figure was enveloped in a chintz dressing-gown, below which his trowsers, which looked as if made for a much taller man, hung in loose folds over an immense pair of shoes, into which his legs seemed to have shrunk down. His head was covered with a blue silk night-cap, and from under that and his projecting brows, his sharp black eyes peered at me with a whimsical expression of inquiry. There he stood, with his palette and brushes in one hand, and a mahl-stick, twice as long as himself, in the other ; his attitude and look saying, for he did not speak, " What do you want ? " On telling him that I had been elected an Associate of the Academy, he said quickly, " And who's the other ? " " Mr. Clint," I replied. " And so Clint's got it at last. You are an architect, I believe." I set him right ; and he continued, " Well, sir, you owe nothing to me ; I never go near them ; indeed I never go out at night anywhere." I told him I knew that, but thought it right to pay my respects to all the Academicians, and hoped I was not interrupting him. He said, " By no means ; " and asked me into his painting-room, where he was at work on an equestrian picture of George IV., as large as life, which he must have made up from busts and pictures. " I was desirous," he said, " to paint the King, for there is no picture that is like him " (I could not help contrasting to myself Lawrence's pictures of his Majesty with the one before me, and by no means to its advantage) ; " and he is by far," continued Northcote, " the best King of his family we have had. It has been remarked that this country is best governed by a woman, for then the government is carried on by able men ; and George IV. is like a woman, for he minds only his own amusements, and leaves the affairs of the country to his ministers, instead of meddling himself, as his father did. He is just what a King of England should be, something to look grand, and to hang the robes on."

He talked of Sir Joshua Reynolds, and I asked him whether he thought Sir Joshua was fully aware of his own great excellence. He said, " Perhaps not; I believe Sir Joshua did not, in his own estimation, rank himself as high as Vandyke. When young artists asked him to lend them his pictures to copy, he did not refuse, but was accustomed to say, ' If you can get a fine Vandyke, it will be much more useful to you.' "

. Northcote showed me what I supposed to be a picture by Reynolds ; but he told me it was a copy by Jackson, and said, " I have been myself deceived by his copies."

I asked leave to repeat my visit, which was readily granted, and from that time we were very good friends. He talked better than he painted.

When I first found myself painting in the exhibition rooms of the Royal Academy, where most of its members were at work, retouching their pictures, I was a good deal puzzled at the very opposite advice I received from authorities equally high. North-cote came in, and it was the only time I ever saw him at the Academy. He had a large picture there, and not hung in the best of places, at which he was much dissatisfied. I told him of my difficulties, and that Wilkie and Lawrence had just given me extraordinary advice. " Everybody," he said, " will advise you to do what he himself would do, but you are to consider and judge for yourself whether you are likely to do it as he would, and if not you may spoil your picture."

Northcote then complained to Phillips of the ill-usage he had received from the Academy, and said, " I have scarcely ever had a picture well hung. I wish I had never belonged to you."

Phillips said, laughing, " We can turn you out."

" The sooner you do so the better; only think of the men you
have turned out; you turned out Sir Joshua, you turned out
Barry, and you turned out West; and I shall be very glad to
make a fourth in such company."

The truth is, Sir Joshua and West had each resigned the chair
for a short time, in consequence of some displeasure with the
Academy; and therefore what Northcote said was more ingenious
than true; but it was not a bad specimen of his readiness in
reply.

When Mr. Shee paid him some compliments, with the adroit-
ness which was natural to him, Northcote said, " Very well,
indeed; you are just the man to write a tragedy, you know how
to make a speech." At another time, Northcote complimented
Shee in his own peculiar manner by saying, " You should have
been in Parliament instead of the Academy."

I lived still in Buckingham Place, Fitzroy Square, and was,
therefore, a very near neighbour to Flaxman, whose studio I
often visited. I remember seeing there some beautiful casts, in
plaster of Paris, from real flowers, branches of laurel, ivy, &c.
Being attached to backgrounds, they had the appearance of exquisite carvings in high relief. The firmer flowers and leaves
were perfectly moulded, as the lily, laurels, &c.; and even roses
were cast with surprising success.

Flaxman was always very kind in giving me his advice; but
his manner was almost painfully polite; he would say, " If I
might presume to suggest," &c. In this he resembled Lawrence,
and such a manner had the effect, though not intended, of keeping
people at a distance. I felt that it would be difficult to become
intimate either with Flaxman or Lawrence.

Though Flaxman's art is in a great degree eclectic, yet he had,
unquestionably, an exquisite feeling, entirely his own, for whatever is most graceful in nature. His imitation of the antique,
and of early Italian art, occasionally betrayed him into a manner
somewhat pedantic; yet it is not that mere mimicry which the
Germans of the present day (I am writing in 1843), have fallen
into. He imitated classical art as N. Poussin did, with constant
reference to nature. Allston told me that, having complimented
Flaxman on his designs from Homer, Dante, &c., the latter said,

"I will now show you the sources of many of them," and he laid
before him a great number of sketches from nature, of accidental
groups, attitudes, &c., which he had seen in the streets, and in
rooms. I have myself seen Flaxman stop in the street to make a
sketch of some attitude that struck him. There can be no doubt
that his outlines, particularly the series from Dante, led the way
to what the Germans are now doing. They began by outlines
from Faust, &c., and are now all becoming *little children in art*,
as they seem to fancy, by imitating the infancy of the Italian
schools. But they forget that the charms of infancy cannot be
assumed. Hence, though their works, by a mere *external* resemblance to early art, may deceive the superficial, all who are
really capable of separating that which is the essence, from that
which only belongs to the accidents of the age, the country, &c.,
must see that nothing can, in reality, be less like the art of Giotto,
and the infancy of Raphael's style, than what the Germans seem
almost desirous of palming on the world for veritable designs by
those masters. The mantle of Raphael has not yet fallen among
them.

Flaxman and Stothard would have been among the foremost
artists in the days of Julius II. and Leo X., but England, in the
times of George III. and IV., was utterly unworthy of them.
The British aristocracy, with the exception of Lord Egremont,
patronised Canova, and almost every English sculptor rather than
Flaxman, the greatest of all. He was, indeed, above their comprehension, and thus he found time, while his chisel was unem-
ployed, for his outline compositions; works which are looked to
as a mine of wealth by all European sculptors, and from which
painters as well as sculptors, British and foreign, have largely
helped themselves.

Canova, who was a noble-minded man, took every opportunity
of pointing out the merits of Flaxman to the English nobility
while they were crowding his studio, and giving him commissions
which he was sometimes obliged to refuse. "You English," he
said, " see with your ears." *

Lord Egremont, an exception to this reproach, employed Flaxman on his noble group of the Archangel Michael piercing Satan,
        * This I was told by Mr. Rogers.

and on a beautiful figure of a pastoral Apollo; but whatever other patronage he may have received from the nobility, it was miserably scanty for so great a genius. What must foreigners think who visit London (and who, if they have any taste, must be well acquainted with the powers of Flaxman) when they walk through our streets and squares, and meet with no work of his hand excepting only one of the statues and the bas-reliefs in front of Covent Garden Theatre, for which his country is indebted solely to the private regard of the architect, and John Kemble, for Flaxman?

I have been told by Mr. Baily, that Flaxman would not have been employed on the statue of Nelson for St. Paul's, had it not been that the hero himself was acquainted with him, and was known to have said, " If ever there should be a statue erected of me, I hope, Flaxman, you will carve it." He had competed unsuccessfully for the monument in St. Paul's, and when, for the reason mentioned, it was agreed by the committee of *taste* that he should make the statue of Nelson, he was desired to work from Westmacott's design, which the committee preferred to his own!!

He submitted, but never competed again. Chantrey was wiser, and never competed on any occasion. As a man, he was as different from Flaxman in manner as in appearance. Handsome (his mouth exceedingly beautiful), with a bluff John Bull look, and a bluntness of manner not quite pleasant, but playful, witty, and in general good natured. His strong native sense and tact compensated for his entire want of book learning. He was an admirable speaker; always clear, forcible, and to the purpose, with not a word too many or too few, the effect of what he said being aided by a fine, deep voice.

With respect to his art, he seems to me the Reynolds of portrait sculpture. Excepting the first portrait Lawrence painted of West, and the one he painted of the Duke of Wellington for Sir R. Peel, all the portraits I have seen by his hand are far surpassed by Chantrey's busts, whenever the same people sat to both. It is much to be regretted that Chantrey made so few busts of women. One I remember of a German princess, a relation, I think, of Queen Adelaide, was exceedingly lovely. It

4

was posthumous, and made from a cast taken after death. The
bust of Queen Victoria I thought also a charming work. It is
saying but little for it, that it is by far the best yet made.
Chantrey often showed his powers most when he had an indifferent subject. His bust of William IV. appeared to me a
great triumph of art. He managed to preserve a very strong
likeness, and without gross flattery contrived to give a kingly
air to it, of which certainly honest King William had very
little.

I had painted a portrait of a nobleman, of whom Chantrey
had just made a bust, and I asked him if I could do anything to
make my picture more like. He had not formed a very high
opinion of the inside of his Lordship's head, and pointing to the
ears, he said, " Make them longer."

The friends of a lad who had determined on applying himself
to sculpture, consulted me about placing him with a master. I
recommended Chantrey, and meeting him a day or two afterwards
in the Antique School at the Academy, I asked him if he took
pupils. " No; why do you ask?" I told him that a young
friend of mine would be glad to study with him. " I can teach
him nothing," he said, " let him come here." " He does, but how
is he to learn the use of the chisel?" "Any stone mason can teach
him that better than I can. He must become a workman before
he can be a sculptor. One great fault of our sculptors is that
few of them are workmen."

Edwin Landseer, the best of mimics, gave a capital specimen
of Chantrey's manner, and at Chantrey's own table. Dining at
his house with a large party, after the cloth was removed from
the beautifully polished mahogany — Chantrey's furniture was all
beautiful — Landseer's attention was called by him to the re-
flections, in the table, of the company, furniture, lamps, &c.
" Come and sit in my place and study perspective," said our
host, and went himself to the fire. As soon as Landseer was
seated in Chantrey's chair, he turned round, and imitating his
voice and manner, said to him, · " Come young man, you think
yourself ornamental; now make yourself useful, and ring the
bell." Chantrey did as he was desired — the butler appeared,
and was perfectly bewildered at hearing his master's voice, from

the head of the table, order more claret, while he saw him standing before the fire.

The only time I ever met Lord Jeffrey, was at Chantrey's. I
sat next to him at dinner, and found him delightful.

I also met Colonel Gurwood there. He could talk of nothing
but the Duke of Wellington. Speaking of the publication of his
Dispatches, he said, " I have unveiled a great man to the world.
He is the greatest creature God Almighty ever created. But
he don't write so well now as he did, for he thinks every thing he
writes will be printed, and he takes pains."

If proof were wanted of the superiority of Chantrey's mind, it
would be found in the fact that his most intimate associates were
such men as Davy and Wollaston; and that such men delighted
in his conversation. He, on the other hand, delighted to learn
from them, for, like every artist who deserves the title of an artist,
he was greatly interested in all natural science. On such subjects, I have so often heard him quote Davy and Wollaston, that
I feel sure nothing he heard them say was lost on him.

If Chantrey's busts possess many of the highest qualities of
the portraits of Reynolds, Jackson's best pictures approach them
the nearest in colour.

The first time I remember to have seen Jackson was in the
autumn of 1813, and at the British Institution, where we were
at the same time engaged in copying the same picture, the portrait of John Hunter, by Sir Joshua Reynolds. I knew nothing
then of Jackson's merits as a portrait painter, and was not disposed to rate him highly from what I saw of his mode of proceeding at the Institution. He seemed to me to be going on very
much at random, smearing asphaltum and lake over his canvass
in what I thought a very unartistlike manner, and I fancied my
copy would be much the best of the two. In short, I formed an
opinion of Jackson as opposite as possible to that which he really
deserved. I supposed him to be a conceited fellow, who affected
singularity not only as an artist, but as a man, for at that time he
wore knee breeches with brown silk stockings. Breeches were
then sometimes worn, but the brown stockings puzzled me.

Many years afterwards, I saw his copy of the John Hunter at
the house of Sir Charles Bell, and had I not been told what it

was, I might have mistaken it for the original. Still later in life, I met with my own copy. There is certainly no danger that it will ever pass for a work of Reynolds. I afterwards learned to value Jackson's art as well as himself. As a man, he was most amiable. It seemed scarcely possible that the serenity of his temper could be ruffled. I saw him often, but I never saw him in an ill humour under any circumstances. Though inclined to taciturnity, he had a great deal of natural drollery, and the soundness of his sense may be shown by a single sentence, whether it originated with him or whether he quoted it. " Whatever is worth doing," he said, " for the sake of example, *must* be worth doing for its own sake." What a contrast is this to the sophistry of Horace Walpole, who says, " I go to church sometimes in order to induce my servants to go to church. I am no hypocrite. I do not go in order to persuade them to believe what I do not believe myself. A good moral sermon may instruct and benefit them. I only set them an example of listening, not of believing."

I often spent my Sundays at Walthamstow, in the family of William Dillwyn, a venerable Quaker gentleman. He was from Philadelphia, and had known West before he left America ; and it was from him I heard the singular story of the first meeting between John West and his eldest son, who had never seen each other till the latter was fifty years of age. A strict adherence to the rules of his sect had not quenched the natural vivacity of Mr. Dillwyn. He had known Dr. Franklin, who carried him one day to the gallery of the House of Commons. As soon as they were seated, the Doctor whispered to him that a gentleman, immediately before them, was Garrick. The great actor had a friend with him, and Mr. Dillwyn overheard snatches of his conversation. On Garrick being asked how it was that with his abilities he had never thought of getting into Parliament, he said, " I have quite farce enough at my own house."

Mr. Dillwyn's son told me that his father, in his younger days, was in a stage coach with a party of military officers. One of them, a pert, effeminate, young dandy, undertook to quiz the plain Quaker, and after some indifferent jokes, asked him at an inn where they stopped, to hold his sword for a minute, supposing he would consider it an abomination to touch it. Mr. Dillwyn, however, eying the young man from head to foot said, " As I believe from thy appearance it has never shed human blood, and is not in the least likely to do so, I have not the smallest objection."

CHAPTER IV.

LORD EGREMONT had asked Phillips to go fifty miles into the country to make a sketch of one of his grandchildren, who was at the point of death. Phillips, unable to leave town, proposed that I should go, and this circumstance first made me known to Lord Egremont. When I reached the house of Colonel Wyndham, the father of the little girl, she had just died. I sat up all night, making sketches from her very beautiful face, and afterwards painted a small picture from them. When Lord Egremont asked me what he was to pay for it, I said twenty guineas. "But your travelling expenses must be paid." I told him they were five guineas, as I had posted to the house, and he immediately wrote me a cheque for fifty.

Soon after this he desired me to paint him a picture, leaving the subject and size to my own choice, and I painted "Sancho Panza in the Apartment of the Duchess." A few days before the picture went to the Exhibition Wilkie called on me, and, after paying me some compliments, with which I was greatly delighted, as coming from him, he said: "I think you may improve your picture very much by giving it more depth and richness of tone. Don't be afraid of glazing. The practice of our artists is running too much into a light and vapid style which will, in the end, ruin the art. I am trying, in my own pictures, to avoid this as much as possible, and I should be glad *to talk you over*. I have a picture by Isaac Ostade, which has exactly the qualities I should like to see you give to this. Can you come to Kensington this afternoon and look at it, for there is no time to be lost?" I said I would gladly do so, and as Newton intended to call on him to

see the pictures he was about to send to the exhibition, I would
ask him to go with me.   " No," said Wilkie, " I would rather see
him at some other time; I can talk better to one than to two."   I
went, and saw his beautiful little picture from Allan Ramsay's
" Gentle Shepherd," of Jenny and Peggy dressing themselves, a
fine specimen of richness and depth of *chiaroscuro*.   Indeed, but
for Wilkie's modesty, he might just as well have explained to me
all his notions of tone and effect from this picture as from the
Isaac Ostade.   But he dwelt eloquently on the beauties of the
latter, and concluded by exclaiming, in a voice of despair, " Are
we never to see this done again ? "   I might have answered, " No ;
but we may see something equally good though different in kind,
as your own pictures prove.   No form of art has ever been *exactly* repeated with success."   But I was more disposed to listen
with respect to all he said than to interrupt him, even with a compliment.   I felt the distance between us as artists, and I felt
greatly obliged by his taking the trouble to help me where I
knew I wanted help.   I was struck with the warmth, earnestness,
and animation of his manner, so unlike anything I had before
observed in him, and I felt convinced that he, like all first-rate
men, had nothing more seriously at heart than the advance of
every member of his profession.   As well, indeed, might we expect to find a sincerely religious man indifferent to the advancement of piety, as to meet with a really great artist unconcerned
for the general advancement of art.   It would be absurd to claim
for my own profession any exemption from the infirmities of human nature, — and it must be admitted that the greatest painters,
and very good men among them, have not been free from jealousies of their contemporaries, — but, to judge from my own experience, I should say that bad feelings rankle most among the
inferior artists, where their effects, from the comparative obscurity
of the individuals, are least known or noticed.   I remember an
amateur painter making a great noise in the hall of the Academy,
during the arrangement of an exhibition, because he had heard
that his picture was not well hung.   Constable and I went down
to pacify him.   He accused several of the members of jealousy,
and said, " I cannot but feel as I do, for painting is a passion with
me."   " Yes," said Constable, " and a *bad* passion."

While my picture of "Sancho and the Duchess" was in the Exhibition, Lord Egremont called on me and asked if I had received any commission for a similar picture. I told him I had not, and he said : "Then paint me a companion to it, and if anybody should wish to have it, let it go, and paint me another. I wish to keep you employed on such subjects instead of portraits."

Soon after this I received commissions for fancy subjects from Lord Essex, the Duke of Bedford, and others, and Lord Egremont desired me to execute them and reserve the one he had given me until I should be in want of employment.

In the autumn of 1824 I visited Scotland for the purpose of painting a portrait of Sir Walter Scott for Mr. Ticknor of Boston. Newton had gone with Irving on an excursion, which he afterwards extended to Scotland, and as Edwin Landseer was also bound for the north, he and I left London together, in the steamboat, for Edinburgh. I there found Newton, and, as I learned that Sir Walter was not at Abbotsford, we agreed to make a short trip to the Highlands. We passed through Glasgow, visited Loch Lomond and Loch Katrine, whence we walked across the mountains to Loch Earn, to be present at an annual meeting of Highlanders, under the patronage of Lord Gwydyr, at which prizes were distributed to the best performers on the bagpipes, the best dancers, broadswordsmen, &c.

It was a bright fresh autumnal morning when we left Loch Earn head for the other end of the lake, a distance of seven miles, in a large row-boat, in which, besides ourselves, were a number of Highlanders — men, women, and children. As we passed down the lake, the rowers amused us with stories of the fairies that inhabited its shores ; these stories being matters of serious belief with them. Occasionally we heard the distant sound of bagpipes, and as they neared us the hills were enlivened by the appearance of parties of Highlanders in full costume, each headed by a piper, and all bound for the place of rendezvous. This little voyage afforded us an enjoyment of the Highlands, with all that is native to them, in perfection. The amusement of the games which we afterwards witnessed was nothing to the delight of gliding gently down the clear smooth lake with such accompaniments.

We afterwards visited Stirling and Ayr; the latter being to me the most interesting spot in Scotland, associated as the town itself and the scenery of its neighbourhood is with Burns. A lover of Burns (and who does not love him) may imagine the feelings with which we crossed the "Brigs of Ayr," listened to "the drowsie donjon clock," looked up to Wallace Tower, visited the cottage in which the bard was born, and Kirk Alloway, and strolled by the side of the "Bonny Doon," where Burns had so often strayed, composing his enchanting songs. I bathed in its exquisitely clear stream. "What are those mountains?" I asked of an old man, who said he had often had a gill of whiskey with Burns. They were "the Cumnock Hills." "What a delightful companion Burns must have been." "Oh, not at all; he was a silly chiel; but his brother Gilbert was quite a gentleman — like you," he said, looking at Newton, whose appearance and manner were remarkably good.

A Scotch gardener told me that he knew the original Tam-o'-Shanter. I forget his name, but he was very proud of being immortalized by Burns, though he said that part of the poem in which his wife rates him for his drunkenness, was "a lee; for there never was a better-tempered woman, and she never scolded me in a' her life."

From Ayr I returned direct to Edinburgh, where I left Newton, and proceeded to Abbotsford. I carried from John Murray to Sir Walter a mourning ring, which had been left to him by Lord Byron.

The following is a quotation from a letter I wrote from Abbotsford: "The Countess of Compton, her mother (Mrs. Clephane), and her two sisters, have been here for the last three days. Mr. and Mrs. Terry are here: Lady Alvanley and her two daughters arrived yesterday to dinner: and late in the evening came Mrs. Coutts, attended by a lady, a secretary, a doctor, and I don't know how many servants. Mr. Stewart Rose is also here. This list will give you some notion of the hospitalities of Abbotsford. Mr. Canning is expected, but not till October, and so I shall not see him. I have had three sittings from Sir Walter, and the general opinion is that the portrait will be like."

During one of these sittings, there came on a thunder-storm;

and as the peals followed more and more closely the flashes of
lightning, Scott became uneasy, and at last rose from his chair,
saying, "I must go to Lady Scott, she is always frightened when
it thunders."

It is curious that the only circumstance connected with Scott
and related by Lockhart, of which I was a witness, is incorrectly
stated in his Life of Sir Walter.   Lockhart places Mrs. Coutts's
visit to Abbotsford in 1825, instead of 1824; and tells us she
was accompanied by the Duke of St. Albans and one of his
grace's sisters, and by "a brace of physicians," evidently con-
founding this visit with one she paid to Sir Walter in Edinburgh
in the following year, when the Duke and one of his sisters were
of her party, and when she may have had two physicians, which
was certainly not the case when she was at Abbotsford in 1824.

But Lockhart's chief inaccuracy is in the account he gives of
the ill-manners of some of Scott's lady visitors towards Mrs.
Coutts, and the result.   After saying that they contrived to mor-
tify her "without doing or saying anything that could expose
them to the charge of actual incivility," he tells us that Sir Walter remonstrated with the "youngest, gayest, and cleverest (a
lovely Marchioness)," that she took the remonstrance in good
part, promised better behaviour, and that she and the rest directly
became as civil to Mrs. Coutts as they had before been the reverse ; that Mrs. Coutts was pacified, and "stayed her three
days."

Now I have no doubt Sir Walter did remonstrate with the
beautiful Lady Compton (who was not then a Marchioness), for
I remember that Lady Compton was very polite to Mrs. Coutts
in the evening, and sat down to the piano to accompany her in a
song which she made an ineffectual attempt to sing, but could not
utter a note.   Her wounded spirit, in fact, was not healed ; and
instead of staying "her three days," she slept at Abbotsford but
one night, after the night of her arrival, and went away the next
morning.

Stuart Newton was at Abbotsford at the time.   About a year
afterwards he was taken by a friend to one of Mrs. Coutts's fêtes
at Holly Lodge, and on saying that he had "had the honour of
meeting her at Sir Walter Scott's," she said, "Oh ! I remember,

it was when those horrible women were there. Sir Walter was very kind, and did all in his power, but I could not stay in the house with them."

I believe the rudeness Mrs. Coutts suffered at Abbotsford was chiefly occasioned by what had occurred before she came. She was expected the day before she did arrive; the dinner hour, seven o'clock, came, but not Mrs. Coutts; at first, nobody could feel aggrieved that Sir Walter would not allow dinner to be served. But no doubt the ladies (two of them titled ladies) thought it too much that dinner was deferred till nine o'clock, and might have been longer postponed, had not a messenger arrived from Mrs. Coutts, to say that she was delayed on the road by the want of horses, and could not reach Abbotsford that night.

It was not unnatural, therefore, that ladies, by no means prepossessed in her favour, and feeling that more deference had been paid her by their host than was due to anything less than Royalty, should be somewhat out of humour with her beforehand; and though this is no excuse for their ill-breeding, it may account for it.

Constable, the publisher, spent a day at Abbotsford while I was there. He told Sir Walter that Meg Dodds, a name given to the mistress of an inn halfway between Edinburgh and Abbotsford, and who was supposed to have furnished the original of that character, said " Sir Walter had ill-obliged her by not giving her notice that so great a lady as Mrs. Coutts was coming, in order that she might be prepared to receive her properly. She was taken by surprise, when she ought to have been informed that the greatest woman in all England was on her way to visit the greatest man in all Scotland; indeed she might say Sir Walter was the greatest man in the world, now Bonaparte was dead."

The following is from one of my letters: —

" I am painting in the library. When Sir Walter is seated I always place a chair in the direction in which I wish him to look, which is never long unoccupied by some one of his visitors, who is sure to keep him in conversation. At the other end of the room there is generally a group round the harp or piano. Imagine how delightful these sittings are to me.

" This morning, being Sunday, Sir Walter read the Church

Service to the whole family and his guests, in an impressive manner."

When I began the portrait, Scott suggested that for the background I should take "Thomas the Rhymer's Glen," one of his
favourite haunts. I went with him and Mr. Rose to see it, and
when we came near the spot where Thomas was supposed to
have met the Queen of the Fairies, Sir Walter and I dismounted
from our ponies, and as the descent into the glen was steep, I
offered to help him; but he declined assistance, saying, he could
get along best in his own way; and, indeed, he displayed more
activity than I could have expected, considering his lameness,
scrambling down the sides of the glen, often on all fours. He
told me that in his youth he had been an adventurous climber,
though no one would suppose it, as his lame leg was of scarcely
any use to him.

The glen was beautiful, and as he rested himself in his
favourite seat near a little succession of waterfalls, he said, with
a strong emphasis of satisfaction on the two last words, " a poor
thing, but *mine own*." I told him the dimensions of my picture
would not admit the scene as a background, as its leading features
could nôt be brought into so small a compass. I might, however,
have made a sketch of it with Sir Walter in the spot he loved,
and my only excuse for not doing it is that Mr. Rose, who was
too infirm to descend into the glen, was waiting for us above.
As we returned, I remember Rose saying he had never known
anybody who had read Voltaire's " Henriade" through. Scott
replied, " I have read it, *and live;* but, indeed, in my youth I
read everything."

Sir Walter had appropriated to his friend Rose, whose infirmities were occasioned by paralysis, a sitting-room with a bed-
room adjoining it on the ground floor, the latticed windows of
which, shaded by flowers, looked into the garden. Here Rose
could seclude himself when he liked, and pursue a task Scott had
engaged him in, a translation, I think, of Ariosto. Scott thought
that some such easy employment of the mind would be service-
able to his health. The luxurious table at Abbotsford would,
however, have rendered Sir Walter's kind intentions useless, had
not Rose practised a rigid system of self-denial.

When Lady Scott offered to help him to some rich delicacy, he said — " No, madam, I believe in a *hereafter*."

Rose was able to shoot, with the assistance of his man, Henviss, who carried his gun; and when he went out for a morning's sport, he wore a great coat without sleeves, for the better convenience of using his arms. His under-coat, differing in colour from the outer one, gave him a very odd appearance, his body being brown and his arms black. Henviss raised the gun to his shoulder for him, and Rose said — " When I fire I never know whether the birds are to fall or myself." But he generally managed to kill them notwithstanding his lameness. Henviss was an odd, half-witted fellow, and Scott said he reminded him, more than any man he had ever met with, of the motley fools in Shakespeare. Rose had, in fact, provided Henviss with some sort of antic dress which he made him wear by way of punishment, when he had behaved amiss; but Henviss took a fancy to it, and would often put it on for his own gratification. He wanted to wear it at Abbotsford, but to this Sir Walter objected, saying — " I have no reputation for wisdom to spare in my own neighbourhood, and I cannot afford to fall lower in the estimation of the country-people by permitting Henviss to be seen about the place in a fool's dress." Rose told many droll stories of Henviss; but, as he related many out of the way things of other people, it was thought these stories owed quite as much to the master as to the man. Lady Anna Maria Elliott, herself a wit, said, after listening for some time to Rose : —

" What a great number of very odd people you have known."

" I don't know that," he replied.

" Well, then, I am very sure all Mr. Rose's acquaintance know *one* very odd person."

During one 'of Sir Walter's sittings to me, the conversation turned on Quakers, and he was surprised to hear that I had painted the portraits of several, for he thought they objected to pictures, as well as to music. He said, " They must have been what are called wet Quakers." I assured him they were not, but he would have it that " at least, they were *damp* Quakers."

Scott told me he had known a labouring man who was with Burns when he turned up the mouse with his plough.

Burns's first impulse was to kill it, but checking himself, as his eye followed the little creature, he said, "I'll make that mouse immortal." He mentioned this as an instance of Burns's confidence in his own powers.

I was much interested by seeing in the library at Abbotsford, an autograph manuscript of "Tam O'Shanter." There were, either in this MS., or Scott had noted that there were in some other copy, two lines that had never been printed. They occurred after

"The landlord's laugh was ready chorus:"

and ran thus:

"The cricket join'd his chirping cry,
The kittling chas'd its tail wi' joy."

Scott had remarked, in a note, that Burns probably rejected them from the resemblance to Goldsmith's line, —

"The cricket chirrup'd on the hearth."

He had once seen Burns, and described his eye as remarkably fine; it was dark, and seemed to dilate when he became excited. I have lately met Major Burns, one of the poet's sons. I looked at him with great interest, which was increased by his modest and unassuming manners, in which I am sure he must have resembled his father, whose genius was of too high an order to be accompanied by any personal assumption or display.

While strolling with Sir Walter about his own grounds, a pleasure I often enjoyed, he would frequently stop and point out exactly that object or effect that would strike the eye of a painter. He said he always liked to have a dog with him in his walks, if for nothing else but to furnish a living object in the *foreground of the picture;* and he noticed to me, when we were among the hills, how much interest was given to the scene by the occasional appearance of his black greyhound, Hamlet, at unexpected points. He talked of scenery as he wrote of it — like a painter; and yet for pictures, as works of art, he had little or no taste, nor did he pretend to any. To him they were interesting merely as representing some particular scene, person, or event; and very moderate merit in their execution contented him. There were things hanging on the walls of his dining-room, which no eye possessing sensibility to what is excellent in art could have endured. In this respect his house presented a striking contrast to that of Mr. Rogers, where nothing met the eye which was not of high excellence. I am inclined to think that in music also, Scott's enjoyment arose chiefly from the associations called up by the air, or the words of a song. I have seen him stand beside the piano or harp when Lady Compton, Miss Clephane, or Mrs. Lockhart were playing Highland music, or a military march, his head and whole figure slightly moving in unison with the instrument, and with an expression in his face of inward delight, that told, more plainly than any words could tell, how thoroughly he relished the performance. He had kept a piper, but this personage was dismissed before the time of which I am writing: I believe for drunkenness. Sir Walter, as might be supposed, was fond of the bagpipe, and contended that it was really a fine instrument, independently of all national associations.

His conversation was enriched with quotations, often made highly humorous by their application. I remember his comparing the sound of the dinner-bell, for which, he said, he had "a very quick ear," to

> " the sweet south,
> That breathes upon a bank of violets,
> Stealing and giving odour."

There was more benevolence expressed in Scott's face than is given in any portrait of him; and I am sure there was much in his heart. It showed itself in little daily acts of quiet kindness to everybody about him. As an instance, I may mention that there was a young man, educated for the Church, but as yet without a curacy, living at Abbotsford. He was so deaf as to be obliged to use an ear-trumpet. Sir Walter always placed him at his side at dinner; and when anything was said that he thought would interest Mr. ——, he turned to him, and dropped it into his trumpet. "Look at Scott," Newton whispered to me, "dropping something into ——'s charity-box."

I asked Sir Walter where I should be likely to meet with a haggis. "I don't know a more likely place than the house you are in," he said; and the next day a haggis appeared on the

table. It was placed before him, and he greeted it with the first
lines of Burns's address to the " Chieftain of the Pudding Race."
He repeated them with great effect ; and at the words

> " Weel are ye worthy of a grace
> As lang 's my arm,"

he extended his arm over the haggis.

It was curious that Mr. Leycester Adolphus's " Letter to Richard Heber," so satisfactorily proving Scott to be the author of
the Waverley Novels, was lying on the table of the Abbotsford
Library at that time, when the novels were never mentioned in
Scott's presence. This admirable essay not only carries conviction on the point it was written to establish, but contains the best
critique on Scott's prose and poetry (for an entirely favourable
one) ever written.

Sir Walter's old and faithful servant, Tom Purdey, is mentioned by Lockhart. I made a small whole-length sketch of Tom
for Sir Walter. Purdey was in bad health, and his master was
much grieved at the thoughts of losing him ; but Tom lived till
after the authorship of the novels was acknowledged. Mr. Cadell
told me that, as Sir Walter was leaning on Purdey's arm, in one
of his walks, Tom said, " Them are fine novels of yours, Sir
Walter ; they are just invaluable to me." " I am glad to hear it,
Tom." " Yes, sir, for when I have been out all day, hard at
work, and come home, vara tired, if I sit down with a pot of porter by the fire, and take up one of your novels, I'm asleep directly."

Somebody spoke of clubs, and Scott said, " I belong to many,
but I don't frequent them, for there is always a scum of bores
floating on the surface of club life. And yet I don't dislike a
good bore, for it requires a clever man to be one."

He said, " I never knew a man of genius — and I have known
many — who could be regular in all his habits, but I have known
many a blockhead who could."

Cadell told me that, in allusion to the opinion that Lord Byron's lameness was the occasion of his misanthropy, he said to
Scott, " Your temper has not suffered from the same misfortune,"
and Scott replied, " When I was of the age at which lads like to
shine in the eyes of the girls, I have felt some envy, in a ball-

room, of the young fellows who had the use of their legs; but I generally found when I was beside the lasses I had the advantage with my tongue."

When I left Abbotsford for Edinburgh, Scott gave me a packet for Constable, which, no doubt, contained manuscript. I think he was then writing the " Tales of the Crusaders."

At Edinburgh I met with much kind attention from the artists. Wilkie was there, for the purpose of making studies of the Scottish Regalia, &c., for his picture of George the Fourth entering Holyrood House, and I was delighted to meet him in the capital of his own country. We talked of Scott and of Burns, and he remarked that it was a fine piece of art in Burns to make an exaggerated account of Tam O'Shanter's excesses *dramatically* natural, by putting it into the mouth of his angry wife.

At the time of which I am writing, my sister Ann was living with me, and as I had the prospect of marrying I had taken a small house in Lisson Grove, which had the convenience of a large painting room attached to it. This had been built by the owner of the house, Mr. Rossi, R.A., for Mr. Haydon, and it was there Haydon painted his " Christ entering Jerusalem."

The last letter I received from my sister, while on my visit to Scotland, hastened my return, as it told me she had heard that our mother was dangerously ill. On arriving at my own door, my sister met me in deep mourning. She had been sorrowing at home, while I had been revelling in enjoyment.

My mother died on the 24th July, aged fifty-seven, at the house of my brother, Captain Leslie, at West Point. My sister heard this soon after I went to Scotland; but did not acquaint me with it, knowing that it would defeat the object for which I had gone.

CHAPTER V.

On the 11th April, 1825, I was married ; and in the course of
the same year I received a visit from my third sister Mrs. Henry
Carey, her husband, and his sister Maria. I had not seen my
sister Carey for fourteen years, and was greatly struck with the
uncommon sweetness of her face and manner. I had not, when
a boy, thought her even pretty, but she now appeared to me
beautiful. I was perhaps by this time a better judge of beauty.
Her figure was slight and petite, her features not regular, and
her complexion dark, though very clear. But her eyes were
lovely, full' and grey, with long black lashes ; she had beautiful
dimples ; and at all times an expression of so much good sense,
whether joyous or sad, and manners so perfectly natural and engaging, that I thought her one of the most charming women I
had ever seen. She had always been a favourite with my brother
and myself, but I had never entirely appreciated her till, after our
long separation, we met again as new acquaintances. My relations made a short excursion in England through some of the
scenes my wife and I had visited on our wedding excursion ; and,
after a trip to Paris, they returned to America, taking my sister
Ann with them.

Not long before my marriage, I had been introduced to Lord
Holland. I painted small portraits of his lordship, of his beautiful daughter Mary (now Lady Lilford), and of Lady Affleck
(Lady Holland's mother), for Lady Holland. These were all
painted at Holland House ; and from that time I had frequent
opportunities of being present at the delightful breakfast and

dinner parties that took place every day in that fine old mansion. Among the guests whom I met there most often, were Sir James Mackintosh, Mr. Richard Sharpe, Mr. Rogers, Mr. Luttrell, and Mr. Thomas Moore.

Lord Holland was, without any exception, the very best tempered man I have ever known. How much more he was than merely a good-tempered man, has been, and will no doubt again be, recorded by persons far better able than I am to describe him. Of the grace with which he could confer a favour, the following letter addressed to me, affords a specimen. It enclosed a cheque for one hundred guineas for the portraits I had painted of himself and of his daughter, that sum being forty guineas more than I expected to receive.

"10th *June*, 1829.

"DEAR SIR,

"When you were so good as to undertake to paint a portrait of my daughter, I understood from Lord Egremont that you charged only thirty guineas for works of that nature and size. But after the great trouble you have taken, and the great success you have had in those you have painted for me, I am really ashamed of repaying such works at so low a rate; and I hope you will do me the favour of accepting the enclosed for the two pictures finished and framed as you will deliver them to me. The price, even in its amended shape, bears no proportion whatever to the value I annex to the works; but it unfortunately does bear a more correct one to the sum that I can with any prudence devote to such objects.

"I am, Dear sir, with many thanks,

"Your obliged and obedient servant,

"VASSALL HOLLAND."

Lord Holland was fond of talking of his uncle, Charles Fox, and repeating his *bon mots*. But Lord Holland had a wit's relish for wit. When Stuart the painter died, a eulogium on his character appeared in one of the American papers, in which it was said that he left the brightest prospects in England, and returned to his own country, from his admiration of her new institutions,

and a desire to paint the portrait of Washington. On hearing
this, Sir Thomas Lawrence said : " I knew Stuart well ; and I
believe the real cause of his leaving England was his having
become ·tired of the inside of some of our prisons." " Well,
then," said Lord Holland, " after all, it was his love of freedom
that took him to America."

A saying that perhaps was invented for Lady Holland, is still
so like her, and so good, that I will put it down. When Moore's
" Lalla Rookh " appeared, she is reported to have said to him :
" Mr. Moore, I don't intend to read your *Larry O'Rourke*, I don't
like Irish stories." She was hard to please in all kinds of stories ;
few people told them as well as she did.

In the autumn of 1826, Lord Egremont invited Mrs. Leslie and
myself to Petworth, where we spent a month. From that time
to the end of Lord Egremont's life, we were regularly invited to
Petworth, with our children, every year. Besides the picture I
had painted for him of " Sancho and the Duchess," I painted
three others of the same class,* and was engaged on a fourth at
the time of his death. I painted also small portraits of his daughters, Lady Burrell and Mrs. King.

He was the most munificent, and at the same time the least
ostentatious, nobleman in England. Plain spoken, often to a degree of bluntness, he never wasted words, nor would he let others
waste words on him. After conferring the greatest favours, he was
out of the room before there was time to thank him. When he
first noticed me, he had almost entirely retired from London,
living at Petworth, and benefiting the people about him, in every
way in his power.

His personal habits were the most simple possible; and his
manner naturally shy and retiring. He might easily be mistaken, by those who knew him but slightly, for a proud person ;
but, as Sir William Beechey said of him, he " had more ' put-up-
ability ' than almost any other man." He would bear a great
deal before he would take the trouble to be angry ; but when
angry it was to the purpose, and I have known him, in more than

---

* Scene from the " Taming of the Shrew;" Gulliver's introduction to the
Queen of Brobdignag; Charles II. at Tillietudlem Castle, from " Old Mortality." — ED.

one instance, order persons to leave his house, who, encouraged by his good-nature and the easy footing on which they found themselves at Petworth, had forgotten where they were, and behaved as if that noble mansion were but a great hotel.

His liveries were extremely plain, and there were neither arms nor coronet on any of his carriages. Wilkie was at Petworth during one of our visits, and Lord Egremont took him and me, one morning, to Chichester. On the way, he stopped to show us Goodwood; but the Duke and Duchess of Richmond being from home, he asked for the housekeeper. The servants did not know him, and we were kept waiting for a quarter of an hour in the hall. Lord Egremont showed some impatience, ordered his footman to ring the bell again, and said: "I would go away, only they will think we are a parcel of thieves." He had some business to transact at Chichester; but one of his objects was to show us a young girl, the daughter of an upholsterer, who was devoted to painting, and considered to be a genius by her friends. She was not at home; but her mother said she could soon be found, "if his lordship would have the goodness to wait a short time." The young lady soon appeared, breathless and exhausted with running. Lord Egremont mentioned our names, and she said, looking up to Wilkie with an expression of great respect, "Oh, sir! it was but yesterday I had your head in my hands." This puzzled him, as he did not know she was a phrenologist.

"And what bumps did you find?" said Lord Egremont.

"The organ of veneration, very large," was her answer; and Wilkie, making her a profound bow, said:

"Madam, I have a great veneration for genius."

She showed us an unfinished picture from "The Bride of Lammermoor." The figure of Lucy Ashton was completed, and, she told us, was the portrait of a young friend of hers; but Ravenswood was without a head, and this she explained by saying, "there are no handsome men in Chichester. But," she continued, her countenance brightening, "the Tenth * are expected here soon."

All this was uttered with an air so perfectly simple and inno-

* A regiment noted for its handsome officers.

cent, that it was the more amusing, and Lord Egremont was highly diverted.

As his lordship, from that "put-up-*ability*" of his character which Beechey noticed, seldom changed his servants, some of the upper ones were as old as himself; and these not being in livery, and his own dress, in the morning, being very plain, he was sometimes by strangers mistaken for one of them. This happened with a maid of one of his lady guests, who had not been at Petworth before. She met him, crossing the hall, as the bell was ringing for the servants' dinner, and said : " Come, old gentleman, you and I will go to dinner together, for I can't find my way in this great house." He gave her his arm, and led her to the room where the other maids were assembled at their table, and said : " You dine here, I don't dine till seven o'clock."

He was very fond of children, and while he was dressing, his grandchildren were generally brought into his room. He asked for ours at the same time, and they always came away each with a sugar-plum, or some other little present.

On matters of art Lord Egremont thought for himself; and his remarks were worth remembering. He said to me : " I look upon Raphael and Hogarth as the two greatest painters that ever lived." When the picture of the " Vision of St. Jerome," by Parmegiano, now in the National Gallery, was bought for a large sum by the Directors of the British Institution, Lord Egremont, who happened to be in London, called on me, and asked me if I had a catalogue of the British Institution. " I want to see," he said, " who are the men who have given so much money for that broken-backed St. John. A poor way, I think, of encouraging the art."

The following is one of his letters relating to a picture he wished me to paint as a companion to " Sancho and the Duchess : "

" DEAR SIR,

" You said that you would show me a design when you came to Petworth, and I wish to explain that, by a companion picture, I did not mean to confine you to the story of Don Quixote. On the contrary, I have never seen any representation of the Don that satisfied me, and I believe that it is impossible to represent all the absurdity and ridicule of his character, and at the same time the dignity of his mind, and the grandeur of his sentiments, by painting only, without the addition of language.

"Ever yours truly, &c.

"EGREMONT."

The kind manner in which we were invited to Petworth will be seen in the following note, in answer to one which I wrote declining an invitation, in consequence of our having spent as much time as I could then spare from home at Brighton. My letter accompanied a picture I had painted.

"DEAR SIR,

"The picture is quite safe, and wants nothing. I hope you have some great works in hand, but whenever you feel an inclination for some country air for your children, I hope you will give the preference to Petworth, where you will find me at any time, and always happy to see you.

"Ever truly yours,

"EGREMONT."

"*Petworth, August 14th, 1832.*"

It was impossible to move many steps in the town of Petworth without meeting with something to remind one of the benevolent feelings of him who might be called its king. Mr. Sockett, the rector, pointed out to me on a tomb this epitaph, written by Lord Egremont : —

HERE LIETH THE BODY

OF

WILLIAM ANDRE,

A man of the most blameless conduct, and the most inoffensive manners. To his professional skill hundreds have been indebted for health and life. From his hands thousands have received, by Vaccination, security against that most destructive of all diseases, the small-pox. Reader, if thou art a stranger, learn that these benefits were gratuitously conferred; if thou art a neighbour, remember them with gratitude, and respect his tomb.

HE DIED DEC. 4, 1807,

AGED 64 YEARS.

I at this time became acquainted with Sidney Smith, through

my friend Newton. His wit and humour were always unpremed-
itated, and seemed not so much the result of efforts to amuse, as
the overflowing of a mind full of imagery, instantly ready to
combine with whatever passed in conversation. His very exag-
gerations took away the sting of his most personal witticisms, and
I suppose no man was ever so amusing with so little offence ; for
those who were the subjects of his jokes were often the most ready
to relate them. When a discussion took place among the clergy
of St. Paul's, as to the expediency of surrounding the cathedral
with a pavement of blocks of wood, Smith said, " If the bishops
would lay their heads together, the thing would be done : " and
this was so often repeated, and with so much unction, by the
Bishop of London, that he was suspected of having invented it.

I happened to be in Newton's room when Mr. Smith came in
to sit for his portrait. He looked, in the arm chair, very like
Newton's picture of Abbot Boniface ; and indeed he suspected
Newton of taking a hint for the portly figure of the Abbot from
him. " I sit here," he said, " a personification of piety and absti-
nence."

Newton told me that at a dinner party at Lord Lyndhurst's, at
which he was present, the conversation turned on the custom, in
India, of widows burning themselves, an instance of which was
recent. When the subject was pretty well exhausted, Smith
began to defend the practice, asserting that no wife who truly
loved her husband could wish to survive him.

" But, if Lord Lyndhurst were to die, you would be sorry that
Lady Lyndhurst should burn herself."

" Lady Lyndhurst," he replied, " would no doubt, as an affectionate wife, consider it her duty to burn herself, but it would be
our duty to put her out ; and, as the wife of the Lord Chancellor,
Lady Lyndhurst should not be put out like an ordinary widow.
It should be a state affair. First, a procession of the judges, and
then of the lawyers."

" But where, Mr. Smith, are the clergy ? "

" All gone to congratulate the new Chancellor."

At the back of Holland House, a window is distinguished from
all the rest by an iron grating over it. This window communi-
cates with Lady Holland's bedroom, and she had it grated when

she heard of a gentleman and his wife being murdered in their bed by a servant, who entered their room through a back window. Sidney Smith gave another account of this window. "Allen," he said, "keeps a clergyman in confinement there, upon bread and water." Mr. Allen's dislike to the clergy was no secret.

I met Sidney Smith at a dinner party at Mr. Rogers's. Sidney's brother was there, and told us of his having been at school with the Duke of Wellington, with whom he had the honour of fighting, but the Duke beat him. "He began with you," said Sidney, "and ended with Bonaparte."

Mr. Luttrell mentioned an Irish clergyman who was much offended at being called a "*pluralist*," and said, "if you don't take care you will find me a *duelist*." Smith took this up, and said, "I suppose there is scarcely a clergyman in Ireland who has not *been out*." I am told they settle these matters when the afternoon's service is over. I have seen a parson's challenge : — "Sir, meet me on the first Sunday after the Epiphany."

I was greatly amused with him at a large evening party at Mrs. Bates's house. He had been suffering from gout, and remained seated near the door, watching the arrivals of the guests, and their reception by the hostess. "Is it possible," he said to her, "that you know all these people?" "Oh, no!" "Well, then, you do it remarkably well, for you not only seem to *know* them all, but to *love* them all. Can you tell an American at first sight? I'm sure I can't." And then, observing a lady with an uncommonly splendid turban on her head, he added, "I should say there is a bit of U. S." — and he happened to be right.

Many things were invented for him which he never said, among them the story of Landseer asking to paint him, and his reply — "Is thy servant a *dog* that he should do this thing?"

This was in the newspapers, and Sidney Smith meeting Landseer in the Park, said : —

"Have you seen our little joke in the papers?"

"Are you disposed to acknowledge it?"

"I have no objection."

Soon after his pamphlet appeared against American repudiation, my friend, Captain Morgan, arrived, and brought from New York some very fine apples. I suggested to him to send a barrel

to Sidney Smith, and beg his acceptance of them as his share of
the American debt. Morgan received two notes in reply. The
first is published, and the second ran thus —

" SIR,
            When I told my company that your apples came from
a solvent State, they were eaten with great applause."

He enclosed his poetical receipt for a salad.

Sidney Smith, after travelling for some hours in a stage coach
with one other passenger only, a lady, said, as he was about to
leave the coach :

" We have been some time together, and I dare say you think
me a very odd fellow, and would like to know who I am."

" Indeed, sir, I should."

" Well then, madam," he said, as the coach stopped, and he
was getting out, " I must inform you that I am the stout gentleman who was seen by Mr. Washington Irving's nervous friend."

Mr. Rogers told me that Smith received invitations to dine with
Whitbread and with some peer at the same time. He accepted
Whitbread's, and wrote to the peer that he " was engaged to dine
with the great fermentator in Chiswell Street." But, putting his
answers into the wrong covers, his excuse to the peer went to the
brewer, and Lady Elizabeth Whitbread replied, " The *great fermentator* is much obliged to Mr. Smith for giving him the preference." He answered, " I have received your ladyship's note, and
kill myself on the spot."

Edwin Landseer said to him : " With your love of humour, it
must be a great act of self-denial to abstain the theatres."

" The managers," he replied, " are very polite ; they send me
free admissions, which I can't use ; and, in return, I send them
free admissions to St. Paul's."

Like Sterne's Yorick, Sidney Smith has been thought to indulge too much in a levity unbecoming a clergyman, and by some
people the sincerity of his faith has been, like Yorick's, doubted.
It is true he assumed no outward garb of sanctity ; and if to be a
Christian, it be necessary to be a Methodist, he was not one. But
those who knew him most intimately, speak of him as not neg-

lecting any of his serious duties; and Lady Bell, who soon after
the death of her husband passed some time with his family at his
living, spoke in the highest terms of his active benevolence among
his parishioners.   It must be remembered, also, how constantly
his wit was employed against enormous abuses, and particularly
in the Church; how constantly he raised his voice in behalf of
the poor and hard-working clergy.

A friend of mine, who had opportunities of knowing him well,
characterised him as " *the greatest disperser of humbug that ever
lived.*"

I had heard, and with great admiration, Sidney Smith preach,
many years before the time of which I am writing.   I thought
him the best preacher I ever heard, and I know of no better sermons than those he has published.

There are passages in them tinged with the wit which made
him so delightful a companion out of the pulpit, but this does not
in the least impair their seriousness.   He seems to me, in these
discourses, to be at all times equally earnest, eloquent, and sound
in the view he takes of his subject, and the more I read them the
more I find them to contain.

He carried the natural cheerfulness of his mind into his religion.   I remember, the first time I heard him preach, — and before I knew anything else of him than that he was an admirable
preacher, — he strongly objected to melancholy views of religion.
He said with great emphasis, " I want you to *enjoy* your religion."

Among my brother artists, the two with whom I was the most
intimately associated, at the time of which I am writing, were
Newton and Constable; but Newton lived so much in society, and
in that respect his habits were so different from my own, that I
found myself less with him than with Constable.

Of all the painters I have known — and I have been intimate
with all the most eminent of my time — Constable was to me the
most interesting, both as a man and an artist.   I have been told
that my great admiration of his pictures arose out of my personal
acquaintance with him; but the reverse was really the case; my
acquaintance with him arose out of my admiration of his pictures.
I cultivated his friendship because I liked his art.   There are

many estimable men, artists, for whom I have the greatest regard, but of whose works that regard cannot make me an admirer.

A lively Quaker lady, a daughter of my excellent friend, Mr. Dillwyn, considered the world as composed of two classes — "those who have souls, and those who have none;" and wherever she may have drawn the line of separation, I am sure, could she have known Constable as I did, she would have admitted him into the first of these classes. He was not without a body either, and one of genuine flesh and blood, but he put his soul into his art. When he said he "thanked Heaven he had no imagination," he meant only that his imagination did not lead him into what he called "the vacant fields of idealism." Nobody knew better than Constable that without imagination there could be no true art. His manner of expressing himself, in this instance, must, therefore, be taken in reference to what he saw in the works of many of his contemporaries, who, because they could not imitate nature (the most difficult of all things), pretended to do something better, — that is, to produce works of imagination.

· I will say thus much for myself, that I always preferred to associate as much as I could with my superiors. This was another reason for my cultivating the friendship of Constable, and I never felt more happy than when I found he gave it me. He had not a very large circle of friends; but his friends, like the admirers of his pictures, compensated for their fewness by their sincerity and their warmth.

The impression his character made, and the impression his art made, and I may say the impression they did *not* make, were proofs to me of the truth of Roscoe's remark, that "genius assimilates not with the character of the age." No man more earnestly desired to stand well with the world; no artist was more solicitous of popularity. He had, as the phrenologists would say, *the love of approbation* very strongly developed. But he could not conceal his opinions of himself and of others; and what he said had too much point not to be repeated, and too much truth not to give offence. It is not, then, to be wondered at, that some of his competitors hated him, and most were afraid of him. There was also that about him which led all who had not known him well and long to consider him an odd fellow, and a great egotist; and an egotist he was; but then, if the expression may be allowed, he was not a *selfish* egotist. " By self he often meant," as Charles Lamb says of the poet Wither, " a great deal more than self — his friends, his principles, his country, the human race." Few, however, knew or studied him sufficiently to perceive this. He was opposed to all cant in art, to all that is merely specious and fashionable, and to all that is false in taste. He followed, and for his future fame he was right in following, his own feelings in the choice of subject and the mode of treatment. With great appearance of docility, he was an uncontrollable man. He said of himself, " If I were bound with chains I should break them, and with a single hair round me I should feel uncomfortable." I always felt inclined to say to him, " Do all that it is in thine heart to do ; " and I was happy that to me he said all that it was in his heart to say. Turner was a very different man from Constable, and yet quite like him in one respect, namely, his entire reliance on a guide within himself— always a characteristic of genius.· But Constable could not help talking of his feelings, of his views of art, &c. He talked well, and this made him extremely interesting to those who could feel with him, but either tiresome or repulsive to those who could not. Turner did not talk well, and never talked of his own art, or of the art of others. To me, therefore, he was far less interesting than his pictures, but, at the same time, his prudence prevented his giving offence. It was impossible, however, not to like Turner, there was something so social and cordial in his nature. I believe him to have had an excellent heart.

In the spring of 1828 Sir Walter Scott was in London, and I had the pleasure of meeting him at the house of Mr. Rogers, where were also Sir James Mackintosh, Lord John Russell, Mr. Richard Sharpe, Fennimore Cooper, Chantrey, Mrs. Siddons, Miss Fanshawe, and Miss Rogers — such an assembly as I can never hope to meet again.

During this visit to London, Sir Walter was present at the anniversary dinner at the Royal Academy as a member, having been elected antiquary to the Academy the year before. After the usual toasts, Sir Thomas Lawrence said : " Before we part, I have to propose the health of one with whose presence we are

honoured, and of whom it may well be said, in the words of the
poet he most resembles, —

> "If *he* had been forgotten,
> It had been as a gap in our great feast,
> And all things unbecoming."

The enthusiasm with which the toast was received exceeded
anything of the kind I ever witnessed, and when Scott rose to
reply, the applause, for some time, prevented his speaking. As
soon as he could be heard, he said: " Mr. President, — When
you acquainted me with the honour the Royal Academy had done
me by including me among its members, you led me to believe
that the place would be a *sinecure*. But I now find that I then
reckoned without my host, for on my first appearance here, as a
member, I am called on to perform one of the most arduous of
duties, that of making a speech." He then, in a few words, returned thanks. This was the last time I ever saw him.

Of the many portraits of him Chantrey's bust is, to my mind,
the most perfect. Lawrence gave him a pomposity of manner
which he never assumed ; but in Chantrey's bust, the gentle turn
of the head, inclined a little forwards and down, and the lurking
humour in the eye and about the mouth, are Scott's own. Chantrey watched Sir Walter in company, and invited him to breakfast previous to the sittings, and by these means caught the
expression that was most characteristic. The first bust was a
commission from Scott, and when breakfasting with Chantrey, he
said : " You and I reverse the case supposed in Scripture, for I
have asked you for a stone, and you give me bread."

On the 7th January, 1830, Sir Thomas Lawrence died suddenly. An eminent surgeon told me he believed that he was
bled and physicked to death — not an uncommon occurrence in
those good old times. The Royal Academy had now to choose a
President, and the election took place on the 25th, when Mr.
Shee had eighteen votes, Sir William Beechey six, Wilkie two,
Phillips one, and Calcott one. Allan Cunningham, in his " Life
of Wilkie," has made a mistake in saying he had but one vote,
that of Collins. I also voted for him, for I considered that he
united more requisites for the high office than any other man in

the Academy. But Sir Martin Shee made so incomparable a President, that I am glad the majority did not think as Collins and I did at the time of the election.

I should have mentioned that, in 1828, I joined a small society of artists that had then been established for twenty years. Its meetings are held weekly, on Friday nights, during the months of November, December, January, February, March, and April. The members assemble, at six o'clock, at each other's houses in rotation. All the materials for drawing are prepared by the host of the evening, who is, for that night, President. He gives a subject, from which each makes a design. The sketching concludes at ten o'clock, then there is supper, and after that the drawings are reviewed, and remain the property of him at whose house they are made.

I had been acquainted with Alfred and John Chalon for many years before joining this society, but I was now brought into a closer intimacy with them — an intimacy that I count among the best things of my life.

These pleasant evenings also enabled me to appreciate the delightful social qualities of Stanfield, whose friendship from that time I have been so fortunate as to possess; and, though indifferent health and the distance at which I live from most of the members, led me, in 1842, to withdraw from the society, I am still admitted to its meetings, as an honorary member, when I can attend them.

CHAPTER VI.

In the year 1833 my brother, without consulting me (indeed there was no time), obtained for me the appointment of teacher of drawing at the Military Academy at West Point, on the Hudson River; and he and my sisters, as well as others of my friends in America, strongly urged me to accept it.

The inducements they held out were, that it would give me a fixed income for life, that I should have the greater part of my time to myself, being obliged to attend the school only for two hours, on five days in the week; that I should be enabled to procure an excellent education for my sons at the Academy, free of expense; that the situation was a very healthy and beautiful one, and that in America the opportunities of settling my children for life were better than in England; that I should have a convenient house to live in, to which a commodious painting-room would (no doubt) be added at the expense of Government; and that I should be once more among my relations and early friends. They represented to me that I could form no notion of the great improvements in all respects that had taken place in America since I had left it; that at least the experiment was worth a trial; and that if I did not like the change, I could return to England, having had an opportunity of visiting my relations at a less expense of time and money than would be possible under other circumstances. It was recommended to me that I should go alone, and, if I determined to remain, my wife and children should follow me.

After a long and very harassing consideration of the matter, and after consulting those of my friends on whose judgment I placed the greatest reliance, I resolved to accept the situation, and my wife, great as the sacrifice was to her, determined to go with me, though her own relations, and particularly her brother, did not think very favourably of the scheme.

I had not consulted Lord Egremont on this important subject, as I ought to have done. But the distance his high rank created between us made it seem to me that it would be taking too great a liberty. I might have known him better; for after I had made up my mind and written to my brother on the subject, I received the following letter : —

" Dear Sir,

" It is a long time since I have had the pleasure of seeing Mrs. Leslie and you, and as I may probably never go so far as London again, I have no chance of it unless you will come here at any time of the summer that may suit you, and I shall be very happy to receive you at any time. It seems to me that you have but one picture in your own style in the Exhibition, and the others are a scripture subject and a portrait.

" Ever truly yours, &c.,

" Egremont."

" *Petworth, June 10th, 1833.*"

In my reply to this kind letter, I acquainted Lord Egremont with my intention of visiting America, and this brought me another letter, which I really think, had I received it while my mind was wavering, would have kept me in England.

" Dear Sir,

" It is but a groundless regret at my age, when the course of nature will probably settle the point without any act of yours or mine ; but I cannot help regretting that your promised visit to Petworth will probably be the last time that I shall have the pleasure of seeing you. But I cannot disguise to myself that in the irritated state of feeling in this country,* in the midst

---

* In the present quiet state of things (in 1844), it would be difficult for those who do not remember the excitement produced by the state of political parties

of the greatest wealth and prosperity, if we had but the good
sense and good temper to make the best of it, and enjoy it, even
if it should subside without any fatal effects, the prospect is anything but encouraging; and I believe it is the condition of human nature, that almost every great improvement in society is
counterbalanced by some evil arising from it, which is not
thought of till it happens, and so now the great diffusion of wealth
and health, and comfort and education, produces a much greater
number of young persons seeking situations adapted to their cultivated habits and manners, than there are situations to employ
them.

" On the other hand, the situation to which you are going, at a
considerable distance from the society of the metropolis, and with
two or three hundred troublesome boys under your care, does not
seem to me to be a very agreeable one."

After some very kind expressions intimating his fear that I was
about to leave England on account of want of employment, Lord
Egremont thus concludes :

" I can only say that I will gladly give a thousand pounds for a
companion picture to Sancho and the Duchess.

                    " Yours ever truly, &c.,
                                        " EGREMONT."

" *Petworth, June 24th, 1833.*"

This letter made me almost feel as if I were about to commit
an act of ingratitude in leaving a country where greater patronage
had been, and was still, extended towards me than was, in many
instances, bestowed on my superiors in art.   In reply, I explained
to Lord Egremont that I was not leaving England for want of
employment.   With regard to his noble offer of one thousand
pounds for a companion picture to " Sancho and the Duchess,"
I told him I should be guilty of a robbery were I to receive
such a sum for such a picture ; that I should be most happy
to paint him one of that size in America; but that it must be

on the subject of Reform in 1833, to conceive of the consternation that prevailed throughout the country.

on the condition that its price should not exceed five hundred guineas.

Mrs. Leslie and I paid our last visit, as we thought, to Petworth, and on our taking leave of Lord Egremont, all he said was, "I am very sorry for this." The day after our return to town, I received a letter, which had followed me to Petworth, enclosed in the following:

"DEAR SIR,

"I take the opportunity of this letter to write a line, and to assure you, that although I could say but little at the time, there are very few things which could give me greater pain than pronouncing the last farewell to you and Mrs. Leslie. I heartily wish you success, but if you are to be disappointed, I hope it may be soon, that I may have a chance of seeing you again, which will not admit of much delay.

"Ever truly yours, &c.,

"EGREMONT."

"*Petworth, September 8th, 1833.*

Strange as it may seem, I had so little expectation of returning to England, that I considered it my duty to resign my Academic diploma, and on this subject I consulted Sir Martin Shee, who told me he thought such a step by no means imperative, even if I were certain of remaining in America, but that at any rate it was quite unnecessary to take it now.

We sailed from London on the 21st September, in the ship *Philadelphia*, Captain Morgan, and after a favourable passage of five weeks arrived at New York. Our little Mary was at that time but two months old, and her mother was fortunately able to nurse her during the whole of the passage.

My brother came to New York to receive us on the morning after our arrival; but before going to West Point, we paid a visit to my sisters in Philadelphia. Nothing was omitted on the part of my relations and friends to make us as happy and comfortable as possible; but still, on returning to the scenes of my boyhood, after so long an absence, I felt like a stranger. I met some of my old school-fellows, but my lively playmates had now

become grave plodding men of business, and we could never be
to each other as in the days of our youth. This I might have
foreseen, and also that it would be a long time before I could
make a new home of my old home. At West Point, I was delighted with the beautiful scenery, though the trees, when we
arrived, were nearly bare of foliage. My brother saved me
almost all trouble in furnishing and fitting up our house; which
I found, however, less commodious than the one I had left in
London. For my painting-room, I had only a small attic, but I
was assured a convenient one should be built.

I soon found that the school occupied much more of my time than
I had expected. Saturday, it is true, was a holiday to the cadets,
but it was less so to me than any other day in the week, for I had
on that day to make a report of the conduct of my pupils. If, in
this report, I censured any for misbehaviour, they appealed, and
I was obliged on the Monday to answer their appeals. When
the examination, at the close of the year took place, I was obliged
to attend with the other teachers and the professors from eight
o'clock in the morning until four in the afternoon, for two or three
weeks; and I was told I should be subject to the same attendance
at the Midsummer examination; but of this I had not been informed before I accepted the appointment.

In the course of the winter my wife suffered a more severe illness than she had ever before experienced, and I began to doubt
·whether the climate of West Point was so healthy as my brother
considered it. ·I found that where there was any predisposi-
tion to consumption in any of the cadets, it soon became necessary to remove them, and those who were removed never
returned.*

Colonel de Russey, the Superintendent, was very desirous
that the promised painting-room should be built, and assured
me it should be done as soon as the season would permit. He
had a plan drawn for it, and submitted to the Secretary of
War at Washington, but without success. There existed, at
that time, a party in Congress opposed to the very existence of

* My brother, who was educated at West Point, and had become so much
attached to it as to wish to pass his life there, has since left it, being obliged to
remove with his family to New York on account of his wife's health.

the · West Point Academy; and that party was just then making a strong effort to destroy it. This effort failed; but it was so far unlucky for me, that it prevented an application to Congress for the money necessary to build my room.

I did not find that the expense of living in America was likely to be so much less than in England as I had been led to suppose. All articles of clothing were greatly dearer, and dress is a serious item in a large family.

One hope which had weighed very much with me when I accepted the situation, was that I should find · less difficulty in settling my children for life in America than in England; but from what I heard during my sojourn at West Point, I was inclined to doubt this. Our reasoning is generally on the side of our inclinations; and so entirely did I now feel that England had become my home — so anxious was I to be again among my brother artists (the best in the world) — that had prudential reasons weighed more strongly than they seemed to do on the side of my remaining in America, I should probably have disregarded them. I felt assured also that I should make my wife happy by returning; and Lord Egremont's letter had its due weight in determining me to go back.

So much was I occupied in arranging matters for my departure, that I had not time to revisit Philadelphia; but my sister, Mrs. Carey, and her husband, paid us a visit.

We sailed for England on the 14th of April, 1834, with our good friend, Captain Morgan, who gave us the same berths in his fine ship we had occupied on our passage out; and when my wife found herself on board the *Philadelphia*, she said, "Now I feel at home again." After being a week at sea, the wind became westerly; and from that time our course continued in one direct line to Portsmouth, which we reached in twenty days from New York. When we left West Point not a leaf was out, and the landscape still bore the appearance of winter; but on our arrival in England, the country was clothed with foliage and ·blossom; and this, apparently, abrupt transition from winter to summer was very striking. The first land we saw closely was ·the Isle of Wight, in its

greatest beauty, for we passed between the Needle Rocks and
the main land. These circumstances, and the delightful weather, increased our joy at finding ourselves again in England,
from which I have felt, from that moment, no inclination to
estrange myself.

Soon after my return I visited Lord Egremont. He was
then in his eighty-second year. A few days before my arrival he had given a dinner in the park to 4000 poor women
and children, and marks were on the grass, made by the
tables, of which there could not have been less than 100, ranged in a triple semicircle opposite the house. At that time
the direct entrance to the house was closed, in consequence of
the illness of the porter and his wife, who were both dying of
old age. As they lived at the lodge, Lord Egremont would
not allow them to be disturbed, neither would he have them
removed. Had I not learned all this from the stage-coachman,
I should have been greatly astonished to find " *No Admittance* "
posted upon any gate leading to his residence.

The guests I found at Petworth consisted entirely of poor
relations and poor friends; indeed, all that I noticed strongly
illustrated the character of its benevolent master.

I made this visit alone, as my wife could not leave town, in
consequence of the children having brought the whooping-cough
from West Point; but in two months we were all at Petworth
together; and on this occasion it happened, very pleasantly to
me, that Constable was one of Lord Egremont's guests.

In the early part of 1834, Stothard was released, at an advanced age, from a world in which his gentle nature had met
with an unusual share of domestic affliction, and but little just
appreciation of his lovely art.

Every great painter carries us into a world of his own, where, if
we give ourselves up to his guidance, we shall find much enjoy
ment; but if we cavil at every step, we may be sure there is a
greater fault in ourselves than any we discover in him. I have
known people who, I have fancied, would not be quite satisfied
with heaven itself, if they should ever come there; fault-finders,
insensible to beauty, and, nine times in ten, finders of imaginary faults only. For such people Stothard did not paint. But

he did paint for all who can feel and see what is best and most beautiful in this world, and who long for something still better than the present condition of humanity.

Few could feel this longing more intensely than he did, and this feeling made his art what it was.

Mr. Rogers was always his warm admirer and steady friend; and among artists he was admired by all whose admiration was of value. Flaxman sought his acquaintance early in life, from seeing one of his designs for " The Novelist's Magazine" in a shop window. He procured him the commission to paint the Burleigh staircase, and every year, on his wife's birth-day, he presented her with a small picture by Stothard. Lawrence, Constable, Wilkie, and Chantrey were his great admirers; and Turner proved the sincerity of his admiration by painting a picture in avowed imitation of him. While retouching it in the Academy, Turner said to me, " If I thought he liked my pictures half as well as I like his, I should be satisfied. He is the Giotto of England."

On the other hand, the aristocracy knew little and cared less for him. Sir George Beaumont was loud in his condemnation; and when the great Duke was showing the Wellington shield to some friends, and was asked who designed it, he said, " Ward and Green." Mr. Rogers (who told me this) interposed " Stothard;" and the Duke said, " Ah, yes, *Stoddart*" — not even giving him his right name.

For some years before his death I had the happiness of being intimate with him, and often spent evenings at his house, looking over his sketch-books. They were filled with every variety of subject; landscape, architecture, groups of figures and flowers, all drawn with exquisite taste. On my asking the name of a flower, which struck me as peculiarly elegant, he said, " A weed, sir; I have a great respect for weeds." Many of his sketches were made from the windows of inns where he had halted while travelling; and to judge from the materials which filled his books, he did not appear to have ever gone in search of the picturesque, but to have sketched whatever his leisure permitted, and chance presented to him.

I was often surprised by seeing the most ordinary objects and

personages, such as an inferior artist would not think worth his
notice, rendered interesting by the hand and eye of this great
master. Chantrey told me that soon after the peace with France,
Stothard and he visited Paris together. On leaving Calais, Stothard tied his pencil to his finger, and began to sketch as well as
the motion of the carriage permitted him. He was very quick in
noting down, in two or three lines, the general forms of objects,
and after sketching rapidly every single apple tree of a long line
which bordered the road from Amiens, he said, " Now, sir, I
shall remember the character of an apple tree as long as I live."
Among his sketches he showed me some early drawings from the
antique, made while he was a student of the Academy. They
were begun and finished with pen and ink only, and looked like
beautiful line engravings. He said, " I adopted this plan, because,
as I could not alter a line, it obliged me to *think* before I touched
the paper." To this practice he, no doubt, owed that certainty of
hand which is a beauty in all his works.

Stothard told me that when a lad, he and another youth spent
a summer on the banks of the Medway, in a hut which they built
in imitation of Robinson Crusoe's dwelling. They purchased a
small boat, and amused themselves with sailing when the weather
permitted it. This anecdote gives an additional interest to his
illustrations of Robinson Crusoe.

He said to Constable that when he was engaged in making
drawings for " The Novelist's Magazine," he walked the streets
for his subjects.

I believe that during the whole of his life, the time not passed
in his studio was, for the most part, spent in long walks ; in the
winter through the streets of London, and in the summer through
the fields.

Though his deafness disabled him from enjoying society, except that of a single friend at a time, his disposition was social.
He never missed attending the meetings of the Royal Academy,
though he could catch nothing of the discussions that took place,
except as far as some friend would explain them. I have often
walked home with him from these meetings, and the first question he would ask me was, " What have we been doing to-
night ? "

Full as his countless work are of exquisite sentiment, I never heard him use the word *sentiment* in his life. I spoke to him one day of his touching picture of a sailor taking leave of his wife or sweetheart, and he said, "I am glad you like it, sir; it was painted with japanner's gold size."

Though utterly careless of dress, Stothard always looked like a gentleman, and as he grew old, his appearance became very venerable; his head, or rather the expression of his face, resembling the antique in the British Museum called Homer.

As he heard little that passed in conversation, he said little; but that little was always well said. When an eminent painter of the four-legged creation, presented to the Academy, on his election, a picture of two little naked, bilious, dirty-looking boys, intended for Bacchanals, a member regretted that he had not sent "some of his pigs." Stothard said, "I think he has."

I was amused with an account Constable gave me of a walk he took with him in 1824, from London to Coombe Wood, where they dined by the side of a spring. They set out early in the day, provided with some sandwiches for their dinner. Before they reached the wood, Stothard, seeing Constable eating a sandwich, called him "a young traveller," for breaking in on their store so early. When they got to the spring, they found the water low and difficult to reach; but Constable took from his pocket a tin cup, which he had bought at Putney unnoticed by Stothard. The day was hot, and the water intensely cold; and Stothard said, "Hold it in your mouth, sir, some time before you swallow it. A little brandy or rum now would be invaluable." "And you shall have some, sir, if you will retract what you said of my being a 'young traveller;' I have brought a bottle of rum from town, a thing you never thought of:" for though Constable carried their fare, Stothard was the caterer.

As they lay on the grass, enjoying their meal under the trees that screened them from a midsummer's sun, Stothard, looking up to the splendid colour of the foliage over their heads, said, "That's all glazing, sir." I am not afraid that these anecdotes will be thought trifling. The sandwiches and the rum are ordinary things, but they serve to show the frugal habits of two remarkable men, who were enjoying the beauties of nature with a

relish of which the most refined voluptuary cannot form a distant
conception. I have heard that Stothard, hardy and thrifty, never
got into a hackney coach in his life, and never wore a great coat.
He was, as I have said, a daily walker, and Constable was the
chosen companion of his walks. Stothard, indeed, fully appreciated the originality of Constable's mind, and well knew that he
was a friend on whom he could rely to the utmost.

I witnessed at the Academy a trifling proof of the respect felt
for Stothard by his colleagues. He was at one of the meetings
which take place on every 1st of December to ballot for the
prizes to the students. This is always held in the day-time, and
in the largest of the exhibition rooms, which, at Somerset House,
there were no means of warming. Sir Thomas Lawrence putting on his hat begged us all to do the same; but Stothard, who
had left his in the ante-room, did not hear him. " Which of you,
gentlemen," said Lawrence, "will bring Mr. Stothard's hat?"
There was a general rush to the door, and Shee, who ran the
quickest, brought it to the old gentleman before he knew what
the bustle meant.

I doubt whether there exists an entire collection of the thousands of engravings of Stothard's lovely conceptions, though
there are many large ones; and in looking over these, the impression is, that the life of a man of such a mind as they display
could not have been an unhappy one — nor was it; notwithstanding a series of domestic afflictions of such weight as would have
crushed most men; and these trials were continued to the close of
his life. Constable, in a letter to a friend, written in 1833, says,
" I passed an hour or two with Mr. Stothard on Sunday evening.
Poor man! the only Elysium he has in this world he finds in his
own enchanting works. His daughter does all in her power to
make him happy and comfortable."

He must have possessed great constitutional serenity of mind,
and he was also, no doubt, much supported by his art. His
easel, indeed, bore evidence of the many years he had passed before it; the lower bar, on which his foot rested, being nearly
worn through.

What a contrast does such a man offer, preserving his cheerfulness through a long and troubled life — a life throughout which

his great merits were very imperfectly appreciated — to the
many, who,

> " When no real ills perplex them,
> Can make enough themselves to vex them."

On my return from America, I commenced writing a diary,
which I continued for two or three years. The following account
of Lady Cork (the Hon. Miss Moncton mentioned in Boswell's
Life of Johnson) is from it:

" Sunday, June 1st, 1834. My wife and I dined with Miss
Rogers. Met Mr. S. Rogers, Lady Cork, the Ladies Jane and
Fanny Harley, and Mr. Wilkinson.* Lady Cork very old, infirm, and diminutive; dressed all in white, with a white bonnet,
which she wore at the table. No doubt she had been pretty in
her youth. Her features are delicate and her skin fair, and notwithstanding her great age, she is very animated. She was attended by a boy page, in a fantastical green livéry, with a cap and
a high plume of black feathers. Mr. Rogers asked her about
Sir Joshua Reynolds, whom she knew very well, and who had
painted a whole length portrait of her. She told us nothing of
him, except that he was a very pleasant man. The truth is, the
old lady, who was a lion-hunter in her youth, is as much one now
as ever, and was wholly taken up with Mr. Wilkinson, who, Mr.
Rogers told her, was accustomed to ride on a tame crocodile in
Egypt; but he, being shy, preferred talking, in a low tone, to the
Ladies Harley, to bawling out to the deaf Lady Cork. She was,
however, not to be put off, but contrived to carry him away in
her carriage."

The saddest change that had taken place among my friends in
England, while I was at West Point, was that which had over-
taken poor Newton. He was insane.

On my visit to him at the asylum at Chelsea, where he was
placed, his conversation was, for the most part, rational, but he
always uttered something, sufficiently flighty to show the state of
his mind. At one time, his friends had some hope, from his
having taken up his pencil, which he had long laid aside. Dr.
Sutherland considered this a favourable symptom.

* Now Sir Gardner Wilkinson.

On calling to see him in October, 1834, he showed me many pencil sketches, and one begun in oil. The subject of the oil sketch was the widow of Lord Strafford showing her son his father's portrait. He told me that Lord Strafford * was not exe-cuted, but had vanished from the scaffold and was still living; that he was the same person as Lorenzo de' Medici, who had ap-peared in the world many times in different characters. With the exception of this flight, his conversation was rational. A profile of Walter Scott, drawn by him in lead pencil, I had seen before, and had asked him to give it me. He had promised that he would, when he had made a copy of it, and he now showed me the copy, and said I might have that or the first. I chose the first, but they were both very like Sir Walter. The following lines of Newton's composition, are on the back of the sketch : —

> " 'Tis thine, renowned being, the task, the privilege,
>   ' To hold the mirror up to nature.'
>   Whether thy pen instruct us or thy conduct,
>   Alike we are taught. First by the magic of that pen
>   What man has been; then by thy fair career,
>   The more important lesson what he should be."

The subject of his other sketches were, " Christ blessing little children," " Lear in the Storm," " Miranda and Prospero on the summit of a rock looking at the Shipwreck," " Falconbridge upbraiding Hubert with the murder of Arthur," " Uncle Toby, Mrs. Wadman, and Trim," " La Fleur taking leave of his Sweet-hearts " (the figure of La Fleur very good), " The nurse lament-ing over Juliet, whom she supposes dead," " A child marching through a garden of flowers, fancying himself a soldier, and salut-ing the flowers " (this Newton said was himself, and what he did when a child), " Bardolph moralising to Falstaff," " Edie Ochil-tree making toys for children," " The Antiquary waiting for the coach," and other sketches, several of which were of mothers and children.

I took care that all the materials required for drawing and painting should be placed in his room; but he never again sketched or painted.

He died in August, 1835. A few days before his death, his

* If I recollect aright, Lord Strafford had no son.

mind seemed somewhat restored, though I did not hear that it was ever entirely so. During the rapid consumption that ended his life, he read only the Bible and Prayer-book; and when he became too weak to read, they were read to him by an attendant. The day before he died, he desired to hear the funeral service, saying, " It will soon be read over me." He listened with great attention, and remarked that it was " very fine." ·

Newton, like Constable, was misunderstood by those who did not know him thoroughly. I knew enough of him, and of his actions, to know that his heart was noble, and his mind a pure one. His pleasantry and good manners made him very acceptable in society. He was a most amusing companion, and though the two or three things I recollect him to have said may not be the least worth noting, I will put them down at a venture. He happened to remark to a friend, that he was often in want of rags to clean his palette.

" What do you do with your old shirts? "

" I wear them."

A gentleman showing him his pictures, and discovering from his manner that he did not think highly of them, said, " At least you will allow that it is a *tolerable* collection."

" True, sir; but would you eat a tolerable egg? "

When Sir Thomas Lawrence died, and we were speculating as to his successor in the chair of the Academy, Newton said, " It must be either Phillips or Shee, for they are the only Academicians who wear powder."

Speaking of art to me, and when in the asylum, he said, " A painter cannot do better than attend to the advice of Polonius, ' Be thou familiar, but by no means vulgar.' "

On his return from America, and when he was quite himself, an Englishman asking him about the society in Boston, said, " You must have felt the difference; you did not meet such people there as you associate with here."

" I met such people there," he said, " *every day*, as I am glad to meet here *occasionally*."

This was not said merely for the sake of making an unexpected answer, for I know that, in Boston at that time, the best society included many men of rare intellectual attainments; and in a place so much smaller than London, Newton's opportunities of meeting such men were much more frequent than here.

Newton was, to my eye, a handsome man, though his features were far from regular. He was tall, and his hands, like Wilkie's, were beautifully formed and very white.

CHAPTER VII.

I SCARCELY know whether the following passages from my journal are worth preserving, but I feel inclined to take them from among many others which I am sure are not.

"*December 24th*, 1834. — Dined with Constable. Mr. Rogers and Mr. and Miss Wilkie, and Mr. Bannister were there. Bannister amused us very much with a comic song as sung by 'Mr. Killjoy,' a person wholly destitute of humour. He spoke of Mrs. Siddons, and Mrs. Jordan, whose first appearances he remembers. He acquits Garrick of behaving ill to Mrs. Siddons in not engaging her, for he said Garrick could not guess at her future eminence, as she displayed very little talent at first. Mrs. Jordan's voice was the most delightful he ever heard on the stage. Wilkie asked Bannister if he had seen Dr. Johnson. He said, 'once in the street,' and knew him from Sir Joshua Reynolds's portrait. Bannister was intended by his father for an artist. He drew in the Academy, and remembers sitting behind Bartollozzi and Cipriani in the Life-School, and thinking their drawings wonderful. He gave us an imitation of an old Jew, and in doing this so altered his features, and even his figure, as to lose, to appearance, his own identity. He raised his shoulders, which gave him the look of a tall man, whose head was sunk in his chest with age. He described the Jew, as complimenting him on his acting, 'And your fader, Mr. Bannister, oh! what an actor he was! what a voice he had! So beautiful — so melodious! He could go as low as a bull.'

"*August 5th*, 1835. — At Cashiobury. Mr. Rogers there. I walked with him for two hours in the garden. He remembers

Sir Joshua Reynolds; but was only twice in his company. He once breakfasted with him, and he was present at his last discourse. On that occasion the room was crowded, and Burke and Boswell were there. As Sir Joshua descended from the reading-desk, Burke stepped forward, and taking his hand, said: —

> " The angel ended, and in Adam's ear
> So charming left his voice, that he a while
> Thought him still speaking, still stood fixt to hear."

" It was on this evening that the sinking of the floor of the great room a few inches so much alarmed the company. All rushed to the door, and it was some time before it was ascertained there was no danger. When the fright was over, Mr. Rogers obtained a much better situation than he had before.

"At dinner the conversation turned on the trial of Queen Caroline. A gentleman mentioned a reply made by a Quaker who was asked, what the Society of Friends thought of the Queen, while that disgraceful business was going on. ' We are of opinion,' said he, ' that she is not good enough for our Queen, but too good for our King.'

" Lord Essex told us that, when it became the fashion for the nobility to marry actresses, Lady Spencer said, ' If my daughters don't go off this season, I shall bring them out on the stage.'

" Mr. Rogers, speaking of the stage, remarked that, in the performance of a fine play we receive a greater amount of intellectual gratification, the result of a greater variety of genius and ingenuity, than we can from any other entertainment that has ever been devised. Take, for instance, ' Macbeth,' as we have all seen it acted, — the poetry of Shakespeare, the acting of Mrs. Siddons, and John and Charles Kemble, the music of Lock, the beauty of the scenery and ingenuity of the mechanism.

" I was amused to hear Lord Essex, speaking of happiness, say: ' The secret is to be content with the little one has. The Duke of Bedford and Lord Egremont, with all their wealth, are not happier than I am.'

" *October* 19*th.* — At the painting-school at the Academy are Sir Joshua Reynolds's splendid picture of Iphigenia, belonging to the king, and a small picture of a child by him. Oliver, who is keeper of the painting-school, told me that he used to go to Sir

Joshua, when a student, to show him his pictures, and request advice, and was always very kindly received. It was Sir Joshua's practice to admit young artists in the morning before he commenced painting, and he most readily lent them his finest works to copy. Turner also told me that he copied many of his pictures when he was a student. Oliver says Sir Joshua's manner was, on these occasions, exactly as Goldsmith has described it:

'Gentle, complying, and bland.'

"Allan Cunningham's 'Life of Reynolds' being the last, and published in a popular form, would be injurious to the memory of Sir Joshua, disfigured as it is by prejudices, were it not that the writer seldom fails to confute his own reasoning where it is erroneous, and that his misrepresentations of Sir Joshua's words are too glaring to escape the notice of even a hasty reader. For instance, he quotes the following passage from the account the great painter gives of his sensations on visiting the Vatican: 'On inquiring further of other students, I found that those persons only who, from natural imbecility, appeared to be incapable of relishing those divine performances (the frescos of Raphael) made pretensions to instantaneous raptures on first beholding them,' and on the next page Cunningham says, 'the conclusion which Reynolds draws, viz., that none but an imbecile person can be alive at first sight to the genius of Raphael, is certainly rash, and, most probably, erroneous.' And yet Allan Cunningham was an honest and well-meaning man. But the passage I have quoted, as well as many others in his 'Life of Reynolds,' and some in the 'Life of Wilkie,' in which the Royal Academy is spoken of, show how far an honest mind may be carried away from the truth by prejudice. Such unfairness to the personal character of Reynolds, and to the Academy, is equally unaccountable.

"*November 9th.* — Dined at Holland House. Lord Seaford, who was there, remembers dining in company with Dr. Johnson, at Dr. Brocklesby's. Lord Seaford was then a boy of twelve or thirteen. He was impressed with the superiority of Johnson, and his knocking everybody down in argument.

"Lord Holland said, Mr. Fox always avoided talking with Dr. Johnson on account of his over-bearing manner. Johnson heard

somebody say Mr. Fox was 'Aut Cæsar aut nihil.' He remarked
that Fox was 'nihil' whenever he met him.

"Lord Holland said he saw Kean and Kemble play the last
scene in 'A New Way to Pay Old Debts,' on the same night.
As Kemble was slower than Kean, Lord Holland went, the instant the curtain fell at Drury Lane, to Covent Garden, and was
in time for Kemble.

"On being asked which he preferred, he replied, 'I hardly like
to say, for I had always a friendship for Kemble.'

"*November* 16*th.* — Dined at Cartwright's, with my wife. Mr.
and Mrs. Bannister there. Bannister talked of Garrick. He
said, it seemed invidious to speak of his acting compared with
that of others, it was, in general, so superior. Kean, he said,
had flashes of power equal to Garrick, but he could not sustain a
character throughout as Garrick did.*

"In Lear, Bannister said, Garrick's very stick acted. The
scene with Cordelia and the physician, as Garrick played it, was
the most pathetic he ever saw on the stage.† Garrick instructed
Barry in Romeo, and afterwards when Barry played it in rivalry
with him he was obliged to alter his own manner, notwithstanding
which he beat Barry. A lady (I forget her name), who had performed Juliet with them both, said, she thought she must have
jumped out of the balcony to Barry, and that she thought Garrick would have jumped into the balcony to her.

"Garrick instructed Bannister, when the latter was about

---

* My own impression is, that I never saw finer acting than Kean's *Othello*,
not even excepting any performance of Mrs. Siddons. His finest passages were
those most deeply pathetic.

  † I was told by Mr. Harness (Lord Byron's friend), who in early life was
much in theatrical society, of the manner in which Garrick gave a passage
from *Lear* (Mr. Harness, no doubt, had it from the Kembles). When *Lear*
curses his daughter, and wishes, if she should have a child, that it may prove
ungrateful, "that she may feel," &c., Garrick repeated these words thus:

> "That she may *feel* — that she may *feel* —
> How sharper than a serpent's tooth it is
> To have a thankless child."

Both times he dwelt with the strongest emphasis on *feel*, first raising his voice
to the highest key, and the second time sinking it to the deepest bass, and paus-
ing for a moment after that word. Let this be tried, and the effect will be at
once perceived.

seventeen, in three characters, one of which was Zaphne, in
'Mahomet.' In this he first appeared, and with great success.
A day or two afterwards meeting Garrick in the street, the man-
ager said : —

"'Well now, I suppose you are on the top of St. Paul's, but
don't be vain. What character do you think of next?'

"Bannister mentioned 'Oronooko.'

"'Oronooko,' said Garrick, 'why, you will look like a chimney-
sweeper in a consumption.' (Bannister was at that time very
thin.)

"Garrick's manner of saying this was dramatic, and that of a
man who was conscious he was known and looked at. 'Dick, the
Apprentice,' was one of the characters in which Garrick instructed Bannister, and when he first played it, he gave imitations of
living actors; that of Bensley, in particular, was thought very
good; but finding that public mimickry often hurt the feelings of
those he mimicked, more than he could have supposed, he gave it
up entirely.

"Though I had the great pleasure of seeing much of Mr. Ban-
nister, after his retirement, I only saw him on the stage twice.
The first time was in a little interlude, 'The Purse, or the Benev-
olent Tar,' and the second in 'Wild Oats,' in which he played *John
Dory*, and the scenes between him and Dowton (*Sir George
Thunder*) were matchless for genuine humour.

"Bannister was remarkably handsome, even as an old man;
his dark eyes, still full of animation, were the more striking from
the contrast with his white hair. His nature was a thoroughly
genial one. 'When I first attracted notice on the stage,' he
said, 'I was told of such and such people who were my *enemies ;*
but I never would listen to such reports, for I was determined to
go through life without enemies, and I *have* done so.'

"He said to Constable, 'they say it is my wife who has taken
care of my money and made me comfortable in my old age ; and
so she has ; but I think I deserve a little of the credit, for I *let*
her do it.'"

Though with the help of his wife he was careful, yet he was
very generous. I remember hearing Terry relate that he put a
bond for a sum of money, and not a small sum, which he had

lent to a friend, into the fire, on finding that its payment was in-
convenient; but in doing this, he said, " Don't tell my wife."
    To return to my diary : —
    "*July* 26*th.* — In the evening I took little Harriet and Caro-
line, with Rebecca and William Clark, to the gardens of the
Eyre Arms Hotel, where there was an exhibition of fireworks,
&c.   A woman was to ascend a rope across the gardens, 300
feet in length, and 60 feet from the ground at its greatest height.
She proceeded slowly, in consequence, as I afterwards learned,
of the rope not being sufficiently tight; and when she was within a short distance of the end she stopped, being unable either to
advance or to go back.   The ascent had become so steep from the
slackness of the rope, that she could not proceed a step higher,
neither could she stoop to take hold of it without throwing away
the balance-pole, and had she done that she must have fallen.
For some minutes she continued stationary, her husband calling
to her from below to go back.   I was too far off to hear her reply; but it was evident she could not venture to turn round.
Her situation became every instant more perilous; and I was
about to leave the garden, fearing she would lose her presence of
mind, and dreading to see her fall, and that my little girls should
witness so horrid a sight.   I should mention, that, as it was quite
dark, she was only made visible by fireworks exploding around
and below her.   The top of a ladder now rose from the midst of
the crowd; but when perpendicular it was not long enough to
reach her feet; and there was another dreadful minute or two of
suspense, with cries and screams from the crowd.   A table was
then brought from the inn, and the ladder placed on it, and kept
in a perpendicular position by two men at the foot, while another
ascended.   There were loud cries of " Don't let the ladder touch
the rope ! " as he went up.   The top of it rose but a foot above
the rope ; and he could use but one arm in saving her, as with
the other he had to keep hold of the ladder.   It seemed, therefore, scarcely possible that he could help her.   After a few moments' consultation, he called to the crowd to stand from below.
She threw away the balance-pole, and at the same instant stooped
towards the ladder, and, falling across the rope, remained suspended, with one leg over it, and her arms holding to the ladder.

It was with some difficulty that her preserver managed to remove her to the ladder; but as soon as he did, she descended rapidly, amidst the cheering of the crowd; while the gallant fellow who had saved her seemed in some danger himself, for he remained for a short time suspended by his hands to the rope, with only one foot on the step of the ladder. But he soon righted himself, and reached the ground. I left the children in the care of Mr. Danforth, who had accompanied us to the garden, and, mixing with the crowd, asked her preserver if he was related to her; he said ' No,' and that he was only a servant. He was a fine-looking young man, and I was told had been a sailor. Having half a sovereign in my pocket, I put it into his hand.

" *July* 28*th.*— Dined with my neighbor Richard Cook: Wilkie, Phillips, Hilton, and Blore were there. In speaking of the ceiling of the Sistine Chapel, Wilkie praised its *chiaroscuro* and colour. He said in many of the pictures there were bright lights, so intense, that it was thought, generally, other parts had become faint or low in tone from time; and these effects were not, therefore, copied by the engravers, who probably thought them accidental. Wilkie, however, was of a different opinion, and believed that the general effect of the pictures was not materially altered by time. He observed, that no engravings of them gave the *chiaroscuro.*

" *July* 31*st.*— In the evening I went to Mr. Dunlop's. Mr. Dunlop had been sitting to Chantrey, who fixed the back of his head in a wooden machine to keep him perfectly still, and then drew with a camera lucida the profile and front face of the size of life. He afterwards gave a little light and shade to the drawings, and said, ' I shall not require you to sit still after this.' He said, ' I always determine in my mind the expression to be given; and unless I can see the face distinctly, and with that expression when I close my eyes, I can do nothing. If I can, I can often make the face more like in the absence of the sitter than in his presence.' Thus it is that a certain degree of imagination is required to make a fine portrait. Chantrey's portraits were of the best kind, *characteristic* and not *literal ;* and so I am convinced were Reynolds's, who, I have no doubt, often gave to his heads touches of the greatest value when the sitter was away.

He who can only work with his model before him can never produce an elevated work, either in history, portraits, or landscape.

"But a great portrait painter or sculptor must look to have the works of inferior artists often preferred to his. I am told Reynolds's portraits frequently disappointed the people for whom they were painted, and I know that Chantrey's busts sometimes did. The family of Lord Egremont preferred a bust of his lordship, by Behnes, to the noble one by Chantrey, one of the very best of his works, and, to my mind, possessing all the character of Lord Egremont's fine head. If, as I think, it be true, that a great artist will often give the happiest touches to his work in the absence of his model, it is equally true that he who trusts to imagination *alone*, is in great danger of falling into irreclaimable mannerism or insipid vagueness. The greatest artist is the one who knows how to avail himself of every means towards his end, and who is quickest at taking advantage of every favourable accident that nature presents. The results of such powers will make every work of his hand a work of imagination, whatever the subject may be. For my own part, I have always felt that there is more poetry in the portraits of Reynolds than in nine-tenths of the pictures professedly poetic in subject. . . . .

"In the course of a walk with Mr. Rogers, he talked much of Canova, whom he described as a most amiable man. Canova told him that he was in love when he was but five years old.

"At dinner, Mr. Rogers related a story of a nervous gentleman who kept a fire-escape — a kind of sack in which he could lower himself from his window. Being suddenly awakened, one night, by the sound, as he thought, of the wheels of a fire-engine, followed by a tremendous knocking at the door, he descended in his sack in great haste, and reached the street just in time to hand his wife (who had been to the opera) out of her carriage.

"Another story related by Rogers was of a wretch who, for some atrocious crime, was hanged in chains. His whole life had been so desperately wicked that the country people believed his body would be carried away by the Devil. The day after his execution their prediction seemed verified, for the corpse was gone; but, strange to say, in about eight or ten days it was there again, safely enclosed within the irons and as if but newly dead. The truth was, that on the night of the execution, a farmer and his son who had been for some days from home, were returning in a cart, and passing close to the gibbet were startled by a groan from the body, and then a feeble voice imploring help. When they got the fellow home, they nursed him with the greatest care, till, in the middle of one night, his deliverer was disturbed by a noise, and discovered the villain in the act of packing up every article of value in the house which he could conveniently carry away. The farmer had just time to awake his son, who agreed with him that they had better put their new friend into his chains again.

"In looking over a large collection of prints from Sir Joshua, Mr. Rogers observed of a common-place-looking General among them, 'That is one of the men of whom Lord North said, when a list was presented to him of officers to be sent to America, "I know not what effect these names may have on the enemy, but they make me tremble."'

"I noticed that Mr. Neat, in speaking of the music of Handel and Beethoven, made use of the words *outline* and *colour*. Thus, the arts borrow terms from each other. So painters speak of tone and harmony. Neat said, that eminent musicians were sometimes insensible to the beauties of a fine piece of music on first hearing it; and he had known them dislike a piece, which afterwards gave them the greatest delight. I told him what Sir Joshua said of his great disappointment on seeing the frescos of Raphael.

"Mrs. Malaprop's axiom, that 'it is best to begin with a little hate,' is not altogether absurd. Certainly, when we do change in anything from such a beginning, our liking is always the stronger.

"*September 7th.* — Dined at Holland House. * * * Lord Holland speaking of Boswell, whom he remembered, said that whenever he came into a company where Horace Walpole was, Walpole would throw back his head, purse up his mouth very significantly, and not speak a word while Boswell remained.

"*September 13th.* — Looking into D'Israeli's 'Curiosities of Literature,' I find an article entitled 'Poets, Philosophers, and

Artists made by Accident.' D'Israeli begins truly enough by
saying, 'accident has frequently occasioned the most eminent
geniuses to display their power,' and then gives about a dozen
instances. If, however, he means that but for those accidents the
powers of such men might have remained unknown to themselves, and therefore unused; or that men differently constituted,
meeting with similar accidents, would have done what they did,
he is, I think, mistaken. We learn to talk by the accident of
hearing others talk ; but, without a natural capability of speech,
we should remain dumb as our cats and dogs do, though they
hear us speak. Gibbon, it is true, might not have written his
' Decline of the Roman Empire,' but for the accident of hearing
the bare-footed friars singing vespers in the temple of Jupiter ;
but he would have written something else in which the same
powers of mind and turn of thinking would have been displayed.
The accident did not make Gibbon an historian, it only directed
him in the choice of a subject.   Neither is it to be supposed, that
Sir Joshua Reynolds would not have been a painter, and every
whit as great a one, had he never seen ' Richardson's Treatise.'
He read the treatise with interest, because his mind was naturally turned more towards painting than to anything else.   Dr.
Franklin, another of D'Israeli's instances, might have taken up
Richardson fifty times, and fifty times laid him aside without
reading a page ; but, when Defoe's ' Essay on Projects' came in
his way, he read it with avidity ; and as he himself says, ' derived impressions that influenced some of the principal events of
his life.' Yet we cannot suppose, that, but for this book, the
world would not have known Franklin as a philosopher. But to
return to Reynolds and Richardson, it must be admitted that if
even books could infuse a love of art, and an ambition to shine
as a painter, into a mind hitherto insensible to such things, Richardson's discourses would be the most likely to do so.

"*December 1st.* — Dined with Constable. He mentioned that
Wilkie and he were students together at the Academy. Wilkie
told him that when he studied at the Scottish Academy, Graham,
the master of it, was accustomed to say to the students, in the
words of Reynolds — ' If you have genius, industry will improve
it ; if you have none, industry will supply its place.' ' So,' said

Wilkie, 'I was determined to be very industrious, for I knew I had no genius.' Wilkie said, also, to Constable — 'When Linnell, and Burnet' (who were his fellow students in London), 'are talking about art, I always get as close as I can, to hear all they say, for they know a great deal, and I know very little.' This was said with perfect sincerity, for Wilkie was modest.

"It was not because Sir George Beaumont was a man of rank and wealth, that Wilkie was so docile to his teaching. Sir George was, in the first place, a much older man; and, besides being a clever amateur painter, had known, intimately, Reynolds and Gainsborough, indeed all the first artists, and many of his own opinions were therefore derived from the highest authorities; added to which he was an admirable talker, and in every way a very delightful person."

On the 1st of April, 1837, as I was dressing, I saw from my window, Pitt (a man employed by Constable to carry messages) at the gate. He sent up word that he wished to speak to me, and I ran down expecting one of Constable's amusing notes, or a message from him; but the message was from his children, and to tell me that he had died suddenly the night before. My wife and I were in Charlotte Street as soon as possible. I went up into his bed-room, where he lay, looking as if in a tranquil sleep; his watch, which his hand had so lately wound up, ticking on a table by his side, on which also lay a book he had been reading scarcely an hour before his death.* He had died as he lived, surrounded by art, for the walls of the little attic were covered with engravings, and his feet nearly touched a print of the beautiful moonlight by Rubens, belonging to Mr. Rogers. I remained the whole of the day in the house, and the greater part of it in his room, watching the progress of the casts that were made from his face by his neighbour, Mr. Joseph, and by Mr. Davis. I felt his loss far less then than I have since done — than I do even now. Its suddenness produced the effect of a blow which stuns at first and pains afterwards; and I have lived to learn how much more I have lost in him, than at that time I supposed. Those personal qualities that attached me to him gained more and more on me

* It was a volume of Southey's "Life of Cowper," containing many of the poet's letters.

while he lived, and the examination of his papers and letters
since his death, has increased my esteem for him in proportion
as they gave me a deeper insight into his character.   It is a gratification to me to believe that some of my feelings and tastes are
like his ; indeed, if this be not true, I know not how to account
for the great delight his pictures give me, a delight distinct from,
and I almost think superior to, that which I receive from any
other pictures whatever.

Among all the landscape painters, ancient or modern, no one
carries me so entirely to nature; and I can truly say, that since
I have known his works I have never looked at a tree or the sky
without being reminded of him.

We talk of untimely deaths ; but all deaths I believe to be
merciful, for God, no doubt, takes every one of us at the time
best for ourselves.   The bodily sufferings that immediately preceded Constable's death, though acute, were of very short duration ; and he was spared a world of anxiety which the thought
of leaving his children young, and orphans, must have occasioned,
had he lingered on a sick bed with no hope of recovery —
anxiety which, with such feelings as his, would have been extreme.

I have said in another place that Constable was a gentleman,
everywhere and at all times, and as much to the humblest as to
the greatest people.   He even conciliated that untractable class,
the hackney coachmen ; for, in his time, there were no cabs.   He
would say on getting into a coach : —

" Now, my good fellow, drive me a shilling fare towards só and
so, and don't cheat yourself."

Not long after his death, I was coming away from his house,
and sent for a coach from the stand near it.   When I got home
the driver said : — " I knew Mr. Constable ; and, when I heard
he was dead, I was as sorry as if he had been my own father —
he was as nice a man as that, sir."

To the selection from Constable's letters which I printed in
the form of a memoir, I added recollections of some of his pithy
sayings.   In addition to those, I remember two that may be worth
preserving.   He numbered among his friends Doctors Bailey and
Gooch, and had a great respect for the abilities of such men.

But this did not hinder him from saying, " As every animal has its peculiar food, or prey, provided by nature, I look upon women and children to be the natural prey of doctors."

Lord Northwick met him in an auction room, and said : — " I shall be glad, Mr. Constable, to take advantage of your judgment here."

" I am afraid, my lord," he said, " the judgment of a painter is of very little value in such a place as this, for *we* only know good pictures from bad ones. We know nothing of their pedigrees, of their market value, or how far certain masters are in fashion."

In the room in which this was said, and at the same time, a picture by Bonnington was placed as a pendant to one by Constable, and he said to a friend — " Bonnington's picture will sell high and mine low ; " and this happened, but the reverse would happen now.

He said of a portrait painter who had worked his way to some eminence, but whose art was of the tamest and most commonplace kind, that, when he painted a head, " he took out all the bones and all the brains." In this saying he characterised an entire class of portraiture, and not a small one.

CHAPTER VIII.

IN the summer of 1837 I was at Petworth, and saw Lord Egremont for the last time. He had just put up a marble slab, in the church, bearing inscriptions to the memories of the 9th, 10th, and 11th Earls of Northumberland, their wives and children, and some other members of the Percy family. They concluded thus : —

" This Monument was erected to their memory by their descendant, George, Earl of Egremont, in the year 1837, the 86th of his age.
" *Mortuis Moriturus.*"

My next journey to Petworth was to attend his funeral. On that occasion all the shops in the town were closed, and business entirely suspended. Indeed all the inhabitants were present, either following the procession, or lining the way as it passed. There was not a single carriage. All the mourners followed the coffin on foot, and the line was continued to a great length. The many artists who had enjoyed his patronage, Turner, Phillips, Carew, Clint, and myself, were present.

For more than ten years I had, nearly every season, spent from one to two months at Petworth, with my wife and children ; and we were always made to feel quite at home there. Such a friend, in such a sphere of life, we can never hope to find again.

One little circumstance I cannot help mentioning, because it marks the character of Lord Egremont, and shows that to the last moment of his life he was, as he had always been, studying the good of others. He was remarkably fond of children ; and, as I have mentioned, was accustomed to have all that were in the house brought into his room while he was dressing. On the day of his death those of his grand-children who were at Petworth were brought to him ; but when they were about to kiss him as usual, he motioned them away, no doubt thinking his breath might do them harm.

After what I had known of Lord Egremont, I was amused to see him characterised in one of Walpole's letters to Sir Horace Mann as "*a most worthless young fellow.*" * He had made a proposal of marriage to Walpole's niece, lady Maria Waldegrave, second daughter of the Duchess of Gloucester. Walpole, in mentioning that the offer was accepted, says, " He is eight-and-twenty, is handsome, and has between twenty and thirty thousand a-year." In less than three weeks, however, Sir Horace Mann is told that the match is broken off. Lord Egremont, who is " weak and irresolute, has behaved with so much neglect and want of attention, that Lady Maria heroically took the resolution of writing to the Duchess, who was in the country, to desire her leave to break off the match. The Duchess, who had disliked the conduct of her future son-in-law, but could not refuse her consent to so advantageous a match, gladly assented ; but the foolish boy, by new indiscretion, has drawn universal odium on himself. He instantly published the rupture, but said nothing of Lady Maria's having been the first to declare off ; and everybody thinks he broke off the match, and condemns him ten times more than would have been the case if he had told the truth, though he was guilty enough in giving the provocation."

Now Lord Egremont was certainly, when I had the happiness of knowing him, anything but a foolish, a weak, or an irresolute man ; but he was shy and taciturn, and probably had been still more so in his youth. It seems probable, then, that the lady rejected him solely from not understanding his character. He was not a man to talk sentiment, or to throw himself on his knees at the feet of a woman ; not that he was in the least insensible to the charms of the sex, but for the reasons I have mentioned. What attentions she may have expected, and how far he failed in them, it is impossible to guess ; but it is clear, from her uncle's account, that Lord Egremont did not in the least consider *himself* to blame.

* Letter 333, dated July 24th, 1780.

In the summer of 1838 Lady Holland sent for me to breakfast, as she had something to tell me. This was, that the Queen
had expressed a wish to see the portrait I had painted of Lord
.Holland. "I thought," said Lady Holland, "she might as well
see the artist with it; and Lord Melbourne has just written to me
to say she will see you to-morrow at two o'clock." I saw that all
this was kindly managed by Lady Holland for my advantage;
and so it turned out.

Lady Holland, without my asking or expecting it, procured for
me a ticket to see the Coronation from the Earl Marshal's box.
A ticket had also been sent to me, as a member of the Academy,
for another part of the Abbey, which enabled my wife to see the
ceremony. We set out together, at four o'clock in the morning,
for Westminster. On this one occasion in my life I wore a court
dress. My wife was in a full evening dress, and it seemed very
odd to find ourselves walking in the street (for we walked, when
near the Abbey, to save time) such odd figures, at so early an
hour of the day. We were, however, kept in countenance by a
long procession of ladies and gentlemen, most of them much more
finely dressed than we.

The ceremony was well worth seeing, but I made up my mind
that if another Coronation should take place during my life, I
certainly should not put on a court dress, get up at three o'clock
in the morning, and remain in Westminster Abbey till four in the
afternoon, to see it.

It led, however, to my painting the Queen receiving the Sacrament; and the doing this procured me opportunities of seeing
something of Her Majesty, and of several members of the Royal
family; for I was obliged to take the picture to the houses of the
Dukes of Sussex and Cambridge, and the Princess Augusta.
With the Princess Augusta I was perfectly delighted. I never
met with any lady, old or young, of more charming manners.

The Duke of Cambridge reminded me, in his manner of talking, of Peter Pindar's account of his father. While he sat to
me, there was always a gentleman in the room (not one of his
household) to whom he addressed himself, sometimes in English
and sometimes in German, and his talk was nothing but a series
of questions. One day he sent this gentleman out of the room

for something, and then talked to me, which he had not done before. " Do you paint all day? Are you a Royal Academician? Are you painting any other picture? Do you walk here or ride?" &c., &c.

The Duke of Sussex, talked better and was very pleasant. It was impossible not to like him, but he wasted my time miserably; keeping me three entire days doing nothing, by not sitting when he had appointed. About once an hour a servant came to me in the library, where I had the picture, to tell me the Duke had visitors, but would be with me very soon.

I wrote to the Duke of Wellington to say that I was commanded by the Queen to introduce his portrait into a picture I was painting for Her Majesty. He answered my note by return of post, and the next day he called. His first words were: " You live a great way from my house; five miles, I should say." I said I did not think it was more than three. " Oh, you're mistaken, it's five miles." I then said, as I was fully aware of the value of his time, I would take the picture to Apsley House, if agreeable to him. He was pleased with this, and appointed an early day; " but," he added, " my time is so little my own that I may not be able to sit. However, if I can't, I will send you word before you leave home in the morning; for your time is of as much consequence to you, as mine is to me." On the morning appointed, as I heard nothing from him to prevent me, I took the picture to Apsley House, and the first thing he said was, " Well, don't you find it five miles?" I said as before, and what was the truth, that the distance was not more than three miles, but he repeated that I was mistaken; he would have it to be but five.

When I had sketched his figure, I asked him to look at it. He said, " You have made my head too large, and this is what all the painters have done to whom I have sat. Painters are not aware how very small a part of the human figure the head is. Titian was the only painter who understood this, and by making his heads small he did wonders."

The Duke could talk more to the purpose on his own subjects. I was told that he said, when describing the Battle of Waterloo at his own table, to some coxcomb who asked him how it was that the French did not, at such a time, attack him in such a place — " Because they were not d——d fools."

Next to the Duke of Wellington, the most remarkable man in the picture was Lord Melbourne. I had seen him, for the first time, years before in Murray's drawing-room in Albemarle Street. In that room, Murray held, every morning, such levees as were not to be matched in London. Everybody who knew him, and had any business with him, walked into it without announcement or ceremony; and there were to be found the most eminent authors and politicians of all parties, drawn together by the common bond of literature. It was then that Murray was receiving MSS. and frequent letters from Lord Byron, and it may be conceived how interesting were the fragments of these with which the great publisher treated his company.

At later periods I saw much of Lord Melbourne at Holland House. His head was a truly noble one. I think, indeed, he was the finest specimen of manly beauty in the meridian of life I ever saw. Not only were his features eminently handsome, but his expression was in the highest degree intellectual. His laugh was frequent, and the most joyous possible, and his voice so deep and musical, that to hear him say the most ordinary things was a pleasure. • But his frankness, his freedom from affectation, and his peculiar humour, rendered almost everything he said, though it seemed perfectly natural, yet quite original. At Holland House he was abusing women to Lady Holland. His strong charge against the sex, was the want of charity of women for women. He called them "devils to each other."

" But," said Lady Holland, " what nurses they are. What would you do without women in your illnesses ? "

" I would rather have men about me when I am ill ; I think it requires very strong health to put up with women."

" Oh ! " said the lady, tapping him with her fan, " you have lived among such a rantipole set."

I met Lord Melbourne at Lady Holland's a day or two after he ceased to be prime minister. He was as joyous as ever, and only took part in the conversation respecting the changes in the Royal household (which were not then completed) to make every body laugh.

· " I hear," said a lady " that ——," naming a duke of not the most correct habits, " is quite scurrilous at not getting an appointment."

" No," said Lady Holland, " he can't be scurrilous."

" Well, then, he is very angry."

" It serves him right," said Lord Melbourne, " for being a tory. None of these immoral men ought to be tories. If he had come to me I would not have refused him."

While sitting to me, he said he remembered, when a child, sitting to Sir Joshua Reynolds. Sir Joshua played with him and rode him on his foot, and said, " Now be a good boy, and sit a little longer, and you shall have another ride."

He asked me how it was that Raphael was employed by the Pope to paint the walls of the Vatican.

I said, " Because of his great excellence."

" But was not his uncle, Bramante, architect to the Pope ? "

I replied, " I believe Bramante was his uncle."

" Then it was a job, you may be sure," he said, with his hearty laugh.

Lord Melbourne, with all his abilities, his good sense, and his scholarship — for I am told he was an accomplished scholar — did not value art, and seemed to have a bad opinion of mankind. Perhaps what Lady Holland said to him, when he expressed his opinion of women, may account for his small belief in human goodness. He had lived among a bad set.

I found the Archbishop of Canterbury, Dr. Howley, a most agreeable sitter. He talked of Burns, and quoted passages from his poems as instances of exceeding refinement of taste. He had known Kemble and Mrs. Siddons, and been much with Fuseli in the early part of his life. Fuseli, speaking of Dr. Howley, said, " Before he became a dignitary of the church, he used to come to my house frequently, and sit there for hours together ; but for some years he seems to forget even my person." *

The Archbishop, without reference to this passage, which perhaps he had not seen, told me that, greatly as he admired the genius of Fuseli, he was obliged to withdraw from him on account of his ungovernable temper, which was apt to explode in downright insult on his associates.

I had the pleasure of being much at Lambeth while Dr. Howley lived. Mrs. Howley asked me to paint a small portrait of

* Knowles's " Life of Fuseli."

him for herself. "He has always been painted," she said, "in his
robes, but I don't want a portrait of the Archbishop; I want a
portrait of *my husband.*" I painted him for her in his ordinary
dress, and she was so good as to pay me much more for it than
the price I asked.

In 1841, I painted a second picture for the Queen—the Christening of the Princess Royal. I was admitted to see the ceremony, and made a slight sketch of the Royal personages as they
stood round the font in the room. I made a study from the little
Princess a few days afterwards. She was then three months old,
and a finer child of that age I never saw. It is a curious proof
of the readiness with which people believe whatever they hear to
the disadvantage of those placed high in rank above them, that at
the time at which I made the sketch, it was said everywhere but
in the palace and by those who belonged to the Royal household,
that the Princess was born blind, and by many it was even believed that she was born without feet. The sketch was shown at
a party at Mr. Moon's the evening after I made it, and the ladies
all said "What a pity so fine a child should be entirely blind." It
was in vain I told them that her eyes were beautifully clear and
bright, and that she took notice of everything about her;—I was
told that though her eyes looked bright, and though she might appear to turn them to every object, it was *certain* she was blind. I
remembered that it had been said, two years before, that the Queen
herself could scarcely walk, although I knew, from good authority,
that she had danced out a pair of shoes at one of her own balls,
and when the company thought she had retired for the evening,
she reappeared with a new pair.

It is by the ready credence given to such tales, that people
balance the account between their own lot and the splendour of
high station. When the marriage between the Queen and Prince
Albert took place, bets were laid in the club houses that in six
months they would be living separately.

The most agreeable part of my task in painting the christening
of the Princess Royal was, in studying the fine head of the wisest
and best of living kings, Leopold, a man whom the people he
reigns over scarcely seem to deserve. Nothing could be more
agreeable than his manner, and that of his amiable queen, who

was in the room all the time he sat. He speaks English very
well, and she also spoke it. After I had painted for some time,
she said, " May I look ? " and, on suggesting some alteration, she
said, " You must excuse me, I speak honest; but if I am wrong
don't mind me."

In the summer of 1841, the country, by the death of Wilkie,
lost a great artist, and his friends lost a most amiable and honourable man.

When his last works, his Asiatic sketches, were exhibited at
Christie's Rooms, I was struck with the contrast they presented
to the common-place materials that had been for years brought
by other painters from the countries Wilkie had last visited, and
from which he never returned. Their grandeur and breadth of
style were as striking as their truth of character and expression,
and in all there was a degree of novelty, from his choice of subject and mode of treatment, which I was not prepared to see
after the numerous studies that had been brought from the East
by other artists.

I was glad to see the sincere homage paid to his genius in the
high prices that were given for these last sketches, though it was
melancholy to think that the industry that produced them, added
to the excitement of the scenes in which they were made, and
the effects of the climate, must have hastened his death.

The recollections of all my intercourse with Wilkie, and I
knew him for about twenty years, are altogether delightful. I
had no reason ever to alter the opinion I first formed of him, that
he was a truly great artist and a truly good man. The little
peculiarities of his character, as they all arose from the best intentions, rather endeared him to his friends than otherwise. He
was a modest man, and had no wish to attract attention by eccen-
tricity; and indeed all his oddity, and he was in many things
very odd, arose from an extreme desire to be exactly like other
people. Naturally shy and reserved, he forced himself to talk.
I can easily conceive, from what I knew of him, that he had a
great repugnance to making speeches at dinners or public meetings,
yet knowing that from the station he had acquired he must do
such things, he made public speaking a study. He carried
the same desire of being correct into lessser things, not from

vanity, but from a respect for society, for he considered that genius did not give a man the right to be negligent in his manners, even in trifles. When quadrilles were introduced, Wilkie, who like most other people of his rank had danced reels and country dances only, set himself in the most serious manner to study them. His mind was not a quick one, and I am told he drew ground plans and elevations of the new dances to aid his memory in retaining the lessons of his master. Then, in dancing them, he never omitted the proper step, never for an instant walked, and never took a lady's hand without bowing. All this, so different from common ball-room habits, gave a formality to his manner that was extremely amusing, and his dancing, as indeed his mode of doing most things, was, from the same cause, very unlike that of any body else. He was always ceremonious; but, as I have said, from modesty, and not from pride or affectation, for no man had less of either. Long as I knew him, and latterly in very close intimacy, he never addressed me but as Mr. Leslie.

How admirably he performed every duty of a son, a brother, and a friend, is sufficiently shown in Allan Cunningham's memoirs of him; and that his strictly economical habits were consistent with a noble liberality, is clear from a passage in the "Autobiography of Abraham Raimbach," from which, as a less known work, I transcribe the following account of Wilkie's conduct to him respecting the first plate from one of his pictures which Raimbach engraved: —

"The mutual conditions of our engagement were promptly arranged upon the basis, with various modifications, of one-third share to Wilkie, and two-thirds to me; which were afterwards changed to one-fourth and three-fourths respectively, at the generous and unsolicited suggestion of Wilkie."

Raimbach also mentions that when, in order to engrave the "Village Politicians," it became necessary to pay to Sam. Reynolds one hundred guineas in consideration of the right to engrave it which had been granted to him, and it was agreed that this sum should be jointly paid by Raimbach and Wilkie, the latter "subsequently took the whole most liberally on himself."

Wilkie was always thinking of his art, and it may raise a smile to say that he had a true artist's appreciation of the capabilities of a *cocked hat*. A cocked hat is not only one of the most picturesque coverings for the head ever invented, but by the variety of ways in which it may be worn, it gives expression to greater varieties of character than anything else that ever man put on.

We have only to turn over the works of Hogarth to be convinced of this. I believe the cocked hats of the Chelsea pensioners were among Wilkie's inducements to paint his picture of the " Reading of the News of Waterloo." His " Parish Beadle " also, and his " Napoleon and the Pope," each had, to him, the advantage of a very characteristic cocked hat. Had Napoleon worn a round hat, Wilkie would never have put in on his head. Indeed, these execrable round hats, which have now been worn for more than half a century, almost preclude any modern outdoor subject from being painted.

At the funeral of Sir Thomas Lawrence, Wilkie and Constable walked together. The cocked hat of the city marshal, on that occasion, was dressed out with a large quantity of black silk. At the conclusion of the ceremony, when the company were ranged in a circle under the dome of St. Paul's, this officer stepped forward to speak to the undertaker. As he stood for a minute holding this awful hat behind him, it caught the downcast eye of Wilkie, who whispered to Constable, " Don't you find a cocked hat a very difficult thing to manage in a picture ? " He soon became almost loud as he pointed out the fine effect of Mr. Wontner's hat, with its sable trappings.

Wilkie and Newton made an excursion together into Derbyshire, and visited Chatsworth. After they had been conducted over the house, Newton inquired for a picture painted by himself, and was told it was in the Duke's sitting-room, and could not be shown without his permission.

I should here mention, that when this picture was exhibited at the Academy, it was placed much higher than Newton liked ; and he remarked that if it should be sold, the purchaser must be a very tall man ; the Duke of Devonshire is above six feet high. Newton was pleased to find that he kept it in the room he most constantly occupied, and Wilkie said, " If there were a picture of mine here, I would not go away without seeing it." The Duke, they were told, was out, but not away from his own grounds, so they determined to look for him ; but when they saw him at a distance, Wilkie hesitated, " The Duke," he said, " will think we came for an invitation. He *must* ask us to dine."

" We can decline," replied Newton.

" True," said Wilkie ; " but suppose he should *not* ask us ? " And they went away without speaking to his Grace.

With Newton, Landseer, Callcott, and myself, Wilkie had passed a few days in a visit to the Duke and Duchess of Bedford at Woburn, and as he and I had engagements that called us to town before the party broke up, he proposed that we should post home together, to which I very gladly agreed. The uninterrupted conversation by this means enjoyed with him was delightful, and highly as I had previously thought of him, raised him still higher in my estimation. He spoke of many of our mutual friends and acquaintances with equal judgment and good feeling, and whenever he touched on art, I felt that I was listening to a rare and an original minded man.

It is not to be supposed that Wilkie, having made himself a great name, could pass through life without detraction, and he was accused of bowing rather too low to rank. He certainly had a sufficient respect for the aristocracy, among whom he had found many sincere and liberal friends ; but I never heard of his really degrading himself by servility ; and I know that, where his art was concerned, he would not give up a point that he thought of consequence in deference to the opinions or wishes of people of title. When he painted " George IV. entering Holyrood House," he had a good deal of difficulty respecting matters of costume with the Duke of Argyle, whose fine face and figure are conspicuous in that picture. The duke, among other things, protested strongly against the round Highland shield, because he had not carried one on the occasion ; but Wilkie, who wanted its form in the composition, persisted in retaining it. So when he was engaged on one of his last pictures, — " The Queen's First Council," — he told me that Mr. Croker made so many objections to this and that in the composition, " that," said Wilkie, " though I don't like to have words with any man, I was really obliged to have words with *him*." Mr. Croker, it is true, did not belong to the aristocracy, but he had so much influence in high circles, and particularly in circles in which Wilkie has always stood well, that to oppose him in opinion was quite as bold as to oppose any nobleman, or even bolder.

The different estimates which Constable and Wilkie formed of the value of public opinion, arose naturally from the treatment each met with from the public; — Wilkie being, from the commencement of his career, as popular as Constable was the reverse, it was natural that the one should think more favourably of public opinion than the other. Still I fear Constable was the nearer to a right judgment in this matter. Wilkie, in one of his published letters, says, " The applause of the exquisite few, is better than that of the ignorant many. But I like to reverse received maxims; give me the many who have admired in different ages Raphael and Claude." But have the *many*, in any age, admired Raphael and Claude? I certainly believe not. Their reputations are established, and everybody, therefore, speaks alike concerning them, as all Englishmen do of Shakespeare. But can we suppose that the public, without their guide books or other directions, would ever find out that the Cartoons are, beyond all comparison, the most valuable works of art at Hampton Court, — or that they would go at once to the St. Ursula of Claude in the National Gallery, as to the finest picture there of its class, without being told that it is? I am as sure they would not, as I am sure that when John Kemble was playing Hamlet or Brutus, those personations were not felt by the public to be above his Rolla — I mean the characters themselves — for, could his audience have been made to believe " Pizarro " to be the work of Shakespeare, they would have received it with 'all the reverence due to his name. In the diary of Cooke, the actor, is the following : " The general veneration for Shakespeare is a nominal one ; his faults are, by the million, esteemed, and his beauties little understood."

All that can be said is, that genius in some of its forms is more understood by the public than in some others; that Ra-

phael's works are addressed to a larger class than Michael
Angelo's; and that Shakespeare is more read than Milton.

Wilkie's works were popular from the first, because the public
could understand his subjects, and natural expression is always'
responded to. But the beauty of his composition, the truth of
his effects, the taste of his execution, were no more felt by the
multitude than such qualities are felt in any class of painting, by
any but those whose perceptions of art are cultivated. There
can be no stronger proof of this than the fact that the companion
prints, designed by Burnet, to one or two of Wilkie's subjects,
were just as popular as his; indeed, the engraving from Wilkie's
picture of the Chelsea pensioner reading to his companions the
news from Waterloo, was less liked, as I was told by the publishers, and had a less extensive sale than its companion the
Greenwich pensioners. An artist must belong to the multitude
to please the multitude.

CHAPTER IX.

" OFFICE OF WOODS, &c., *October*, 1846.

" LORD MORPETH presents his compliments to Mr. Leslie, and would feel extremely obliged to him if he would be good enough to give him the benefit of his judgment upon the appearance and effect of the Statue of the Duke of Wellington in its present position upon the Triumphal Arch on Constitution Hill.

" Lord Morpeth feels that the distinction implied in Mr. Leslie's being a member of the Royal Academy must be his warrant for the trouble which he thus ventures to give.

" Charles R. Leslie, Esq., &c. &c."

When the Wellington statue was placed, upon trial, on the arch opposite Apsley House, and the general opinion, as far as it could be ascertained by the Press, was strongly manifested against its remaining there, Lord Morpeth (now Earl of Carlisle), who was at that time the Chief Commissioner of the Woods and Forests, wrote letters to all the Academicians, before any part of the scaffolding was removed, requesting to have their opinions on the matter. The question asked of us had nothing to do with the merits or demerits of Mr. Wyatt's work, but related merely to its situation ; and, with but one or two exceptions, we all agreed in recommending its removal. In my reply to Lord Morpeth, after remarking that I thought that place not only injurious to the effect of the statue itself, but to all the architectural objects about it, I added : " There is another reason entirely distinct from these, and one that appears to me a sufficient ground of itself for the removal of the statue. It seems to me to be an act of great

injustice to any artist who has executed an approved public work
to allow any alteration to be made in his design, or any feature
to be added to it, unless with his concurrence ; and I understand
that very strong objections from the gentleman who designed the
arch have not prevented the statue with its pedestal from being
placed on his work."

Some of the members of the Academy evaded a distinct reply
to Lord Morpeth, by stating that they could not judge fairly of
its appearance in consequence of the scaffolding that so closely
surrounded it. The scaffolding was then partially removed, and
his Lordship addressed a second letter to each. In that which I
received I was asked whether I *now* saw any reason to alter my
opinion. I replied that I did not ; and, I believe, that in no instance was any objection that had previously been felt to placing
the statue on the arch done away by the removal of the scaffolding. There, however, it remains — to the disgrace of the age.
A Frenchman, on seeing it, said, " France is now avenged for the
Battle of Waterloo."

The gigantic bronze cast in Hyde Park is an equal disgrace to
the taste of the nation. Will it be believed by posterity that
Flaxman was living when Westmacott was employed to waste the
brass of the cannon captured by the Duke on a cast from an antique figure that could not, in any way, be made to allude to any
event in the Duke's history ? The action of the figure is that of
retreat. And then the bad taste of casting the figure without the
horse, and of putting a shield on the upraised arm, when the
action of the hand proves that that arm could not have held a
shield !

In the year 1844 or '45, Mr. Smirk died. I visited him not
long before his death. He was upwards of ninety, and in perfect
possession of all his faculties ; indeed, he might pass for a man
under eighty. Even then he amused himself with painting, and,
though he did not show his last productions, I was told they displayed no signs of imbecility. He talked most agreeably, and
told me he was old enough to have known a man who, in his
youth, had known William Vandervelde when he was in England,
and this man told him that Vandervelde used to go to Hampstead
Heath to study skies.

One very agreeable result of our visit to America, in 1833, was its making us acquainted with Captain Morgan, whose friendship has been among our greatest enjoyments. I have known very few men so constantly agreeable, for his intelligence and sense are equal to his cheerfulness, and that is unceasing. He may not be always so happy as he appears, for no man can be, but he seems to consider it a duty to be always cheerful.

Our delightful friend had a good story à propos to everything that happened. As a specimen, I will put down one of his amusing inventions.

Single ladies often cross the water under the especial care of the captain of the ship, and if a love affair occurs among the passengers, the captain is usually the confidante of one or both parties. A very fascinating young lady was placed under Morgan's care, and three young gentlemen fell desperately in love with her. They were all equally agreeable, and the young lady was puzzled which to encourage. She asked the captain's advice. " Come on deck," he said, " the first day when it is perfectly calm — the gentlemen will, of course, all be near you. I will have a boat quietly lowered down ; then do you jump overboard and see which of the gentlemen will be the first to jump after you. I will take care of you."

A calm day soon came, the captain's suggestion was followed, and two of the lovers jumped after the lady at the same instant. But between these two the lady could not decide, so exactly equal had been their devotion. She again consulted the captain. " Take the man that didn't jump ; — he's the most sensible fellow, and will make the best husband."

Morgan had often noticed, in our walks together, that no shepherd's dog we ever met had a tail. I had told him they were born without tails, and that Bewick was my authority. Still he would not believe it; and meeting a shepherd, and having laid a wager on the result of his answer, Morgan put the question thus : " At what age do you cut these dogs' tails ? " " About eight or nine months." I submitted. But " No," said Morgan, " you give up too soon ; much depends on how a question is put. That man possibly knows nothing of the matter, but he would not appear ignorant. His answer, therefore, does not prove that

you are wrong. If I had asked him if the dogs were born
without tails, perhaps he would have said yes."

When at sea with Captain Morgan, I said: "In such a ship as
this, and with such a captain as you, there seems to me to be no
risk but from fire, and that, at sea, must be fearful." *

" And it is at sea only," he said, " that I never fear fire. As
soon as I land, and find myself in a hotel, I can't sleep for a night
or two, for fear of being burned. We are very strict about lights
in the ship, and, though the rules may be broken, there are
always people awake in every part of the vessel. If some of
the steerage passengers will smoke, contrary to orders, there are
timid ones who lie awake to watch them. No; you are safer at
sea than anywhere else."

June 9th, 1849. — To-day I had the gratification of seeing the
principal works of my old friend and fellow-student, William
Etty, collected in the great room of the Society of Arts, in the
Adelphi.

Etty was in the room, and on my saying I was delighted to see
him so surrounded, he said, " by my children." I might have
farther congratulated him on having so large and fine a family of
daughters. There can be no doubt but that to these daughters,
and to the unreserved manner in which their charms are displayed, much of his popularity may be attributed. Still there is
often far more that is objectionable indicated in a single female
face by Greuze, where the figure is entirely draped, than in all
the nudities of Etty, whose mind was anything but a gross one.
Not that his choice of subject, in many instances, is in any degree
more defensible than that of Titian, of Correggio, or of Rubens.

But the excuses that may be offered for those great painters,
when treading on forbidden ground, — namely, that they elevated
their subjects, instead of allowing their subjects to debase their
art, — may, in a great degree, be advanced for Etty ; though in
many respects his taste is much below theirs, excepting always in
his colour, which is sufficiently fine in its own way to place him
beside them. And yet he commenced his practice in a school
unpropitious to colour, — that of Lawrence.

* This was before the days of steamboats. Now the great risk is from colli-
sions, which never happened then.

The impression made on me by this exhibition, and which, from all that I heard in the room, was the general impression on my brother painters, was that the pictures that had pleased formerly, now pleased still more, and those we had least liked gained on us.

Up to the time at which Etty was elected an associate of the Royal Academy, he had attended the Life-School with more regularity than any other student. It was supposed that, on becoming a full member, he would discontinue this habit, and some of the old Academicians thought he ought to give it up. I told him what I had heard on the subject, and he replied, "I do not mean to leave off studying in the Life-Academy. It fills up a couple of hours in the evening that I should find myself at a loss to employ otherwise. I am very fond of it, nor do I think it beneath the dignity of any rank to which my brethren may think fit to raise me. I hope I shall never disgrace the Academy by my conduct; but if my continuing to paint in the Life-School is considered wrong, let them not make me an Academician, for I will not give it up."

Nor did he discontinue the practice until compelled to do so by the state of his health, no doubt impaired by so regularly breathing the heated atmosphere of our ill-ventilated school-room.

As a member of the Academy, his conduct was invariably marked by the most unremitting and disinterested zeal for its welfare and honour, which he always considered identical with the general wellbeing of British art.

At our meetings he never spoke without a great effort, yet he was never silent on any question in which he thought he could serve the Academy. The first speech he made at a general meeting was to propose a very useful measure, which he carried; but he was so nervous that he could scarcely articulate, and it was painful to witness how much the effort cost him. He was warmly thanked by the President.

There was a simplicity and sincerity in the manner of Etty that attached his friends firmly to him, and I never heard that he had an enemy. In speaking of his own life he compares it to a long sunshiny holiday; and, indeed, we need but look at his productions, to feel sure that with him industry has never been

labour. And yet I remember him at a time previous to the
existence of any work of his hand now in the Adelphi, when he
was looked on by some of his fellow-students as a worthy but dull
plodding person, who would never distinguish himself. I recollect
his making a pasticcio at the British Institution, from the Paul
Veronese, "The Communion of St. Nicholas," now in the
National Gallery, which he turned into an "Adoration of the
Magi," on which it was remarked that "it was very plain *he* was
not one of the Magi."

He died in the November that followed his exhibition.

In this year occurred the sad accident that terminated the life
of Sir Robert Peel. Within my recollection no death in England,
with the exception of that of the Princess Charlotte, had occasioned such general sorrow as this unexpected event. The cases,
however, were widely different. The real character of the young
princess could only be imperfectly understood. But she was
looked to as the future sovereign, and being taken from the world
with her child at the time of its birth, her death could not but
excite an unusual degree of feeling throughout the country. Her
short life, however, from the privacy in which it had passed, had
as yet offered little more than promise.

On the contrary, the great talents of Peel had long been admired by his friends and admitted by his opponents, but his political changes had subjected him to severe censure ; and though his
conduct and motives were beginning to be more justly appreciated
than they had been, it seemed that his real worth was far from
being fully felt till, at a time of life when his services might fairly
have been counted on for years to come, his country was suddenly
deprived of them.

It is much to be regretted that there is no portrait that does
him justice, for he had a fine head. Lawrence's half-length is the
best ; but in that the dress challenges equal attention with the
face. The late statues, busts, and pictures of him are miserable
things ; indeed, his face, like his conduct, has been subject to more
misrepresentation than has been the case with most public men.
Lawrence, by the emphasis which he laid on the tie of his cravat,
the velvet waistcoat, and the glittering watch-guard, made a dandy
of him. Now, though there were some peculiarities in his man-

ner of dressing, Sir Robert Peel was so far from dandyism, that George the Fourth (no incompetent judge) remarked that his clothes never fitted him. The truth I believe to be, that the King, though glad to avail himself of Peel's great talents, looked on him as a plebeian, and *therefore* deficient in that taste, in small as well as in great things, which is supposed by some to be the birthright only of Royal or noble blood.

Sidney Smith related a pleasant invention illustrative of this,— which represented Peel, when in the ministry, and on a visit at the Brighton Pavilion, as called out of bed in the middle of the night to attend his Majesty in what—his dinner having disagreed with him in a very alarming manner—the King supposed to be his last moments. Peel was much affected, and the King, after a few words, which he could scarcely utter, said, " Go, my dear Peel,—God bless you! I shall never see you again:" and, as Peel turned to leave the room, he added faintly, " Who made that dressing-gown, my dear Peel? It sits very badly behind. God bless you, my dear fellow! Never employ that tailor again."

Not long after the death of this admirable man, died one whose conduct, in a much smaller, yet not unimportant sphere, was marked by the same disinterested zeal for the interests committed to him that at all times distinguished the great statesman. On his own account, the death of Sir Martin Shee could not be regretted, as it was the release, in old age, and from years of suffering, of a faithful steward of all of which he had the care. His devotion to the welfare of the Academy was never more conspicuous than when he was examined by a committee of the House of Commons, headed by Mr. Ewart, before which were summoned all the enemies of the Academy, some of whom no doubt from conscientious motives, and others perhaps from a mere wish to pull down a body which had not admitted them among its members, suggested the most impracticable and senseless changes. I regret that I do not possess a copy of the minutes of evidence before this notable committee. But the manner in which Sir Martin there repelled every unjust accusation against the Academy,—answered, in detail, every objection brought forward against its constitution,—and exposed the absurdity of the proposed plans for its amendment, does equal honour to his courage and his judgment. And he was well supported by the secretary and keeper, Howard and Hilton; who, though they could not vie with him in eloquence, went fully along with him in zeal for the cause they were called on to defend.

One word more about Sir Martin Shee. At the first Academy dinner, at which he took the chair as President, Lord Holland and Lord Grey sat next each other. After Shee's first address to the company, Lord Holland said to his neighbour, " I never heard a better speech." " And I," said Lord Grey, " never heard so good a one."

In August, 1850, my wife and I, with our daughter Mary, visited Oxford and Blenheim, with a party of friends, among whom were Mr. Doyle (H. B.), and his son Richard, the admirable artist of " Pipps's Diary " and " Brown, Jones, and Robinson."

While looking at the collection of pictures, not remarkable for their excellence, belonging to Christ Church College, a gentleman in a gown and cap, accompanied by two ladies, passed through the gallery. " That is Dr. Pusey," whispered our guide. " He has gone up into the library: you can go up." This, however, we did not choose to do, immediately; but, after looking at all the pictures, in the vain hope of finding something good, we ascended to the library, where the Doctor was writing at a window in the centre of the room. " He will turn round directly, and then you will see his face," said our guide. This happened accordingly; and when the doctor left the room, we were shown his autograph, in the book in which volumes borrowed are entered. It seemed, indeed, as if we had come on a pilgrimage to Oxford, *as the residence of Dr. Pusey ;* for another of the guides asked if we wished to see the house in which he lived, and was astonished to find we did not care to go out of our way for it.

Towards the end of September in this year, I was in Paris for a week with my daughter Mary. The best part of the Louvre being closed, in consequence of alterations and repairs (for the French, whatever form of Government may prevail, do not neglect the arts,) I spent more time than I had done when last in Paris in the gardens and streets, and was more than ever struck with the architectural beauty of Paris. How generally dingy,

low, and tasteless do the houses in London appear on a return
from Paris! How heavy and cumbrous where ornament is attempted, either on house or shop fronts! And how disagreeable
to the eye is the dirty drab that so much prevails in London, and
which, under the name of stone-colour, so soon degenerates, by
the aid of the smoke, into the colour of mud! In Paris you see
pure white or grey; and where tints are used, which is always
sparingly, pale reds, blues, yellows, or greens; but I never observed drabs.

On our return to England we spent a week at Sandgate, at the
house of my old friend James Foster. While there I saw, for
the first time in my life, a lunar rainbow. Looking towards
Folkestone, the light of the rising moon was visible, though her
orb was hidden from us by the cliffs; and on turning in the opposite direction the bow appeared partly over the sea. The arch
was nearly perfect, and, as the moon had but just risen, almost a
semicircle; and there seemed a very faint appearance of an outward arch. I remarked, as we often see it in the solar bow, that
the mist on which it appeared was of a uniformly darker shade
outside of the arch. The prismatic colours were not perceptible
to my eye, but it appeared of a soft pale light, nearly white. It
seemed the ghost of a magnificent double bow which I had seen
in the morning, not very far from the same place in the heavens.

On the 4th of November, this year, Eastlake was elected
President of the Academy. He had long been considered by
most of the members as pre-eminently qualified for this high
office; while, at the same time, it was well known to most of us
that he did not desire it. Sir Martin Shee died in August; and
the reason why so long an interval was allowed to pass before the
election of a President, was that many members were out of
town, and it was desirable that the meeting for the election should
be as full as possible. The vacancy occurred at a time of the
year when the Academy was least occupied with business that required a chairman, and it was proposed by Eastlake himself that
the choice should be deferred till we assembled in November to
elect associates, when it was likely most of the academicians
would be present. There were many discussions among the
members, who, like myself, were anxious for Eastlake's election.

9

It was thought by some, that it would be best to ascertain beforehand whether he would accept the presidency in case of a majority in his favour; but others, and I with them, feared that this
might draw from him a refusal, to which he might feel bound to
adhere, even if circumstances should afterwards occur to induce
him to change his mind. Edwin Landseer was in Scotland in
the autumn, and at Balmoral, where he heard the Queen and
Prince Albert express a hope that the choice of the Academy
would fall on Eastlake. As Landseer knew that these wishes
would have great weight with him, he sent me a note, written to
him by Colonel Phipps, stating how highly agreeable it would be
to the Queen and the Prince that Eastlake should be placed at
the head of the Academy. Landseer authorised me to make
whatever use I thought best of this note; and I sent it to Eastlake a short time before the election, begging him not to reply
to me unless he could reply as he must well know was desired by most of the members of the Academy. Until he saw
Colonel Phipps's note, I have no doubt he had determined to decline the chair. There were, of course, some persons dissatisfied
with his election, as is always the case in every such event; and
they and their friends affected to lament that the members of the
Academy had been influenced in their choice by the expressed
wishes of royalty. But the note I sent to Eastlake was seen *only*
by him. No other member of the Academy, excepting Landseer,
his brother, and myself, knew of it; and we had determined to
vote for him, whenever the vacancy should occur, long before we
knew how acceptable the choice would be to the Queen. Immediately on his election, the sum of 300*l.* per annum, which had
for some years been given to Sir Martin Shee, was voted to the
President, until the bequest of Sir Francis Chantrey of that sum
annually to the office should come into effect. This was unpala-
table to some of the academicians, who considered it undignified
that the President of the Royal Academy should be paid for his
services; a view, I confess, entirely opposite to that which I take
of the matter. In the first place, 300*l.* is no payment for the
time and money the President is now called on to expend in the
service of the Academy; and, in the second, it seems to me that
it would be much less dignified in that body, to allow a distin-

guished artist to make the great sacrifices he must make, for the benefit of the institution, wholly without compensation.

The rare qualities essential to the President of such a body may possibly be found united in a man who is by no means rich. Sir Martin Shee undertook what he could not afford; and the Academy, very properly, during the last years of his life, gave him what ought to have been given him at first. *They* must have strange notions of dignity who would call this conduct un-dignified.

On the evening of the election, before we proceeded to vote, I gave notice that I should propose at the next meeting that the sum voted annually to Sir Martin Shee should be continued to his successor; and when the time came this was agreed to without opposition. Having taken an active part in these matters, I think it right to leave some record of the facts.

At the election, the votes were for Eastlake, 26; for Edwin Landseer, 1; for Pickersgill, 1; and for Jones, 2.

The month of May, 1851, will remain memorable on account of the opening of the Great Exhibition of the Industry of all Nations, in Hyde Park — an event, the success of which has so greatly surpassed expectation and falsified prophecy.

Soon after the Exhibition was opened, I was informed that I had been nominated a juryman for the American Commission. I concluded, as a matter of course, that the jury on which my name was placed were to decide on the merits of works of art; but when I took my seat at the board, I found myself entirely among strangers — ordinary-looking men, at least, such at the first glance, they appeared to me. I soon found, however, they were discussing matters of science; and, on looking round the table again, their looks improved. It then occurred to me to refer to the voluminous catalogue, which I had found of little use in the Exhibition, and in the last page of it I discovered my own name in the list of Jury, Class X, of which Sir David Brewster was chairman; and among it the members were Sir John Herschel, Baron Seguier, Professor Potter, and other eminent men; and I found also by my catalogue, that I was to decide, with these gentlemen, on the merits of "Philosophical, Musical, Horological, and Surgical Instruments."

I sat out the meeting, determined to resign a situation for which I was unfit. I listened to discussions on matters of which I was wholly ignorant, and came away with the impression that the gentlemen round the table were remarkably wise-looking men — so true it is that the character is rarely seen in the face at the first acquaintance, and never so truly seen as when we know it beforehand. The maid-servant of the Misses Cotterell who mistook Dr. Johnson for a robber, is not to be too hastily censured.

On inquiring of the Commissioners why I had been nominated upon such a jury, I was told it was because they could think of no other resident in London connected with America but me; and that I might be of use by drawing the attention of the jury to objects which in the enormous collection might by chance escape their notice. It was earnestly wished that I should continue to serve, and I therefore did so; not sorry to have frequent opportunities of sitting at the same table with my distinguished colleagues.

CHAPTER X.

On the 19th of December in this year died the greatest painter of the time, by some thought the greatest of all the English painters. By many, however, and perhaps by the best judges, Turner will be placed in that class

" whose genius is such
That we never can praise it or blame it too much."

The artists, with scarcely an exception, had, from the beginning of his career, done him justice. But he passed through life little noticed by the aristocracy (Lord Egremont being, as he had been in the case of Flaxman, the principal exception), and never by Royalty. Callcott and other painters, immeasurably below him, were knighted; and, whether Turner desired such a distinction or not, I think it probable he was hurt by its not having been offered to him. Probably, also, he expected to fill the chair of the Academy, on the death of Sir Martin Shee; but, greatly as his genius would have adorned it, on almost every other account he was incapable of occupying it with credit to himself or to the institution, for he was a confused speaker, and wayward and peculiar in many of his opinions, and expected a degree of deference on account of his age and high standing as a painter, which the members could not invariably pay him, consistently with the interests of the Academy and of the Arts.

Having said that he received but little notice from the nobility, with the exception of much patronage from Lord Egremont, I must not omit to mention that he painted one of his largest and grandest pictures for Lord Yarborough, and another, as fine, for

the Marquis of Stafford. Mr. Rogers, with less means of patronage, was always his great admirer, and has associated his
name with that of Turner in one of the most beautifully illustrated volumes that has ever appeared.

It is remarkable that the poet was equally the friend and admirer of Flaxman and Stothard, while the titled and wealthy of
the country lost for themselves the honour of connecting themselves with names that will probably outlive their own.   ·

Sir George Beaumont was a sincere friend to the Arts, but in
many things a mistaken one. IIe was right in his patronage of
Wilkie and of Haydon, but he ridiculed Turner, whom he endeavoured to talk down. IIe did the same with respect to Stothard, and though personally very friendly to Constable, he never
seems to have had much perception of his extraordinary genius.

In the year 1822, Constable thus wrote: " The art will go out :
there will be no genuine painting in England in thirty years."
And it is remarkable that, within a few months of the date thus
specified, Turner should have died, almost literally fulfilling, as
some of his admirers may think, Constable's prophecy.

It is difficult to judge of the condition of Art in our own time ;
but I think it cannot be denied that painting is in a much lower
state in this country now than in the year 1822. At that time
Stothard, Fuseli, Wilkie, Turner, Lawrence, Owen, Jackson,
Constable, and Etty were living, James Ward was in the full
possession of his great powers, as were also most among the
present eminent painters. But those who have since come forward, however they may hereafter rank, cannot, I think, at present be considered as forming anything like such an assemblage
of excellence, as the English school could boast of thirty years
ago.

Turner was very amusing on the varnishing, or rather the
painting days, at the Academy. Singular as were his habits, for
nobody knew where or how he lived, his nature was social, and
at our lunch on those anniversaries, he was the life of the table.
The Academy has relinquished, very justly, a privilege for its
own members which it could not extend to all exhibitors. But I
believe, had the varnishing days been abolished while Turner
lived, it would almost have broken his heart. When such a

measure was hinted to him, he said, " Then you will do away
with the only social meetings we have, the only occasions on
which we all come together in an easy unrestrained manner.
When we have no varnishing days we shall not know one
another."

In 1832, when Constable exhibited his " Opening of Waterloo
Bridge," it was placed in the school of painting — one of the
small rooms at Somerset House. A sea-piece, by Turner, was
next to it — a grey picture, beautiful and true, but with no
positive colour in any part of it. Constable's " Waterloo " seemed
as if painted with liquid gold and silver, and Turner came several
times into the room while he was heightening with vermilion and
lake the decorations and flags of the city barges. Turner stood
behind him, looking from the " Waterloo " to his own picture,
and at last brought his palette from the great room where he was
touching another picture, and putting a round daub of red lead,
somewhat bigger than a shilling, on his grey sea, went away
without saying a word. The intensity of the red lead, made
more vivid by the coolness of his picture, caused even the vermilion and lake of Constable to look weak. I came into the
room just as Turner left it. " He has been here," said Constable, " and fired a gun." On the opposite wall was a picture,
by Jones, of Shadrach, Meshach, and Abednego in the furnace.
" A coal," said Cooper, " has bounced across the room from
Jones's picture, and set fire to Turner's sea." The great man
did not come again into the room for a day and a half ; and then,
in the last moments that were allowed for painting, he glazed the
scarlet seal he had put on his picture, and shaped it into a
buoy.

In finishing the " Waterloo Bridge " Constable used the palette
knife more than the pencil. He found it the only instrument by
which he could express, as he wished, the sparkle of the water.

Parsimonious as were Turner's habits, he was not a miser. It
was often remarked, that he had never been known to give a
dinner. But when dining with a large party at Blackwall, the
bill, a heavy one, being handed to Chantrey (who headed the
table), he threw it to Turner by way of joke, and Turner paid it,
and would not allow the company to pay their share. I know,

also, that he refused large offers for his "Téméraire," because he intended to leave it to the nation.

Like Sir Joshua Reynolds, he avoided expressing his opinions of living artists. I never heard him praise any living painter but Stothard; neither did I ever hear him disparage any living painter, nor any living man.

Mr. Ruskin, in a lecture he delivered at Edinburgh, draws a touching picture of the neglect and loneliness in which Turner died.* This picture, however, must lose much of its intended effect when it is known that such seclusion was Turner's own fault. No death-bed could be more surrounded by attentive friends than his might have been, had he chosen to let his friends know where he lived. He had constantly dinner invitations, which he seldom even answered, but appeared at the table of the inviter or not as it suited him. His letters were addressed to him at his house in Queen Ann Street; but the writers never knew where he really resided. It may well be supposed that a man so rich, advanced in life, and, as was thought, without near relations, should be much courted. He had for many years quoted in the Academy catalogues a MS. poem, "The Fallacies of Hope;" and I believe that among his papers such a MS., though not in poetic form, was found by some of his friends to be his will.

I am very far from supposing that Mr. Ruskin belonged to this class of Turner's friends; for I have not a doubt that his enthusiastic admiration of his art and mind was genuine; and expressed with no other feeling of self-interest than the pride of being known to be capable of appreciating him.

It is greatly to be regretted that Turner never would sit for a portrait, excepting when he was a young man, and then only for a profile drawing by Dance. This is, therefore, the only satisfactory likeness of him extant.

It happened, of course, as with every eminent man, that as soon as he was dead the shop-windows exhibited wretched libels

* " Cut off, in great part," says Mr. Ruskin, " from all society, first by labour, and last by sickness, hunted to his grave by the malignity of small critics and the jealousies of hopeless rivalry, he died in the house of a stranger."

on his face and figure, the most execrable of which was from a sketch by Count D'Orsay.

Turner was short and stout, and he had a sturdy sailor-like walk. There was, in fact, nothing elegant in his appearance, full of elegance as he was in art; he might be taken for the captain of a river steamboat at a first glance; but a second would find far more in his face than belongs to any ordinary mind. There was that peculiar keenness of expression in his eye that is only seen in men of constant habits of observation. His voice was deep and musical, but he was the most confused and tedious speaker I ever heard. In careless conversation he often expressed himself happily, and he was very playful: at a dinner table nobody more joyous. He was, as I have said, a social man in his nature; and it is probable that his recluse manner of living arose very much from the strong wish, which every artist must feel, to have his time entirely at his own command.

It fell to my lot to select the first of his pictures that went to America. Mr. James Lenox, of New York, who knew his works only from engravings, wished very much to possess one, and wrote to me to that effect. I replied, that his rooms were full of unsold works, and I had no doubt he would part with one. Mr. Lenox expressed his willingness to give 500*l.*, and left the choice to me. I called on Turner, and asked if he would let a picture go to America. " No; they won't come up to the scratch." I knew what he meant, for another American had offered him a low price for the " Téméraire." I told him a friend of mine would give 500*l.* for anything he would part with. His countenance brightened, and he said at once, " He may have that, or that, or that," — pointing to three not small pictures. I chose a sunset view of Staffa, which I had admired more than most of his works from the time when it was first exhibited. It was in an old frame, but Turner would have a very handsome new one made for it. When it reached New York, Mr. Lenox was out of town; and we were in suspense some time about its reception. About a fortnight after its arrival he returned to New York, but only for an hour, and wrote to me, after a first hasty glance, to express his great disappointment. He said he could almost fancy the picture had sustained some damage on the voyage, it ap-

peared to him so indistinct throughout. Still he did not doubt
its being very fine, and he hoped to see its merits on farther
acquaintance; but for the present he could not write to Mr. Turner, as he could only state his present impression.

Unfortunately, I met Turner, at the Academy, a night or two
after I received this letter, and he asked if I had heard from Mr.
Lenox. I was obliged to say yes.

" Well, and how does he like the picture ? "

" He thinks it indistinct."

" You should tell him," he replied, " that indistinctness is my
fault."

In the meantime, I had answered Mr. Lenox's letter, pointing
out, as well as I could, the merits of the picture, and concluded
by saying, " If, on a second view, it gains in your estimation, it
will assuredly gain more and more every time you look at it."
Mr. Lenox, in reply, said, " You have exactly described what has
taken place, I now admire the picture greatly, and I have brought
one or two of my friends to see it as I do, but it will never be a
favourite with the multitude. I can now write to Mr. Turner,
and tell him conscientiously how much I am delighted with it."

Mr. Lenox soon afterwards came to London, and bought another picture of Turner's, at a sale, and, I think, another of himself, and would have bought " The Téméraire," but Turner had
then determined not to sell it.

It was reported that Turner had declared his intention of being
buried in his " Carthage," the picture now in the National Gallery. I was told that he said to Chantrey, " I have appointed
you one of my executors. Will you promise to see me rolled up
in it ? " " Yes," said Chantrey; " and I promise you also that as
soon as you are buried I will see you taken up and unrolled."

This was very like Chantrey, and the story was so generally
believed, that when Turner died, and Dean Milman heard he was
to be buried in St. Paul's, he said, " I will not read the service
over him if he is wrapped up in that picture."

I have said Turner often expressed himself happily. I remember that when it was proposed that the new Houses of Parliament were to be decorated with pictures, he said, " Painting
can never show her nose in company with architecture but to
have it snubbed."

How true this is! No architect ever seems capable of understanding in what light, and at what distance, painting can be seen; and it is a great pity that first-rate art, either sculpture or painting, should ever be employed in the decoration of architecture. The Elgin Marbles were never seen till now, when they are in ruins. The coarsest art would have as well ornamented the Parthenon, and Lucca Giordano might have been better employed in decorating the Sistine Chapel and the chambers of the Vatican than Michael Angelo and Raphael.*

An attempt has lately been made in Italy to rescue some of the great works of art from the decay and injury to which they are exposed in churches, but without success. I never saw an altar-piece in a light in which it could be fairly seen. There are always windows on each side, to say nothing of the picture being too high, and the lower part generally hid by the decorations of the altar.

In the year 1852, being, for the fourth time, one of the Council of the Academy, I proposed that the exclusion of engravers from the highest academic honours should be reconsidered. I was induced to do so on account of a vacancy occurring in the list of Associate engravers, by the death of Mr. Landseer, and I hoped that an alteration of the laws of the Academy might be effected before that vacancy should be filled up, so as to induce engravers of first-rate excellence to become candidates.

On a former occasion, when such an alteration was proposed, I was among its opponents. But I had since reconsidered the subject in all its relations to the arts and to the Academy, and, having changed my opinion, was now anxious to repair my share of what I considered the perseverance of the Academy in an error committed at its formation.

I was farther encouraged to take up this matter by what fell from Sir Charles Eastlake, at a council, upon the vacancy among the Associate engravers being mentioned. He said: " I suppose the question respecting the admission of engravers to the highest honours of the Academy will, some time or other, be again brought forward." I had before known that he was in favour of such a

* I should think few lovers of art would agree with Mr. Leslie in this opinion. — ED.

change, and the hint thus thrown out determined me to lose no
time in bringing the matter forward.

Sir Robert Strange attributed the exclusion of engravers from
among the Academicians to the determination to keep him out of
the Academy, he not being acceptable to the King on account of
his Jacobite principles. But I cannot believe that Sir Joshua
Reynolds and other eminent artists were not sincere in their opinion that engraving should receive an inferior distinction to that
conferred on Painting, Sculpture, and Architecture, because it is
an art not requiring inventive powers.

The Academicians were not, however, unanimous in this
opinion, for West spoke strongly in favour of placing engraving
on the same footing with the other arts, and Bartolozzi, though
he did paint a picture to entitle him to admission, owed his election, in reality, only to his eminence as an engraver. The Society,
by this proceeding, practically acknowledged what their constitution denied. Whether or not this was done to appease the anger
of the engravers, many of whom were members of the society
out of which the Academy sprung, the inconsistency of the act
was very unfortunate. The engravers were only the more irritated, and in the second year of its existence the Academy made
a second mistake in an alteration of its constitution, by which six
engravers were eligible to the rank of Associate only.

That this law was a mistake has been abundantly proved from
its working. For some time no candidate for the intended honour
could be induced to come forward ; and the first that offered himself was an artist eminent only as a seal-engraver to the King.
He was followed by an obscure foreigner, and eighteen years
elapsed before the entire number could be filled up, nor did
it then include any engraver who stood at the head of his profession.

In 1802 a vacancy occurred among the Associate engravers
which was not supplied till 1806, when the late Mr. Landseer
became a candidate, in the hope of influencing the Academicians
to change the law relating to his art. The same motive had previously induced James Heath to accept the diploma, and both ex-
erted themselves to promote such a change.

Mr. Landseer memorialised the Academy, and suggested that

four engravers should be made Academicians, and that a professorship of engraving should be established.

The advocates for a change of the law increased as years rolled on, and among these Wilkie may be mentioned as one who possessed, more than any other painter, a practical knowledge of the difficulties and requirements of the art of engraving.

The opponents to a change in the constitution of the Academy favourable to engraving, have always laid much stress on the wisdom of such men among its founders as Reynolds and Chambers. But these eminent men might — could they have lived to the present day — see cause to acknowledge their mistake, and to place themselves among those now disposed to listen to the opinions of the engravers. The Academy had reached its eighty-fourth year, and, with very few exceptions, engravers of eminence had not accepted the place it offered to them, while the list of distinguished engravers who have stood aloof from it is a large one.

First on the list are the names of Woollett, Strange, and Schiavonetti, artists of unrivalled excellence, and to these may be added the names of others who, if not so great, have yet done much honour to the British school. Vivares, Medland, Charles Warren, Raimbach, Charles Heath, William Finden, Le Keux, George and William Cook, line-engravers; Cardon, Agar, Scriven, Jones, and Caroline Watson, chalk-engravers; and Earlom, M'Ardell, Fisher, and Reynolds, mezzotint-engravers.

A title for so long a time refused by the leading men of the profession for which it was created could clearly be no honour. If the Academy was not, after much experience, disposed to confer a distinction on engraving, which those who practised it best would accept, it seemed to me and others that it would be more to the credit of the Institution to discontinue the offer of a rank to engravers that was generally considered by them as an insult.

The great battle was about the relative dignity of the art. Whatever that may be, I cannot look at the best works of the best engravers and not feel that they are the productions of genius. If the Academy could be filled with artists like Reynolds, Gainsborough, Wilson, Chambers, Banks, and Flaxman,

there would unquestionably be no room even for the best of engravers. But it is most unfortunate for the Academy that such
persons as Baker, a flower painter; Chamberlain, a portrait
painter; Hayman, a historical painter; Richards, a scene
painter; Meyer, an enamel painter; Yeo, an architect; and
many others now equally forgotten, were Academicians, when
men who have done so much honour and service to the Arts as
Strange, Woollett, and Sharpe, were not permitted to confer the
honour of their names upon it.

Nor was it only in the first years of the Institution that its
ranks were swelled by mediocre artists. Down to the present
day there have always been Academicians, whose diplomas would
have been more worthily bestowed upon first-rate engravers.

There *have been* such artists as Piranesi and Bewick, engravers
not only of consummate skill in the use of their tools, but possessing great powers of invention and great fertility of imagination.
There have been such men, and there may be again, and under
its original constitution the Academy had no place for them.

When the proposed alteration was in the course of discussion,
I said I considered that England had produced the best engravers
in the world, and the Academy had treated them as if they were
the worst. Sir Richard Westmacott attributed the interest I took
in their cause to gratitude, and he was right. But the gratitude
I feel is not merely towards a few who have ably engraved some
of my pictures, but to the art itself. For I believe that in no
country have the other arts ever owed so much to engraving as
in England.

The greatest patron of painters that has appeared in this country, since the time of Charles I., was an engraver, who acquired
a fortune as a publisher, which he spent entirely in the encouragement of art. It would take a long time to enumerate the magnificent things done by Boydell during upwards of half a century;
while all that was done within the same time for historic or poetic
art by the British aristocracy, may be stated very shortly — it
was next to *nothing*.

Had there been no such art as engraving, there would have
been no such patronage as Boydell's, which gave birth to some
of the greatest works of the British school; and to this same art

of engraving it is scarcely too much to say we owe the very existence of Hogarth. His patrons were the million. The great people were told by Walpole that he was no painter; and Walpole, being one of themselves, they believed him. But for engraving, therefore, Hogarth must have confined himself to portraits on which he might have starved, for he was never popular as a portrait painter. But when the prints of "The Harlot's Progress" appeared, 1200 copies were immediately subscribed for. This was the beginning of the patronage produced for painting by engraving. Its benefits appeared next in the case of Stothard, who lived and died scarcely employed except by publishers, to whom we owe the thousands of his enchanting conceptions now so eagerly sought by collectors.

Even Wilkie would not have been what he was but for this art. The prices he received for his finest pictures, at the time when he painted but one a year, would never have enabled him to give them their admirable finish, but for the remuneration he received from his prints. It is remarkable (as illustrating the history of patronage in England) that the Directors of the British Institution bought his "Distraining for Rent," and soon after put it in their cellar, where it remained till Raimbach repurchased it for the purpose of engraving — the right to do which had before been refused by the Directors. The great excellence of this picture had, at first, induced the Directors of the Institution to buy it as soon as it was seen at Somerset House. But they were afterwards frightened at what they had done, on its being suggested that the subject was a satire on landlords, and the picture was placed in a large dark lumber-room under the gallery, where the students were allowed to wash their brushes. I saw it there; and told Young (the keeper) that if it remained long in so dark a place it would turn yellow. He accordingly allowed it to be hung in one of the upper rooms during the intervals between the exhibitions. Washington Irving saw it there. I was present at the time, and I remember that he stood for some minutes before it without saying a word; and, when he turned round, tears were streaming down his cheeks.

Turner's large fortune was acquired very much through the means of engraving; nor has, what I cannot but call, the patron-

age of this art been extended to painting only. Flaxman, neglected by the Court, the Government, and the aristocracy, was
enabled by engravers to spread all over the world those exquisite
conceptions which have supplied materials to less inventive sculptors and painters of classical subjects.

Such are the grounds of my gratitude to the art of engraving.
I was told, however, that if painters owe much to this art, it owes
its very existence to them. True; but the benefits between living
painters and engravers are not necessarily mutual. *They* can do
without *us* much better than *we* can do without *them*. They can,
as Strange did, employ themselves wholly, and with great advantage to their reputations, on the works of the old masters.

The injustice of the original laws of the Academy towards
engravers was very remarkable. While painters, sculptors, and
architects were elected by painters, sculptors, and architects, no
engraver could be present at the election of a member of his own
profession. The choice was made by artists who had no practical
knowledge of the engraver's craft. Thus, while the Academy
offered to a profession what was considered no honour by most
who belong to it, the gift, to such as were willing to receive it,
carried less guarantee of merit than the gift of any other distinction in the Academy.

Eastlake was of opinion, and I entirely agreed with him, that
there always had been, and always would be, room among the
forty for a few first-rate engravers. The majority, however,
thought otherwise, and it was otherwise determined. But there
was one thing required of candidates for the engravers' associate-
ships to which I was strongly opposed, namely, that they should
exhibit original compositions, or drawings, from nature. This
part of the law appears to me so unreasonable, and so much
worse than useless, that I cannot but believe it will, sooner or
later, be rescinded.

CHAPTER XL

THE "Autobiography of Haydon" recalls to mind my first acquaintance with its author, then young and full of promise, in his own eyes and in those of all who knew him, of great future eminence.

But here I must digress to another early acquaintance, John Howard Payne, whose career resembled Haydon's in its many years of the extremest misery of debt, incurred by the bad management of good natural talents.

The success of Master Betty, who, for a time, carried the public away from Kemble and Mrs. Siddons, excited a youth in America, like Betty, of handsome features and graceful manners, and with a charming voice, to come forward as an *American Young Roscius*. Master Payne, in a very short time realised a small fortune by his personations of *Romeo*, *Hamlet*, *Young Norval*, and the other characters in which Betty had attracted such crowds in London. I saw him play *Romeo* in Philadelphia, and was perfectly delighted. Whether he equalled Betty on the stage, I know not; but he was superior to him off the stage; for while yet in his teens, he became the editor of a newspaper or magazine — I forget which — and was a favourite associate of the foremost literary men in Boston, New York, and Philadelphia.

I think it was in 1813 that Payne came to England to try his fate on the London Boards. But he was no longer a boy; and as Betty lost his attractiveness with the growth of his beard, so it

. 10

was with Howard Payne. He played two or three nights at
Drury Lane, but with little applause, excepting from the American friends who mustered to support him. Mr. West was in a
stage-box, and I sat by his side. The old gentleman had not
been in a theatre for many years. He expressed himself pleased
with Payne, but he was delighted — and well he might be —
with Knight (the father of the present secretary of the Academy), who played the principal character in the farce.

Though Payne failed as an actor, he afterwards acquired fame
as an author by his tragedy of " Brutus," in which Edmund
Kean thrilled the audience by his inimitable personation of the
hero.

Soon after his arrival in England, Payne, as had happened in
America, became a favourite in a large circle of young men of
talent, artists, and literary aspirants. Among these were Haydon ; Dr. Croly (now Rector of St. Stephen's, Walbrook), then
a poet, and without a living ; Shiel, the Irish orator, who died
Master of the Mint ; Scott, the editor of the " Champion," who
fell in a duel in consequence of an attack upon Lockhart ; and
Procter (the amiable Barry Cornwall). I remember also seeing
at Payne's lodgings, at a breakfast which he gave to a large
party, the then celebrated Robert Owen, who was at that time
filling the papers with his schemes for re-modelling society on a
plan that was to transcend Utopia. I remember Payne telling me
that when Wilberforce, on being urged to bring this plan before
Parliament, replied that it was too late in the session, Owen exclaimed, " What, sir ! put off the happiness of mankind till
another session of Parliament ! "

After failing as an actor, Payne tried what he could do as a
manager, and undertook the direction of Sadler's Wells for a
season. But Grimaldi was the only attractive person in his
company, and the manager incurred nightly losses. He gave his
friends very amusing accounts of his difficulties and embarrassments ; and the melancholy though often laughable incidents he
related of this part of his life furnished Washington Irving with
much of the theatrical adventure introduced in his " Buckthorne
and his friends."

It was through Payne that I became acquainted with Haydon.

I had admired the power displayed in Haydon's "Macbeth," and still more that shown in his "Solomon." When I first saw him he was engaged on his "Christ entering Jerusalem."

Payne, who attributed his failure on the boards of Drury Lane to everything but want of talent, had given Haydon a long account of the way in which he had been thwarted by the jealousy of English actors, and the illiberality of the English press. To all this, Haydon very characteristically replied: "Sir, I regret from my soul the treatment you have met with; I regret it as an Englishman, and am ashamed of my country. I wish it were in my power to do anything that could make you the slightest amends; but the only way in which I can show my sense of the injustice you have suffered, is to make you the St. John in my picture."

I was captivated with Haydon's art, which was then certainly at its best, and tried, but with no success, to imitate the richness of his colour and impasto. Allston, Morse, and I, often spent evenings with him, and very pleasant evenings they were. At a much later period I was struck with his resemblance to Charles Lamb's "Ralph Bigod, Esq.," that noble type of the great race of men — "the men who borrow." I even thought, before Lamb declared Fenwick to be the prototype of Bigod, that Haydon was the man; and I am not sure that Lamb did not think of him as well as of Fenwick; — all the traits were Haydon's. "Bigod had an UNDENIABLE way with him. He had a cheerful, open exterior, a quick, jovial eye, a bald forehead, just touched with grey (*cana fides*). He anticipated no excuse, and found none. . . . . When I think of this man, — his fiery glow of heart, his swell of feeling, — how magnificent, how *ideal* he was; how great at the midnight hour! And when I compare with him the companions with whom I have associated since, I grudge the saving of a few idle ducats, and think that I am fallen into the society of *lenders* and *little* men."

Haydon never asked me to lend him money; perhaps he knew I had none to lend; for, indeed, being a bad economist, I was often obliged to borrow myself: and I may here say, that had it not been for very kind friends, belonging to what Lamb calls the LITTLE class of men, I must have been often as badly off as

Haydon was at the worst. The only thing he ever borrowed of
me was a picture — a copy from a Paul Veronese. He kept it
long, but it came safely back to me.

His " Christ entering Jerusalem " did not equal his " Solomon," as a whole; but there were very fine things in it. The
head of Jairus, and the head and figure of his daughter, were
inimitably painted; and there was a noble, matronly Jewess,
kneeling and spreading drapery, in the foreground. It seemed to
me that there was an almost regular decrease of excellence in
his pictures, from the " Solomon " to the end of his life, parallel
with his increasing troubles. The " Raising of Lazarus " was
inferior to the " Entry into Jerusalem," though, had the conception and execution, throughout, been equal to the conception
and execution of the figure of Lazarus, it would have been one
of the finest pictures in the world. The introduction of the father
and mother of Lazarus, persons who have no place in the history,
was a great mistake.

Haydon's journal, like his pictures, displays great powers of
mind, and in it, as in his pictures, passages of truth and of false-
hood often stand side by side. According to the feeling that is
uppermost he does the amplest justice, or the grossest injustice,
to those of whom he writes. This is most often the case in what
he says of Wilkie, because of Wilkie he speaks most often.

In a very touching anecdote, he gives a true character of West.
While he was at work on the " Solomon," he says, " West called,
and was affected to tears at the mother. He said there were
points in the picture equal to anything in the art. But," said
this good old man, " get into better air; you will never recover
with this eternal anxiety before you. Have you any resources ? "
" They are exhausted." " D'ye want money ? " " Indeed I do."
" So do I," said he; " they have stopped my income from the
King, but Fauntleroy is arranging an advance, and if I succeed,
my young friend, you shall hear. Don't be cast down ; such a
work must not be forgotten ! " In the course of the same day
West sent him a cheque for £15.

But ·Haydon repeats the story of the withdrawal of a little
picture by Wilkie from the exhibition, which Allan Cunningham
tells in a manner wholly distorted by *his* prejudices against the

Academy. Haydon acknowledges that he advised Wilkie not to send the picture, because it was unworthy of his reputation, and then accuses West of intrigue, because he recommended Wilkie to withdraw it. He speaks of West's *"pretended"* regard for Wilkie. It was a real regard, as I well know, founded on respect for him as a man, and the highest admiration of his genius. I have more than once heard West say, " There is but one Wilkie."

In Haydon's account also of his interview with Flaxman, he gives the grossest caricature of that great artist.

In some published remarks on Haydon's journal, I have said that " all the charges " contained in it, " unfavourable to the Royal Academy, are unfounded." But a reperusal of it shows me that in one instance I was mistaken. Haydon says, " in 1810," he " first put down his name for Associate, Arnold was elected."

The fact, as thus stated, is inaccurate ; but not so the implied charge of injustice. It was 1809, the year in which he exhibited his " Dentatus," that he first put down his name. In that year there were two vacancies among the Associates. The first was very justly given to Wilkie, but the second very unjustly to Dawe. This was certainly disgraceful to the Academy, and I doubt whether a single man who voted for Dawe did not afterwards repent it. Haydon's " Dentatus," though much inferior to his " Solomon," should assuredly have made him an Associate. His indignation, however, on account of its place in the Exhibition, was what no man with as much genius, and less of vanity, would have felt. It had a central situation in a room where pictures by Reynolds and Gainsborough had often been placed, and where one of Lawrence's finest portraits was hung, when he was President of the Academy. Haydon says the ante-room had no decent light for a picture, which is untrue, for the light in which the " Dentatus " was hung was as good as possible ; nor can I acquit him of wilful misrepresentation, when he says the ante-room had " no window," for this, though in one sense true, is substantially false, the ante-room being lighted by a sky-light, the best of all windows for pictures.

In judging of Haydon's character, it is fair to consider what he did *not,* as well as what he *did;* and it is to his credit that, through all the extremes of mental agony he suffered, and with his sanguine and ardent temperament, he never gamed, or sought relief from his sufferings by drinking. Indeed, whatever were his faults, he seems to have had no low vices; and in his family he was as good a husband and father as a man always over head and ears in debt could be; no doubt a much better husband and father than many a man who never knew any but easy or affluent circumstances.

Lord John Russell's "Life of Moore" reminds me of the opportunities I have had of meeting another eminent man. I saw Moore most often at Holland House, and at the House of Mr. Rogers; but at neither was there a piano, and it was only two or three times at Mr. Murray's that I had opportunities of hearing him sing. I shall never forget a small dinner party, in Albemarle Street, of which Moore and James Smith (the chief author of the "Rejected Addresses") were the life and soul. They sat opposite each other at the table, and kept up a constant interchange of anecdote and pleasantry.

After dinner they sung their own songs alternately, Moore accompanying Smith on the piano, though he knew nothing of the airs. But Smith hummed them over in an under tone, previous to singing, and that was sufficient to produce a beautiful accompaniment from Moore's dextrous little fingers. One of Smith's songs was made up of men's actions contradicting their names, *e. g.:*

> "Mr. Metcalf ran off upon meeting a cow,
> With pale Mr. Turnbull behind him."

and —

> "Over poor Mr. Lightfoot, confined by the gout,
> Mr. Heaviside danced a bolero."

So much has been said of the taste and feeling with which Moore sung his own songs, that I will say nothing but that too much could not be said of it.

When his "Life of Byron" first appeared, it was in two large quarto volumes, and the first came out alone. Murray told me that a lady said to him, "I hear it is dull;" and he told her the scandal was all to be in the second volume. "And is the second volume to be had separately?" asked the lady.

This last touch was probably given to the story by Murray himself.

In 1855 Alfred Chalon exhibited his own works with those of his brother John, at the rooms of the Society of Arts in the Adelphi.

Death had separated the brothers, whose affection for each other was the strongest I ever witnessed between relations. Indeed, the love and harmony in that family, of which Alfred is now the sole survivor, was such as, were it universal, would make this world a paradise.

It was to me a proof — if I had wanted one — of the non-appreciation of colour at the present time, that the exhibition of Alfred and John. Chalon's pictures failed to attract notice.

Except at the private view, I doubt whether any artist entered the rooms, though there is not one living who might not have learned much by studying the pictures there. I went, as to a school, and indeed I always felt myself in a school in the house of the Chalons. To my mind, Alfred Chalon has long been the first among painters in water-colours; and yet, though his beautiful drawing of the Queen was in the great Paris Exhibition, this year, the prize for water-colour art was given to Cattermole! But it could scarcely be expected that an artist, so little understood by his countrymen, should meet with more justice from the jurors of a nation where no taste or feeling for the beauties of colour at present exists. Injustice was done by this decision not only to Chalon but to John Lewis, whose admirable drawing of "the Hareem" was wholly unnoticed.

In November, this year, I visited Paris in company with my wife, who had never before been in France. We staid about ten days, and though the weather was cold, enjoyed the many enjoyable things there greatly.

The enormous collection of pictures and sculpture confirmed what I had before thought, that these arts have gradually declined in England and advanced on the Continent, since the peace of 1815.

When it was proposed to adorn the houses of Parliament with

frescoes, Haydon thus wrote: " English art never stood higher
than at the end of the war.   Foreigners were astonished at our
condition, and well might be.   The reason was, blockading kept
the rich from running over the Continent; our energies were
compressed and devoted to ourselves, and we flourished accordingly. . . . . We escaped the contagion of David's brickdust
which infected the Continent, and the frescoes are but a branch
of the same Upas root grafted upon Albert Durer's hardness,
Cimabue's gothicism, and the gilt ground inanity of the middle
ages.   All the vast comprehensiveness of Velasquez, Rubens and
Titian, are now to be set aside, and we are not to go on where
they left off, but to begin where their predecessors began."

It is certain that before the Continent was thrown open to our
artists, and our patrons of art, there was an immense difference
in favour of the British school, between its productions and those
of any other school; a difference not only in degree, but in kind;
and that, now, though some remains of colour are still left to us,
as well as some feeling for what is natural in expression, yet this
great difference no longer exists.

It is as if the British school had possessed the wine, and the
other schools the water only of art, and that the peace, by mingling these, had strengthened the art of the Continent exactly in
the degree in which it had diluted art with us.   This amalgama-
tion may be one cause of the change; but the rise and decline of
art, like the rise and decline of nations, is never the effect of a
single cause.

Combinations of circumstances, which can never be thoroughly
understood, bring these things about.

I am quite aware that, to many, my premises resting on the
great superiority of the British school will appear doubtful.
Those who take an opposite view to mine will contrast the cor-
rectness of drawing of the French and German artists with our
inaccuracies in form, and will insist much also on the cultivation
in those schools of high art — namely, historical and religious art.
With respect to the first point, power in drawing, I heard an eminent English painter praise the works of Horace Vernet, while
he admitted, with me, that his colouring was disagreeable, and
that he had no feeling whatever for that breadth of chiaro-scuro,

which has always been a distinction of every great painter. But he praised, and very justly, his facility of composition.

Now it is clear that the deficiencies he admitted in the art of this very clever Frenchman, must deprive him of any claim to the name of a painter, because as the admission leaves him only the power of expressing forms and combining them well, it leaves him only so much of art as may be given by outline compositions like those of Flaxman, and much better given in that manner; an entire absence of colour, and chiaro-scuro being very much better than the presence of these qualities without harmony or breath.

As to the cultivation of historic and religious art by the Continental painters, it will be time enough to call it the cultivation of *High* art when they produce pictures that will bear even a distant comparison with the works of the great old masters; while we may say, with pride, that the works of — I will not go back to Hogarth, Reynolds, Wilson, and Gainsborough, for they are now numbered with the old and great masters, — but the works of men whom many of us living have had the happiness of knowing personally, as Fuseli, Stothard, Turner, Constable, Wilkie, Etty, and the best of Haydon's, will hang with credit among those of the greatest painters that ever lived.

Mrs. Leslie and I slept at Calais on our way home, and passed the greater part of a day there. We were at Dessin's hotel, and after the hurry and bustle of Paris there was much in this quiet old house to charm us, independently of all associations — its old-fashioned simple elegance — so unlike the style of the Parisian hotels — the beautiful garden through which we had to pass to and from our bed-room, all looking as if no change had been made in the house or its decorations for a century. It seemed, indeed, exactly as it must have been when Sterne wrote of it. In the very room where the monk first addressed him, we read the story, and the poor Franciscan's " courteous figure seemed to re-enter." We went into the coachyard where Yorick apologised for his harshness to Father Lorenzo, and we felt that, though Sterne might have been, as Mr. Thackeray calls him, " an old scamp," he has left, in that inimitable story, much atonement to the world for his vices, and for those passages in his writings which it is a pity he had not blotted.

The present master of the hotel is a grandson of the Monsieur
Dessin of Sterne, who, by the way, spells the name incorrectly—
Dessein ; and in the quarto copy of the " Sentimental Journey,"
printed both in French and English, which lies in the coffee-
room, wherever the name occurs it is corrected with a pencil.

The head waiter, an old man who has lived at the hotel forty
years, followed us into the street when we took leave. He had
noticed that we felt interested in the hotel, and placing his hand
on my shoulder, he said :

" You will come here again ? "

I said : " I hope so, and tell M. Dessin that, if I do, I will
bring him some engravings from the ' Sentimental Journey ' " (I
meant those from Stothard) " to hang up in his rooms."

Another object of interest to me was the old gate, painted by
Hogarth. The drawbridge, with its chains depending from the
projecting beams, is exactly like that in the picture ; but the portcullis is gone, and the gate much altered. Whatever remains
there may have been of the English arms upon it in Hogarth's
time are now wholly removed.

In this year (1855) we lost an old and valued friend, Peter
Powell, who never entered our doors without bringing cheerfulness, and who often, by his extraordinary powers of amusing, at
our little parties, made entire evenings pass as if we formed an
audience at a comedy. His songs, all his own, were unsurpassed
in humour ; but his great performances were an imitation of an
oratorio (in which he gave an idea of all the instruments of the
orchestra, and of Braham on the stage,) and an imitation of a
melo-drama. The last was indeed a wonderful affair. Without
scenery or any change of his dress he acted an entire melo-drama
far more amusingly than any melo-drama was ever acted before.
He began with a syllabus in rhyme of what was to come :

> " A Baron — mustachoes —
> A great hat and feather —
> A maid in despair —
> And a deal of foul weather.
>
> A castle — a village —
> A wedding — a dance
> A little like England,
> A good deal like France.

> Then thunder and lightning,
> And just in the middle,
> A scream from a maid,
> And a squeak from a fiddle."

But how he would give the dialogue, with the most ludicrous imitation of the melo-dramatic style, express in his own single comical little person an entire *corps de ballet* and the march of a stage army, and conclude all with a grand battle of infantry and cavalry, ending in a single combat between the perfidious Baron and Lindor, the lover of the piece, in which the Baron falls and dies — how he contrived to do all this can never be described.

My friendship with Powell began nearly forty years ago, and was never interrupted, though there were subjects (and, as we both considered them, important ones,) on which we never agreed. He was a thoroughly honest, good-hearted, benevolent man, of a most happy temperament, and always delighted to spread happiness about him. He died at a good old age (I believe not far from eighty) with little suffering, and preserving the cheerfulness of his nature to the last.

Another aged friend — for friend I feel sure I may call him — died in this year, whose death was more like a mere dissolution of nature, without disease, than any death within my recollection. Whatever place may be assigned to Samuel Rogers among poets, he deserves to hold the highest place among men of taste; not merely of taste for this or that, but of general good taste in all things. He was the only man I have ever known (not an artist) who felt the beauties of art like an artist. He was too quiet to exercise the influence he should have maintained among the patrons of art; but, as far as his own patronage extended, it was most useful. He employed, and always spoke his mind in favour of, Flaxman, Stothard, and Turner, when they were little appreciated by their countrymen. The proof of his superior judgment to that of any contemporary collector of art or *vertu* is to be found in the fact that there was nothing in his house that was not valuable. In most other collections with which I am acquainted, however fine the works of art, or however rare the objects of curiosity, I have always found something that betrayed a want of taste — an indifferent picture, a copy passing for an original, or something vulgar in the way of ornament. Then, too, his collection was entirely formed by himself, whereas most of the great collections of pictures of the beginning of the present century were formed under the direction of the most respectable dealers — men whose characters warranted their honesty.

Those who are disposed to think the worst of Mr. Rogers, say that, by the severity of his remarks, he delighted in giving pain. I know that, by the kindliness of his remarks, and still more by the kindliness of his acts, he delighted to give pleasure.

It has been said that temperance, the bath, the flesh-brush, and, above all, to avoid fretting, were his receipts for health. To these I can add another — fresh air; for he was a great walker, and it was his daily custom after breakfast (which was often a long meal, as he was fond of company at his breakfast-table,) to go out and spend the greater part of the day in the open air, quite regardless of the weather, of which he never complained. I have heard him express his surprise that the most religious people were often among those who most abused the weather. " They forget," he said, " who sends it. And when it is fine, if you remark how pleasant it is, they say, ' Yes ; *but we shall pay for it.*' "

Lord Byron thought Rogers's taste must have been "the misery of his existence." Never was a greater mistake. True taste, such as his, *must* contribute to a man's happiness ; but beside the possession of this, Rogers had a happily-constituted mind, and no one who knew much of the last years of his life, and who saw the sweet smile on his venerable countenance, when his memory was gone, and when, at times, he did not know that he was in his own house — no one could see that sweet smile without a conviction that he had much of Heaven within his breast.

While he retained his faculties, I heard him more than once repeat the concluding lines of Mrs. Barbauld's " Address to Life." *

> Life! we have been long together,
> Through pleasant and through cloudy weather;
> 'Tis hard to part when friends are dear;
> Perhaps 'twill cost a sigh, a tear;

---

* I once met Mrs. Barbauld at the house of Mr. Wm. Vaughan, at Clapham. She was a little old lady, still handsome in age, and a perfect gentlewoman in manners.

> Then steal away, give little warning,
>   Choose thine own time —
> Say not Good night, but in some brighter clime
>   Bid me Good morning.

The last time I heard him recite this passage was at Brighton. My daughters and I were at breakfast with him. I sat so as to command the view from the window : and while he was repeating the lines a funeral was passing. He did not see it.

During our stay at Brighton, he took me to the Dyke, which I had never before seen. As we sat in his carriage looking over the vast expanse of country below us, he pointed down to a village that seemed all peace and beauty in the tranquil sun-set.

" Do you see," he said, " those three large tombstones close to the tower of the church ? My father, my mother, and my grand-father are buried there."

" Really ? "

" No, but I should like to be buried there."

On telling this to a literary friend, a man, too, who aspired occasionally to be poetical, he exclaimed, " What a lying old rascal ! "

Several times, at Petworth, we met Mr. Rogers. I recollect that, one evening, all the young ladies in the house, formed a circle round him, listening with extreme interest to a series of ghost stories which he told with great effect. Indeed, while he staid at Petworth, the beaux there had little chance of engaging the attention of the belles, when he was in the room. His manner of telling a story was perfect. I remember only one other person, the late Lady Holland, who, like him, used the fewest words with the greatest possible effect ; sometimes more than supplying the omission of a word by a look, or a gesture. Rogers *told* his stories as, in prose he *wrote* them. The story of " Marcolini " in his " Italy " for instance, could not have better words, nor fewer, without loss of interest. Walter Scott's manner was different. He amplified, digressed, and in relating any-thing he had heard, added touches of his own that were always charming. Lord Eldin (John Clerk), once said to him — " Why, Sir Walter, that's a story of mine you've been telling ; but you have so decorated it, that I scarcely knew it again."

" Do you think," said Scott, " I'd tell one of your stories,
·or of any body's, and not put a laced coat and a cocked hat upon
it ? "

In the " Table Talk " of Mr. Rogers, published in March,
1856, every anecdote that I have heard him relate, is more or
less spoilt by the editor. In the story of Lord Ellenborough and
the wig box, which he threw so angrily out of his carriage window, mistaking it for his wife's bonnet-box, Mr. Rogers used to
wind up with " Lady Ellenborough bore it like an angel ; " but
this is omitted.

The story of Sidney Smith asking his doctor on whose stomach
he should take a walk, is so falsified as to be turned into utter
nonsense. The story of George IV. talking of his youthful ex-
ploits and telling the Duke of Wellington that he had made a
body of troops charge down the Devil's Dyke, is very inferior to
the story as Mr. Rogers told it to me while we were together at
the Dyke. The King said to the Duke : —

" I once galloped down that hill at the head of my regiment."

" Very steep, sir," said the Duke.

There is one other anecdote which, though it may be correctly
reported, must not pass without notice. Mr. Rogers was told
that a gentleman, passing the door of Sir Joshua Reynolds, saw
a poor woman sitting on the steps and crying. She said she had
been sitting to Sir Joshua, he had given her a shilling, it was a
bad one, and he refused to change it. Now there are two implica-
tions against Reynolds in this story ; first his meanness in giving
her *only* a shilling ; and, secondly, his dishonesty in refusing to
change it. As to the first insinuation — if, which is very probable, the woman had sat but an hour, a shilling was, in those
days, ample payment, for no more is expected by persons who sit
to artists now ; and, as to the last, it is utterly incredible. There
cannot be a doubt that the woman told a lie to excite charity.
That such an anecdote should have found a place in the " Table
Talk," is not surprising ; but I am surprised that Mr. Rogers
should have told it without noticing the palpable lie of the
woman.

Those who know Rogers only from his writings, can have no
conception of his humour. I have seen him, in his old age, imi-

tate the style of dancing of a very great lady with an exactness
that made it much more ludicrous than any caricature ; and I remember, when I met him at Cassiobury, that he made some droll
attack, I quite forget what it was about, on one of the company,
and went on heightening the ridicule at every sentence, till his
face " was like a wet cloak ill laid up," as were the faces of all
present, and especially the face of the gentleman he was at-
tacking.

At an evening party, at which I met him, the oddest looking
little old lady, for she was as broad as she was long, and most
absurdly dressed, as she was leaving the room saw him near the
door, and accosted him :

" How do you do, Mr. Rogers, it is very long since I have
seen you, and I don't think, now, you know who I am."

" Could I ever forget you ! "   He said it with such an emphasis that she squeezed his hand with delight.

I think it was in the summer of 1842 that Rogers, Wordsworth, and Washington Irving were all under my roof together.
I had met them at breakfast at Miss Rogers's, and as we came
away at the same time, Rogers walked home with me, and Wordsworth and Irving, promising to come, took a cab.   As they got
into it, Rogers said : —

" They are a couple of humbugs, I believe, we shall see no
more of them."

They came, however, and Wordsworth's eye on entering my
painting-room was caught by copies by Jackson of Reynolds's
portraits of Sir George and Lady Beaumont.   But I must interrupt my story to mention a peculiarity of Rogers.   He, and it is
common to men of taste, liked to find out something to admire
that had escaped others.   I have known him at Holland House,
when Lord Holland was quoting, with praise, something affecting
in prose or poetry, take up a newspaper, and read one of those
anonymous appeals that daily appear among the advertisements.

" If J. C. will return to the home which is made desolate by
her absence, all will be forgotten, &c."

" There," he would say, " is real pathos."

To make what happened in my room, further understood, I
must mention also that Rogers, though he admitted the genius of

Constable, did not admire his works; the only indication, as I
thought, of his want of taste. Indeed he often told me that my
admiration of Constable did harm to my own practice. And now
for my story: —

"Ah!" said Wordsworth, "there are my old friends Sir
George and Lady Beaumont."

"But not a bit like," said Rogers. "You look at them, because they are a fine lady and gentleman, but you don't notice
those sweet cottage children. Who painted that charming picture?" (Turning to me.)

"Constable."

I confess that I enjoyed the triumph of being able to give such
an answer. The picture was an early one by Constable of two
little girls, children of his father's coachman. It belonged to Mr.
Hering, who lent it to me. He afterwards had it cut, and each
child framed in an oval. The youngest he gave to me.

Mr. Rogers was very fond of children. On his visits to us,
when ours were little ones, his first ceremony was to rub noses
with them.

"Now," he would say, "we are friends for life. If you will
come and live with me, you shall have as much cherry-pie as you
can eat, and a white poney to ride."

At a later period, my eldest daughter reminded him of these
promises, and said: —

"We believed you, Mr. Rogers."

"Yes," he said, "how wrong it is to deceive children; but will
you come and live with me now?"

He offered her his arm, she took it, and as they were going out
of the door, he turned to me, and said: —

"Good bye, papa."

It was reported, that about this time he made an offer of marriage to a young lady; most probably founded on something like
this. I was told, with reference to the reports, that Lady Holland asked him if he intended to marry Miss ——, and that he
said: —

"I'm not old enough."

His stories of children, of which he told many, were very

pretty. The prettiest was of a little girl, who was a great favourite of every one who knew her. Some one said to her : —

" Why does everybody love you so much ? " She answered : —
" I think it is because I love everybody so much."

He spent most of his time in society, or in walking. He told me that he never read excepting when confined to his house by illness, and " then," he said, " it is a new pleasure."

I once dined in the chambers Mr. Rogers occupied in the Temple, before he took the house in St. James's Place. The dining-room was a large and cheerful one, on the ground-floor, in Paper Buildings (I think), and commanded a fine view of the river. He had faced the window-shutters with looking-glass, so that from every part of the room there were to be seen views of the river, up and down.

11

CHAPTER XII.

On the 1st of October, 1856, our daughter Caroline was married to Mr. Alexander Pearson Fletcher, a young man whom we all greatly like, and not the less for his being a Scotchman. . They went to Paris, where Caroline was so ill that her mother and I joined them, and staid till she was well enough to return.

Like all old people, I now live much in the past, and constantly recall to mind persons and scenes of which I have said nothing in these pages.

Nearly forty years ago, a Boston negro, named Prince Saunders, came to England, I think, with the intention of going to Africa as a missionary. He had education enough to keep a little school in Boston, where, I believe, he had also preached. He, however, went not to Africa, but to Hayti, where he obtained the favour of the king, and returned to England with a great deal of money. He was noticed by Mr. Wilberforce, and soon became a lion of the first magnitude in fashionable circles. The Countess of Cork could not have a party without " his Highness Prince Saunders ; " for as he put his Christian name " Prince " on his cards without the addition of Mr., he was believed to be a native African Prince, and he did not undeceive those who chose to think him one. In short, his whole career here was an amusing instance of humbug ; on his part, however, no otherwise than by his silently allowing his admirers to humbug themselves.

This was very amusing to the Americans who had known him at home. A great Boston lady was in England, who, when Saunders last called on her in Boston, would send him into the kitchen to have lunch with her servants. He called on her early one morning in London. She was at breakfast, and with extreme condescension (as she thought) offered him a cup of tea. "No, thank you, ma'am," he said, "I am going to breakfast at Carlton House."

I was taken by my friend Dr. Francis, of New York, to one of Sir Joseph Banks's conversazioni. The old gentleman received his company sitting (being very gouty), in his library, at one end of which hung a portrait of Captain Cook.

> " Lamented and with tears as just,
> As ever mingled with heroic dust."

The room was filled with the most eminent scientific and literary men, but Prince Saunders, the coal black Boston negro, was the great man of the evening; a negro too of the most moderate abilities. Everybody asked to be presented to "his Highness." I got near to hear what passed in his circle, and a gentleman, with a star and ribbon, said to him, "What surprises me is that you speak English so well." Saunders, who had never spoken any other language in his life, bowed, and smiled acceptance of the compliment.

He had a large party one evening at his lodgings; but the Countess of Cork, having a party the same night, as she could not go to Saunders, sent her carriage for him, and he left his company, and went to the Lady Cork.

From Prince Saunders, a nobody, who was made much of, my recollections go back to a man who was somebody, and (comparatively) made little of while he lived — Alexander Wilson, the ornithologist.

Mr. Bradford, the same liberal patron who enabled me to study painting, enabled Wilson to publish the most interesting account of birds, and to illustrate it with the best representations of their forms and colours, that has ever appeared. Wilson was engaged by Mr. Bradford as tutor to his sons, and as editor of the American edition of " Rees's Cyclopædia;" while at the same time he was advancing his Ornithology for publication. I assisted him to colour some of its first plates. We worked from birds which he had shot and stuffed, and I well remember the extreme accuracy of his drawings, and how carefully he had counted the number of scales on the tiny legs and feet of his subject.

He looked like a bird; his eyes were piercing, dark, and lumin-

ous, and his nose shaped like a beak. He was of a spare bony
form, very erect in his carriage, inclining to be tall; and with a
light elastic step, he seemed perfectly qualified by nature for his
extraordinary pedestrian achievements.

Alexander Wilson belonged to a class of men of which Scotland seems to have produced a greater number than any other
country— men from the humble and middle classes of life, of
poetic minds, lovers of nature, of science, and of art — men of
unconquerable perseverance, who succeed at last in acquiring
fame, and sometimes fortune, often in despite of the most adverse
circumstances in early life.

Wilson's ardour in the pursuit of science was too much for his
bodily strength, and he died at the age of forty-five.

His biographer, George Ord, speaks thus of him: — " Mr.
Wilson possessed the nicest sense of honour. In all his dealings
he was not only scrupulously just, but highly generous. His veneration for truth was exemplary. His disposition was sociable
and affectionate. His benevolence extensive. He was remarkably temperate in eating and drinking; his love of retirement
preserving him from the contamination of the convivial circle.
And unlike the majority of his countrymen, he abstained from
the use of tobacco in every shape. But as no one is perfect, he
partook in a small degree of the weakness of humanity. He
was of the *genus irritabile,* and was obstinate in opinion. It
ever gave him pleasure to acknowledge error when the conviction
resulted from his own judgment alone, but he could not endure to
be told of mistakes. Hence his associates had to be sparing of
their criticisms, through fear of forfeiting his friendship. With
almost all his friends he had occasionally, arising from a collision
of opinion, some slight misunderstanding, which was soon passed
over, leaving no disagreeable impression. But an act of disre-
spect, or wilful injury, he would seldom forgive."

Mr. Bradford was the most enterprising publisher in America,
and determined to make the " Ornithology," as far as he had to
do with it, in the highest degree creditable to his country.

The types, which were very beautiful, were cast in America;
and though at that time paper was largely imported, he determined
that the paper should be of American manufacture; and I re-

member that Amies, the paper maker, carried his patriotism so far that he declared he would use only American rags in making it. The result was that the book far surpassed any other that had appeared in that country, and I apprehend, though it may have been equalled in typography, has not before or since been equalled in its matter or its plates.

Bewick comes nearest to it; but his accounts of birds are not so full and complete, and his figures, admirably characteristic and complete as they are in form, have not the advantage of the much larger scale of Wilson's, or of colour.

Unfortunately Wilson's book was necessarily expensive, and therefore not remunerative; but nothing discouraged him, as will be seen by an extract from a letter which must, from its date, have been written when the first volume only had appeared, which was followed by eight more.

" If I have been mistaken in publishing a work too good for the country, it is a fault not likely to be soon repeated, and will pretty severely correct itself. But whatever may be the result of these matters, I shall not sit down with folded hands while anything can be done to carry my point, since God helps them who help themselves. I am fixing correspondents in every corner of these remote regions,* like so many pickets or outposts, so that scarcely a *wren* or *tit* shall be able to pass along from York to Canada but I shall get intelligence of it."

Before I left America I was well acquainted with Peter Pindar's verses, and indeed knew many of them by heart; for (notwithstanding his ill-nature) his humour and his excellent sense, when not influenced by a bad motive, made me read him with delight and I think with some profit. A short time before Dr. Wolcott's death I became acquainted with a young Irishman, a literary man, named Desmoulins, who was intimate with him, and who, knowing my admiration of his poems, offered to take me to see him. The doctor appointed a day to receive us, and we called at his lodgings in a small house in an obscure street in Somerstown. But he was too ill to see a stranger. Mr. Desmoulins went up to his bed room, and I stayed in his little sitting room which was furnished as might be expected. There were shelves

---

* He was writing from Boston.

with books, a piano, on which lay a violin, and there were pictures and drawings on the walls, of which some were small copies from Reynolds, and some landscapes in water-colours by Wolcott himself. As well as I recollect, these were good, their effects of light and shade broad and powerful. He died soon after.

I was standing one day with Mr. Sockett, the rector of Petworth, before his house, when an old-fashioned chair upon wheels was drawn past by a labouring man, a crippled pauper being in it. "Go and put your hand on the back of that chair," said Mr. Sockett. I did so, and "Now," he said, "your hand has been where the hand of the poet Cowper has often been. I have often drawn Mrs. Unwin in that chair round Hayley's grounds at Eartham, with Cowper and Hayley pushing at the back of it. The old lady had an attack of paralysis while she and Cowper were on a visit to Hayley. Cowper remembered to have heard that electricity was good in such attacks, and the nearest electrical machine being at my mother's house it was sent for, and I (then a boy) being the only person who knew how to make use of it was sent for to work it. Hayley took a fancy to me, and afterwards recommended me to Lord Egremont as a tutor to his three sons. Lord Egremont sent me to college with them, I took orders, and he gave me this living; and all this followed from the accident of Mrs. Unwin's attack at Hayley's house.

Mr. Sockett has a set of chairs which had belonged to Hayley. They are of carved mahogany, and designed by Flaxman. The centre of every back is a lyre.

I have been at many pleasant dinner parties, as I suppose everybody who has reached the age of sixty-three may say, but at few more amusing than one at Mr. Cartwright's, at which Charles Kemble and Matthews the elder were present. Edwin Landseer was there and Mr. Z., as I shall call a person of some note in his day.

Matthews was preparing a new "At Home," and rehearsing his songs in private companies according to his custom, and we had the benefit of one of these rehearsals. He sung several after dinner. One, as I remember, described a fox-hunt, and concluded with an enumeration of the mishaps of the day incurred by a dandy who had never hunted before. "He had been fatigued to death, thrown into a ditch, lost his boa, his hat, and one of his boots, and all because a parcel of dogs chose to follow an unpleasant smell." These compositions of Matthews consisted of alternate singing and speaking. I think he invented that kind of song, and I believe he was assisted in them and in the getting up of his entire entertainment by his son, now so deservedly popular.

Mrs. Trollope's book on America was just published, and Mr. Z. took occasion to eulogise it and abuse the Americans. Matthews defended them. As to Americanisms, he said, he once made out a pretty long list, but had since met with every one of them in England excepting only "Slick right away." Then Z. attacked their mispronunciations, and Matthews mentioned several words in which they are more correct than Englishmen. For instance *engine*, in which they give the true sounds of the vowels, while here it is commonly pronounced *ingin*. Edwin Landseer mentioned *Lunnon* for London, *charot* for chariot, as not unfrequent among fashionable people, and *potticary* also. "Sir," said Z., with an expression of great contempt, "you must have lived among potticaries." "Did you ever hear ——" (naming a lady of high rank) "say potticary?" "Yes," said Landseer. Z. then, without knowing the least about the matter, doubted whether the eating and drinking in America were to be compared to ours — "You never sat down to such a dinner as this in America." Matthews made him very angry by asserting that he had often done so, and with wine as good, "and such Madeira as you never tasted, and never will taste till you go there." He added something more that made Z., who had by this time taken quite wine enough, so angry that he rose on his feet and exclaimed, "That's not true, you stupid old Mr. Matthews;" and Matthews answered with the most perfect good humour, "It *is* true, you sensible old Mr. Z."

A friend of mine wrote a farce, I think some five and forty years ago, and sent it to the managers of Covent Garden Theatre, who kept it for some time and returned it with a civil refusal. Not long after, a new farce was announced at Covent Garden, called "Love, Law, and Physick." Now a lawyer and a doctor

were the principal personages in my friend's production, and of
course there was love in it; so we were almost certain it had
been pirated. We formed a party, therefore, for the first night,
to detect the villany of the managers and the author, and I am
not sure that my friend had not prepared a rough draft of an
indignant letter to some newspaper. There was not however the
remotest resemblance between Kenney's admirable after-piece and
our friend's ; and, instead of the luxury of a first rate grievance,
we saw " Love, Law, and Physick " acted more amusingly than
it was ever acted again; for Matthews, as the lawyer, gave an
imitation of Lord Ellenborough, summing up a case and charging
a jury, which he was not permitted to repeat. The other actors
were Liston, Emery, and Blanchard; and there was Mrs. Gibbs,
to see whom and to hear whose joyous laugh would have been
worth our tickets, had the rest been bad actors instead of the very
best.

Many years after this I became acquainted with Kenney, and
found him always delightful. His health was bad, and he suffered from a nervous affection which showed itself very oddly ;
sometimes it seemed impossible for him to make up his mind to
step over a gutter or to get into a carriage. But he always talked
well, was always ready to amuse or be amused, and every moment of his life he was a perfect gentleman.

His abilities, however, failed to do for him what infinitely
smaller abilities constantly do for other men, and he was always,
at least while I knew him, struggling with pecuniary difficulties.
His indifferent health no doubt precluded much effort, and he had
a large family to support.

At last, when worn out with fruitless exertion, his friends made
arrangements to give him a benefit at Drury Lane. I saw him a
day or two before it took place. He was ill, but not in bed, and
hoped to be at the theatre ; but on the very morning of the day
of his benefit he died.

The first thought of his family was to postpone the performance, but Mr. Rogers, who had taken a great interest in the
affair, said " No ; " and the " Beggars' Opera," and " Love, Law,
and Physick " were acted to an overflowing house, in which
what had happened that morning was known only behind the

scenes. Wright played Liston's part in the farce, and better than any body but Liston could play it.

In Charles Lamb's "Two Races of Men," there is an amusing allusion to Kenney and to Mrs. Kenney, "that part-French, better-part English woman," as Lamb calls her.

I think it was Kenney who said of Luttrell's "Advice to Julia," a poem aiming at humour, that "it was too long and not broad enough."

Poor Kenney! the sufferings of so sensitive and fine a mind as his, sufferings which were never obtruded on his friends, must have been very great. But he enjoyed society, and adorned it in his quiet modest way.

I constantly recall anecdotes of those who are gone, and I shall put down at a venture things that amused me in the hope that they may amuse others.

Mr. Rogers told me that when the "Pleasures of Memory" was first published, one of those busy gentlemen, who are vain of knowing everybody, came up to him at a party, and said, "Lady ——— is dying to be introduced to the author of the 'Pleasures of Memory.'" "Pray let her live," said Rogers, and with difficulty they made their way through the crowd to the lady. "Mr. Rogers, madam, author of the 'Pleasures of Memory.'" "Pleasures of what?" "I felt for my friend," said Rogers.

Not many years before his death he visited Paris with his friend Mr. Maltby. Maltby was a year or two the elder, and their friendship began (I think Mr. Rogers told me) when he was but nine, and lasted without the slightest interruption till the death of Maltby at upwards of ninety.

Maltby was one of the most absent of men. While in Paris together Rogers dined at a party, where a lady who sat next him did not know him at first, but after hearing him talk for some time discovered who he was. Maltby was not at this dinner, and Rogers telling him of this lady said, "she asked if my name was not Rogers." "And was it?" inquired Maltby.

Mr. Rogers said he preferred the mode in Roman Catholic churches of seats without pews; and a gentleman who preferred pews said, "If there were seats only, I might find myself sitting by my coachman." "And perhaps you may be glad to find your-self beside him in the next world."

I remember also his saying, "those who go to heaven will be very much surprised at the people they find there, and very much surprised at those they do not find there."

*   *   *   *   *   *   *

EXTRACTS

FROM

LESLIE'S CORRESPONDENCE.

WHEN a little above seventeen Leslie landed in England, as we read in his Autobiography, in December, 1811. He kept up a regular correspondence with his family at Philadelphia, from which, however, only extracts have been placed at my disposal. It is principally from these extracts and his correspondence with Washington Irving, that the following selections have been made. Leslie was a regular exhibitor at the Royal Academy from 1813 to 1859, the year of his death, with the exception of 1815, 1817, 1818, 1823, 1828, 1830, 1834, and 1853. His life was uneventful; spent in the affectionate discharge of family duties — which no man ever fulfilled better.— and in the happy practice of his art. Its public interest lies entirely in its connection with his pictures. I have therefore enumerated, for each year, the pictures of that year, with selections from his letters which throw light on the progress of his pictures, or on the occupations, ideas, and associations of the painter. I have been fuller in my extracts from the earlier letters, as of importance in illustrating the growth of the writer's mind, both as regards art and general culture.

Leslie's letters paint the man — affectionate, social, candid, modest, and eager for instruction and improvement; always seeking the society of the best and most eminent persons to whom he could gain access, without intrusion or forwardness.

1812.

Pictures Painted this Year.

TIMON OF ATHENS. — HERCULES. — PORTRAITS OF MRS. VISSCHER; MISS
SMYTHE; MR. INSKEEP; MR. COATE; BENJAMIN WEST, P. R. A.; MR.
WEST (of Salem, Massachusetts); MR. EARLE.

Leslie's first year in London was a memorable one, especially
to citizens of the United States residing in England. On the
the 29th of June, 1812, the orders in council, affecting the trade
of neutrals were revoked, as regards America, in consequence of
the revocation of Napoleon's Berlin and Milan decrees. But unluckily for the specific effect of our revocation in the United
States, Congress had already declared war with England on the
18th of the same month.

This war continued till the conclusion of the treaty of Ghent,
on December the 24th, 1814. Leslie's letters extending over this
period contain allusions to the hostile relations of the two countries and regrets at the obstruction to correspondence thus caused,
but it is remarkable that these allusions show scarcely any trace
of bitterness against this country. The young writer, though
thoroughly national, seems, already, to have felt that, let the governments differ as they might, the nations were kindred. To him
London was, above all, the seat and nursery of the arts he loved.
Politics occupy him little.

His chief associates were the American artists, Allston, King
and Morse. His days were spent in study at the Academy, the
British Museum, and Burlington House, where the Elgin marbles were then deposited, or in portrait painting. Before beginning work, he tells his sister, he often bathed in the Serpentine.
The favourite amusement of his evenings was the play. This
was the year of Mrs. Siddons' retirement from the stage, and he
followed her through the round of her farewell performances.
His earliest letters are almost equally divided between his own
art and the theatre.

Thus, writing to Miss Leslie, 19th April, 1812, he tells her

" I have just returned from seeing ' The Gamester.' It is the last time Mrs. Siddons is ever to perform the character of Mrs. Beverley; I never saw so perfect a piece of acting. She appeared very much affected at the commencement, and really shed tears. In the scene between her and Stukely, she was uncommonly fine. Although she is now very large, she appears as easy in her motions as a young girl, and is extremely graceful. In the last scene, she almost surpassed herself. A lady in the boxes went into hysterics and was carried out. The look of speechless agony she cast on the body of Beverley as she went off, surpassed everything I had ever seen. Beverley was played by Young, who is very like Wood * in his manners (the latter I believe copies him,) though a much better stage figure, and has a fine head, though I will not say a more expressive countenance. His voice too is very good. He stands certainly next to Kemble in tragedy. Lewson was very well played by C. Kemble. Stukely, by Egerton, was but ordinary. King has seen Cooke in that character, with Kemble and Mrs. Siddons. What a treat! I can scarcely bear to think of it. I did not stay to see the farce, which was the ' Child of Nature.'

" In the Exhibition, which will open in a few days, there is to be a picture of Kemble in ' Cato,' by Lawrence, which he has just finished. I have seen that of him in Hamlet — it is very fine.

"A new romance by Murphy has appeared, called ' The Milesian Chief.' Allston, who is a great admirer of this man's works, says it is much better than ' The Fatal Revenge.' It is a modern story; the scene is in Ireland. I have seen the first volume, but have not been able to get the others from the library. The language abounds in poetical images. Morse and myself subscribe jointly to a very large library in Bond Street. We take out seven volumes at a time. The days now are quite long, and the weather begins to be very fine.

" When it grows warmer I shall go to the British Museum every day, to draw from the antiques, of which there is a fine collection there. I have begun to study the Vault Scene in Marmion, which I shall finish for the next Exhibition. I wished to have done something for this year; but it was impossible.

* An Actor in Philadelphia. — Ed.

You know it requires some time to use oil colours with facility, and as I never painted in that way until I came here, my first essays were wretched daubs, and I could have sent out nothing that would not have disgraced me. I have painted several portraits, and have improved myself so much that I shall soon be able to earn something in that way.

"You wish there may be an accommodation between the two countries. I think there will soon be. You can have no idea of the distress our non-intercourse has caused here. There is nothing to be heard of but riots in the manufacturing towns. The poor are in a state of starvation. The Prince is abused by everybody. You would be astonished at the audacity of the public papers against him. He is caricatured in all the print shops. I am sure he cannot be less popular in America than he is here. The 'Examiner,' a violent opposition paper, said the other day, 'it was reported that the Prince and his brothers were going to the Continent in person.' He observed that, 'it would be a most refreshing sight to see those royal personages quitting the country for the good of the state.' Cooper will be a very great loser by his bet. The King may live these twenty years yet, for aught I know; he is now doing very well. I dare say I shall not stay here long enough to witness his funeral. I went the other day to see Barker's Panorama of Lisbon. It is admirably painted, and said to be exactly like it. I think I mentioned in another letter that I had seen two other paintings of the sort. They are certainly perfect in their way. The objects appear so real, that it is impossible to imagine at what distance the canvas is from the eye.

"I went lately to see an Exhibition of Water Colour Drawings, from the Old Masters. They have brought that kind of painting to greater perfection in this country than, I believe, ever was known before.

"The colours appear equally brilliant with oil, but I cannot see any advantage in it, as it is quite as much trouble to use them as oil, and the pictures will not last so long." *

On May the 11th, Perceval was assassinated. Leslie writes next day

* They sometimes last longer. — LESLIE.

TO MISS LESLIE.

LONDON, *May 12th*, 1812.

*   *   *   *   *   *   *

"There has been a violent sensation excited here to-day by the assassination of Mr. Perceval. You will no doubt have heard of this shocking affair before this reaches you. He was shot last evening in the passage to the House of Commons just as he was entering, by a man who had posted himself there for the purpose, said to be a bankrupt merchant of Liverpool. The ball penetrated his heart, and he instantly expired. The perpetrator of the deed surrendered himself immediately to the officers of justice; indeed it was very evident he had no wish to escape. As soon as it reached the ears of the mob they assembled in vast bodies about the house crying out, 'Burdett for ever.' I am told there has been chalked on many of the walls near it, 'Peace, or the Regent's Head.' There seems to be some mighty event about to take place here. It appears to me like a great play, at which I am an unconcerned spectator.

"I have just returned from seeing Mrs. Siddons in 'Venice Preserved.' The afterpiece being one I had seen before, I thought I should much better employ the remainder of this evening in writing home. I have beheld Belvidera herself to-night. It is the fourth time I have seen this play and by very far the best. Kemble was uncommonly animated in Pierre. I think the scene of the Senate and that between him and Jaffier afterwards were inimitable. The words of Aufidius seemed exactly to apply to him : —

> Thy face
> Bears a command in 't; tho' thy tackle 's torn.
> Thou show'st a noble vessel.

"I like him equally well with Cooke, but I think it is hardly right to draw a comparison between them, as the line of characters they each excel in is quite different. Kemble could not play Sir Pertinax like Cooke, nor could the latter perform Pierre or Coriolanus like Kemble. I saw Mrs. Siddons about a week ago in the 'Grecian Daughter,' in which character I have sent you a drawing of her. She played the character as well as possible, though it is not a play that I like much. It appears to me to be one of those works which you cannot find fault with, and yet has no striking beauties. Young played Evander extremely well, and Charles Kemble Dionysius. The scenery, dresses, &c., were very splendid and perfectly classical. The afterpiece was the ' Secret Mine,' a foolish melodrame they have got up for the sake of exhibiting the horses. The scenery, &c., were as usual very superb. They are performing this piece again to-night, which caused me to come away, for I never wish to see anything after a tragedy excepting a good broad farce.

" I have sent you two other drawings, one of Young as Rolla, and the other Liston as Diego in ' The Virgins of the Sun.' They are thought to be pretty good likenesses. Liston is the first comic performer at Covent Garden. He is equivalent to Jefferson with us. The moment he comes on, the whole house begins to roar with laughter.

" I have just begun to copy a small picture of Mr. West's of ' Arethusa Bathing;' it is a most beautiful thing; when it is finished I shall endeavour to send it over, together with a design I intend making. Mr. West gave Morse and myself a recommendation to the British Museum, which we delivered this morning, and shall go there in a day or two to commence drawing. I have just finished a half-length portrait of Mrs. Visscher, an American lady, whom I mentioned in a former letter as looking so much like Anna. I have also begun to paint Miss Smythe, a daughter of Mr. Maxwell's, whom I also mentioned.

" This young lady is governess in a family, and owing to her engagements through the week, she can only sit to me on Sundays; her portrait therefore will proceed but slowly. She has many accomplishments, among which, her drawing very well is not the least. She is a beautiful girl, and appears to be very amiable.

" I have two acquaintances that I believe I did not mention in my former list, Collard and Lonsdale. The first is a musician and a partner in the house of Clementi and Co., from whom Bradford imports pianos. He is a man of excellent sense, though generally so facetious that one feels inclined to laugh at everything he says. Lonsdale is a portrait painter, though rather mediocre in his profession. He is, however, excellent company — a good deal like Collard in his manner. They are both Englishmen, so you see I am not altogether among Americans here. We frequently have evening parties composed of these two gentlemen, Allston, King, Morse, and myself; sometimes at their respective houses and sometimes at ours. In this circle my time always passes delightfully.

" The Exhibition at Somerset House has just opened. I went there the first day; but the rooms were so crowded I could not enjoy it at all — I shall go again soon. Lawrence's portrait of Kemble in ' Cato,' is very fine, and the best likeness I have ever seen of him. He is seated in his study with a scroll in his hand, and his dagger lying on the table. His eyes are raised, and he appears to be just exclaiming, ' It must be so — Plato, thou reason'st well.' There are a great number of other fine portraits by Lawrence and Sir William Beechey. Mr. West has only two pictures there, ' Saul Prophesying,' and a portrait of Mr. Wilmot, who settled the claims of the American Loyalists. There is a grand Landscape by Turner,* representing a scene in the Alps in a snow storm, with Hannibal's army crossing; but as this picture is placed very low, I could not see it at the proper distance, owing to the crowd of people. Allston says it is a wonderfully fine thing: he thinks Turner the greatest painter since the days of Claude. I intend soon going to his gallery which is now just opened. There is also a large picture of ' Christ Blessing Children,' by Trumbull,† but I do not like it — his Scripture pieces are, I think, very far inferior to his battles. The number of pictures amount to 940 at this Exhibition. In the model-room there is a bust of Mr. West, by Mr. Nollekens, I think the best likeness · I ever saw of him.

" I frequently see an old beggar, without legs, in Holborn, who was one of the rioters at the time Newgate was burnt, and had both his legs shot by a chain-shot in that very street. He was

---

* Now in the Turner Gallery, South Kensington.

† Col. Trumbull, an American painter, and during the War of Independence a member of General Washington's staff, some of whose battle-pieces ornament the Capitol at Washington.

afterwards condemned to be hung, but pardoned on account of his maimed condition. I dare say mother or you may recollect seeing this man. I am told his body is remarkably fine, and that he has frequently sat to artists — very often to Mr. West.

" When I called on Mr. West the other day, I asked him to let me make an outline from his great picture to send to you. I told him what a miserable thing they had in America. He said the etching by Heath was now made, and I am in hopes I shall be able to procure one of them through his interest.

" He told me he had one or two small pictures that he was finishing out of the way, and as soon as they were done he would go to work immediately on the picture for America, and not quit it until he finished it, which could be by next autumn."

TO MISS LESLIE.

LONDON, 6th August, 1812.

" The news has just arrived of the declaration of war; and as there is an embargo laid on all American vessels that have not licenses, this will probably be the last opportunity I shall have of writing for some time. I am in hopes, however, that as affairs between the two countries have at length advanced to a crisis, they will be more speedily settled in some way or other, and we shall be relieved from the state of uncertainty that has so long existed. The interruption of our correspondence will be a dreadful thing to me, but I must bear it as well as I can, in hopes that the time is not far distant when the intercourse will be opened much more freely than ever, when our country shall have inspired some respect by its decisive and firm measures. I have almost finished my picture of ' Timon,' and have considerably advanced with one of ' Hercules reclining on his Club,' from the famous statue. It will be the largest figure I have painted ; I am copying it from a small cast (the same as that in the Academy) and have a living model to colour it from. They have a very fine cast from the original at Somerset House, which is colossal, I suppose twelve feet high.

" I intend making drawings from that to finish my hands and

feet from. I believe I mentioned to you before that Allston was about a large picture (the dead man revived by touching the bones of Elisha). Mr. West called on him the other day to see it, and was quite astonished. ' Why, sir,' he exclaimed, ' this reminds me of the fifteenth century ; you have been studying in the highest schools of art.' He added, ' There are eyes in this country that will be able to see so much excellence ; ' and then, turning round, he saw a head Allston had modelled in clay for one of his figures, and asked what it was, taking it to be an antique. Allston told him it was one of his, at which, after examining it carefully, he said there was not a sculptor in England could do anything like it. He did not find fault with any part of the picture, but merely suggested the introduction of another figure.

" I never was more delighted in my life than when I heard this praise coming from Mr. West, and so perfectly agreeing with my own opinion of Allston. He has been in high spirits ever since, and his picture has advanced amazingly rapid for these two or three days. He intends sending it to the exhibition of the British Gallery, where it will no doubt obtain the prize of 400 guineas, besides which he will have an opportunity of selling it. I have just heard that David has finished the most excellent likeness of Bonaparte that ever was painted, and that that monarch intends sending it to the Prince Regent. He is represented just rising from his chair to go to bed, and looking at a clock, the hand of which points to four in the morning ; before him is a table covered with papers, mathematical instruments, &c. It is said that the countenance possesses the minutest shades of his character. This is the account one person gives of it, but I am told others say it is not at all like him. I suppose the Prince means to send his in return. Lucien Bonaparte, who has been ordered out of this country, I am told, wants to go to America, and has offered to present his collection of pictures to the government there, to establish a National Gallery. Allston, who has seen it, says it is quite an indifferent collection.

" Morse and I find ourselves very comfortable in our new lodgings, and I hope we shall not change again very soon. Our landlady has a very pretty daughter, which is one very great recom-

mendation to her lodgings. By the bye, we shall not now be
able to hear of King's arrival very soon. If he delivers the
letter I gave him to mother, I hope you will all show him a good
deal of attention, as he was a very great friend to me here. I
am sure you will like him, for he is very agreeable, has read a
good deal, and, from the opportunities I have had of judging,
I think he has an excellent heart as well as head. He will
be able to give you a good account of me, of the manner in
which I live, &c. There is one quality that I found in King
which pleased me much, because it is a scarce one, *he does not
flatter.*

" I am now reading Telemachus again, and intend to paint
some subjects from it. These subjects are much more advanta·
geous for me to paint than those from Gothic poems such as Scott's,
because I have an opportunity of making parts of my figures
naked, and I am now studying the human form as much as possible. It was for this reason that I chose 'Timon of Athens'
and ' Hercules.' I intend, in the next picture I paint, to follow
Sir Joshua Reynolds's advice, and take all my figures from Michael
Angelo's works, altering some of them slightly ; or perhaps considering them as statues, and taking other views of them, and I
think I shall also model some of them in clay. Sir J. says that
by this means you imperceptibly acquire a habit of thinking like
him from whom you select your figures, and that when you come
to introduce one of your own in the picture it will necessarily
partake somewhat of the grandeur of the others. It is for this
reason that sculptors consider it a valuable lesson to supply the
limbs of the Torso. Speaking of this noble fragment, many
people think that it was made by Michael Angelo and buried, but
I think it hardly probable that had it been so, that great man
would have kept it so profound a secret.

" It is very certain that he studied it intensely, and the resemblance his manner has to something in that 'mass of breathing
stone,' was much more probably the result of his studies from it,
than given to *it* by *him.*"

The fashion of the day in art was classical. ' The Antique,'
' the Nude,' ' High Art,' and ' Michael Angelo,' were dinned into

the ears of the student. Leslie began with a boy's belief in the orthodoxy of these doctrines; and was as yet without a suspicion, apparently, that a painter's style and subject must be determined by the painter's own bent and capacity. This was the period at which, as he tells us in his lectures, he considered Mr. West equal to Raffaelle. In deference to the fashion of the day, we have seen him beginning with the classical subjects of 'Timon' and 'Hercules.' The following letters are illustrative of the implicitness with which Leslie at first accepted the fashionable faith in the matter of his art, and of his sincere youthful veneration for West, who treated him, as he did all young artists, with genuine kindness, all the greater, no doubt in Leslie's case, for his American blood.

But, for all his classicality, and reverence for authority, Leslie's judgment was not quite asleep, as appears from his criticism on Westall in the following letter.

LONDON, *Sept. 14th,* 1812.

DEAR BETSEY, — I was much disappointed at not hearing what effect the rescinding of the orders in council had in America. It is fully expected here that an amicable adjustment will take place. Mr. Morse has been in the country for this week past; and in my solitary situation, a letter from you would have been the greatest possible treat to me. As soon as he returns, we shall take a little trip to Hampton Court, Windsor, &c.

I have finished my pictures of 'Timon' and 'Hercules,' and am now painting a portrait (Mr. West of Salem, Massachusetts) and one of Mr. Inskeep. The head of the former, which is finished, Allston says is by far the best thing I have done. I have been to Westall's house to look at his pictures; you recollect Sully told me I should find some clever things amongst them, and indeed I was much pleased with many parts of his works, and fancied that he showed the feeling of a poet in many of his inventions.

But I, no doubt, often admired when I should have condemned, for his style is very specious and imposing, and I have frequently found that when I have been dazzled at first sight by the gaudiness of his colouring, upon looking into the picture I have been astonished at his want of real science. In his flesh, though very unequal, he seems always at the same distance from nature. He is either too hot, too cold, too red, too gray, or too yellow. Some of his figures, particularly children, appear to have their deepest shadows made of vermilion alone, others have so great a proportion of gray or blue tints that one almost freezes to look at them. When free from other faults his flesh often inclines too much to purple. I should call him a mannerist in every part of his art. He is mannered where it is the least pardonable, in the character and air of his heads, and in the grace of his figures; dreadfully so in his draperies, which all appear carved from stone.

His faults seem to arise chiefly from a wish to improve upon nature, not knowing that what generally goes by the name of improving upon nature, is nothing more than being able to select all that is good from her, and that to obtain this end the artist cannot have too much intercourse with her. Now *he* seems to attempt it by avoiding her as much as possible. His style of painting is showy, and perhaps pleasing to those who are not in the habit of thinking when they look at a picture : — but to those of real taste (which Sir Joshua says, 'is nothing more than an appetite for truth '), his pictures must seem meretricious, and instead of possessing only those casual faults which are to be met with in every work of art, appear to be built entirely upon a foundation of error. The consequence is, that as his figures have a kind of fashionable appearance, they will please a few as long as the present fashions last, and then be forgotten. While painting Mr. West's portrait, I called to see Owen's pictures, who stands very high as a portrait painter. He has not so much skill as Lawrence in the drawing of his heads, nor is he so happy in improving their expression, but he certainly colours better, and the subordinate parts of his pictures, his draperies, &c., are painted with more truth. I find it a great advantage to me to go thus constantly to the houses of artists and look at their pictures, particularly when I am about anything of the same kind myself. I expect Mr. West will make me some compensation for painting him, and whatever he gives me I shall lay out in buying a collection of prints, particularly the heads of Van Dyk and Sir Joshua. I suppose the last volumes of Miss Edgeworth's ' Tales ' have not yet appeared in America. I have just read one of them containing ' Vivian,' and I need only say that I think it quite equal to any other of her works to give you an idea of its excellence. There are two other volumes which I have not yet been able to get from the library. If you have not already got them I know it will gratify you to hear of their appearance in the present dearth of anything good in the book way. By the bye, it is said Walter Scott is just going to publish another poem; what it is I have not heard.

I have not been for some time at any of the theatres. Covent Garden is again opened, but as they have lost Mrs. Siddons and Kemble, I feel very little inclination to go there. My hopes now rest on Drury Lane, which is to open next month, and which will, I suppose, totally eclipse its "huge classical rival" as they have engaged both Kemble and Elliston. I have been to Sadler's Wells to see the Aquatic scene, that is so much talked of. Excepting by Grimaldi (the clown), I was very little entertained. I take but little delight in pantomime changes, which, to do them justice, they manage here in the greatest perfection. The after-piece was a melodrama, the dialogue of which was in blank verse, with now and then a foolish rhyme coming out in order to call it *recitative.** The water scene pleased me better than I expected, it represented a castle with a moat and drawbridge; the castle of course attacked by troops who came on in boats. Many of the combatants contrived to get themselves into the water by the breaking of the drawbridge, where they fought up to their chins. This theatre is quite small, and ornamented in the most showy manner, with a plentiful lack of taste. I lately had the pleasure of seeing their mightiness the *mob* in all their glory at Bartholomew Fair, and really such a scene of riot and confusion I never before beheld. * * *

" When the news of Lord Wellington's victory at Salamanca arrived, there were universal illuminations for several nights. I did not, however, go to any of the public buildings where I might have seen them in their greatest perfection. I am now sorry I did not go to the Admiralty, where the standards were dis-

---

* This was necessary, to evade the penalties for infringement of the patent right of the two great Theatres.

played that were taken from the enemy. Had I gone out on those nights, I should have seen the *mobility* in their highest glory. Mr. Inskeep and another gentleman, passing Somerset House, in a hackney-coach, were made to pull off their hats, and not content with this, the rabble forced open the coach door, and threw in squibs, &c., until they set fire to the straw in the bottom.

Mr. Inskeep had one of his whiskers burnt off (what a loss!) and was struck on the breast by a fire-brand which, "dismal horror to relate," burnt through his waistcoat. I am told, that one of their civilest tricks was firing off a pistol between the heads of any two well-dressed people that happened to be walking together. In Fitzroy Square, opposite to us, they had a cannon which they kept constantly firing, with lesser accompaniments on the blunderbuss, pistols, &c., to our great amusement. Captain and Mrs. Visscher have sailed about a week ago for America. Morse and myself feel their loss very much, as they were extremely attentive and kind to us. If they may be taken as a sample of the New England people, I am inclined to have a much better opinion of them than I ever had before.

Mr. and Mrs. Allston are the only friends we have left that are very near us, and if I were to lose the society of Mr. Allston, I should not wish to remain any longer in England. Since Morse has been among us he (*i. e.* Allston) has very kindly spent every evening with me. He is advancing very rapidly with his large picture and will be able to exhibit it in the British Institution next year, where it will, no doubt, obtain the prize of 400 guineas, besides standing a good chance of its being sold. Sir George Beaumont (one of the first connoisseurs of the day, and who is in fact an excellent artist himself), having seen the outline, wrote to Mr. Allston a very complimentary letter from his country seat, and concluded by requesting him to paint a small picture of some church, for which he offered him 200*l*. Mr. Brown (whom, I believe, I mentioned in a former letter) has been very attentive to Morse and myself. He mentioned to me, the last time I saw him, that he should like me to spend a few days at Snaresbrook, and paint Mrs. Brown and her dog, which is a great favourite, as they have no children. The last time I dined there, I met Mr. Zantzinger, a brother to J. Barton. He told me he had my plate of Blisset and Jefferson,* which he would show me, but I have not yet called on him. I have become acquainted with a Mr. Coate, from Montreal. He is originally from Philadelphia, and is related to the Cotes' family, though he spells his name differently. He has been a clergyman and has travelled among the Indians as a missionary, but being of a consumptive habit he was obliged to give up preaching, and is here publishing a number of specimens of ornamental penmanship, which indeed, are the most elegant things of the kind I ever saw. He brought out letters to many of the nobility, Sir Wm. Beechey has particularly interested himself in obtaining him subscribers, and Mr. West has been a great friend to him. He obtained permission for Morse and myself to look at a very fine collection of pictures, which are about to be sold. Among them is one of the finest of Claude's landscapes, two very fine Titians, several Guidos, a Portrait and a Madonna by Van Dyk, a large Rubens, and a number of small Flemish paintings, a 'Danaë' by Correggio, and a great number of other pictures.

This Mr. Coate lives in Warren Street, which is very near us. He appears to be a very friendly, good-hearted, pleasant man.

Farewell.

During this year Leslie and his friend Morse were lodged together at No. 8, Buckingham Place, Fitzroy Square, in " the very centre of almost all the artists in London," to which Leslie removed from his first lodgings in Warren Street, in the same neighbourhood.

LONDON, *Sep.* 29, 1812.

" DEAR BETSEY, — Mr. West has kindly consented to take charge of my ' Hercules' and ' Timon of Athens,' which I have sent with his own portrait to Mr. Bradford, and which I suppose will be in the next exhibition. I called a few days since, with the portrait of Mr. West and the ' Hercules,' on Sir Wm. Beechey, who is extremely kind in giving advice to young artists. However, I must say I received very little encouragement from

---

* Portraits painted by Leslie in Philadelphia (?)

him, as he pointed out innumerable faults, and not one part in which I had succeeded. He looked principally at the portrait, as the other was not so much in his line of painting. Sir William is extremely open and candid even to bluntness. He told me when I was coming away, that whenever I wanted another *set down* he would be very happy to accommodate me. I shall certainly call frequently on him, although I must confess I felt somewhat dispirited, yet I consider it very wholesome chastisement, and am certain that I shall benefit much from it.

Allston tells me that when he was in England before, he showed a picture to Sir William, who said to him, " Sir, that is not flesh but mud; it is as much mud as if you had taken it out of the kennel and painted your picture." * * I afterwards took my picture to Mr. West, from whom I received more encouragement, for though he pointed out a great many errors in my ' Hercules,' he gave me praise for the left leg and foot. If Tom, his still surviving brother, is present at the unpacking of my pictures, he will perceive on the back of ' Hercules ' a ball drawn by Mr. West himself, who was explaining to me his principle for the light and shadow and colour, and by this simple diagram he can assign his reasons for the arrangement of every part of his immense pictures. Mr. West kept me for several hours while he illustrated all he said in the clearest manner by constantly recurring to nature. I really pitied the poor porter who carried my pictures there, and whom Mr. West used as a model, placing him in various lights, and poking at him with his mahl-stick to point out the different effects of light and shadow upon him.

He directed me how I might alter my ' Hercules ' to the best advantage, and I worked on it till the very day it was packed up. * * * I am going to paint another ' Hercules ' for Mr. Coate, who has offered to pay for my models, canvasses, &c.

I have finished his portrait, which is thought extremely like, and I am now about one of Mr. Earle, and a small one of myself, which will, I think, be like. Mr. West gave me six pounds for his picture which I have laid out in prints of Van Dyk's and Sir Joshua Reynolds's portraits, and a few from Raphael. Among the Sir Joshuas are his ' Mrs. Siddons as the Tragic Muse,' and his ' Infant Academy,' two of his finest works.

Among the Raphaels is his 'Incendio del Borgo,' which Sir
Joshua speaks of in his Lectures.

1813.

Pictures Painted this Year.

MURDER: Macbeth, Act II., Scene 1. — PORTRAIT OF MR. EMLEN, of Philadelphia. (Exhibited at the Royal Academy.)

The following letters for this year need no introduction or connecting remark. What Leslie says in that of May of the necessity that a picture should tell some scriptural or classic story in
order to insure it " currency," shows the cramping influence of
the conventionalism of that day. One may remark too on the
rise, shown by the letters of this year, in the level of the painter's
studies. The eighteen-year-old lad of last year was content with
his subscription to the Bond Street circulating library. He tells·
his sister only of the novels he is reading. This year his studies
lie in Homer, Milton, and Dante, among the poets ; while Smollett and Swift are his prose authors. Then, too, he has made the
acquaintance of Coleridge. With such books and such compan-
ionship it is not to be wondered at if we find Leslie at nineteen
ripening gradually into juster appreciation both of the painters
and the Art-maxims of the day.

TO MISS LESLIE.

LONDON, *Feb.* 25, 1813.

YOUR letter by the ' Catharine Ray ' came duly to hand, and
was doubly welcome to me, as I had not heard from you for a
very long time. I rejoice to hear you like King so well, and I
sincerely hope he will get business in Philadelphia. I think his
close intimacy with Sully will be of very great advantage to him.
You will perceive that King's greatest excellence is in his colouring of flesh. His drawing is very correct, and his heads are generally very like ; but they have not always a happiness of ex-

pression, and his attitudes generally want ease. Now in these
two points Sully is very excellent, and as they are not to be
imparted by rules, King will be more likely to acquire a feeling
for them by having pictures that possess them constantly before
him than he would by any other means. He is also deficient in
the management of draperies, which Sully paints very beautifully. Since Mr. Inskeep's picture I have begun a picture for
the Exhibition at Somerset House. I scarcely know what name
to give it, but the subject was suggested by these lines from
Shakespeare : —

> ———— now wither'd Murder
> Alarum'd by his sentinel, the wolf,
> Who howls his watch, thus with his stealthy pace,
> With Tarquin's ravishing stride, towards his design
> Moves like a ghost ——.

I have represented an assassin stealing from a cave at midnight,
with a drawn sword in one hand, and holding his breath with the
other. The horizon is formed by the sea, and the moon, just
rising, illuminates the distance and middle ground, while the
figure is quite in shadow against the light sky and sea. All the
foreground is also in shadow, produced by a projection of the rock.
I have modelled a head in clay for my figure, and made a small
sketch of the whole. The picture will be the same size as my
' Hercules.' As it will be necessary to send it to the Academy in
the beginning of April, and I wish to bestow every possible pains
on it, it will occupy every moment of time till that period. Morse
and I intend going to Hampton Court as soon as we have sent
our pictures in, and Allston having promised to accompany us, we
shall have a very pleasant little jaunt. The exhibition at the
British Gallery is now open, and I have been twice to it, but as I
intend writing an account of some of the principal pictures to
King, who will communicate it to you, I shall say nothing here
of them. As soon as this Exhibition closes, they are to open one
consisting of all the works of Sir Joshua Reynolds in this country,
which are to be borrowed for the purpose from the different possessors of them. I esteem myself particularly fortunate that I am
here at this time, for if it was not for this collection, I should, no
doubt, miss seeing a great many of these treasures. I only regret

that my advancement is not sufficient, at present, for me to profit from them as much as I might hope to do in a few more years.

A new tragedy has appeared at Drury Lane this season called 'Remorse,' though no doubt you will have heard of, if not received, it before you get this. It is by Coleridge, who I believe I have before told you is an intimate friend of Allston's. As it is many years since a tragedy has been received, and there were no very first-rate performers in this line to support the characters, the author was not very sanguine in his expectations of success. It was received, however, with the most rapturous applause, and has had a very capital run. I went to see it the second or third night, and was quite as well pleased with it as I expected to be from the excellent accounts I had heard of it. Rae, who performed the principal male character, I had never seen before ; he is a young man, who after playing with great success at some of the provincial theatres, made his debût in London the beginning of this season. He is a good actor and has much judgment, but fails to seize the feelings and carry one away as Kemble or poor Cooke would have done. When they were on the stage it was impossible to look at or think of any body else. Each of them seemed to say " I am myself alone ; " but this is not the case with Rae. Allston says the reason of it is, that he has not the proper inflections of the voice. His face appeared good for the stage and capable of great variety of expression ; it seemed to me to have the character of Kemble's, though I was much too far off to distinguish his features, being in the upper row of boxes. His figure, as well as I could see, — it being disguised in a bad dress, — I thought good, though it seemed to me to want importance. It is impossible however to judge of an actor from only once seeing him, and at such a distance, and it is therefore very likely that upon a second and better sight of him I may find myself mistaken in many respects. Mrs. Glover played Alhadra uncommonly well ; it appeared to me to be the most prominent character in the piece. This lady has, however, not a tragic voice, and very far from a tragic face. She was dressed well, however, and is a commanding figure, though monstrously fat. Elliston in a Moorish dress looked so like Cooper in 'Othello,' that had they both been on the stage I think I should scarcely

have known the difference. He played Alvar. As I have very
little doubt that you will have read the tragedy when you get this,
I have written as if you were acquainted with the characters. I
have not yet seen 'Rokeby,' but the truth is, I have applied
repeatedly at the library and it is never at home; it is published
in so expensive a form that I cannot purchase it.

March 8th, 1813.

As I have just heard of an opportunity, I hasten to close this
letter. I should have made it much longer, but owing to the
picture I have now on hand at which I am obliged to work very
hard, and the lectures at the Academy where I am a constant
attendant, and some other things which I will mention another
time, I am just at present more engaged than I ever have been
since my residence here. Writing letters with me is not a thing
that can be done at odd scraps of time, but I must sit down and
compose myself to it and collect all my thoughts about me.

Mrs. Jordan has returned to the stage, and is now playing at
Covent Garden. Bannister and Braham are at Drury Lane, and
they are now performing some of the finest comedies at both houses.
The opposition makes each one bring forth all their best actors. I
have not had time to see either Mrs. Jordan or Bannister, and
think I shall not until the Academy closes. Adieu.

TO MISS LESLIE.

Loxdon, *April* 4, 1813.

*   *   *   *   *   *

I expect to go about the middle of next week, with Mr. and
Mrs. Allston and Morse, upon a little trip to Hampton Court,
Windsor, &c., from which we all promise ourselves much pleasure.
I am extremely pleased with young Payne,* who is now here;
from what I have seen of him, I think him very amiable and
agreeable, independently of his talents. Mr. and Mrs. Allston
knew him and all his family very well in America, and it was

* Howard Payne, for whose career, see the Autobiography.

with much pleasure that they renewed their acquaintance with him.

I am going to paint his portrait when I return from Hampton Court; we have already taken a plaster cast of his face. I have finished and sent to Somerset House my picture from Shakespeare, which I described in my last letter. A few days before I sent it I took it to Mr. West. He did me the honour to praise it a good deal, and advised me by all means to exhibit it, without which I should not have sent it. He suggested to me to introduce the wolf, howling in an obscure part of the cave, which he said was necessary to mark the subject. He also advised me to show part of the moon, which was hid by a fragment of rock. Both these things I did, and upon showing it to him again he told me my subject was now complete. From the good opinion Mr. West expressed, I have little doubt it will be admitted. My only fear is, that it will be crammed into some obscure place, or lost amid the blaze of pictures that crowd the great room. There were last year upwards of a thousand pictures exhibited, and, I have heard, about five hundred rejected that were sent there. Mr. West has been painting a picture for the Exhibition which nobody has yet seen. For a week past he locked himself up entirely, and has been denied to everybody. When I called on him, the servant told me I could not possibly see him; but I begged him to show him the picture and mention my name; that if Mr. West, could not see me then, I would call in the evening. I waited in his gallery, and the old gentleman presently came out to me with my picture. He told me that he had shut himself up, but he was so well pleased with my picture that he could not help seeing me.

I went a short time ago to see Mrs. Jordan in 'As You Like It,' and was quite as much pleased with her as I expected; indeed, more so, for I had been taught to expect an immensely fat woman, and she is but moderately so. Her face is still very fine, no print that I ever saw of her is much like. Her performance of Rosalind was in my mind perfect, though I am convinced the character from its nature did not call forth half Mrs. Jordan's powers. I long to see her in the 'Country Girl,' 'Miss Prue,' or something of that kind. The other characters were extremely

well supported, particularly Touchstone by Faucett, and Audrey
by Mrs. Chas. Kemble, who was even superior to Mrs. Francis.
Young played Jacques very well, and Chas. Kemble looked
Orlando better than he played it. Incledon played Amiens,
and sung his songs delightfully. He is one of the worst looking
men I ever saw, and has indeed completely the face and figure
of a low sailor. He is likewise a wretched actor, and always appears on the stage with that kind of awkward stiffness that arises
from a man being in better company than he is accustomed to.
He is, however, a very charming singer, and has the most manly,
and at the same time, agreeable voice that I ever heard. He
was, I am told, in reality a common sailor originally. I have
also heard he has other talents than that of singing, and can eat
and drink more at a meal than any other man. He was one of
poor Cooke's most intimate friends. The nation is at present in
mourning for the Duchess of Brunswick. Fortunately for me, I
always wear black, so that I am at no trouble on the present
occasion. One of my reasons indeed for wearing it was, that I
might be prepared for the demise of the King, but that I believe
is never to happen. I have not observed more black than usual
in the streets, but I am told in company it is always expected.
The dress boxes at the theatres exhibit nothing else. The
duchess was buried at Windsor (not in state), and I missed
seeing the funeral move from her house here, supposing there
would be no parade.

I have lately read the 'Mysteries of Udolpho' for the first
time, and with very great pleasure. I am now going through
Homer, Milton, and Dante's works, which every painter should
be well acquainted with.

I suppose you will not believe me when I say that I have not
seen 'Rokeby.' I have applied incessantly at the library, but it
is always out, and they have constantly promised to send it me,
but never have.

I have lately been made a Student in the Academy, by showing a chalk drawing, a skeleton, and an anatomical figure. I have
now access to the library every Monday, besides the privilege of
wearing my hat in the Academy, and coming in with a greater
swagger than before.

As the drawing Academy is at present shut, and of course will continue so until the Exhibition closes, I have now resumed drawing at the British Museum every Tuesday and Thursday as I did last summer. Remember to all his friends.

Your C. R. L.

TO MISS LESLIE.

LONDON, *May* 6, 1813.

I HAD written a long letter to Jane, giving a detail of my jaunt to Windsor, Oxford, and Blenheim, with Mr. and Mrs. Allston and Morse. With this party I was out of town about ten days, and the weather being uncommonly fine made it a very delightful trip.

Morse's picture of the 'Hercules,' and mine of 'Murder,' are in very excellent situations at Somerset House; they have already been noticed in a newspaper. The exhibition is very good: the greater part of the pictures here, as usual, are portraits. Mr. West has but one picture, and that is quite small. I long to hear how our little Academy in Philadelphia has got on this year. Morse and I have found, after a good deal of experience, that we cannot paint with as much advantage both in one room, as we could separately; and I have, therefore, hired a painting-room directly opposite to us.

It is about twice the size of Morse's, and, being at the back of the house, has of course the same light. I pay 17*l.* a-year for it. Since my return from the country, I have begun a portrait of Payne, which promises to be the best likeness I have ever painted; and one of a Mr. Emlen, of Philadelphia, who is studying physic here. I have lately been a good deal in company with Coleridge, and have had opportunities of seeing the man as well as the poet.

I really do not know which most to admire, the goodness of his heart or the soundness of his head. He is a man of the most exquisite feelings, which give a cast of melancholy to his character always visible in his countenance, excepting when he is carried away by sprightly conversation. He has greater colloquial talents than I have ever before met with, and with the most

13

consummate eloquence, possessing all the graces of conversation, he exhibits on every subject the deepest philosophical thinking. Allston says, that when in the vein to exercise it, there are no bounds to his wit. He was secretary to Sir Alexander Ball, governor of Malta, during the bombardment of Tripoli, at which place he had an opportunity of seeing many of our naval officers. He was particularly pleased with Decatur, of whom he often speaks in the highest terms as a gentleman and a hero. I am at present hard set to think of a subject for a pretty large picture that I want to paint for the next exhibition. I find that pictures from modern poets do not take, and even if they should, it is uncertain how long they may continue in vogue. To insure a picture currency, therefore, it is necessary that it should tell either some scriptural or classic story. Even Shakespeare, Dante, and Milton, are scarcely sufficiently canonised to be firm ground.

I have at length read Scott's ' Rokeby,' and was of course very much pleased with it. I must, however, read it again, for the interest the story excited made me gallop to the end as hard as I could, and I had not the opportunity to admire the beauties of imagery, or observe the nicer shades of character that a second reading will afford me.

I have lately read ' Humphrey Clinker,' for the first time, and liked it exceedingly; the story of Mr. and Mrs. Baynard is admirable. I have also read Swift's ' Tale of a Tub,' and ' Battle with the Books,' with great laughter. I have not been at the theatre for a long time until a few nights ago, when I went to see ' Education,' a new comedy by Morton ; and ' Aladdin, or the Wonderful Lamp.' The comedy I was not greatly pleased with, although they had lugged into it all the best actors. It appeared to me to be made up from the ' Road to Ruin ' and the ' Sons of Erin.' ' Aladdin ' is a melodrama, and, as you may suppose, splendid in the extreme. With these kind of things they spare no expense at Covent Garden.

1814.

Pictures Exhibited this Year.

THE WOMAN OF ENDOR RAISING THE GHOST SAMUEL BEFORE SAUL. " Then said Samuel, Wherefore then dost thou ask of me, seeing the Lord is departed from thee and is become thine enêmy." 1 Samuel, ch. vii. v. 16. (Rejected by the British Institution, but afterwards exhibited at the Royal Academy.) — PORTRAIT OF HOWARD PAYNE as NORVAL.

Leslie, in his ' Recollections,' speaks of the ' Saul ' as his first large picture, and of its fate in being at first rejected at the British Institution, owing to its unfinished appearance — attributed by the painter to its want of varnish — of its improvement, under the advice of Mr. West, and of its ultimate sale for one hundred guineas, to Sir John Leicester, afterwards Lord de Tabley.

Of Payne and his portrait we have heard already, in the Autobiography, as well as in the letters of 1813.

I have had entrusted to me no letters of Leslie's for this year, nor for   .

1815.

A PORTRAIT OF A LADY (not exhibited) is the solitary picture recorded for this year. But in the interval between 1813 and 1815 he had qualified himself to carry off the two medals at the Academy, which he received in the following year.

1816.

Pictures of this Year.

DEATH OF RUTLAND.

Rutland. — Oh, let me pray before I take my death : —
       To thee I pray; Sweet Clifford, pity me !
Clifford. — Such pity as my rapier's point affords.
               *   *   *   *   *   *
       Thy father slew my father; therefore, die !
                 Third Part of Henry VI.   Act 1.   Scene 3.

The choice of subject for this year's picture is worth noting.

It was Leslie's first venture on his most congenial work — the illustration of our English classics. From this time we hear no more from him of the antique and the classical in subjects. Shakespeare, Cervantes, Molière, Le Sage, Addison, Fielding, Goldsmith, and Smollett, are henceforth to prompt the young painter's conceptions. He followed his bent in choosing this field, and speedily displayed his real power of keenly apprehending and gracefully representing characters and humours in the creations of those great masters. But the incident of this picture of 1816 was a painful one, the murder of the young son of Plantagenet by the revengeful Clifford. Sir Edwin Landseer, then a curly-headed youngster, dividing his time between Polito's wild-beasts at Exeter Change and the Royal Academy Schools, tells me that he sat for the pleading boy, with a rope round his wrists. Leslie appears to have thought more of his conception of the murderer than of that of the victim, for he speaks of the picture as " my Clifford." The picture was sent to Philadelphia, and, to his great gratification, purchased by the Academy of his native place.

It was in this year that the controversy as to the Elgin marbles raged so loudly, on the occasion of their purchase by the Government. Haydon was foremost in blowing the flames of the controversy, and fiercely sounding the praises of these divine works, as he has fully recorded in his Autobiography. The casts to which Leslie alludes in his letter of June 3rd, were probably casts from the moulds of the Thescus, Ilyssus, and other fragments, taken under Haydon's direction.

LONDON, *June 3rd*, 1816.

DEAR BETSEY, — I have just received your letter of April 23rd, by the ' Superior.' I am on every account delighted with the sale of Mr. Allston's large picture to the Academy, first, for the service to so excellent a man, then for the promise it gives of encouragement for historical painting in America, and, lastly, for the honour it does to the city of Philadelphia. I have lately been leading quite a dissipated life, and having spent almost every evening out for some time past, I have let a longer time elapse since writing to you than I ought, or wished to have done, which I hope you will excuse with your usual goodness. I have heard a debate in the House of Commons, and have been to the opera for the first and, I think, last time. At the former place I heard Lord Castlereagh, Mr. Vansittart, Mr. Brougham, &c., speak, and saw Sir Francis Burdett. At the latter I heard Braham, Madame Foder, Signor Naldi, &c., sing, but at both places the *acting* was so bad, and the people appeared so little like what they represented, that I grew very tired of listening to them. Imagine, if you can, Lord Castlereagh, that great diplomatist and negotiator, in the likeness of a Bond-street lounger, blue cossack pantaloons gathered in front like the old English dresses, a blue coat, the skirts and pockets edged with white and black, and a black velvet collar! — rather a small man, with something of a fashionable lisp. Mr. Brougham, leader of the Opposition, the thunders of whose eloquence must have reached America long ago, is as follows.* The room in which they meet is very small and plain, and by no means gives an idea of a place in which the affairs of a great nation are settled. I had here an opportunity that never occurred to me before, that of hearing several genuine Irish bulls, made by a member of the house. The Opera House is the most splendid theatre I was ever in. Each box is separated by a crimson curtain, which gives a most magnificent appearance to the whole. I sat in the gallery, which is quite a respectable place, and nearly as expensive as the boxes at the other theatres. It reminded me of ' Evelina and the Branghtons.' I had an English translation of the piece (which was called ' La Cosa Rara') in my hand, so that I could understand the performers, but the acting was so execrable that it destroyed all the effect of the music, excepting in some of the songs. A few nights ago I had a ticket given me for a private concert at Lady Saltoun's, near Grosvenor Square, where I had an opportunity of mingling with lords and ladies for a few hours. There were stars glittering on the breasts of gentlemen, and diamonds on the necks of ladies, and to say the truth, the ladies had need of them, for I never saw a more ordinary set. They reminded me of those subordinate characters in Miss Edgeworth's novels, in which she is so happy.

* A pen-and-ink sketch followed.

Some of the music was very fine, particularly a duet by two
French girls, which was divine. They had taste enough to
encore it, and I could have listened to it all night. I had also the
pleasure of again hearing Drouet, the celebrated performer on
the flute. I felt that this was the proper way to enjoy music, one
such concert to me is worth fifty operas with the same performers.
When the ear is delighted, nothing else is wanted. Scenery,
gesture, costume, and everything of that kind, hurts the effect
instead of improving it. Fine music always carries me into
other regions, but at the opera I felt chained down to the earth.
Some time ago, I went to see a new tragedy ('Bertram'), which
bears some resemblance to Lord Byron's 'Corsair.' It is written
by the author of the 'Milesian.' We were very near the stage,
where I could enjoy and appreciate Kean's acting. He has the disadvantage of a small person, but with an amazing power of expression in his face. He is less noble and dignified than Kemble,
but I think his genius is as great in its way. Every word he
utters is full of power, and I know not whether he most excels
in the terrific or in the tender and pathetic. His face, though
not handsome, is picturesque, and the manner in which he wore
his hair was peculiarly so.

*

The above sketch, though caricatured, is a little like him. A
few nights ago, Mrs. Siddons performed Queen Katharine for
Charles Kemble's benefit. I could not resist the temptation of
going, and actually endangered my life to see her, in a most tremendous crowd. She played gloriously, so as to bring back all
my former recollections of her. She is very little altered, and I
believe there are hopes of her return to the stage. Kemble
played Cardinal Wolsey in his best manner, and his voice was in
excellent condition. This play is got up in the most classical and
magnificent style. The banquet scene was splendid in the extreme, and Anne Boleyn was performed by Miss Foster (a perfectly beautiful girl). Egerton who played Harry resembles his
person, and was dressed precisely like the pictures and statues of
him. Charles Kemble played Cromwell; by the by he is no
great actor; the only character I ever liked him in was Falcon-

* Here followed a pen-and-ink sketch.

bridge. I am in great hopes of getting an introduction to Mrs. Siddons, to make a sketch of her face, through Payne. However, there are many difficulties in the way, as she is as much of the Princess off the stage as she is on. Payne knows Charles Kemble very well, but Charles is not sufficiently intimate with his sister to take the liberty of asking such a favour of her. He did not even ask her to play for his benefit. I am therefore in hopes of obtaining it through John Kemble. Mr. Coleridge is at present here; he has just published his poem of 'Cristabel.' He lives at Highgate (about three miles from us) in a most delightful family. He requested me to sketch his face, which I did, out there, and by that means became acquainted with Mr. and Mrs. Gilman, who are the sort of people that you become intimate with at once. They have invited me in the most friendly manner to visit them at all times, and to spend weeks with them. There are some beautiful scenes about Highgate, and I shall in future make it my resort for landscape studies. Mrs. Gilman has a very fine face, and she will sit to me whenever I wish. She is a very excellent, charming woman; and to do the English justice, I believe hers is not an uncommon character among them. I have met with four such women myself, and I think I could right safely add more to the number, and my English acquaintance is not very extensive. If I had any right to speak from my limited observation, I should say, that the women here far exceed the men in virtue. Caroline Percy, Belinda, and Grace Nugent, are, I am convinced, not ideal characters. They have just opened a very fine exhibition of the Italian masters at the British Gallery. It contains two of the cartoons of Raphael,* and a cabinet picture by him of Saint Catherine, which is the most divine head I have ever seen, one or two fine Titians, a number of glorious Paul Veroneses, and all the original cartoons of the heads of Leonardo da Vinci's 'Last Supper,' which give me a higher opinion of him than anything I have seen, and, though last not least, some very fine Claudes, Salvators, and Poussins. This exhibition affords a most delicious treat to us

---

* Got up from Hampton Court, Haydon says — in his biography — at his suggestion. — ED.

artists,* and I hope some of the best pictures will be left at the close of it, for the students to copy. I shall soon send to Sully a little oil copy from a Paul Veronese, which I think he will find useful. I am going on much as usual. Portrait is the order of the day.

I have just received a long and kind letter from Mr. Bradford, which I shall answer immediately. I shall be extremely glad to see Henry Carey, and shall render him every service in my power. Remember me affectionately to him when you see him. Nothing has occurred to alter my determination of returning . at the time I have fixed; on the contrary, I grow more and more anxious for its approach, and the sale of Mr. Allston's picture has very much brightened my prospects.

I am exceedingly anxious that our Academy should send for casts from the finest Antiques in the world, which are now in London, and were brought from Athens by Lord Elgin. I have written to Sully on the subject, and hope he will exert his influence with them to that end. It will be an incalculable advantage to our artists, and their being in Philadelphia would make me quite content to fix my residence there for the remainder of my life. I know an artist † who says, he thanks God every morning that he did not die before they arrived in England.

Tell Sully that I entreat him not to lose a moment's time in persuading the Academy to procure them. He will look upon their arrival as a sure prognostic of the rise of the Arts among us. We want to establish a correct public taste, and I know nothing so likely to do it. I sent Sully an extract from one of the weekly papers upon the subject of them,‡ since which there has appeared in the last number of the 'Quarterly Review' a full account of them, which I wish he could obtain a sight of. No doubt many of his acquaintances receive that work. Farewell, remember me as usual to all relations and friends.

C. R. L.

* This was the first year in which such an opportunity of copying was given. — ED.

† Haydon. — ED.

‡ One of Haydon's articles from the 'Examiner.' — ED.

TO MISS LESLIE.

LONDON, *Dec.* 12, 1816.

I HAVE just received your letters of October 8th and 19th, rendered doubly welcome by so long an interval since the last.

I am glad to hear of the safe arrival of the pictures, and still more so that the Academy is inclined to purchase my Clifford. Tell Sully I will accept the thousand dollars in preference to the other proposal. Your criticisms on the picture are very just. I am only afraid that your diffidence as to your own judgment prevents your pointing out many other faults that you see. Do not be afraid of saying exactly what you think. I am used to having my pictures remarked on, and when people can see some merit in them it does not annoy me to have a great many faults pointed out; on the contrary I have, in most instances, reason to be pleased with it. Your commendations were very gratifying to me, as they were bestowed upon those parts of my picture which I was best satisfied with myself. I think, therefore, they were just, though somewhat too warm, from the natural and amiable prejudice of a sister, and from your not having had opportunities of seeing a great deal of art. You will be pleased to hear that the silver medal which I was a candidate for has been awarded to me. The evening of the 10th, I received it from the hand of Mr. Fuseli, who presided in Mr. West's absence (on account of ill-health). The copying at the British Gallery is over. I have finished my Paul Veronese. It is rather a pleasant mode of study, and has considerable advantages. There were thirty artists there on an average every day, eight or ten of them ladies. It is useful to see the different modes of painting that are practised, and to hear the various opinions that are advanced. From those that are better and further advanced than myself, I have learnt in many instances what to aim at, and from those that are inferior what to avoid. There were two of the cartoons left there, but I had not time to make any studies from them. My principal pursuit at present is colour, and I find there is more to be learned in that from the Venetians than all the other schools put together. They have a painting-school at the Academy now,

on a similar plan to that at the Gallery, and they have lately received one of the cartoons, the Death of Ananias, — one of the
finest — from Hampton Court. There is a picture there of Mr.
West's, — a Head by Guido, — which I am going to copy for
Mr. MacMurtrie.

I lately requested to see Fuseli's pictures at the Academy.
He received me very politely and took me into his painting-room.
He is at present about a picture of Perseus flying off with the
head of Medusa. The figure of Medusa is very happily conceived, and he has contrived to hide all the disgusting part, — the
stump of the neck and the blood, — very judiciously. He has in
his room the finest picture I ever saw of his, ' The Lazar House,'
I believe from Milton. It is one of the most tremendous exhibitions of appalling sights I ever beheld. The figures glare
across the picture like a horrible dream. He has certainly never
been equalled in the visionary, and there it is he shines as a
genius, but whenever he attempts commonplace he is contemptible.

Fuseli, I believe, never has painted from nature, and conse-
quently does not know what it is. His illustrations of Cowper
are ridiculous in the extreme. He is a great master of light and
shadow, and colour, as far as it can be made an engine of the terrific. His paintings are very coarse, and have an uncertain kind
of execution which is very fine in ghosts and witches, but very
bad in gentlemen and ladies. Turner, however, is my great
favourite of all the painters here.

I went to see his pictures yesterday, and was delighted as I
always am with them. He combines the highest poetical imagination with an exquisite feeling for all the truth and individuality
of nature, and he has shown that the ideal, as it is called, is not
the improving of nature, but the selecting and combining objects
that are most in harmony and character with each other. To
wind up the matter, I will sketch the heads of the two great men
I have been describing.* Alas! I have failed in the likeness of
Turner ; the other is Fuseli, and though a little in caricature,
gives some idea of him. His front face has very much the character of a lion. I find I have written about one subject only,

* Here follow two pen-and-ink sketches.

and that though the most interesting to me may not be equally so to you, and so good bye.

TO MISS LESLIE.

LONDON, *Dec.* 23, 1816.

My last letter I believe was solely about the Arts. There were several other things I had intended to say in it when I began, but I soon found myself over head and ears in paint, and accordingly reserved them for another letter.

I am very much pleased with the subject you proposed in your last, of William Tell, and shall probably paint it some time or other. It will be very difficult to compose it.

I have often intended to ask my mother for a description of the places where my father lived, and where Tom and I were born. I wish she may recollect the numbers of the houses. I remember that just before we sailed, we had lodgings in Cheapside, at a china shop. I think the name of the people was Anice, but I have looked in vain for such a name or such a shop in Cheapside. I should like also to know the church in which I was christened. * * * * I often amuse myself by dreaming of my return, and how you will all look, and what you will all say: delightful reveries —

> When I think of my own native land,
> In a moment I seem to be there;
> But alas! recollection at hand,
> Soon hurries me back to ———.

no, not to " despair," but to old England. Farewell for the present. Remember me to all friends and relations.

C. R. L.

1817.

Pictures of this Year.

PORTRAITS PAINTED AT PARIS OF MISS WELLER, MRS. CARNES, MR. GREEN, AND OTHER AMERICANS.

LESLIE exhibited no picture at the Academy this year, though

he painted the above enumerated portraits of his countrymen and
women during a visit to Paris, where he spent two months. He
made the excursion in company with his friends Allston and William Collins, afterwards the Royal Academician. In a letter to
his sister, of September 22, after describing their journey, *via*
Brighton and Dieppe, he says, —

" The day after our arrival we were not able to get into the
Louvre, and we visited the church of Notre Dame, a fine Gothic
structure, but inferior to Westminster Abbey. The following day
we went to the Louvre, and revelled all the morning in the richest luxury of art. It is impossible for me to describe my feelings ; had my whole life before been one of misery, it seemed as
if this day would have balanced the account, and made me consider myself the happiest of human beings. But all this may
appear to you extravagant, and perhaps is so ; but as I believe
that in many instances it is of advantage to be led away by our
feelings (provided they do not lead us away from our duties), I
gave myself entirely up to them. In the cartoons of Raphael, I
had before had frequent opportunities of seeing all that part of
the art which addresses itself to the mind, and now I saw, in its
fullest perfection, all that part which can delight the eye, in the
picture of the ' Marriage at Cana ' by Paul Veronese. It is an
immense picture, about thirty feet by twenty, and the figures are
as large as life. The colouring is quite perfect, and far exceeds
any picture of the kind that I have ever seen, or expect to see.
There are many other very fine pictures, and, it must be owned,
a great deal of trash, which has been substituted for the pictures
which were removed. The gallery itself is a most splendid
building, and does very great honour to the nation it belongs to."

Of this year, too, is the first letter I find from him addressed to
his friend Washington Irving. It would seem from allusions to the
' Dutch Courtship,' and other passages in this letter, to have been
already settled that a series of illustrations to ' Knickerbocker '
and the ' Sketch Book ' were to be executed by Allston and
Leslie. We shall find frequent references to this work in a
year or two.

LONDON, *Dec.* 20, 1817.

MY DEAR SIR,—I ought to be very clever at making apologies for delaying to answer the letters of my friends, if practice is as useful in this as in other things; but I am really quite at a loss in the present instance, for the truth is I have no excuse to offer but laziness, which is inexcusable. I shall therefore plead guilty, and hope that as the fault carries with it the heavy punishment of its own consciousness, you will forgive me.

I arrived in London about three weeks ago, by the way of Brussels and Antwerp, after a very gratifying, and I hope profitable, residence of two months in Paris. The Louvre is more rich than I expected. I painted a portrait of Miss Weller, but as I did not come back direct, I left it, with some sketches I made in the Louvre, to be sent after me, and they have not yet arrived.

I had the pleasure of meeting Preston there; he gave me some very interesting descriptions of scenes that you· enjoyed together in Scotland. You must have been very much delighted with the society of Edinburgh. I hope your tour has roused you into the writing mood.

I have put the sketch of the ' Dutch Courtship' into the hands of a very excellent engraver. It will be done in two months; the price will be twenty-five guineas, which is not high for the style in which he will do it.

Mr. Allston is afraid that his drawing cannot be reduced without losing the expression, and intends therefore doing another of the size of mine as soon as he can choose a subject. He has not yet got to work on his large picture, but has just finished a very grand and poetical figure of the angel Uriel sitting in the sun. The figure is colossal, the attitude and air very noble, and the form heroic without being overcharged. In the colour he has been equally successful, and with a very rich and glowing tone he has avoided *positive* colours, which would have made him too material. There is neither red, blue, nor yellow in the picture, and yet it possesses a harmony equal to the best pictures of Paul Veronese. I hope you will be in London ere long to see it. I cannot in this letter make any observations on ' Jacob's Dream,'

but I will write to you again very soon, and in the meantime,
endeavour to put together some remarks upon painting generally.

We met Verplank at Paris, whom we found a very agreeable
and intelligent companion. I painted there the portraits of Mrs.
Carnes, a pretty countrywoman of ours, and Mr. Green. I am
at present engaged in the same way here, and shall probably do
nothing else till my return to America, which I expect will be in
the spring, when I hope to undertake the plans I communicated
to you when you were in London.

Allston sends his warmest regards to you, in which he is
heartily joined by

Yours, very truly,

CHAS. R. LESLIE.

To WASHINGTON IRVING, ESQ.,
    At HENRY VAN WART'S, ESQ.,
        Birmingham.

1818.

Pictures of this Year.

ANNE PAGE AND MASTER SLENDER. (Not exhibited). — GIRL WITH DEAD
BIRD. (Not exhibited.)

As to the former,* which was no doubt the first conception of
the more important picture on this subject, which he painted and
exhibited in 1825, I find nothing in the correspondence under the
date of this year, except the allusion to it in the following letter
from Washington Irving, who was now at Birmingham, in very
bad health, and labouring under great depression of spirits. Leslie
had no doubt written to tell his friend of the progress of the illus-

---

* I think it likely to have been the first engraved picture of Leslie's, from
the ' Merry Wives of Windsor.' The engraving is by Finden. The scene is in
Page's garden, where Anne invites Slender in to dinner. He stands with
crossed legs lackadaisically, and turns his back on Anne, who points towards
the house. The Slender has a great deal of character. The Anne Page is
conventional, and smacks of George the Third's London and 1818, more than
Elizabeth's Windsor and 1592. — ED.

trations, but I do not find the letter in the extracts I have from
Leslie's correspondence with Irving.

Irving writes from Birmingham (July 29, 1818) :

" I wish the plates put in the printer's hands as soon as possible, and to be executed on the best paper.   Two thousand of
each.   I should like to have three hundred proof impressions of
each struck off in such manner that they would do to frame,
should any person like to have them in that manner ; if not,
they can hereafter be cut down to the size of the volume.   You
and Allston will have as many struck off for yourselves as you
please.   Let me know the whole expense, and I will send the
money immediately.

" I have had my trunk packed to come to London, and should
have attended to all this myself, but one circumstance or other
continually occurs to baffle my plans, and I am at this moment in
a little uncertainty when I shall get them.

" I shall try hard to see Allston before he sails.   Had he been
going to embark at Liverpool the thing would have been certain.
I regret excessively that he goes to America, now that his prospects are opening so promisingly in this country ; but perhaps it
is all for the best.

" His ' Jacob's Dream ' was a particular favourite of mine.   I
have gazed on it again and again, and the more I gazed the more
I was delighted with it.   I believe if I was a painter, I could at
this moment take a pencil and delineate the whole with the attitude and expression of every figure.

" Allston gives me a charming account of your picture of
' Anne Page and Master Slender.'   I hope you will take frequent opportunities to steal away from the painting of portraits,
to give full scope to your taste and imagination."

In this year Leslie made a pleasure-excursion into the West of
England, of which the letter to his sister gives some pretty landscape sketches in pen and ink.

TO MISS LESLIE.

LONDON, *Nov.* 21, 1818.

IN my last I informed you that I had just returned from a trip through Devonshire, the particulars of which I had not then time to relate. I will endeavour (now that I have a little more leisure) to give you some account of it. I had received an invitation from Mr. Dunlop, to spend a short time with him at Dawlish, where he had taken lodgings for a fortnight. I arrived at Exeter from London in twenty-four hours, where I hired a gig and a man to drive me to Dawlish, which is at the sea-side, and about twelve miles from Exeter. This part of the country is all hill and valley, very luxuriant and beautifully diversified with gentlemen's seats and villages. The cottages and churches are of the most brilliant white, and a kind of vine which is generally seen spreading over the walls of the former, the leaves of which are at this season of a bright crimson, produces a beautiful effect. I spent a fortnight of uninterrupted enjoyment at Dawlish, bathed in the sea almost every morning, and after breakfast went out to some one of the fine views with which we were surrounded, sometimes alone, and sometimes with Mr. and Mrs. Dunlop. We visited Powderham Castle, and the grounds belonging to it, beautifully situated on the River Exe. The castle is an ancient Gothic one, but as it has been constantly occupied, the interior has been modernised.

On the opposite side of the river, stands the seat of the late Lord Heathfield. We also visited Mamhead, the highest hill in the neighbourhood. On the summit stands an obelisk surrounded by pines and other forest trees, among which is the evergreen oak, a remarkably elegant tree. This place is more like an American wood than anything I have seen in England.

At Mamhead there is a pretty little church, in the yard of which stands the largest yew tree I ever saw. The trunk is thirty-six feet in circumference. There were also some of the finest elms I ever saw. Dawlish itself is a small place, with nothing particularly beautiful about it ; but as it is well sheltered and affords conveniences for bathing, it is a good deal resorted to by invalids. The climate is considered the finest of any part of

. England. The shops at these small places are like our American country stores. I bought a pair of gloves at a grocer's who was likewise an undertaker, and I had my hair cut by a barber who kept horses for hire and sold pianos.

Mr. and Mrs. Dunlop having given up their intention of going to Plymouth, I set out by myself. Mr. Dunlop lent me a horse and accompanied me as far as Newton Bushel, about ten miles from Dawlish, in the course of which ride I saw some of the beautiful scenery on the River Teign. I had sent my trunk back to London, and took with me only a few shirts and cravats tied in a handkerchief, and my sketch book.

Thus equipped I left Newton on the top of one of the coaches, and about four o'clock got down within two miles of Totness to visit Berry Pomeroy Castle. After proceeding about half-a-mile on foot, I came within sight of the ruins, which crown the summit of a hill, richly wooded, and over-topped by another equally luxuriant rising behind it, and forming a back-ground to the castle. Fearful that I should not have time before dark to explore the beauties of the place, I endeavoured to procure a lodging at some cottages I saw before me. This I found impracticable, but was directed to the lodge of the castle as the only likely place to obtain a bed, and where the woman lived whose business it is to show the castle to strangers. To the lodge I therefore repaired, through a long avenue of trees, but found I could not procure a bed nearer than at Totness. My guide took me into the castle through a modern wooden gate, which supplies the place of the ancient portcullis. The ruined walls and towers are in most places completely covered with ivy. Not a vestige of the roof remains. Tall trees are growing in the principal apartments, and bushes of various kinds on the tops of the walls. We ascended and descended flights of steps, in some places almost impassable, traversed narrow and winding passages, sometimes in perfect darkness. In the guard-room, over the entrance, my guide pointed out the long narrow opening through which the portcullis had formerly descended. Sunset was approaching and the

> Loop-hole tower, the donjon-keep,
> In yellow lustre shone.

14

That part of the castle which we first entered was built in the .
year 1070. The rest, though of more modern date, was nearly
in an equally ruinous state. The view from one of the towers
was very fine : the surrounding hills swelling and steep. The
day had been a little misty, but the sun was setting beautifully
behind the bold outline of a hill. Upon one side of the castle
the hill on which it stands is nearly perpendicular, and the appearance of the valley as seen from above is very romantic ; the
wildness of the foliage which covers the descent, and some
picturesque rocks of limestone opposite, — separated from the
hill on which the castle stands by a broad level green, which in
days of old had been covered with water forming the moat, —
combine to make it so. The lulling sound of the stream to which
the moat is now shrunk, and which winds through the valley entirely concealed by foliage, and the distant clink of a mill, were
the only sounds, excepting the notes of the castle's feathered inhabitants.

We now descended to the opposite rocks, from which is the
best view of the whole place. The sun had set, but left a mellow light which streamed along the horizon, behind the dark grey
walls and still darker ivy which mantled them, and threw a faint
tinge on the tops of some of the tallest trees that rose to the base
of the ruins. The feeling I had in beholding a scene so perfectly poetical for the first time, and knowing all that to be real
which looked so like a vision, was indescribable. We traversed
the valley and passed the mill, part of which is coeval with the
castle and belonged to it. The wall still remains round a part of
the castle ground, and my guide pointed out what had been the
garden — now a desolate field. By the time we regained the
lodge it was dark, and I proceeded to Totness without delay,
passing through the village of Berry, about half a mile from the
castle. I met one or two country people on the road, who saluted
me with a ' good night. ' In the daytime the Devonshire people
always bow or courtesy to you, down to the youngest children. I
had made up my mind to return to Berry Castle the next morning, but when I came, I found Totness such a beautiful place that
I gave up my intention. The day was delightfully fine, and I
employed myself till near two o'clock in wandering through the

charming scenery that surrounds this ancient town, and occasionally attempting a sketch. The bridge is very old, with pointed
arches, and in some parts ruinous. The church is also very
ancient. The custom of tolling the curfew is still kept up in this
part of the country, though it is not followed by putting out the
lights. The church clock at Totness strikes the day of the month
every evening. On the top of a high hill near the church stands
the ruined tower of a castle, so entirely covered with ivy, that at
a distance it has the appearance of a clump of trees. A grassy
walk round the parapet of this tower, commands a very fine view
of the surrounding country, through which the river Dart winds
very beautifully.

I left Totness on one of the coaches that passes through, and
about half-past three o'clock arrived at Ivy-bridge, a pleasant
village situated on a picturesque stream, which dashes over a bed
of rocks in a continual series of waterfalls with a constant roar.
It is crossed by a high picturesque bridge of one arch, clothed
with ivy, from which the village takes its name. I dined at this
beautiful place and strolled about till dark. The next coach
came past at seven, and on that I proceeded to Plymouth, where
I arrived between nine and ten o'clock. The next morning I
took a boat and went on board the 'Impregnable,' by merely asking leave of the commanding officer, which was very politely
granted. She is a 100 gun ship, and was very much shattered
at Algiers in the late bombardment, since when she has been entirely repaired.

I was delighted with the perfect order and cleanliness maintained in every part of her. The second gun-deck was filled
with sailors' wives and children. I afterwards visited the dock-
yard, where I obtained admittance without the least difficulty
by answering in the affirmative when asked if I was a native of
England. I was not aware of what I have since learned, that if I
had called myself an American I could not have got in. Among
other things, I was shown a frigate on the stocks building upon
a large scale, to 'face the Americans,' as my conductor told
me.* *

In this year, much to Leslie's regret, Allston sailed for America. He was an associate of our Royal Academy, but preferred America, and his prospects there, to the certainty of distinction here. He took up his residence in Boston, where he followed his art and cultivated literature. He lived much respected, and died at Cambridge in Massachusetts in 1843. A folio volume of fac-similes of sketches, found in his studio after his death, was published by Steven and Perkins, of Boston, which abundantly shows his grace and antique elegance as a designer. A 'Dido and Æneas,' in particular, might have been traced from a Pompeian Mosaic. Mr. Allston's masterpiece, 'Jacob's Dream,' is in this country, at Petworth; but I confess to having been disappointed in the qualities of the picture, when I saw it for the first time this year, after reading what Irving and Leslie say of it.

1819.

Pictures of the Year.

PORTRAIT OF A LADY (?). — SIR ROGER DE COVERLEY GOING TO CHURCH, ACCOMPANIED BY THE SPECTATOR, AND SURROUNDED BY HIS TENANTS.*
— See *Spectator*, No. 112. (Exhibited R. A.)

THIS year is an epoch in the painter's career, as being that in which Leslie ventured on a class of subjects which none of our painters has treated with so fine a hand as he. We have seen him forsaking the Old Testament and the Pantheon for Shakespeare. But he durst not venture too fast into that region of the familiar, which the pedantic conventionalism of that day almost entirely proscribed. Gainsborough, it is true, had long before this time painted cottage children, and even hazarded 'A Girl and Pigs,' which Sir Joshua had, in the opinion of his contemporaries, lowered himself by buying for a hundred guineas. Morland was great in pigs, and stables, and sheep-pens. Later still, Wilkie had taken the town by storm by his 'Blind Fiddler,' and his other inimitable scenes of Scottish Lowland life. But in spite of these exceptions, it may be said that domestic subjects were

* This picture was exhibited at Manchester in 1857, by its present possessor, John Naylor, Esq.— ED.

tabooed to the mass of painters. The illustration of books — Shakespeare excepted — was thought matter for the publishers and the reading public, rather than for the painter and his patrons. Stothard and Smirke worked at this work, and were both Academicians, but they were ill-paid, and passed over by the scanty picture-buying class of that period.

At a time when the classical and heroic are, in their turn, proscribed, we find it difficult to appreciate the courage of a young painter who dared to deviate from the conventional subjects and style of his times, and to paint what his heart warmed to.

Leslie's first picture of Sir Roger was painted for his good friend Mr. Dunlop, a wealthy tobacco importer, to whom Leslie's American connections had made him known on his arrival in England.

Lord Lansdowne, one of the soundest in judgment and most self-reliant among the nobility, who comprised in their ranks almost all the picture-buyers of that day, saw and admired Mr. Dunlop's picture at the Exhibition, and gave the painter a commission for a repetition of the subject, which now hangs at Bowood.

We have probably a right to consider this year as Leslie's starting-point on the road to fame and fortune. But the only letter I find of this date is the following characteristic one from Washington Irving (who had spent the summer in London), written to Leslie while on a visit to his Quaker friends, the Dillwyns, in Wales, at Penllergare near Swansea. The Lyman, Everett, and Charles Williams mentioned in the letter, were American friends of Irving's and Leslie's; and the Newton referred to, is the painter, one of Leslie's and Irving's most intimate associates.

LONDON, *Sept. 13th*, 1819.

YOU LESLIE! — What's the reason you have not let us hear from you since you set out on your travels? We have been in great anxiety lest you should have started from London on some other route of that six inch square map of the world which you consulted, and through the mistake of a hair's breadth may have wandered the Lord knows where.

Here have been sad evolutions and revolutions since you left us. Newton had his three shirts and six collars packed up in a half of a saddle bag for several days, with the intention of accompanying Lyman, Everett, and Charles Williams to Liverpool, and returning with the latter through Wales, in which case they intended beating up your quarters, and endeavouring to surprise you with your mahl-stick turned into a shepherd's crook, sighing at the feet of Miss Maine. Newton did nothing for two or three days but scamper up and down between Finsbury Square and Sloane Street like a cat in a panic, taking leave of everybody in the morning and calling upon them again in the evening, when to his astonishment he found Charles Williams had the private intention of embarking for America. Charles has actually sailed, and Newton, instead of his Welsh tour, accompanied me on a tour to Deptford and Eltham. He has now resumed his station at the head of Sloane Street. Jones has taken possession of the bottom, and between them both I expect they will tie the two ends of the street into a true lover's knot. For my part I have been almost good for nothing since your departure, and would not pass another summer in London if they would make me Lord Mayor.

I have received the second number of the 'Sketch Book,' and shall be quite satisfied if I deserve half the praise they give me in the American journals ; but they always overdo these matters in America. I am glad to find the second number pleases more than the first. The sale is very rapid, and altogether the success exceeds my most sanguine expectation. Now you suppose I am all on the alert, and full of spirit and excitement. No such thing. I am just as good for nothing as ever I was, and indeed have been flurried and put out of my way by these puffings. I feel something as I suppose you did when your picture met with success — anxious to do something better, and at a loss what to do.

But enough of egotism. Let me know how you find yourself; how you like Wales ; what you are doing, and especially when you intend to return. I hope you will not remain away much longer. Newton's manikin has at length arrived, and he is to have it home in a few days, when it is to be hoped he will give up rambling abroad, and stay at home, drink tea, and play the flute to the lady. William Macdougall means to give her a tea-party, and it is expected she will be introduced into company with as much *éclat* as Peregrine Pickle's *protégée*. I have now fairly filled my sheet with nonsense, and craving a speedy reply,

I am, yours,   W. I.

1820.

Pictures of this Year.

LONDONERS GIPSYING. (Exhibited). — PORTRAIT OF WASHINGTON IRVING.

DURING this year Leslie was much employed with his illustrations for Irving's works — 'Knickerbocker' and the 'Sketch Book' — which had attained a success in London peculiarly gratifying to Leslie's affectionate and admiring friendship for their author. The letters I have of this date run much on this theme. Scott's visit to London this year brought him and Leslie together, and the painter was delighted by Scott's approval of his picture of 'May-day in the time of Queen Elizabeth,' on which he was now engaged. I have inserted the account of Scott's visit to Leslie *in extenso*, as it contains a pen-and-ink portrait of Scott, given with all the sharpness of a first impression. This year, too, died the venerable President of the Academy. I have not been able to ascertain where the 'Gipsying Party' now is, or anything of the way in which the subject is treated.

The edition of Irving's works, with the illustrations by Leslie and Allston, was published by Murray in 1823. Newton contributed the author's portrait; Leslie nine illustrations — the Royal Poet, James the First of Scotland, with the dove flying in at the window; Rip Van Winkle toiling up the hill by the side of the spectral Dutch sailor, keg on shoulder; the Indian chief, Philip of Pokanoket, on his night-watch in the forest; Ichabod Crane giving his singing lesson to Katrine, from 'The Legend of Sleepy Hollow;' a Dutch Fire-side; Dutch Courtship; Antony Van Corlear, trumpet in hand, setting off for the Wars, surrounded by weeping vrows; William Kieft introducing his new mode of punishment for beggars; and Peter Stuyvesant rebuking the Cobbler: all from 'Knickerbocker.' Allston furnished a sin-

gle illustration from the same book — Wouter Van Twiller decid-
ing a law-suit. Leslie's designs are full of his own quiet and
well-directed humour, with just enough of caricature, here and
there, to suit the subject. But in the Dutch Fire-side and Philip
of Pokanoket this element disappears, to give place to good drawing, excellent composition, and, in the former, to a very fine and
subtle effect of *chiaroscuro*. He afterwards painted this subject.
A comparison of Allston's design from ' Knickerbocker,' with
Leslie's, illustrates the difference between the men. Allston has
not the least humour, and tries to make up for it by breadth of
caricature in faces and proportions. Leslie, on the other hand,
keeps his caricature close on the limit which separates that style
from broadly humorous design, and never departs from genuine
and human expression, nor fails to introduce beauty, whenever he
has an opening for it.

                           TO MISS LESLIE.

                                          LONDON, *April* 9, 1820.

    THE last letter I have received from you was that of Feb-
ruary 7th.
    Since I last wrote I have completed my picture of the ' Gipsy-
ing Party,' and sent it to Somerset House. In a few days I hope
to hear where it is placed, and how it is liked by the Academicians. I suppose you will have received the account that was
published in the papers of the funeral of Mr. West. It was
arranged, I believe, exactly on the plan of that of Sir Joshua
Reynolds. An apartment on the ground-floor of the Academy
was hung and carpeted with black, the daylight entirely excluded,
and the room lighted by a number of tall wax candles, placed
at regular distances on the floor, around the coffin, which was
covered by a pall and lid of black feathers. Against the wall, at
the head of the corpse, hung the hatchment bearing the family
arms. No one remained in the room excepting Robert, Mr.
West's old servant, who had sat up there all the preceding night.
My feelings were greatly affected by this scene. The company
who were to attend the funeral assembled in a large upper room,

where they were provided with black silk scarves and hatbands, the Academicians wearing long black cloaks. It was interesting to see persons of different ranks, and of different nations, and of well-known different political sentiments, meeting on this occasion, and uniting in the last tribute of respect to a man of genius. The service was performed by Dr. Wellesley, brother to the Duke of Wellington. In one part of it a very beautiful anthem was sung by the boys of the choir, the effect of which, with the fine organ of St. Paul's (said to be the finest in England), was such as Milton has described in the Penseroso. Nothing certainly raises the imagination so far above this " dim earth " as fine cathedral music heard in a cathedral, and never have I felt its power more than on this occasion. When the service was finished I went down into the crypt, beneath the church, and saw the coffin lowered into the grave. I was not aware at the time that the tombs of Sir Joshua, Opie, and Barry, and Sir Christopher Wren, were all near the same place. The crowd of persons assembled covered them. Sir Thomas Lawrence has been elected President, and has just returned from Italy, where he has been painting whole lengths of the Pope, and I know not how many other high personages.

Walter Scott (now Sir Walter) is in London, and I am to have the honour, and I am sure it will be the very great pleasure, of breakfasting with him at his lodgings on Friday next. Irving, who I suspect of being a very great favourite of Scott's, is to introduce me. It is what I did not venture to ask of him, but Irving, knowing how much such an introduction would gratify me, proposed it himself. I believe we are to meet Crabbe, the poet, there. Scott is one of those men of genius who delights in the genius of others, and is not for having it all to himself. He has expressed the highest opinion of Irving's productions, and perhaps there is not another man in this country whose good opinion is so valuable. You will be glad to hear that there is every prospect of Irving's writings speedily becoming as popular here as they are in America. An edition of the first volume of the ' Sketch Book ' is very nearly sold off here already. One of the stories, ' The Wife,' has been translated into French, and many of the articles have been extracted for the magazines and newspapers. Scott was very much delighted with the sixth number, particularly with the story of ' Brom Bones.' I have just finished reading ' The Monastery.' I do not much like the supernatural agency introduced, but I think there are some scenes very admirably described, particularly the escape of Mysie with Sir Piercie Shafton. The character of Sir Piercie appears to me to be extremely well drawn, and has a good deal of novelty. The Sub-Prior is very finely sustained. From what I have heard, it seems to be less liked than any of the novels, and perhaps with justice, though, for my own part, I read a great deal of it with as much pleasure as any of the others.

I went to see the chairing of Sir Francis Burdett and Mr. Hobhouse, and, as I generally find on these occasions, I was more amused with the crowd than the procession. The show of beautiful women at the windows, their countenances animated by the occasion, waving scarves and handkerchiefs, amply repaid me for a good deal of tramping through the mire, and a ducking from the rain into the bargain. I sent my copy of ' Sir Roger ' home to the Marquis, and a day or two afterwards received a note containing the amount, and his expressions of perfect satisfaction with the picture.

C. R. L.

TO MISS LESLIE.

LONDON, *June* 28, 1820.

WHEN I last wrote I was about to be introduced to Sir Walter Scott. He quite answered all my expectations of him, and you may suppose they were very high. His manners are those of an amiable and unaffected man, and a polished gentleman, and his conversation is something higher, for it is often quite as amusing and interesting as his novels, and without any apparent attempt at display. It flows from him in the most easy and natural manner. As I take it for granted that the most insignificant particulars relating to such a man will be interesting to you, I will give you a description of his personal appearance, and even his dress. He is tall and well formed, excepting one of his ankles and foot (I think the right) which is crippled, and makes him walk very lamely. He is neither fat nor thin. His face is perfectly Scotch, and though some people think it heavy, it struck me as a very agreeable one. He never could have been handsome. His forehead is very high, his nose short, his upper lip long, and the lower part of his face rather fleshy. His complexion is fresh and clear, his eyes very blue, shrewd, and penetrating. I should say the predominant expression of his face is that of strong sense. His hair, which has always been very light (as well as his eyebrows and eyelashes) is now of a silvery whiteness, which makes him look somewhat older than he really is (I believe forty-six is his age). He was dressed in a brown frock coat, blue trowsers, and had on a black cravat. His son was with him; he is a young man of eighteen or nineteen, and in the army — he does not at all resemble his father. Among the company who breakfasted with him the morning we did, was a Mr. Boswell, the son of Dr. Johnson's Bozzy. He is a lawyer, and is said to be cleverer than his father. The breakfast was a very profuse one, and, as I am told, quite in the Scotch style. I would have sent you a sketch of Scott, but, after several attempts, I find I cannot catch his face from recollection. All the portraits I have seen are somewhat like him, but none of them very strongly so.

I have not yet sold my picture of the ' Gipsying Party,' and scarcely expect it now. I am just commencing a picture of the May-day revels in the time of Queen Elizabeth, which will contain a great many figures, and will be an attempt to give the costume and something of the manners of all classes in that age, from the nobility down to the peasantry. I have been studying the subject for several months, and am reading all the old authors I can get hold of who describe manners in that time. I am in hopes it will be popular, as it is a period that Englishmen are fond of recurring to, as one of the most brilliant in the history of their country. They are also more generally acquainted with the manners of that time than any other, on account of the greater popularity of Shakespeare than any other English writer whatever. The picture I am to paint for Mr. Scriven, an engraver, whose object is to make a print of it.

I agree with you in thinking the ' Monastery' inferior to all

the other novels, but still there is a great deal in it that nobody
else could write. Were you not much amused with Sir Piercie
Shafton? I think the description of his flight with Mysie Hap-
per is very good.

C. R. L.

Irving was now in Paris, and the following correspondence
between him and Leslie is creditable on both sides. It gives
glimpses besides of the pleasant social life of Leslie and his circle
— " the lads " as Irving calls them — the affectionate nick-names
— the blind-man's buff under the trees at Dr. Bollman's at Winkfield — and the scrambling bachelor *ménage* of Leslie and his
quaint little chum, Peter Powell, — which seem to me too characteristic to be omitted.

LONDON, Sept. 15th, 1820.

DEAR IRVING, — " What are you at " that you do not write
to some of us? " *There never were such times* " as we have had
lately. 'In the first place, the " Childe " (Newton) was turned
out of house and home by a host of painters and glaziers old
Perkins * let in upon him one day. He agreed to make the tour
of Wales with Charles Williams and the Lymans, but the matter
got perplexed somehow or other between Charles and him, and
Newton, who was to join them on the road, not knowing exactly
where it was to be, determined to go somewhere else. He therefore spent a day in taking the opinions of all his acquaintances as
to whether he should that night set off for Cumberland, Margate,
Paris, the Davidson's, or go to the English Opera. " The
Dusty " (?) being the last man he called on, advised the latter,
which he accomplished, and next morning set off for Hastings,
and from thence to Brighton, where he met all the world, and
returned to London with old Gray in a great panic lest Luke and
myself should have gone to Winkfield (where we were engaged
to pass a few days) without him. We have all three spent a most
delightful week there with the Bollmans, Miss Maine (who is to
be married the 4th of Oct.), and Miss Foote. All that we had

---

* Haydon's most long-suffering of landlords. Newton succeeded him in the
rooms. — ED.

to regret was the absence of yourself and your brother, of which
we were most forcibly reminded by scenes we were sure you
would have enjoyed. Do you recollect an old fragment of an oak
which I believe you christened "Achilles"? On three several
days did that oak hear your name sighed forth as mournfully as
ever poor Yorick's was. You must remember a noble grove of
beech, covering a hill which commands a fine view of the castle,
and separated by the road from a very beautiful group of ash
trees. I am sure you would willingly have exchanged all the
pleasures of Paris to have been one in a game of " puss in the
corner," which succeeded to a considerable destruction of bread
and jam under those beeches. Newton and myself returned to
town yesterday, and he, finding that Perkins had just succeeded
in rendering his rooms completely uninhabitable, was obliged to
sleep with me, and set off again this morning for Winkfield.
Finding that I am not wanted in town, I expect to follow him
to-morrow, and remain there the few days longer that the rest of
the party stay.

LONDON, *Oct.* 18, 1820.

DEAR IRVING, — * * * * * * * * * * I have little to say
about myself since I last wrote. I am going on with my picture,* and now show it to whoever wishes to see it. I find the
subject pleases generally very much, and I am getting still more
interested in it myself. Newton tells me he has written to you.
I suppose he has told you to come back. If I were in your
place (as I am not aware of any important object you have in
staying abroad), I would consult only my inclinations, and not
endeavour to reconcile myself to an absence from England as a
matter of duty if I felt strongly the wish to return. With regard
to writing, I think you will always please yourself best where
you feel most at home. However, all advice of this kind
is most probably useless if not annoying, for we have always
motives for our plans, which cannot be fully understood by others.
I wish, however, you would let me know what is the probable
period of your absence. I feel lopsided without you.

The Americans are all highly pleased by the Edinburgh Review

* The May-day. — ED.

of the 'Sketch Book'; and no one that I have seen appears more gratified by it than the immortal Brockedon, who sends his very best regards to you.

Yours very truly,

C. R. LESLIE.

À MONSIEUR W. IRVING,
　　Aux soins de Messrs. WELLES et WILLIAMS,
　　　26, Rue Faubourg Poissonière,
　　　　à Paris.

PARIS, *Oct.* 31, 1820.

MY DEAR LESLIE, — I have received two letters from you, and ought to have replied long before this, but I have been out of the mood for letter-writing, and so have deferred it from day to day, and so time has run on. I now write in great haste, to avail myself of an opportunity free of expense. I have just received a very long and friendly letter from Mr. Murray, who in fact has overwhelmed me with eulogiums. It appears that my writings are selling well, and he is multiplying editions. I am very glad to find that he has made your acquaintance, and still more, that he has taken a great liking to you. He speaks of you in the most gratifying terms. He has it in his power to be of service to you, and I trust he will be. He tells me he has requested you to look over Knickerbocker for subjects for eight or ten sketches, and the Sketch Book for a couple, and he wishes me to assist you with my opinion on the subject. I will look over the books, and write to you in a day or two. Murray is going to make me so fine in print that I shall hardly know myself. Could not Allston's design be reduced without losing the characteristic humour of it? I am delighted to find that your labours are to be thus interwoven with mine, so that we shall have a kind of joint interest and pride in every volume.

My dear boy, it is a grievous thing to be separated from you, and I feel it more and more. I wish to heaven this world were not so wide, and that we could manage to keep more together in it — this continual separating from those we like is one of the curses of an unsettled life : and with all my vagrant habits I cannot get accustomed to it.

I am glad to hear that you are getting on with your picture, and that you are more and more pleased with it. Depend upon it, it is one of those pictures that will do you very essential service. It will give you a standing with men whose opiuions have great weight in society — men curious in literature and in antiquities. The picture will please them, as showing not merely technical skill, and the ordinary eye for the picturesque ; but as displaying research, mind, and strong literary feeling. It is a highly classical English subject. I hope you will follow it up by something in the same line ; the researches you have made for the picture will make you feel more at home in another. I feel a continual want to be with you and Newton, to see how you both get on.

I had a very acceptable letter from Willis a few days since. Tell him I will write to him soon, but I must first write to Peter Powell, to whom I am in debt. I have so many persons to write to in England and America, that being a very lazy letter-writer, it is but now and then I can bring a letter to bear upon each. Mr. Tappan who bears this letter, told me, that it was the wish of Fairman and yourself, that an engraving should be made from the likeness you have of me. It is a matter I do not feel so much objection to, as I did formerly, having been so much upon the town lately as to have lost much of my modesty. And as I understand, that there has been some spurious print of my phiz in America, I do not care if another is made to push it out of sight. You will only be careful to finish the picture so as not to give it too fixed and precise a fashion of dress. I preferred the costume of Newton's likeness of me, which was trimmed with fur. These modern dresses are apt to give a paltry commonplace air.

Give my love to all the lads, and believe me most affectionately yours, W. I.

P. S. I can give you no idea when I shall return to England. I have no plan on the subject.

PARIS, *Nov. 30th*, 1820.

My Dear Leslie, — I cannot let Mr. Marx depart without scrawling you a line. I hear that you are getting on with the sketches for Knickerbocker, and that you have executed one on

the same subject Allston once chose, viz: 'Peter Stuyvesant rebuking the Cobbler.' I wish you could drop me a line and let
me know what subjects you execute, and how you and Murray
make out together. I hear that you have taken the "Childe" to
Murray's; you have only to make him acquainted with Willis
and Peter Powell, and he will then be able to make one at your
tea-kettle debauches. I have just made a brief but very pleasant
excursion into Lower Normandy in company with Mr. Ritchie.
I must refer you to a letter scribbled to Peter Powell for a full
and faithful narrative of this tour. I have never been more
pleased with any tour that I have made. The little towns of
Lower Normandy seem to have been built and peopled with an
eye to the picturesque. The fine gothic churches, the old quaint
architecture of the private houses, the beauty of the common
people, particularly the peasantry, their peculiar costumes, all
form continual pictures. But I believe you will get a better
idea of them from the sketches of Lewis than from any description that I can furnish. By-the-bye, I saw the card of one of
the Lewises in the hands of a young man of the college at
Falaise, who accompanied me about the beautiful ruins of the
castle where William the Conqueror was born. He told me that
Lewis had taken several sketches of the castle; it certainly is a
most picturesque morsel of antiquity. I anticipate great pleasure
some future day in looking over Lewis's sketches again, and re-
calling some of the curious old buildings and streets of the Nor-
man towns.

I received a letter a few days since from Newton by Miss
Peat. She had been some time on the way to Paris, and the
letter was of an old date. I shall write to Newton the next opportunity, and likewise to Willis, to whom I am indebted for a
most agreeable letter. I find by the Lymans that the Sloane
Street romance * is still unfinished, and that materials are daily
springing up for another volume; that Jones has retired to either
a convent or a nailery in the neighborhood of Birmingham; and
that Newton is busy with a brush in each hand and his hair

---

* *Apropos* of Newton's escapades. The Ann referred to was a beautiful girl
with whom he was in love about this time. Poor Newton's normal state was
one of passionate *furore* for some beauty or other.

standing on end turning Ann's portraits into likenesses of Mary Queen of Scots, General Washington, and the Lord knows who; " there never was such times ! "

Let me hear from you often, and don't wait for my replies, as I am if possible more averse to letter-writing even than Allston. This is written in bed, which must account for its defects.

Paris, 1820.

My Dear Leslie, — I have been intending this long time past to write to you, and a good intention of long standing is a matter to boast of in this naughty world. How comes on your picture? I presume it is nearly finished. Did you call on Sir Walter Scott while he was in town, and ask him to look at it? If not, you have behaved shabbily. I presume before this you have seen Miss Foote; I intended to have written by her, but was occupied at the time, and let the opportunity slip unimproved. I have heard that you are to pass some months at Windsor, to copy several of Sir Peter Lely's pictures, for some lord or other. Is this the case? and if so when do you go there? It will be a charming situation for you during the summer months. Let me know who this lord is who has taken you into favour. I find by Newton's letter, that he and the old Euphuist, the *cidevant jeune homme* that haunts exhibitions, have become sworn friends. I presume the " Childe's " new fledged reputation will introduce him into a great deal of dilettante society, and that good company will come nigh to be the ruin of him. I have been sadly bothered with the same evil of late, and have had to fight shy of invitations that would exhaust time and spirits. The most interesting acquaintance I have made in Paris, is Moore the poet, who is very much to my taste. I see him almost every day, and feel as if I had known him for a lifetime. He is a noble-hearted, manly, spirited, little fellow, with a mind as generous as his fancy is brilliant. I hope you have better weather in London than we have in Paris. Such a spring! Nothing but rain in torrents; and cold boisterous winds. They may say what they please of London weather; I never passed a more dirty, rainy season in London than this last winter has been in Paris; and then the streets are so detestable in dirty weather, that there is no walking in them. My only consolation at such times is the vicinity of the Garden of the Tuileries, which is but a short distance from my lodgings; and which I consider as a park attached to my mansion — though I must own, I prefer my park of St. James' and Kensington Gardens — the latter particularly, as it has glorious lawns of green grass that I can roll on; whereas in the Tuileries, there is no place to rest, except one sit on a cursed cold stone bench; or pays two sous for a vile straw-bottomed chair. I am scrawling as fast as my pen can go, for I find it is near the time of closing the post-office, and I am determined this letter shall go by mail, though it cost me fifteen sous. I wish you would take pen in hand at once, and let me know how you are getting on with your picture, — what else you are about — when you go to Windsor — how long you stay there — who you are to paint the pictures for — what subject you have in view for your next painting — what Newton is doing — what Luke is doing, and what Peter Powell is doing? Answer these questions, and then you may add what you please. I have given you a scheme for a letter; when it is done do not wait for private hand, but send it per post: never mind the postage for once. I want exceedingly to hear from you — the sooner the better.

LONDON, *Dec.* 3, 1820.

DEAR IRVING, — I should have answered your letter sooner, but I hoped to have heard from you again on the subject of the designs for Mr. Murray. The subjects I have chosen are, a Dutch fire-side, with an old negro telling stories to the children; William the Testy, suspending a vagrant by the breeches on his patent gallows; Peter Stuyvesant confuting the Cobbler; and Anthony Van Corlear taking leave of the young vrows. All of these I have finished except the last, and Mr. Murray appears to be highly pleased with them.

He is delighted with Allston's picture of ' Wouter Van Twiller,' which will be engraved with the rest. He talks a great deal about you whenever I see him in terms of the highest praise and friendship. The ' Sketch Book ' is entirely out of print. I do not know whether you will be angry with me or approve what I am going to tell you. Collins, to whom I had lent the ' Sketch

Book,' observed that in the article of the ' Widow's Son ' a passage runs thus, " The service *being ended*, they proceeded to
lower the coffin into the grave." Now he remarked that the
coffin is always lowered into the grave *during* the service or
previous to it, for at the words " ashes to ashes, and dust to
dust" some earth is thrown in upon it. When he came to this passage he said it destroyed the illusion, for the story had taken the
strongest hold of his feelings, and he had been convinced that he
was reading an account of a real scene. I took the liberty therefore of suggesting to Mr. Murray to leave out these few words
" the service being ended," which without any other alteration
does away with the objection to the passage. I am afraid you
will be displeased with my meddling, which I should on no account have dared to do had not the alteration been so very small.
There was not time to write and hear from you, as the volume is
in press, and it is probable after all that the suggestion was too
late for the forthcoming edition.

I enjoyed very much the renewal of my acquaintance with my
old friend ' Diedrich.' I have the highest respect and admiration
for the old gentleman, which is certainly increased by my late intercourse with him, but I must say that in some of *his jokes* he
goes near to be thought a little indelicate. Now these jokes of
the old gentleman being *very few* and not among his best, I
really think he would not suffer by dispensing with them in future.
Forgive this remark if you do not agree with it. * * *

Peter Powell has composed an answer to the letter he expects
from you, and is afraid it won't keep much longer. Whenever
your plans are fixed let us know ; that is, if they tend towards
your return to London. We shall not be so anxious to hear of
any others. For my part I feel the loss of your society as much
as I did at first. You came to London just when I was losing
Allston, and I stood in need of an intimate friend of similar
tastes with my own. I not only owe to you some of the happiest social hours of my life, but you opened to me a new range
of observation in my own art, and a perception of qualities and
characters of things which painters do not always imbibe from
each other.

P. S. Newton, Willis, and Powell send their love. The "Childe" has finished his picture from Molière,* and has been drawing for some time at the Academy.

Remember me affectionately to your brother.

Paris, *Dec.* 19*th*, 1820.

My Dear Leslie, — I have just received yours of the 3rd. I like all the subjects that you have chosen for the designs, except that of William the Testy suspending the vagabond by the breeches. The circumstance is not of sufficient point or character in the history to be illustrated. Still it may have struck you in a different manner, and have afforded scope for humorous sketching. I had hoped to hear from Mr. Murray before this, and to have received a copy of 'Knickerbocker' and of the 'Sketch Book' you mention. I pointed him out a mode of forwarding books to me, but I presume he has been too much hurried to attend to it. When you hear of a private opportunity, I wish you would ask Mr. Murray for copies of the works, and send them to me. I received a letter from Peter Powell, in which he speaks of my portrait being in the engraver's hands, and that it is painted in the old Venetian costume. I hope you have not misunderstood my meaning, when I spoke about the costume in which I should like it to be painted. I believe I spoke something about the costume of Newton's portrait. I meant Newton's portrait of *me*, not of *himself.* If you recollect he painted me as if in some kind of overcoat, with a fur cape — a dress that had nothing in it remarkable, but which merely avoided any present fashion that might in a few years appear stupid. The Venetian dress which Newton painted himself in would have a fantastic appearance, and savour of affectation. If it is not too late, I should like to have the thing altered. Let the costume be simple and picturesque, but such a one as a gentleman might be supposed to wear occasionally at the present day. I only wanted you to avoid the edges and corners and angles with which a modern coat is so oddly and formally clipped out at the present day. ·

I have not the 'Sketch Book' at hand to refer to, so as to see

* The Lovers' Quarrel, from Le Dépit Amoureux. (Engraved.)

that the measure and melody of the sentence is not injured by the omission you mention in the story of the ' Widow and her Son.' I am very much obliged to you for the correction. When I look over ' Knickerbocker,' to prepare the new edition, I will attend to your hint about pruning any indelicate parts. As I have no plan fixed that points immediately to England, it is needless to say anything on the subject. Indeed, my chief care as yet must be to keep quiet, and endeavour to write something more for publication ; if I move about and shift my situation, I disturb my thoughts, unsettle my habits, and lose a great deal of time ; and if I lose much more time, I shall have the spectre of an empty purse haunting me. I am obliged, therefore, to pitch my tent for a time until I can make money enough to secure me from want for two or three years. The change from London to Paris deranged me completely. I am now getting into train again ; but a return to England would unsettle me again for a long time. I received not long since a most flattering invitation from Earl Spencer and his lady to pass the Christmas Holidays at their seat at Althorp. The invitation was forwarded by Mr. Rush, and was given in a manner peculiarly gratifying. If I were in England now, an invitation or two of this kind would make me a good-for-nothing gentlemanly fellow for a month. I understand you have introduced Newton to Mr. Mackay.* He and the " Childe " will like each other. Tell Peter Powell I cannot answer his letter until I have answered one which I received from Willis an age ago. I hope Newton will commence another picture soon, otherwise he will stand a chance of falling into the hands of the ———, or some other pretty girls, and paint himself into a scrape again. Powell speaks of some fine portrait which he has painted of a gentleman, and which is considered his *chef d'œuvre*, but does not say whose portrait it is. I hope it is some one of consequence that may get him into notice.

Give my hearty regards to Newton, Willis, Powell, the Bollmans, the Hoffmans, and all our little circle of intimates. My brother desires likewise to be particularly remembered.

Yours ever,   W. I.

* Author of a very learned book on the ' Progress of the Intellect in relation to Religious Belief ' — a great friend of Leslie's. — ED.

MY DEAR IRVING, — I received yesterday yours of the 19th, and hasten to relieve your mind from any apprehension you may entertain with regard to the costume of your portrait, which is still in my room, exactly in the state in which you last saw it. I shall finish it in a day or two, strictly according to your wishes. The Venetian dress was only a phantom of Peter Powell's imagination, conjured up to disturb your evening dreams.

I called on Mr. Murray yesterday, (who seems to be up to the ears in business), and told him of the opportunities of sending anything to you. My officiously suggested alteration in ' The Widow's Son,' was too late to be introduced into the new edition, which is of a small octavo size and very handsome. Perhaps, as you say, it might have injured the melody of the sentence, and I now see that I was wrong in taking such a liberty.

, The reason I chose the subject of ' William Kieft's Gallows,' was that Mr. Murray wished one design at least from the reign of each governor, and I was a little puzzled in finding one that could be brought within a small compass, from that part of the book. I was somewhat fearful of it myself, but Newton thinks you would like it. Mr. Murray appeared pleased with it ; I will however mention your objection to it, and if he agrees with you I will take something else from the same reign.

It was at Mr. Murray's own request that I introduced Newton to him. The portrait by Newton, that Powell eulogised so highly, is Peter himself ; it is less than life, and perhaps the best, as to likeness, the " Childe " has painted. We had heard a rumour of Earl Spencer's invitation to you, and were very glad to find it confirmed by your letter. Miller says Geoffrey Crayon is the most fashionable fellow of the day. I am very much inclined to think if you were here just now, " company would be the spoil of you." I am very glad to hear you talk of writing. You can be at no loss for subjects where you are ; indeed, I should think your principal difficulty will be to determine what you shall *not* write about. Miller told me of your brother's concern in the steam-boat establishment, which I should think likely to answer his best expectations. Remember me most cordially to him.

All the lads join in wishing you both a merry Christmas and happy new year. I intended appropriating a part of to-morrow to reading your Christmas article. I shall stick up your portrait before my face, and bury myself in an enormous elbow chair I have got, over which "Murphy often sheds his puppies," relying on the book I shall hold in my hand to act as a charm against the seductions of the seat. These associations are the best means by which I can console myself for your absence. I received the drawings safe by Mr. Marx.

1821.

Pictures of the Year.

MAY DAY REVELS IN THE TIME OF QUEEN ELIZABETH.

" The characters in the May Games consisted of Robin Hood, Maid Marian, Friar Tuck, &c. with a hobbyhorse, fool, and dragon. Among the figures in the foreground of the picture, the antiquated beau in the centre, and the old lady on the right hand, are intended as illustrations of some of the fopperies of that age. The latter is followed by two blue-coated serving-men, and a domestic fool.

' At Paske began our Morrice, and ere Penticost our May,
Then Robin Hood, liell John, Friar Tuck and Marian deftly play,
And Lord and Ladie gang till Kirke with lads and lasses gay.' "
— *Warner's Albion's England*, Chap. xxiv. (From R. A. Catalogue, 1821.)

(Exhibited and Engraved, and now in the possession of John Naylor, Esq., Leighton Hall.)

A finished study of ' The May-day ' was painted for Alaric A. Watts, and sold this year at Christie and Manson's.

REBECCA, from Ivanhoe. (Painted for the Marquis of Lansdowne.) — PORTRAITS OF MRS. FRY AND SAMUEL GURNEY. — A CHILD IN A CARDINAL'S DRESS.

This year Washington Irving returned from Paris, to Edgbaston Castle, the seat of his brother-in-law, Mr. Van Wart, where Leslie paid him a visit. Irving was now in bad health, and Leslie, full of solicitude for his friend, was anxious he should come up to London for the best medical advice. Irving's letters show the playfulness of the writer, even under severe suffering; and the correspondence on both sides illustrates the strong attachment of Leslie, Irving, and their " set." The " Childe " is G. S. Newton, now in the rapid development of his great but short-lived power, and materially influencing the colour of Leslie, as is apparent from a comparison of his earlier with his later pictures, when Constable's white chalk had got the better of him. " Father Luke " is Willis, an Irishman, and a landscape painter ; so christened after the jovial Friar in O'Keefe's 'Poor Soldier.'   In the course of this year, Leslie was elected an Associate of the Royal Academy. His ' May Day ' * won him great honour at the year's Exhibition, and with good reason, for it is one of the most inventive, brilliant, and pleasant of his pictures. This picture procured him the pleasure of Scott's acquaintance. The fine engraving from it by Watt, is, no doubt, familiar to most of my readers. It would appear from passages in some of Leslie's letters, that Leslie had it in contemplation to paint a companion picture of English Christmas Revels, but he never carried out the intention. One can perfectly understand Scott's relish of the ' May Day.' It must have been a picture after his own heart, full as it is of old-world rustic manners and merriment, and all astir with the wholesome, fresh, sunshiny, out-door life of the "Merry England," we are all fain to believe in.

LONDON, *April 2nd*, 1821.

IT was a great disappointment to me to hear from Miss Foote that you intend staying abroad all summer ; for I had somehow or other settled it in my mind that we should have had you over with the fine weather, though it is true your letters gave me no reason to think so. Blue-green fair and even Greenwich and Fairlop will lose half their charms for me without you. At Greenwich it is true we shall have Peter Powell, who has taken the attic of a cottage there for the summer ; but there is some danger that Peter will set up a booth for the exhibition of his old women, or else gallant that imaginary bear or flock of sheep through the crowd ;† and if so we shall have but little good of him.

I am now within a week of finishing my ' May Day.' Sir Walter Scott came to see it, and nothing could be more gratifying

---

* See my Introductory Essay.

† Alluding to Peter Powell's Drawing-room Entertainments, described in the Autobiography.

than the opinion he expressed. He said he would come again to see it, and wanted to know where 'Sir Roger'* was that he might pay him a visit. His manner was particularly kind and friendly. He talked a great deal about you, and requested me when I wrote to give you his most affectionate regards. Sir Walter is sitting to Lawrence, which I am very glad of, as we shall now have a more intellectual portrait of him than any of the others. Most of the drawings from 'Knickerbocker' are with the engravers. There is little hope of their being done however before Christmas. I made a more finished one from the sketch of Rip Van Winkle you sent me, with which Murray was much pleased, and am now doing another of Ichabod Crane teaching Katrina to sing, which is the last I am to do for him.

The *Childe* has made a very brilliant little sketch from Molière of a genteel love quarrel. A lady and gentleman returning miniatures, letters, &c., &c. — the lady's maid tittering behind the chair of her mistress. It promises to be his best picture. Martin's picture of ' Belshazzar's Feast ' has gained him great reputation. He has sold it, and received a commission from the Marquis of Buckingham to paint the ' Destruction of Herculaneum,' a very fine subject for him. I find I am writing about nothing but pictures to you, but I have an impression that the *Childe* has written very lately, and has told you whatever other news has occurred in our circle. Remember me most affectionately to your brother.   Yours truly,

C. R. Leslie.

Washington Irving, Esq.,
      Paris.

London, *April 20th*, 1821.

Dear Betsey, — * * * Until within the last fortnight I have been closely engaged with my picture of ' May Day,' which is at last finished and sent to Somerset House. My friends are sanguine as to its success, and I myself consider it the best thing I have done. Did I tell you the purpose for which it is painted? It is for a print; and I am to have two hundred guineas for it, with the privilege of selling it, if I can, for a still higher price, and re-

* The picture of Sir Roger de Coverley going to Church.

ceiving the difference, under the condition of the purchaser's allowing the engraving to be taken either from it or from a copy. Sir
Walter Scott has been lately in London, and came twice to see it
when in progress : the first visit I had taken the liberty to request,
but the second, which you may believe gratified me not a little,
was of his own proposing. He found fault with nothing in my
picture, but suggested the introduction of a few archers, a hint of
which I took advantage. His hearty kindness of manner is peculiarly delightful.

The first day he called, I was so intoxicated with delight by an
honour which, though I had solicited, I scarcely expected, knowing how fully he was engaged, that I could not paint for the remainder of the day. Sir Thomas Lawrence has painted an
inimitable head of him. I am extremely obliged by your candid,
and as I feel them to be very just, remarks on my defects in
colour, chiaroscuro, &c., which, be assured, I shall spare no pains
to correct as much as possible, though in these important points,
I have little hope of ever excelling, least of all in colour, for
which I am afraid I have not a good natural eye.   ·

LONDON, *May* 25, 1821.

MY DEAR IRVING, — I received some time ago the letter you
enclosed in a packet to Newton, and should have answered it
sooner but for various reasons, the principal and best one an utter
distaste to letter-writing, even to you. I have little to say, for
we are all rather dull at present and miss you more than ever. ·

· My picture has been as successful with the public as my most
sanguine friends could have anticipated. It is very well placed,
but I have lately been seeing such fine things of the old masters
at the private galleries, that I am quite out of conceit of it myself. The more I see of the Dutch School, the more I venerate
them, and the more hopeless appears the chance of ever coming
near them. One of the greatest treats I ever had, was lately at
Mr. Hope's Gallery, who has the finest collection in London.
There is a very good exhibition open at the British Gallery of
the old masters. I have not yet been able to think of another
subject; can you help me to one? Mr. Murray wants me to
paint him a picture. He would have bought the ' May Day,' but

it is too large for his room.   The plates for your works are all in the hands of the engravers.

Newton is copying his picture of the ' Importunate 'Author ' for the Earl of Carlisle. · Peter Coxe has volunteered to sit for the poet.   Luke's doings are at present with *closed doors*, enveloped in mystery.

Peter Powell is enjoying the rainy weather at Greenwich. We have heard that you are getting to like Paris, and that you intend spending the summer in Normandy.

The exhibition this year is a very good one, Lawrence has sent his best portraits.   Wilkie has a beautiful little interior. The subject he calls ' Guess my Name.'   There is a fine buxom lass running into the room (which is the inside of a cottage) and blinding the eyes of a young man who sits at the table writing a letter.   The effect of the sun shining into the window is quite magical.   Mulready has a very clever picture of a girl just about to thrash a boy who has been sent of an errand and is playing at marbles.   He has set down a young child and a pound of candles, and both are melting in the sun.

Young Landseer has a most exquisite picture of dogs hunting rats with a ferret, full of expression.   Etty's ' Cleopatra ' is a splendid triumph of colour.   It has some defects of composition, but is full of passages of that exquisite kind of beauty, which he alone can give.

All our clan unite with me in love to you and your brother.

Ever yours,   C. R. LESLIE.

WASHINGTON IRVING,
Paris.

FROM WASHINGTON IRVING.

EDGBASTON CASTLE, *Oct. 9th*, 1821.

MY DEAR LESLIE, — I have been looking for a letter from you every day.   Why don't you drop me a line?   It would be particularly cheering just now.   I have not been out of the house since you left here; having been much indisposed by a cold, I am at the mercy of every breath of air that blows.   I have had pains in my head, my face swollen, and yesterday

passed the greater part of the day in bed, which is a very·extra-
ordinary thing for me. To-day I feel better; but I am sadly out
of order, and what especially annoys me is that I see day after
day and week after week passing away without being able to do
anything. The little folks lament your departure extremely.
George has made his appearance in a new pair of Grimaldi
breèches, with pockets full as deep as the former. To balance
his ball and marbles he has the opposite pocket filled with a peg-
top and a prodigious quantity of dry peas, so that he can only lie
comfortably on his back or his belly. The three eldest boys kept
the house in misery for two or three days by pea-blowers, which
they had bought, at an enormous price, of a tin-man. They at
last broke the blowers, and George pocketed the peas. He says
he means to take care of them till his brothers come home at
Christmas. Have you begun any new picture yet, or, have you
any immediately in contemplation? I received a letter from
Newton, which I presume was forwarded by your direction.
Why did you not open it? It was dated the 15th September.
Ilc had arrived but two or three days; had sailed up the Seine
from Havre to Rouen, with my brothers in the steam-boat. He
had dined with Morse; had passed a day in the Louvre, where
he met Wilkie, and strolled the gallery with him. He speaks in
raptures of the Louvre. He says it strikes him in quite a different way from what it did when he was there before. He intended
to go to work a day or two afterwards, and expected to pass the
greater part of his time there.

Have you seen Murray? When you see him you need not
say where I am. I want the quiet and not to be bothered in any
way. Tell him I am in a country doctor's hands, at Edgbaston,
somewhere in Warwickshire. I think that will puzzle any one,
as Edgbaston has been built only within a year or two. Gₑᵥ‘ me
all the pleasant news you can, and then sit down in the evening
and scribble a letter, without minding points or fine terms. My
sister is very anxious to hear of you. You have quite won her
heart, not so much by your merits, as by your attention to the
children. By the way, the little girls have become very fond of
the pencil since you were here, and are continually taking their
dolls' likenesses.   Ever yours,   W. I.

The following joint letter from Leslie and his quaint little friend and present chum, Peter Powell, gives a pleasant peep into their cheerful, innocent, scrambling student life : —

LONDON, *Oct. 22nd*, 1821.

MY DEAR IRVING, — I should have replied to your letter of the 7th immediately, but as I had written to you the day before I received it, I thought by waiting a few days I might have an answer to that to reply to at the same time. I hope you have now weathered out the severe attack you have had. I regretted very much when I found you had been so ill, that I had not stayed *a* week longer at Birmingham. If I did not know that there may be many causes beside sickness for your delaying to write to me, I should now be in great anxiety from not having received an answer to my letter. I hope, however, you will write immediately to let us know how you are. If you are too busy, or not in the mood to send a regular letter, a single line will do. Powell and I commenced housekeeping a week ago. It is probable that nothing will more astonish you on your return than the metamorphosis at Buckingham Place. Not to speak of window curtains, a pianoforte, *small knives* and plates at breakfast, you will be surprised to find an *academy* established on the principle of mutual education in various branches of learning and the fine arts. During breakfast Powell gives me a lesson in French. At five we both study carving. After tea I teach him to draw the figures, and at odd times he instructs himself in German and the pianoforte, and once a week he unfolds to me the mysteries of political economy according to Cobbett. Instruction is even extended beyond our walls, as far indeed as Sloane Street, where Powell delivers a weekly lecture on perspective. In this way we pass the time ; and I am quite sure that if I get through the winter as I have passed the last week, and with you and Newton here, it will be the most agreeable one I shall have spent in London. I was glad to hear of Newton from you. I did not see his letter or I should have opened it. I am at present painting the portraits of two little girls, and making a drawing from the 'Royal Poet,' the incident of the dove flying into the window.*

* From Irving's ' Sketch Book.'

Powell has promised to fill up the sheet, I must therefore bid you
good-bye. Luke is well, and sends his love to you. I have not
yet seen Mr. Murray. I was very much diverted with your
account of George.

Yours ever,

C. R. LESLIE.

P. S. I know not that it is in *my* power to add much to the
description my affectionate chum has given of our perfect happiness, except that by a new philosophical arrangement of mine,
long legs have been prohibited from engrossing the whole of the
fireplace, and *little* legs stand·a much greater chance than fòrmerly
of getting their shins warmed, and much less of getting them
kicked. The simple means by which I have effected this is truly
admirable, but I.apprehend that a much˙more elaborate and
powerful apparatus will be hereafter required, when the *Leggi*
become accumulated. The Newton alone will demand a great
mechanical power to move. I am beginning to be ashamed of
the prejudices I had imbibed about Buckingham Place. All prejudices are hateful, and people ought to live in every spot they
do not like, in order to ascertain whether their opinions are well
or ill-founded. There are many charms about this place, the
enjoyment of which I never contemplated. While I am now
writing, in addition to the enjoyment of my tea and rolls, a sort
of troubadour is warbling beneath my window, together with the
partner of his bosom and a little natural production between both,
equally regardless of fame and weather, and seemingly smitten
only by the love of halfpence — the pleasure of getting which in
this neighbourhood must, I suppose, like that of angling, be
greatly increased by the rarity of the bite. Those things about
us here, that to the common view appear disagreeable, tend to
increase our happiness. The repose and quiet of our evening
talk or studies is rendered still more so by its contrast with a
matrimonial squabble in the street, or the undisguised acknowledgment of pain in the vociferations of a whipped urchin up the
Court. We are also much more pastoral here than you would
imagine.

We have a *share* in a *cow*, which makes its appearance twice a day in a blue and white *cream*-jug. We eat our own dinners! and *generally* have enough. Yesterday, to be sure, we came a little short, in consequence of Leslie (who acts as *maître d'hôtel*) having ordered a sumptuous hash to be made from a cold shoulder of lamb, the meat of which had been previously stripped from it with surgical dexterity by our host himself during the three preceding days. There have been a great many disputes in all ages about the real situation of Paradise. I have not, to be sure, read all the arguments upon the subject; but if I were to go entirely by my own judgment, I should guess it to be somewhere near the corner of Cambridge Court, Fitzroy Square.

Adieu, and increased health to you.

Yours, &c., &c., &c.,

P. P.

WASHINGTON IRVING, ESQ.,
Birmingham.

EDGBASTON, *Oct.* 25, 1821.

MY DEAR LESLIE, — I thank you a thousand times for your letter. I had intended to have answered your preceding one before; but I am not in mood or condition to write, and had nothing to say worth writing. I am still in the hands of the physician. I have taken draughts and pills enough to kill a horse, yet I cannot determine whether I am not rather worse off than when I began.

On one favourable day of my complaint I rode over to Solihull in a gig to see the boys. I went in a gig with Van Wart and our worthy little friend, George. I wished you with us a dozen times. You would have been delighted with the school-house and the village, and the beautiful old church, and the surrounding landscape. It is all picture. When you are here again you must by all means visit the boys at school. The young rogues are as hearty and happy as ever schoolboys were. They took us about their walks, and the scenes of their enterprises and expeditions; the neighbouring park, and several charming fields and green lanes. The morning's ramble ended at the shop of one of the best old women in the world, who sells cakes and tarts to all the schoolboys. Here they all spoiled their dinners, and nearly ruined their papa; and George, with a citizen-like munificence, having eaten till he was fairly tired, distributed sundry cakes at the door to some of the poor children of the village. I have no doubt that he has left a most excellent name behind him. The little girls talk of you very often, and wish you here. They always wish to know whether you do not mention them in your letters, and beg that I will give their love to you. I am babbling about nothing but children; but, in truth, they are my chief company and amusement at present, and I have little else to talk about.

I cannot at this moment suggest anything for your Christmas piece. I do not know your general plan. Is it to be a daylight piece, or an evening round a hall fire? Is there no news of Newton? If I had thought he would remain so long at Paris I would have written to him. I am glad to hear that you are so snugly fixed with friend Powell for the winter, though I should have been much better pleased to have heard that you were turned neck and heels into the street. Reconcile it to yourself as you may, I shall ever look upon your present residence as a most serious detriment to you; and were you to lose six or even twelve months in looking for another, I should think you a gainer upon the whole.

What prospects are there of the plates being finished for 'Knickerbocker' and the 'Sketch Book'? When do you begin a large picture, and what subject do you attack first? It is time you had something under weigh. I must leave a space to reply to friend Peter, so farewell for the present.

Yours, ever,

W. I.

EDGBASTON, Nov. 2, 1821.

MY DEAR LESLIE, — I wish to heaven you would drop me a line now and then, and give me all the chit-chat you can to cheer and interest me. It would be charity just now, when I am shut up from the world, and suffering in health and spirits. I have dismal letters from America. My sister has lost two of her daughters by sudden and brief illness; the last, her eldest, a fine girl of seventeen. These distresses have affected her own health.

There are no hopes entertained of my brother William's recovery. I received letters yesterday that gave these accounts, and have quenched every spark of animation or cheerfulness in me. I am still preyed upon by this tedious complaint, and find the eruption on my legs worse than ever, while the general tone of my system is relaxed and enervated by this nursing and confinement. I have now given you reasons enough why I cannot write often to you; but why you should write occasionally to me. I have no news to give, and no cheerful feelings to write from. You are in London where everything is news, and can tell me of your own occupations, which are always interesting to me. I want you, therefore, to give me a more gossipping letter. Tell me what news there is of Newton, and when he is expected back. I am surprised at his remaining so long at Paris, since he says he is tired of it.

What pictures are you about?. What one do you intend to paint for the exhibition? Have you done anything to Sir Roger? Do you intend to attack the Christmas piece, and what is your plan; is it to be a fire-side piece or not? Do you think of the Shakespeare subjects? One of these ought to be your choice in preference to the 'Heiress' for your next subject. I do not think the 'Heiress' would be striking enough, at least it has never struck me as being calculated to bring out your powers in any force.

What is Luke doing? Has he any promising subject in hand? I hope you and Peter * are getting comfortably through the honeymoon, and find housekeeping pleasant. I only fear that your not being obliged to go out for your dinner will make you take less exercise than before, and your health will suffer. My own case is a proof how one really loses by overwriting oneself, and keeping too intent upon a sedentary occupation. I attribute all my present indisposition, which is losing me time, spirits, every-thing, to two fits of close application, and neglect of all exercise, while I was at Paris. I am convinced that he who devotes two hours each day to vigorous exercise, will eventually gain those two and a couple more into the bargain.

* Peter Powell.

16

LONDON, *Nov.* 5, 1821.

MY DEAR IRVING, — I was extremely grieved at hearing such bad accounts from you. I hope I need not assure you how much I partake of all your sorrows. I only wish it were possible by so doing to lighten them. I had hoped by this time to have heard of your recovery. Are you sure that you have the best medical advice? In every other respect you must be more comfortable where you are than you could be anywhere else. Jones says there are excellent physicians at Birmingham; and Charles Williams speaks of a Dr. Frere who is very eminent. Mr. Van Wart, however, must be the best judge. Newton tells me he has written to you. The poor fellow has met with a severe blow in the loss of his mother, whose death he heard of the night of his arrival in London. I saw Moore at Newton's; he lately passed through Birmingham, and was very sorry he did not know you were there. Moore is extricated from all his pecuniary difficulties, and has sold his ' Life of Lord Byron ' to Murray for *two thousand guineas ;* the contract was signed by them on Saturday* at Newton's room. Moore expresses the warmest interest in your welfare. Newton has improved my sketch of Paul Veronese wonderfully; it is now invaluable to us as a study of colouring.

Powell and I suit each other extremely well; I do not find that I take less exercise than I used to do. I have painted two portraits since my return, and have made a drawing from the ' Royal Poet ' which I shall show Murray in a day or two. Notwithstanding your objections to my ' Heiress,' I *must* paint it. I have not yet sufficiently made up my mind about a large picture, and it will not do to engage in one prematurely. Don't dissuade me from painting the ' Heiress,' for you will only damp me and prevent my doing it as well as I otherwise should. I do not expect to make a very important picture of it, but it is a commission, and will not take me very long.* Besides, I mean to make it *pay* well.

I went the other day with Peter to see an exhibition of spar-

* He *did* paint it, but not till 1845, for E. Bicknell, Esq., in whose gallery, at Hearne Hill, it now hangs.

ring at ' Fives Court,' and was very much amused. I wished for you, for who should I meet at the door in capacity of check-taker, but our friend the free-and-easy writer at the ' Gipsey House.' *
He turns out to be a bruiser, who at the time we saw him there was in training to fight a pitched battle; so that it is lucky for us we did not take umbrage at his familiarity. He has fought twice, and though beaten both times is considered a " very game man." Among the crowd in the court were two heroes, " Belasco the Jew " and another (whose name I have forgotten), who had fought each other the day before at Moulsey. Belasco has won, though they were both in most woeful plight. Their heads had become too large for their hats, which were balanced on the top of a large bandage of Belcher handkerchief that obscured an eye and cheek of each of them, and it was difficult to imagine the invisible half of their faces to be in worse trim than that which was seen, which shone resplendent with the high polish produced by swelling, exhibiting all the hues of the rainbow. One could not open, nor the other shut his mouth. The bruised carcases of these " knights of the rueful countenance " were enveloped in *wrap-rascals*, in which they moved about stiffly, and occasionally sat down with all the cautiousness of men in whom the sense of touch was delicately alive. Belasco's friends were gathered round him, making up a match for him to fight somebody else as soon as he was well; and the admirers of the other were comforting him by showing him where he had made the grand mistake, and how he might have gained the battle on the preceding day.

Luke is very well, he will write to you soon and speak for himself. He intends painting a large view of Greenwich Hospital, Park, &c. from the hill, where you may recollect his rolling his purse overboard one fine summer day. The " Childe " has begun a portrait of Moore, which will be very like. Murray intends having his picture of you engraved.

Give my love to the " *wee things* " at Edgbaston, and let me know from time to time how the *Citizen* does, and what progress the little ladies are making in the fine arts, and whether Washington still regards your flute with that look of unutterable veneration

---

* Referring to some of their suburban fair experiences.

with which he used to turn up his eyes to it, whether in your
hands or quietly reposing on the top of the bookcase. Write us
a bulletin every day or two of the state of your health. A single
line *will do*, but as much more as you please.   ·

Yours ever,

C. R. LESLIE.

WASHINGTON IRVING, ESQ.,
Birmingham

FROM WASHINGTON IRVING.

EDGBASTON, *Nov.* 8, 1821.

MY DEAR LESLIE, — I congratulate you with all my soul on
your admission to the Royal Academy, of which friend Luke has
just given me the tidings. It is no more than what you have long
deserved, but it is not always that a man gets what he deserves.
I did not mean to undervalue your study of the ' Heiress,' only
in comparison with the other subjects you had in contemplation.
The others are uncommonly rich and striking, and fittest to draw
out your peculiar powers in delineating character, costume, &c.,
&c. I have no doubt but you will make a very excellent thing
of the ' Heiress,' and the landscape that you sketched at Haddon
Hall will enrich it, and give it architectural interest, and picturesque associations.

By-the-by, whenever you want to gather a little information
about Haddon Hall, you will find a description of it with a plate
or two in the sixth volume of the Archæologia. You will find
that work a mine of antiquarian knowledge, and curious facts as
to customs, architecture, dress, &c. It is in many quarto volumes
by the Antiquarian Society. In the ninth and tenth volumes of
the ' Censura Literaria ' are elaborate disquisitions on hawking
and hunting by Hazlewood.   .

Your letter of the 5th was most acceptable and gratifying, and
I thank you for a vast deal of amusement afforded me by the
description of the ' Milling School.' I think Willis has pitched
upon a famous good thing in his contemplated picture ; depend
upon it he will gain himself both honour and profit by it. If he

succeeds, as I am convinced he will, I would advise him to make a companion to it in a view of Paris from one of the neighbouring hills.

As to my medical advices, I have had the advice of one of the best surgeons here, a skilful man; I fear however, I shall be a long time getting rid of this complaint. The Citizen * has been unwell from a cold, but is getting better. He has lately become something of a theologian, and has taken a great notion to talk about the Deity, and asks many very odd questions. I heard him instructing his little sisters the other day on the subject, and assuring them, among other things, "that nothing could hurt God," "a horse could not bite him." He tells me long stories every evening as we lie on the sofa together. They however all turn upon the same things — the adventures of two little girls, who walk in a wood where they are chased by a "savage cart horse" until they run into a gentleman's house, where they have a fine supper, and in setting out the supper-table the Citizen generally exhausts his fancy and the residue of his short evening. All the children talk about you continually, and Marianne begs her mamma, when she writes to you, to tell you that if you don't come to Birmingham, she will come after you to London.

God bless you, my dear Leslie.

Yours ever,

W. I.

LONDON, *Dec.* 5, 1821.

MY DEAR IRVING, — I should have written to you before, but we have been every day expecting to see you for some time past. I am afraid Newton's bed-room would be too small for you to sit in, and in his sitting-room you would be constantly exposed to interruptions from his visitors. I will look about to-morrow to see if I can find anything that I think will suit you, and write you a description of what I see and the terms, without entering into any engagement. I hope you will make up your mind to come to London before the weather gets too cold. I am afraid from the continuance of your complaint you have not good medical advice; here you may have the best. I think if we had you among us

* One of his little nephews so nicknamed.

here we could cheer you up a little, and the change of scene would help to lighten in some degree the heavy affliction you have suffered.

I cannot give a very good account of myself since I last wrote, for I have not yet begun my picture. I found the truth of your remark, that success may sometimes check a man's exertions as well as disappointment. My election threw me out a little. In the first place I had forty visits to pay to the Academicians; in the next I had to attend a council and hear a speech from Sir Thomas, and receive my diploma, and after that to make my appearance among the members at the lectures. I have now got through these ceremonies, and am getting to work again. I find this event has given me a fresh stock of spirits, and I even think of health.

Since writing the above it has occurred to us, that if no other suitable lodgings are to be had, we can make you comfortable (for a short time at least) *here*. Don't start — it is even so. Powell's sitting-room can be made as warm as you please, and you have no idea of the improvement in its appearance since the introduction of window curtains, &c. My advice is, therefore, that you set off, the first fine day, for London, without taking a thought of what is to become of you here — and I am very much mistaken if we can't among us make you comfortable; at least till we can find you suitable apartments to write in.

Yours ever.
C. R. Leslie.

Edgbaston, Dec. 8th, 1821.

My Dear Leslie, — I feel most sensibly the kindness of your letter, which, however, is just like yourself — full of goodness.

I should feel tempted to come to London at once, and to try how I could make out at Newton's quarters, which, upon the whole, I think would best suit me ; but at present it is out of my power.

Everything is done here to make me comfortable ; my good sister almost makes a child of me.

I hope to hear of your getting under weigh with another painting soon; and trust that the good spirits and good health you have picked up will enable you to dispatch the thing with spirit and expedition.

You do not say how the engravings are going on for the new editions of my works, nor whether you have shown Murray your last sketch.

Give my hearty thanks to our worthy friend Powell for the kind offer of his room. I long to be among you all once more. I think a few tea drinkings with the old set would be of great service to me. But the physicians have got hold of me, and I am no longer my own man. I have kept clear of them all my life till now; and now they have got me in their clutches. I fear they will make 'worms' meat' of me before they let me go again.

God bless you, my dear boy.

P. S. — Let me hear from you now and then, for your letters are better than medicine to me. How does Newton come on ? I suppose he has nearly finished his 'Lovers' Quarrels,' and is ready for something else. He must have his mind in good tune for composition after his visit to Paris. I will write to him when next I write. I feel very deeply his kindness with respect to his rooms. Indeed, I feel towards you all more than it is necessary to express. You are often the theme of conversation with them and the children, and I can assure you that a visit from you at any time would be quite a jubilee in the household. "

1822.

Exhibited Picture of the Year.

THE RIVALS.* (Painted for Sir Matthew White Ridley. Engraved by Finden, and lithographed by R. T. Lane, A.R.A.)

DURING the year, Irving was once more on the continent in quest of health. He travelled through Germany in the course of the summer, and writes to Leslie in December from Dresden.

---

* This picture was Exhibited at Manchester in 1857, by its then possessor, E. Rodgett, Esq. There is a small repetition of it, with some variations, in the possession of Edwin Bullock, Esq., of Handsworth, near Birmingham.

FROM WASHINGTON IRVING.

DRESDEN, *Dec. 2nd*, 1822.

MY DEAR LESLIE, — I wrote to Newton from Munich, and
had hoped before this to have had a reply; but have been disappointed. I am very anxious to hear from you all, and to know
what you are still doing. For my part, my whole summer has
been devoted to travelling, gazing about, and endeavouring to acquire a good state of health, in which latter I am happy to say I
have in a great measure succeeded. By dint of bathing, and a
little attention to diet, I have conquered the malady that so long
rendered me almost a cripple; and the exercise, change of air,
and refreshment of spirits incident to travelling, have operated
most favourably on my general health. Since I wrote to Newton, I have been among the Salzbourg Mountains: then by the
way of Linz to Vienna, where I remained nearly a month; then
through part of Moravia and Bohemia, stopping a few days at
the fine old city of Prague, to this place, where I mean to winter.
How I should have liked to have you as a travelling companion
throughout my summer's tour. You would have found continual
exercise for the pencil, and objects of gratification and improvement in the noble galleries that abound in the principal German
cities. I shall now take a master and go to work to study German. If I can get my pen to work, so much the better; but it
has been so long idle that I fear it will take some time to get it
in a working mood. I hope you have made some more designs
for my works, and that the engravings are finished of those that
were in hand. Take care to get for me 'Allston's design for the
' Judgment of Wouter Van Twiller;' and endeavour, if possible,
to get all the originals into your hands. How do you come on in
housekeeping? Have you got to new and comfortable quarters?
How often have I thought of you in exploring some of these old
German towns, where you might have a wing of a deserted
palace almost for nothing. Such glorious painting rooms, that
might be blocked up or pulled to pieces at your humour! The
living in fact is wonderfully cheap in many of the finest cities of
Germany. In Dresden, for example, I have a very neat, com-

fortable, and prettily furnished apartment on the first floor of an hotel; it consists of a cabinet, with a bed in it, and a cheerful sitting room that looks on the finest square. I am offered this apartment for the winter at the rate of thirty-six shillings a month. Would to heaven I could get such quarters in London for anything like the money. I shall probably remain here until the spring opens, as this is one of the pleasantest winter residences, and peculiarly favourable for the study of the German language, which is here spoken in its purity. Which way I shall direct my wanderings when I leave this I cannot say; I find it is useless to project plans of tours, as I seldom follow them, but am apt to be driven completely out of my course by whim or circumstance. Do write to me, and direct your letters, " Poste restante, Dresden." Let me hear all the news you can collect of our acquaintances, and tell me what you are all doing. Have the Bollmans left Paris and returned to America? How goes on Luke's picture of Greenwich? I presume it is nearly finished. What subjects have you on hand, or what on view, &c., &c.? I sent you word in my letter to Newton that I wished you, when the plates illustrating my works were published, to get some sets from Murray for me, and send them to Mr Van Wart, to be forwarded to my brother in America — one set to be given to Mr. Brevoort of New York. I find by a letter from my brother, that he met with that worthy personage, Mr. Peter Powell, at Rouen, and that they had a world of pleasant conversation together.

Farewell, my dear boy.

Give my hearty rememberance to the " Childe," Father Luke, and all the rest of the fraternity; not forgetting my excellent and worthy friend Peter Powell.   Yours ever,   W. I.

I am unable to give any precise particulars as to Leslie's work this year, having no letters of the year to his sisters. But he was certainly engaged on a picture from ' Winter's Tale,' I presume the ' Autolycus,' afterwards painted for Mr. Sheepshanks, and now in the National Gallery at South Kensington; and he may have already commenced his studies for his exquisite picture of ' Sancho in the Apartment of the Duchess,' now at Petworth.

1823.

LESLIE's name does not appear in the Academy catalogue for this year. He was at work on his picture of 'Sir Roger de Coverley and the Gipsies,' but was unable to finish it to his mind. Irving, still at Dresden, writes to him.

(March 15th, 1853.)

I HAVE just been seized with a fit of letter writing, after having nearly forgotten how to use my pen, so I take the earliest stage of the complaint to scribble to you. I had hoped to receive a gratuitous letter from you before this, but you are one of those close codgers who never pay more than the law compels them. I am extremely sorry to hear from Newton that he has been so ill, — though I am by no means surprised at it, as he played all kinds of vagaries with a constitution naturally delicate. I trust this fit of illness will teach him the necessity of daily and regular attention to exercise and diet; which all the advice in the world will not beat into a young man's head.

There is more time lost by these daily attempts to gain time than by anything else; and he who will endeavour to cheat his health out of an hour or two a day in extra fasting, or extra application, will in the end have to pay days and weeks for those hours.

How often I have wished for you and Newton during the last eight or nine months, in the course of which I have been continually mingling in scenes full of character and picture.

The place where I am now passing my time is a complete study. The court of this little kingdom of Saxony is, perhaps, the most ceremonious and old-fashioned in Europe, and one finds here customs and observances in full vigour that have long since faded away in other courts.

The king is a capital character himself — a complete old gentleman of the ancient school, and very tenacious in keeping up the old style. He has treated me with the most marked kindness, and every member of the royal family has shewn me great civility. What would greatly delight you, is the royal hunting establishment, which the king maintains at a vast expense, being his hobby. He has vast forests stocked with game, and a complete forest police, forest masters, chasseurs, piqueurs, jägers, &c., &c., several hunting lodges — packs of hounds — horses, &c., &c. The charm of the thing is, that all this is kept up in the old style — and to go out hunting with him, you might fancy yourself in one of those scenes of old times which we read of in poetry and romance. I have followed him thrice to the boar hunt. The last we had extremely good sport. The boar gave us a chase of upwards of two hours, and was not overpowered until it had killed one dog, and desperately wounded several others. It was a very cold winter day, with much snow on the ground — but as the hunting was in a thick pine forest, and the day was sunny, we did not feel the cold. The king and all his hunting retinue were clad in an old-fashioned hunting uniform of green, with green caps. The sight of the old monarch and his retinue galloping through the alleys of the forest — the jägers dashing singly about in all directions, cheering the hounds — the shouts — the blast of horns — the cry of hounds ringing through the forest, altogether made one of the most animating scenes I ever beheld.

I have become very intimate with one of the king's forest masters, who lives in a picturesque old hunting lodge with towers, formerly a convent, and who has undertaken to shew me all the economy of the hunting establishment. What glorious groupings, and what admirable studies for figures and faces I have seen among these hunters.

By this time your painting of ' Autolycus ' must be nearly finished. I long to have a description of it from Newton. Do tell me something about it yourself. Have you thought of a subject for your next? and have you entirely abandoned the scene of Shakespeare being brought up for deer-stealing? I think it would be a subject that you would treat with peculiar felicity, and you could not have one of a more general nature, since Shakespeare and his scanty biography are known in all parts of the world. Upon my soul, the more I think of it, the more I am convinced it is a subject that you might make a masterpiece of; it is one you should paint at least as large as your ' May Day,' and introduce a great number of figures. Do think of it. You might make a great impression by such a picture.

I have done nothing with my pen since I left you, absolutely *nothing!* I have been gazing about, rather idly, perhaps, but yet among fine scenes of striking character, and I can only hope that some of them may stick to my mind, and furnish me with materials in some future fit of scribbling.

I have been fighting my way into the German language, and am regaining my Italian, and for want of more profitable employment, have turned *play-actor.*

We have been getting up private theatricals here at the house of an English lady. I have already enacted Sir Charles Rackett in 'Three Weeks after Marriage,' with great applause, and am on the point of playing Don Felix in 'The Wonder.' I had no idea of this fund of dramatic talent lurking within me ; and I now console myself that if the worst comes to the worst, I can turn stroller, and pick up a decent maintenance among the barns in England. I verily believe nature intended me to be a vagabond.

P. S.—I hope you intend to make some designs for Bracebridge Hall. I would rather have the work illustrated by you than by any one else."

1824.

Pictures of the Year.

(Exhibited). SANCHO PANZA * IN THE APARTMENT OF THE DUCHESS.—
" First and foremost I must tell you I look on my master, Don Quixote, to be no better than a downright madman, though sometimes he will stumble upon a parcel of sayings so quaint and so tightly put together, that the devil himself could not mend them; but in the main, I cannot beat it out of my noddle, but that he is as mad as a March hare. Now, because I am pretty confident of knowing his blind side, whatever crotchets come into my crown, though without either head or tail, yet can I make them pass on him for Gospel. Such was the answer to his letter and another sham that I put upon him the other day, and is not in print yet, touching my Lady Dulcinea's enchantment; for you must know, between you and I, she is no more enchanted than the man in the moon." — *Don Quixote*, Vol. 3, . Chap. 33. (R. A. Catalogue, 1824.)
Painted for the Earl of Egremont, repeated for Mr. Vernon, and now in

* See Introduction.

the National Collection, South Kensington. Repeated a second time for Mr. Rogers. A third repetition was painted for one of the painter's sisters, in America, and is now in this country, in the possession of John Farnworth, Esq.
(Not exhibited.) PORTRAIT OF LADY HARRIET GURNEY. — PORTRAIT OF SIR WALTER SCOTT (for Mr. Ticknor, of Boston). Repeated.

THIS year was memorable to Leslie for many reasons. It included the death of a mother to whom he was deeply attached; his visit to Sir Walter Scott, at Abbotsford; and the painting of his ' Sancho,' for Lord Egremont. I need add nothing to the tribute which Leslie has paid in his Autobiography to Lord Egremont's munificence, his kindness of heart to all about him, and his little less than paternal kindness to Leslie himself, extended after his marriage to his wife and children. The patronage of Lord Egremont drew after it that of others of his order, and to it Leslie always attributed much of his after success. The best description I know of Lord Egremont and Petworth in his time, is Haydon's. I quote it here, as his emphatic style of describing the place and the owner, and his characteristic letter of acknowledgment, are worth contrasting with Leslie's way of treating the subject, though both descriptions result in giving one the same impression of Lord Egremont's singular geniality and goodness of heart.

" *November* 13*th*. — Set off for Petworth, where I arrived at half-past three. Lord Egremont's reception was frank and noble. The party was quite a family one. All was frank good-humour and benevolence. Lord Egremont presided and helped, laughed and joked, and let others do the same."

" *November* 15*th*. — Sketched and studied all day. I dine with the finest Vandyke in the world — the Lady Ann Carr, Countess of Bedford. It is beyond everything. — I really never saw such a character as Lord Egremont. ' Live and let live ' seems to be his motto. He has placed me in one of the most magnificent bedrooms I ever saw. It speaks more for what he thinks of my talents than anything that ever happened to me. On the left of the bed hangs a portrait of William, Lord Marquis of Hertford,

elected Knight of the Garter 1649, and by act of parliament
restored Duke of Somerset 1660. Over the chimney is a nobleman kneeling. A lady of high rank to the right. Opposite,
Queen Mary. Over the door, a head. On the right of the
cabinet, Sir Somebody. And over the entrance door, another
head. The bed-curtains are different-coloured velvets, let in on
white satin. The walls, sofas, easy chairs, carpets, green damask,
and a beautiful view of the park out of the high windows.

"There is something peculiarly interesting in the inhabiting
these apartments, sacred to antiquity, which have contained a
long list of deceased and illustrious ancestors. As I lay in my
magnificent bed, and saw the old portraits trembling in a sort of
twilight, I almost fancied I heard them breathe, and almost expected they would move out and shake my curtains. What a
destiny is mine! One year in the Bench, the companion of
gamblers and scoundrels, — sleeping in wretchedness and dirt
on a flock bed, low and filthy, with black worms crawling over
my hands, — another, reposing in down and velvet, in a splendid
apartment, in a splendid house, the guest of rank, and fashion,
and beauty! As I laid my head on my down pillow the first
night, I was deeply affected, and could hardly sleep. God in
heaven grant my future may now be steady. At any rate a
nobleman has taken me by the hand, whose friendship generally
increases in proportion to the necessity of its continuance. Such
is Lord Egremont. Literally like the sun. The very flies at
Petworth seem to know there is room for their existence; that
the windows are theirs. Dogs, horses, cows, deer, and pigs, peasantry and servants, guests and family, children and parents, all
share alike his bounty, and opulence, and luxuries. At breakfast,
after the guests have all breakfasted, in walks Lord Egremont;
first comes a grandchild, whom he sends away happy. Outside
the window moan a dozen black Spaniels, who are let in, and to
them he distributes cakes and comfits, giving all equal shares.
After chatting with one guest, and proposing some scheme of
pleasure to others, his leathern gaiters are buttoned on, and away
he walks, leaving everybody to take care of themselves, with all
that opulence and generosity can place at their disposal entirely
within reach. At dinner he meets everybody, and then are re-

counted the feats of the day. All principal dishes he helps, never minding the trouble of carving; he eats heartily and helps liberally. There is plenty, but not absurd profusion; good wines, but not extravagant waste. Everything solid, liberal, rich, and English. At seventy-four he still shoots daily, comes home wet through, and is as active and looks as well as many men of fifty.

"The meanest insect at Petworth feels a ray of his Lordship's fire in the justice of its distribution.

"I never saw such a character, or such a man, nor were there ever many.

"Before leaving that princely seat of magnificent hospitality, I wrote, when I retired to my bed-room last night, the following letter : —

"My Lord,

"I cannot leave Petworth without intruding my gratitude for the princely manner in which I have been treated during my stay, and in earnestly hoping your Lordship may live long, I only add my voice to the voices of thousands, who never utter your Lordship's name without a blessing.

"I am, my Lord,

"Your Lordship's humble and grateful servant,

"B. R. HAYDON."

Leslie started for Abbotsford in August, and met Newton in Edinburgh. The incidents of the journey are fully described in letters to his sister, but Leslie has already drawn so freely on these in his Autobiography, that I refrain from inserting them here. Leslie was at this time an accepted suitor, and from one of his letters to Miss Harriet Stone, soon to be Mrs. Leslie, I extract the following : —

"ABBOTSFORD, *Sept. 12th*, 1824.

* * * * * * * * *

"I HAVE certainly enjoyed myself much more than I expected. Such delightful weather as we have had ever since I have been in Scotland, could not have been anticipated. Still I am very anxious to get back to London, and shall leave Scotland the moment my engagements permit me.

*   *   *   *   *   *   *   *   *

" In my last letter, I gave you some account of this house and its inmates, but said nothing about its situation. It stands close to the Tweed (of which I have a very pretty view from the window of the bed-room from which I am now writing) on the side of a hill, and in the midst of hills, the highest of which are the Eildon, alluded to in the ' Lay of the Last Minstrel,' and the Cowden-knows, which gives the name to an old song. Melrose Abbey, a most beautiful ruin, is situated at the foot of the Eildon hills, about three miles from here, and not far off is a most romantic glen, celebrated by one of the oldest Scottish poets, Thomas the Rhymer, and where he met the Queen of the Fairies. There is a mossy seat near a waterfall at the top of this glen, which is a favourite haunt of the ' Great Unknown,' and which he wished me to introduce into the picture I am painting ; but it is far too good for a background. Near this glen is a very pretty little mountain lake, on which Sir Walter maintains two swans, and tells a story of a water bull that inhabits it ; indeed he has anecdotes to relate of every little spot around him. What the hills most want here are trees, a deficiency Sir W. is doing all in his power to supply, by planting all the ground that belongs to himself full of them. A few years will double the beauty of the scenery here. The Tweed, though not a wide or deep stream, is very ornamental, and makes some beautiful turns among the hills, and the pebbly bed over which it flows gives it a fine *voice*. Some poet calls it ' Well sung Tweed, baronial stream ; ' and I suppose there is no river in Great Britain, the name of which more frequently occurs in poetry, or is more connected with great historical events. Mr. Lockhart, who is married to Sir Walter's eldest daughter, lives in a very pretty cottage near Melrose Abbey. I dined with him yesterday. Newton is staying there, and the two Miss Clephanes (Lady Compton's sisters), who gave us some very delightful music in the evening. Mrs. Lockhart, who has more of her father in her than any of Sir W.'s other children, sings Scottish songs very beautifully. Now that I am on the subject of songs, I must give you the fragments of a

Gloucestershire ditty Sir Walter repeated the other day. I think you will agree with me in regretting there is not more of it. The four first lines are *particularly interesting,* —

> The stones, the stones, the stones, the stones,
> The stones, the stones, the stones, the stones,
> The stones, the stones, the stones, the stones,
> The stones what built Jack Ridley's oven,
> They all was fought (fetch'd) from Barclay quar' (quarry). *

" I must not omit to describe the dogs, who are very important members of the family. Sir Walter is never seen unaccompanied by two *at least*. There are a set of little ugly varlets of black terriers, of the true Dandie Dinmont breed, named Spice, Ginger, Mustard, and Whiskey ; a large greyhound called Hamlet, and a very venerable old deer-hound of gigantic size, named Maida, besides Lady, Scott's own particular dog Risk, and sundry pointers belonging to Charles Scott.

" The picture goes on to the satisfaction of all the family. * *

" I have no wish to go to the church at Melrose, for I am told the parson is a very ridiculous old fellow; and having heard Sir Walter take him off one morning, I am sure I could not help laughing were I to go. Newton, who goes to Edinburgh, will carry this letter enclosed in one to my sister, but as his movements are not so certain as those of the post, it is very probable you may get another from me before this arrives."

*   *   *   *   *   *   *

" ABBOTSFORD, *Sept. 21st*, 1824.

*   *   *   *   *   *   *

" THE portrait of Sir Walter is nearly finished ; but I find it extremely difficult to satisfy myself with it. He dislikes sitting very much. Yesterday he only gave me a quarter of an hour, and then carried me off in his *sociable*, with two other gentlemen who are staying here, to see the ' Yarrow,' famous in song, as, indeed, are all the Scottish rivers. We stopped at a seat of the Duke of Buccleuch's, called Bow Hill, upon the grounds of which stand the ruins of Newark Castle, formerly a palace of the kings

---

* This ditty is given at length in Mr. Hughes's " Scouring of the White Horse." — ED.

17

of Scotland. The ruin is not in itself fine, but it stands, 'bosomed high in tufted trees,' on an eminence, round the base of which the river winds, and dashes away rocks and woods; and the whole together is very picturesque. The Yarrow here resembles the 'bonny Doone,' with the advantage of having much higher hills on each side of it. Sir Walter had ordered a detachment of the 'doggies' (as he calls them), consisting of two greyhounds and as many terriers, that we might have some coursing on the 'braes of Yarrow.' Charles Scott and a friend of his had accompanied us on horseback. Owing to one of the dogs being too old, and the other too young, they only killed one hare, and started two others, which they lost. We saw a great deal of game on the Duke's grounds, consisting of pheasants, blackcocks, and partridges; and I, who am entirely ignorant of all sorts of sporting, was much edi- fied by the conversation of the party on the subject. Sir Walter has been a keen sportsman in his youth. He started one of the hares himself, and gave the view-hallo with the lungs of a Sten- tor. Among the many interesting places pointed out to us by our host on this occasion was the cottage in which Mungo Park, the celebrated African traveller, was born, and where his mother still lives. Sir Walter knew Park well, and describes him as a very fine-looking man, and remarkable for personal strength. A few days ago I made, at the request of Sir Walter, a sketch of his game-keeper, Tom Purdey, who has lived with him sixteen years, and is a very great favourite of his master's. Tom is now in de- clining health, and Sir Walter's extreme solicitude about him, and the attentions he pays him, are strong proofs (if any were wanting) of the goodness of his heart. I was gratified the other day at dinner by what I had been very anxious to see, namely, a *haggis*. It was, however, a small one, by no means answering in appear- ance to the idea Burns gives us of this 'chieftain of the pudding race.' I found its contents, however, very good, and they told me it was a genuine specimen, excepting as to size. I have now tasted the principal Scotch dishes — hodge-podge, porridge (which I never desire to see again), oat-cake, and Miss Scott has prom- ised to have some bannocks of barley this morning at breakfast to complete the list. There is a very patriotic song called the ' Ban- nocks of Barley ' — indeed all the Scotch dishes are rendered classical by their poets. All the company that were here when I last wrote have gone, and there are only the two gentlemen mentioned above (literary men) here at present. I am afraid I shall miss Wilkie, who is in Edinburgh, but will not, in all probability be here till I have left.

" You wonder, you say, how I shall be able to bear London after Scotland ; but in truth I am most anxious to get back. I have enjoyed myself very much; but I am never contented to be long on a visit, even among the most pleasant people in the world. I want to be once more in my painting-room, and to work again in earnest. I want to see my friends, and tell them of all the wonders of Scotland, * * * * * * * and over and above all, I want to see your dear little self again. It required, as you know, a very great temptation to leave London at the time I did, and the trial has only convinced me, more than ever, how entirely my happiness depends upon you.

" I hope to finish Sir Walter's portrait to-morrow ; and if it is dry enough I shall leave Abbotsford the next day. I shall then be obliged to remain in Edinburgh a few days, to make a study from a picture in Holyrood House. I suppose I can go to Culross and return in one day ; and after that I shall set off for London. As, however, I must stop in Norfolk for a few days, to finish Lady Harriet Gurney's picture, I fear it will be a fortnight yet before I shall have the pleasure of seeing you."

On his return home he spent a week in Edinburgh with Edwin Landseer. Sir Walter, who had run up for a day to Edinburgh, took Landseer back with him to Abbotsford, " where I am sure," says Leslie, " he will make himself very popular, both with the master and mistress of the house, by sketching their doggies for them."

Irving, still in Paris, writes to express his satisfaction with the illustrations from ' Knickerbocker.'

FROM WASHINGTON IRVING.

PARIS, *Feb.* 8, 1824.

MY DEAR LESLIE, — It is a long while since I have heard
from either you or Newton. How are you both, and what are
you doing? I see among the pieces to be exhibited at the British
Gallery, a ' Don Quixote ' by Newton, which I presume is the
little picture made from poor Ogilvie, which I have before heard
of. Do you not intend to have anything ready for the next Exhibition? I long to see you again, to have some good long talks with
you. I wish you were here at present, I think you would do me
good. I am trying to get some manuscripts in order for a couple
more volumes of the ' Sketch Book,' but I have been visited by a
fit of sterility for this month past that throws me all aback, and
discourages me as to the hope of getting ready for a spring appearance. I have a Dutch story written, which I have shown to
friend Foy, for I like to consult brother artists. He thinks it
equal' to any of my others. I think you would like it. I have
determined also to introduce my ' History of an Author,' breaking
it into parts and distributing it through the two volumes. It had
grown stale with me, and I never could get into the vein sufficiently to carry it on and finish it as a separate work. Besides,
the time that has elapsed without my either publishing or writing,
obliges me to make the most of what I have in hand and can
soonest turn to account. I have a few other articles sketched out
of minor importance. If I could only get myself into a brisk
writing mood, I could soon furnish the materials for two volumes,
and if these were well received and paid well, I should then have
leisure and means to pursue the literary plans I have in view.
But I am at this moment in a sad heartless mood, and nothing
seems to present to rouse me out of it. Write to me I beg of you,
and say something to stimulate and cheer me up. Do not say
anything of the forgoing literary confidings to any one.

I am sorry to see ' Salmagundi ' is published at London with
all its faults upon its head. I have corrected a copy for Galignani,
whom I found bent upon putting it to press. My corrections consist almost entirely in expunging words and here and there an

offensive sentence. I have a set of your illustrations of my works; they are admirable. I wish you had made others for ' Bracebridge Hall,' or that you would still do so. I still think your ' Dutch Fireside ' worthy of being painted by you as a cabinet picture. It is admirable. The engraving from Newton's portrait of me is thought an excellent likeness by my brother, and by others here.

I see Mr. Foy very frequently, and the more I see of him the better I like him. I thank you for making me acquainted with him. I am very much incommoded by visits and invitations, for in spite of every exertion I find it impossible to keep clear of society entirely without downright churlishness and incivility.

Do let me hear from you, my dear Leslie, as soon as you can spare a moment to the pen. I am sure a letter from you will be of service to me, as a visit from you has often been, when in one of my dispirited moods. Give my best remembrances to your sister, and to Newton when you see him.

Yours ever,   W. I.

FROM WASHINGTON IRVING.

PARIS, RUE RICHELIEU, No. 89,
Dec. 8, 1824.

MY DEAR LESLIE, — I have been for a long time intending to write to you, but my spirit has been so inert as not to be able to summon up a page full of ideas. However, as Brockedon is on the point of starting, and will take a letter free of cost, I will scrawl a line, if it is only in testimony of constant recollection.

The ' Childe ' has given me a mere inkling of his northern visit — just enough to tantalise curiosity. I wish you would give me a few anecdotes on the subject. You must have had a rare time; and I envy above everything your residence at Abbotsford. I am told the Great Unknown was absolutely besieged by a legion of " panthers," that you really surrounded him — one taking a point blank elevation of him in full front — another in profile — another in rear — happy to sketch a likeness, whichever side presented.

To you the visit must have been peculiarly interesting and ad-

vantageous; for, knowing your taste and turn of mind, I am sure
you would find Scott full of precious matter, and would derive a
world of valuable hints from your conversation with him. I long
to hear something of your visit at Abbotsford, and would give
anything for a good long talk with you on the subject.

I wish your 'Sancho' were here in the Exhibition. I should
like to hear what the Frenchmen would say to it: it is so infinitely better than anything which they think good, that I doubt
whether they would know how to appreciate it. There are two
of Lawrence's paintings here, but the French pass by without
noticing them. The only remark I heard made was from two
Frenchmen on Lawrence's head of the late Duc de Richelieu.
One looked at it, with a screw of the mouth, " *Pas mal*," said he ;
" some affectation, something of colouring," and so they passed on.

Have you begun your new picture for Lord Egremont?
Brockedon speaks with great emphasis of your 'Autolycus.' I
do not know whether you have done anything to it since I saw
it, or whether he means the picture in its half-finished state. I
certainly think your head of 'Autolycus' one of your happiest
efforts of character and expression. But, in fact, you have now
but to dash boldly at whatever you conceive ; you have the
power of achieving whatever you attempt, and the certainty of
having whatever you achieve appreciated by the public.

When you see, Newton remember me affectionately to him.
Let me know what he is doing, and how he is doing it. I often
look back with fondness and regret on the times we lived together
in London, in a delightful community of thought and feeling ;
struggling our way onward in the world, but cheering and encouraging each other. I find nothing to supply the place of that
heartfelt fellowship. I trust that you and Newton have a long
career of increasing success and popularity before you. Of my
own fate I sometimes feel a doubt. I am isolated in English literature, without any of the usual aids and influences by which an
author's popularity is maintained and promoted. I have no literary coterie to cry me up ; no partial reviewer to pat me on the
back : the very review of my publisher is hostile to everything
American. I have nothing to depend on but the justice and courtesy of the public ; and how long the public may continue to

favour the writings of a stranger, or how soon it may be preju-
diced by the scribblers of the press, is with me a matter of extreme uncertainty. I have one proud reflection, however, to sustain myself with; — that I have never in any way sought to sue
the praises nor deprecate the censures of reviewers, but have left
my works to rise or fall by their own deserts. If the public will
keep with me a little longer, until I can secure a bare compe-
tency, I feel as if I shall be disposed to throw by the pen, or only
to use it as a mere recreation. Do write to me soon. I long to
hear from you. How often do I miss you in moments when I
feel cast down and out of heart; and how often at times when
some of the odd scenes of life present themselves which we used
to enjoy so heartily together.

Remember me most particularly to your sister. It is with the
greatest concern that I have heard of the afflicting loss * which
both of you have sustained; and I only forbear to dwell on it
because I know that in cases of the kind all consolation by letter
is mere idle formality. God bless you, my dear Leslie.

Believe me, most constantly and affectionately yours,

W. I.

P. S. — My brother is with me, and desires to be particularly
remembered to you.

1825.

Pictures of the Year.

SLENDER, WITH THE ASSISTANCE OF SHALLOW, COURTING ANNE PAGE.†
    Shallow — " Mistress Anne, my cousin loves you." — *Merry Wives of
    Windsor.* Act iii. Scene 4. — (Painted for Sir Willoughby Gordon). Is
    this the picture engraved for the American Art Union in 1858, from the
    collection of Mr. Philip Hone?

(109) SIR HENRY WOTTON PRESENTING THE COUNTESS SABRINA WITH A
    VALUABLE JEWEL ON THE EVE OF HIS DEPARTURE FROM VIENNA. —
    (Painted for Mr. J. Major's illustrated edition of " Walton's Lives.")

    " As for Sir Henry himself, his behaviour had been such during the
    manage of the Treaty, that the Emperor (Ferdinand the 2nd) took him to
    be a person of much honour and merit; and did therefore desire him to
    accept of that jewel, as a testimony of his good opinion of him, which was

* The loss of their mother. — ED.   † See Introductory Essay.

a jewel of diamonds of more value than a thousand pounds. This jewel was received with all outward circumstance and terms of honour by Sir Henry Wotton. But the next morning, on his departing from Vienna, he, at his taking leave of the Countess of Sabrina — an Italian lady in whose house the Emperor had appointed him to be lodged and honourably entertained — acknowledged her merits, and besought her to accept of that jewel as a testimony of his gratitude for her civilities." — *Walton's Life of Sir Henry Wotton.*

SIX DRAWINGS FROM THE WAVERLEY NOVELS. — (For the first Author's Edition.) The subjects of these drawings are from —
    GUY MANNERING. — Dominie Sampson unpacking the books. PEVERIL OF THE PEAK. — Peveril turning from the window, perceives Fenella kneeling at his feet. ROB ROY. — The sudden apparition of Diana Vernon, leaning on her father's arm, to Frank Osbaldiston. ST. RONAN'S WELL. — Mr. Winterblossom exhibiting his drawings to Lady Penelope Penfeather. KENILWORTH. — Amy Robsart toying with Leicester's jewels and orders. — Wayland Smith in the disguise of a pedlar, showing his wares to Amy Robsart and Janet Forster.

IN the course of this year Leslie married Miss Harriet Stone. His first letter to Irving of next year describes his new happiness — a happiness which lasted as long as his life.

.   .

1826.

Pictures of the Year.

(60) DON QUIXOTE HAVING RETIRED INTO THE SIERRA MORENA TO DO PENANCE, IN IMITATION OF AMADIS DE GAUL, IS PREVAILED ON TO RELINQUISH HIS DESIGN BY A STRATAGEM OF THE CURATE AND THE BARBER, ASSISTED BY DOROTHEA.

"I will not arise from hence, thrice valorous and approved knight, until your bounty and courtesie shall grant unto me one boon, which shall much redound to your honour and prize of your person, and to the profit of the most disconsolate and wronged damzel the sun hath ever seen."

    *   *   *   *   *   *   *

"I will not answer you a word, fair lady," quoth Don Quixote, "nor hear a jot of your affair, until you arise from the ground." — "I will not get up hence, my lord," quoth the afflicted lady, "if first of your wonted bounty you do not grant my request." — "I do give and grant it," quoth Don Quixote, "so that it be not a thing that may turn to the damage or hindrance of my king, my country, or of her that keeps the key of my heart and liberty." — "It shall not turn to the damage or hindrance of those you have said, good sir," replied the dolorous damzel; and as she was saying this, Sancho Panza rounded his lord in the ear, saying softly to him, "Sir, you may very well grant the request she asks, for it is a matter of nothing: it is only to kill a monstrous gyant, and she that demands it, is the mighty Princess Micomicona, Queen of the great kingdom of Micomicon, in Ethiopia."

*   *   *   *   *   *   *

" The Barber kneeled all this while, and could with much ado dissemble his laughter, or keep on his beard, that threatened still to fall off, with whose fall perhaps they should all have remained without bringing their good purpose to pass." — *Shelton's Translation of Don Quixote*. Part 4, Chap. 2.

(Painted for the Earl of Essex.)
QUEEN KATHERINE AND HER MAID. — *Henry VIII*. Act iii. Scené 1.
    " Take thy lute, wench: my soul grows sad with troubles;
    Sing, and disperse them, if thou canst."
    (DIPLOMA PICTURE). The same subject was repeated for Mr. Sheep-shanks, and is now in the National Collection at South Kensington.

THIS year Leslie was elected a Member of the Royal Academy, and his first child (Robert Charles) was born on the 14th of May.

> ST. JOHN'S PLACE, LISSON GROVE,
> LONDON, *Jan.* 12*th*, 1826.

MY DEAR IRVING, — Having a wife and picture to attend to might be allowed as excuses for a lazy correspondent among painters and married men — but bachelors and authors may not be so lenient — so have at you. I have heard very good accounts of you from my sisters, and from Mr. and Mrs. Dunlop, and lastly from our friend Foy, who gave me hopes of seeing you before the summer was over, which kept me from writing at that time. But Christmas came and you did not, and now I suppose we must not look for you before the spring. I long to hear from yourself what you have been about, and what you are doing, and when you are really coming. As for myself, I have (as you know) made the greatest change in life that it is in our power to do, and find myself so much the happier, and, I trust, the better for it, that I scarcely seem to have lived before. All the evils of matrimony that I have heard or read of appear to me to be slanders, and all the blessings to have been underrated ; I am now sure I can wish nothing better to all my single friends than a good wife to each of them. As I write to know what you are doing, it is but fair to tell you what I am about. I have for the last six months been very busy with a picture from 'Don Quixote,' on

the same scale as that of 'the Duchess.' The scene is where the
Don has been rusticating in the Sierra Morena, and is drawn
away by the stratagem of the curate and barber, assisted by
Dorothea, who is kneeling at his feet in the disguise of the Princess Micomicona. Those of my friends who have seen it think it
. will be my best picture, but I never know well what I am about
myself till I have done it. It is for Lord Essex. As soon as it
is finished, I am to commence another subject from the Don for
the Duke of Bedford. It is Altisidora pretending to faint at the
presence of Don Quixote, as he passes along a gallery to attend
the Duke and Duchess. I have several other things in embryo
which you shall know all about when you come. I have not
been out of town since the spring, except for a week in the summer, when I took my wife to Hastings. On my wedding expedition I visited old Warwick, Oxford, and Blenheim for the third
time, and went to Birmingham, as I dare say you have heard, to
see Mr. and Mrs. Van Wart and your brother. Give my affectionate regards to him, and my wife's best respects; she was
delighted with the little she saw of him and with your sister's
family. My sisters had a very quick and pleasant passage to
America, and I have had several delightful letters from them.
Newton is quite well, and engaged on a picture * from the ' Beggar's Opera,' — " How happy could I be with either " is the
passage. Powell, as you know, disappears annually at Christmas among a set of friends that we know nothing of, and has not
yet emerged into our circle. If he is not soon heard of, I must
offer a reward for him, for he is one of the few that I find it hard
to be without. I heard from Father Luke in August last : he
was quite well; I dare say you will see him in the spring.
How pleasant an evening you and your brother, Luke, Newton,
Powell, and I, might have together. Think well of it !

Yours ever,

C. R. LESLIE.

WASHINGTON IRVING, ESQ.,
　　　　Paris.

* Now in Lord Lansdowne's gallery at Bowood. — ED.

MY DEAR LESLIE, — I am greatly obliged by your letter, especially as it is so cheerful a one, full of domestic happiness and good news. In return for your kindness, I am about to give you a great deal of trouble, so you must absent yourself from happiness awhile, *i. e.*, from your wife and your painting, and attend to what I request.

There is a very interesting work printing at Madrid, ' The Voyage of Columbus,' compiled from his papers by the famous Bishop Las Casas, and in part composed of extracts from Columbus's journal. It is in Spanish, and I have undertaken to translate it into English, Mr. Everett, our minister at Madrid, having secured it for me. I wish you to make an arrangement with Murray at once for the purchase of the translation, or, if he will not buy it, with Longman or Colburn. I am told it will make about two octavo volumes. Mr. Everett thinks I ought to get 1500 or 1000 guineas for it. I shall be content with the last sum. I should have written to Murray on the subject, but I have had such repeated instances of his inattention to letters, and have been put so much back thereby, that I won't trust to correspondence any more, either with him or any other bookseller. As the case, admits of no delay, I wish you to see him at once. You had better drop him a line, letting him know you have a literary proposition to make on my part, and requesting him to appoint an hour when you can find him at home. *Whichever bookseller you make an arrangement with, get him to announce the work at once as preparing for publication by me.* Let me hear from you as soon as possible ; direct to me, " *Légation des Etats Unis d'Amérique, à Madrid.*" I set off for Madrid in the course of three or four days. My brother accompanies me. Mr. Everett has attached me to the Legation, which will be of service to me in travelling and residing in Spain. I am sorry to inflict such a job upon you, but the case is urgent, and so are my necessities. If I can be of any use to you in Spain in return, either in finding you a part of Don Quixote's armour, or the very helmet of Mambrino, command me. When you write to me, the safest way is by the British Ambassador's bag.

I am delighted with the works which you and Newton have in hand and in prospect. 'Don Quixote' and 'Gil Blas' are uni- • versal works, known throughout the world, and painting from them is like painting from the Bible, or from ancient and classical history.

I have been writing a little of late, but have no prospect of publishing anything original for some time to come; I am not anxious to do so; but I feel the exercise of the pen extremely beneficial to me; I was quite out of spirits for want of the usual stimulus.

When I get to Madrid I will write to you at more length and leisure, — at present I am all in a bustle.

Tell Newton I received his letter, and will likewise reply to him when I come to anchorage. Give my kind regards to Mrs. Leslie, and believe me, my dear Leslie, ever affectionately yours,

•   WASHINGTON IRVING.

LISSON GROVE, Feb. 23rd, 1826.

MY DEAR IRVING, — A week elapsed after I received your letter before I could obtain a sight of Murray, although I called on him and left a note requesting him to let me know when I might. He says it is impossible for him to judge of the value of Columbus's Voyage until he sees it. It might be very interesting or it might be very dry; he therefore cannot make any arrangement until it is done, and that you alone can be the only judge at present whether or not it is worth doing. He had told Mr. Rogers (whom I saw a day or two since) that you had written to him on the subject, and Rogers said to me he thought it would be more advisable for you not to make any bargain until you had done it; as you would then stand a better chance. In consequence of this opinion, I think I had better not apply to any of the other booksellers until I hear from you again ; and the truth is, they are all just now in so great a panic, occasioned by the recent failures here, that it is no time to get them to undertake anything. Murray says he does not know whom to trust among them. He would gladly, he says, receive anything from you of original matter, which he considers certain of success, whatever it might be ; but with regard to 'The Voyage of Columbus,' he cannot form any opinion at present. Let me know as soon as possible what I am to do farther for you in this business, and it shall be done without a moment's delay. I have thoughts of painting something from the life of Cervantes. Can you give me any information about it that I am not likely to get here. I should like very much to know what is the authority for the portrait prefixed to the editions of his life. If you could put up for me an impression of the earliest print of him extant it will be very useful to me.* Why should you not translate some of his works? I believe we have nothing of him in English but 'Don Quixote' and his '*Exemplary Novels.*' I remember when you were in London some years ago, you read me a scene from an old play, in which the two children who were smothered by Richard III. were introduced saying their prayers. What is the name of the play, and where shall I find it? I have just been elected an Academician.

My wife, who is quite well, sends her best respects to yourself and your brother : give my warmest regards to him.

Yours, ever affectionately,

C. R. LESLIE.

P. S. — This is a short letter, but as I hope very soon to hear from you, I shall reserve a great deal I have to say till then.

WASHINGTON IRVING, ESQ.,
    Madrid.

FROM WASHINGTON IRVING.

MADRID, *Feb.* 23rd, 1826

MY DEAR LESLIE, — I gave you a troublesome commission to execute, in a letter from Bordeaux, relative to 'The Voyage of Columbus.' If you have made any arrangement for me, or if there are any demurs on the subject, in consequence of the size and nature of the work not being particularly specified, you may mention that the work makes two volumes of about 450 pages, each page containing forty-five lines, each line forty-nine letters;

---

* There is an admirable portrait of him at Petworth. — ED.

from this a bookseller can make his calculations. The narrative of Las Casas, compiled from the papers, journal, &c., of Columbus, makes but a part of the first volume. The whole work consists of a collection of documents, many of them never before published, among which are private letters of Columbus discovered last year, which give the most ample and satisfactory information relative to the discovery and voyages of Columbus, and set at rest several questions which have hitherto been in dispute, particularly the claim of Americus Vespucius to the discovery of the New World. I shall enrich my translation by some annotations and additions from authentic sources, which will make the English publication still more complete than the Spanish. The Spanish work is by Don Martin Fernandez de Navarrete, Secretary of the Royal Academy of History, &c., and is published under sanction of the Crown. He has promised me any assistance in the prosecution of my undertaking. The London booksellers will perceive by the account given of the amount of letterpress contained in these volumes that they will make two full quarto volumes, such as they sell for three guineas a volume. It will be a work necessary to any library. You can communicate the purport of the above in a note to any one of the booksellers who has entered into the undertaking, or is found disposed to do so. I can furnish manuscript as soon as required. Murray has had a copy of the manuscript of Las Casas offered to him a year or two since, and may be misled by supposing that to be the whole of the present work, whereas it only forms a part of the first volume.

So much for business. We arrived here about a week since, after a journey of five days from Bordeaux. I have been exceedingly interested by what I have seen of Spain, although a great part of our route lay through Old and New Castile, the most bleak and arid part of the peninsula, and as joyless a track as I ever travelled. Biscay and Alava, however, had much to interest, both as to the country and the people. Indeed, the Spaniards seem to surpass even the Italians in picturesqueness; every mother's son of them is a subject for the pencil. It is a continual wish of my brother and myself that we could have you and Newton with us; you might lay up ample materials for your

Spanish pictures. The interiors of the houses, too, are so peculiar and picturesque, that you would have your pencil continually at work.

We are most comfortably situated, having an apartment in the house of the American Consul. We are buried in the very depths of a great rambling Spanish house; our windows look upon a small garden, three parts of which are surrounded by the house. Our windows open to the floor with iron grates to them, through one of which we have a wicket by which we can enter the garden. We have the stillness of a cloister, with now and then the bell of a neighbouring convent to help the illusion. Our Consul, Mr. Rich, is a great collector and vendor of rare books, and I am surrounded by a curious library entirely at my command. He intends coming to London in the spring to sell a stock of Spanish and other works which he has collected, and I intend to give him letters to you and Newton. He is a most obliging and good-hearted man, and one who may be of great service to you should you want sketches, studies, &c., from this country. He has a valuable collection of sketches, studies, &c., of Murillo, Velasquez, &c., which he intends bringing to England for sale, and which he intends submitting to your and Newton's inspection. Should I be able to pick up anything in your way before he sets off I will send it to you, or if there is anything you wish from here in the way of costumes, &c., &c., let me know; as Mr. Rich will be sending boxes and parcels I can easily forward anything you wish. I shall write to Newton as soon as I feel a little more settled, and get through some introductory visits. Mr. Everett has introduced me to the diplomatic circle, and on Sunday next I am to be presented to the King; so if you desire anything at the Spanish court, command me.

With my kind regards to Mrs. Leslie,

I am, my dear Leslie, yours ever,

W. I.

FROM WASHINGTON IRVING.

MADRID, *April 21st*, 1826.

My Dear Leslie, — I take occasion of the departure of Mr. Rich to scribble you a few lines, as much for the purpose of introducing him to you as for anything else. He is American Consul at this place, and a most excellent and amiable man. I have been quartered for a couple of months in the same house with him, and in a manner domesticated with him, and have never been more pleasantly situated. He is a great collector of books, partly as a hobby, but partly, of late years, as a source of profit, having supplied the bibliomaniacs of London with the treasures of old Spanish literature. In this respect you will find him very interesting. He has a number of cases of very rare and curious works with him, and having lately been turning his attention to paintings and engravings, has a few paintings with him as an experiment, and a great number of studies, sketches, and drawings of celebrated masters which he has picked up here, among which are many of Murillo's. He has also a valuable stock of engravings. You will find his collection very interesting to examine, and you may be of great service to him in putting him in the way of disposing of his paintings, sketches, &c., to advantage, as well as of drawing attention of artists, &c., to them. Should you want anything from Spain in the way of costumes, &c., he would be able to procure and send it to you, for he is one of the most obliging men I ever met with.

You wished to know something about a likeness of Cervantes. There is no thoroughly ascertained likeness extant. The most probable one, and which accords with the description given by himself of his physiognomy, is that prefixed to his life, edited by Navarrete, and published, together with his works, in Madrid, in 1819. Mr. Rich has a copy of it for you, and also a collection of various prints and illustrations of Don Quixote.

The old play about which you inquire, as containing scenes relative to the young princes in the Tower,* is by Middleton, en-

* The play is by Heywood, not Middleton, and has been reprinted by the Shakespeare Society. Leslie painted a very touching sketch of the young

titled the ' First and Second Part of Edward IV.' If you wish
the scenes for any professional purpose I can transcribe them for
you in a letter, as I have them by me, but I do not wish to put
any literary forager on the track of this play, as I have an article
on the subject half sketched among my papers, which I intend
some day or other to make use of.

I am occupying myself at present in writing the life and voyages of Columbus ; I do not wish it to be known, however, but
wish it to be supposed I am busied about the translation. In the
curious collection of Mr. Rich I find materials collected together
which I should otherwise have had to hunt for through public
libraries, and I have under my hand the most rare and curious
works relative to the discovery of America. The work which I
had intended to translate is a voluminous mass of mere documents,
which afford excellent materials for a work, but which in their
present form would repel the general class of readers. I am in
hopes of making a work that will be acceptable to the public.

I regret continually, now that you and Newton are engaged in
painting Spanish subjects, that you could not get a peep at the
country and its people. There is a character about them that it
is not easy to gather from mere description. The countenance,
figure, air, attitude, walk, and dress of a Spaniard all have a
peculiar character. The common people are wonderfully picturesque in all their attitudes, groups, and costumes. It is a
source of continual pleasure to my brother and myself in walking the streets to notice the figures and groups around us, and we
are continually regretting that you and Newton are not here to
take sketches.

At the Duke of Bedford's seat (Woburn Abbey) there is a
little gallery of Spanish costumes, represented by small figures
of clay or porcelain, accurately coloured. They are made in
Spain, and are beautiful as specimens of art, while they are
accurate as costumes ; perhaps the same may be met with in
London. There is such national character, however, in the
Spanish dresses even at the present day, that a painter cannot
illustrate Spanish stories without attending to the costumes of

princes at their prayers. It is in the Sheepshanks collection. There is a
repetition of it in the collection of Mr. Joseph Gillot, at Birmingham.

his figures; he would otherwise commit as great blunders as the Flemish painters, who paint Scripture personages in Flemish dresses and armour.

My brother desires to be cordially remembered to you.   Give my kind remembrances to Mrs. Leslie, and believe me, my dear Leslie,

Ever yours affectionately,   W. I.

P. S. — I must not forget to congratulate you on your election to the Royal Academy.   I hope you will rise to the dignity of hangman, and will do your duty by Newton and the rest of your old gang.

1827.

Pictures of the Year.

LADY JANE GREY PREVAILED ON TO ACCEPT THE CROWN.

"The Duke of Suffolk, with much solemnity, explained to his daughter the disposition the late king had made of his crown by letters patent; the clear sense the Privy Council had of her right; and the consent of the magistrates and citizens of London; and in conclusion, himself and Northumberland fell on their knees, and paid homage to her as Queen of England. The poor lady, somewhat astonished at their behaviour and discourse, but in no respect moved by their reasons, or in the least elevated by such unexpected honours, answered them, ' That the laws of the kingdom, and natural right standing for the king's sisters, she would beware of burthening her weak conscience with a yoke that did belong to them; that she understood the infamy of those who had permitted the violation of right to gain a sceptre; that it were to mock God, and deride justice.   Besides,' said she, ' I am not so young, nor so little read in the guiles of Fortune as to suffer myself to be taken by them.   * * *   What she adored but yesterday, is to-day her pastime.   * *   My liberty is better than the chain you proffer me, with what precious stones soever it be adorned, or of what gold soever framed.   I will not exchange my peace for honourable and precious jealousies, for magnificence and glorious fetters.   And if you love me in good earnest, you will rather wish me a secure, a quiet fortune, though mean, than an exalted condition, exposed to the wind, and followed by some dismal fall.'

"All the moving eloquence of this speech had no effect, and the Lady Jane was at length prevailed on, or rather compelled by the exhortations of her father, the intercessions of her mother, the artful persuasions of Northumberland, and, above all, the earnest desires of her husband whom she tenderly loved, to comply with what was proposed to her." — *Life of Lady Jane Grey.*   (Painted for the Duke of Bedford, and engraved.)

(449) STUDY FOR A HEAD OF SANCHO PANZA. — (458) STUDY FOR A HEAD OF DON QUIXOTE.

FROM the correspondence of this year I only extract the following from Leslie's old chum, Peter Powell. It is curious, as showing what a revelation Giotto was to the men of this time. It is a great pity that Leslie never *did* see the great decorative works of Italy in their places. I cannot but think some of his judgments would have been materially modified by the experience.

PADUA, 27*th* *November*, 1827.

DEAR LESLIE, — I hope you will not think me *troublesome*, although it *be* scarcely a twelvemonth since the date of my last letter. I believe, however, I have determined to run all risks, and to indulge my *eternal* scribbling propensity at *your* expense as well as *my own*. Here I am, then, enjoying the luxuries of an Italian climate, with as good a fire as I have the talent to make with *sticks* (which, I confess, please me not so well as *coals*) ; the wind blowing in at the half-shut door, which *must* be left open, or I should soon be all *ham*, from the *curing* properties of the chimney, which smokes marvellously well; out of doors the water is all *ice*, and the opposite mountains are covered with *snow*. Nevertheless, I am pleased with Italy, and really ought not to crack jokes upon so *respectable* a climate on the whole, for up to the middle of this month (*November*) the weather has been delightful ; and, at that period even, the day all through has been frequently warmed by an unclouded sunshine. There are no November *fogs* to be had here for love or money ; to-day the sun is shining charmingly, and the cold has *this* advantage, that I get an opportunity of seeing the men wrapped up in their *magnificent cloaks*. Even those that are *threadbare* are so fine as to the drapery, and are worn in such a style that the beggars here appear to be, what poor Fuseli so eloquently said of Michael Angelo's, the *very patriarchs of poverty*. But the dam'd French (God forgive me for swearing, as the old women say) are making rapid strides here, as well as everywhere else, to destroy everything that is good in taste, particularly in dress, and to substitute their own contemptible frippery. One is truly surprised how they ever could have carried their fashions into countries where the taste was so infinitely greater than their own ; but unaccount-

able as it may be, such is unfortunately the *fact ;* and every
woman above the common class here has thrown aside the graceful drapery of her own country — above all the beautiful veil —
to figure away in a preposterous French bonnet and quilted pet-
ticoats.   I suppose you will have heard something of *me* through
John Chalon, who I met with at Geneva, and with whom I
afterwards visited the Valley of Chamounix and the celebrated
Mont Blanc.   I find *he* is a disappointed candidate, as well as
Newton, for academical honours.   You have, perhaps, also heard
that I *fell in* with Callcott and his wife at Venice, and have not
yet fallen *out* with them, although *they* are at present at *Milan*
and *I* am *here*.   I had been at Venice some time when they arrived,
and the first I heard of *him* was from the English Consul there,
who told me that he was very ill; and accordingly, on going to
his hotel, I found him in·bed, looking very woe-begone and terribly hipped.   It turned out, however, that he was more frightened
than hurt, and the doctor pronounced his disorder to be of
short duration, though poor Callcott's face was as *long* as my arm.
In two days he was quite well, and we *enjoyed* about ten days together at Venice *very much*, as you may suppose.   We are both
somewhat disappointed in *Tintoretto* upon the *whole*, although
some of his pictures are *very* fine ; but certainly *Titian* had nothing to fear from him as a rival, as far as the real excellence of
their works went.   But I must reserve the canvassing these matters more minutely to the period which I anticipate with great
pleasure, that of shaking you by the hand, and, if you will *let* me,
kissing your wife and all the little ones, for I suppose there will
be a lot by that time in addition to Michael Angelo Peter Paul
Antony Raphaelle Charles Robert, who was in his infancy when
I quitted my native land.   I expect to see some proof of early
genius in sketches in water, made with pap-spoons.   I have heard
all about the Exhibition, and some of the proceedings of that
notorious body to which you now have the honour to belong, and
for which you officiated last year in the capacity of sheriff or
hangman ; but, like other hangmen, you must not expect to
please all you hang.   However, you have won poor Collins's
generous heart for ever, I understand.   Mrs. Callcott, who I had
never before seen more than once, I like vastly, and she is cer-

tainly a most extraordinary woman in point of information and
talent; notwithstanding which we are 'become excellent friends!!!
The Callcotts and I left Venice, and visited Padua, Mantua, and
Verona together; after which *they* went to *Milan*, which I *had*
seen, and they had *not*, and we expect to join again either at Bo-
logna or Florence. This unexpected rencountre at Venice has, I
believe, been very agreeable to all of us. Young Lewis (the animal
painter) fell in with us while at Venice. Indeed, if *he* had not
recognised *us* we should never have known *him*, on account of a
huge pair of mustachios which had come to maturity during his
tour in Germany, where he learnt to smoke much and shave
little. We left him at Venice in company with a Mr. Hoskins,
an artist, who has been studying for the last two or three years at
Rome. I have been delighted beyond measure with some of the
fresco paintings of the very early masters. There is a beautiful
chapel in this city entirely painted by the most celebrated of those
great men, namely, *Giotto*, the contemplation of which has made
an entire revolution in my ideas respecting what is termed High
Art. I have been making some imperfect sketches from them,
for I do not draw the figure well enough to do justice to them, or
to what I feel of them. I hope that I may like Raphaelle's
works at Rome *as well*, and I shall be quite satisfied. Raphaelle
evidently studied and formed his own art upon the works of this
extraordinary man, who lived about sixty years before the other.
The frescoes I speak of are most of them in fine preservation,
although more than five hundred years old. This splendid chapel
had been condemned to be dilapidated, with many others in Italy,
but it being represented to Napoleon that it contained Giotto's
frescoes, *he* ordered it to be preserved. My dear fellow, you
ought to visit Italy, if it were only to see this chapel, for I know
no one with whose feelings and taste it would be so congenial,
unless it were Stothard. I have got to the end of my tether,
without doing justice to many of our mutual friends, who I ought
to mention, but to whom (particularly Newton, the Condeys, and
Constable) you will remember me kindly. If you will muster up
resolution a second time to write to me *immediately*, a letter addressed Poste restante, Florence, will reach before I leave; and
I need not, I hope, add that it will give very great pleasure to

one who is with every sincere wish for the happiness of you and
yours,   ·Ever, your affectionate friend,

                                        P. POWELL.

P. S. — Newton owes me a letter; tell him I want to be paid.

                    1828.

The Pictures of this Year were not exhïbited. They are THE BRIDE. (Engraved
by Finden.) — A PORTRAIT OF MISS STEPHENS STANDING AT A HARP-
SICHORD. (Painted for the Earl of Essex, and engraved.) A LADY IN A
DUTCH DRESS, WITH A SCREEN IN HER HAND. — (Engraved by Finden.)

ON the 1st of February in this year was born the painter's second child, Harriet Jane.

                                        MADRID, *Feb.* 16, 1828.

MY DEAR LESLIE, — Your application for the sketch illustrative of your picture has been made at a most unfortunate time,
for my mind is quite diverted from subjects of the kind, and is at
this moment so hurried and occupied with a thousand things,
prior to my leaving Madrid on a tour to the South, that I cannot
for the life of me devise anything to the purpose.* Sketches of
the kind that are to stand by themselves, and take care of themselves, in those collections of *jeux d'esprit*, require some lucky
thought, or something striking either in conception or execution,
and at this moment I can command neither. If I can think of
anything in time, I will send it to you, as I presume the work for
next Christmas will not be immediately put to press.

    Columbus I understand is printed, but the publication deferred
for some weeks. Why, I know not. I can get no letters from
"the Murray;" and "the Newton" to whom I wrote to collect
me information, wrote me a reply without imparting any. I presume when he scribbled his letter, he was on the point of a scamper, either to the east or the west.

    I am glad to hear you have taken in hand your sketch of 'Sir

* Leslie had asked Irving to write something for one of the Annuals to accompany one of his pictures. — ED.

Roger and the Gipsies.' I think you will make a charming picture of it. Wilkie is passing the winter here, and we are daily together, as you and I used to be in old times in London. He has just finished a picture with which I am greatly pleased. I think in some respects he has benefited greatly by his visit to Italy. This painting is in a different style from any of his others, painted with less minute detail, but with great richness, force, and freedom. He looks back upon the minute labour of accessories and details in his earlier pictures as an error, which he should avoid had he to commence his career again. The present picture, however, is meant more as a sketch than a finished painting. It is admirably characteristic of Spain and its inhabitants.

We were greatly amused to hear of the classic expedition of Peter Powell to Italy. Wilkie supposes Peter means to conclude his various entertainments of oratorios, melodramas, &c., by a grand representation of the ' Last Judgment' of Michael Angelo.

I am glad to learn that matrimony sits so lightly and happily upon you. It is a great lottery, but there are invaluable prizes in it; and you appear to have been at the lucky lottery office. Give my kindest regards to Mrs. Leslie, to whom I am much obliged for making you so good a wife, and as your boy advances in understanding, prepare him to look up to me with great respect and veneration when we meet.

I set off for the south of Spain in the course of eight or ten days. I am in hopes my brother Peter will be able to accompany me, though his health has been so delicate for some weeks past, in consequence of an attack of headaches, that he sometimes seems to doubt his being competent to the journey. I have lately been joined by a nephew from America, Theodoric Irving, a fine handsome youngster of between eighteen and nineteen, who, I believe, I shall take on the tour with me.

Yours ever, my dear Leslie,
W. IRVING.

LONDON, March 19th, 1828.

MY DEAR IRVING, — I have lately received your answer to my request in behalf of Alaric Watts, and I beg you will not give yourself any trouble about the little sketch. If anything should occur to you which you can throw off with ease, so much the better; if· not, never mind. If we get nothing from you by the end of June, Watts will ask somebody else to do it.

Murray sent me your 'Life of Columbus' as soon as it was published, and I could scarcely lay it down till I had got through it. I am so much out of the world that I have seen no one else who has read it; and therefore I don't know what is thought of it, but I shall be much surprised if it does not place you in the first rank of biographical and historical writers. To me it had all the fascination of a novel, with the additional interest of real history. My wife was so charmed with the beautiful character you have drawn of Isabella, that she wishes to call our little daughter (who is not yet christened) after her. I am now reading Robertson's 'Charles V.,' and I find by the character he gives of the faithless Ferdinand that you are fully justified in your censures of his conduct to Columbus. I have not been able to finish my picture of 'Sir Roger and the Gipsies' to my mind, and shall not exhibit it this year. Newton's picture I have not seen for some time, but I intend calling on him to-day, to leave this letter for him to forward by Mr. Rich, who I hear is in town.

I am writing in a great hurry, and when more at leisure shall give you a longer sheet. You say I am to teach my boy to look up to you with great respect when you come here. Pray when will that be? I am not without hopes you will be induced to accompany Wilkie, who, I understand, returns this spring. Harriet sends her best respects and good wishes to yourself and brother; to which add the affectionate regards of

Yours, dear Irving, ever,
C. R. Leslie.

Washington Irving, Esq.,
　Madrid.

1829.

Pictures of the Year.

(134) Sir Roger de Coverley and the Gipsies.
　" She told him that he was a bachelor, but would not be so long ; and that he was dearer to somebody than he thought. The knight still re-

peated that she was an idle baggage, but bid her go on." — *Spectator*, No. 180.

THE DUKE AND DUCHESS READING DON QUIXOTE. (Engraved. Now in the possession of Joseph Gillott, Esq., Birmingham.) — PORTRAITS OF MR. AND MRS. DILLWYN AND THEIR FAMILY. — PORTRAITS OF LORD HOLLAND, MISS FOX, AND LADY AFFLECK (Lady Holland's mother.)

Washington Irving was in London this year as Secretary of the American Legation.

TO MISS LESLIE.

Sept. 11*th*, 1829.

MY DEAR BETSEY, — * * * We returned about three weeks since from Mr. Dillwyn's, where I painted a small picture of his whole family, so that to me the excursion was no holiday. To Harriet it was, and she and the children enjoyed the beautiful rambles about the house very much. We were there six weeks; Mrs. Dillwyn had very kindly allotted to the children a large play room to themselves besides their bed-room. Little Robert's greatest delight was walking with me to the farm (which was about half a mile from the house) every morning before breakfast, to see the cows, pigs, geese, ducks, and above all a litter of puppies. On our journey from London we went through Bath and Bristol, and crossed the Severn to Chepstow, which was new to me. We had but one day to stay there, which, unfortunately, was a rainy one. We, however, made an excursion in a postchaise to Tintern Abbey, which is about five miles from Chepstow, and were amply repaid by the sight of the most magnificent ruin we had ever beheld. The showers obscured the beautiful scenery by which it was surrounded, but the Abbey itself we were able to enjoy at intervals. On our return to London we chose an entirely different route, and as Harriet's situation did not admit of very rapid travelling, we were four days on the road. The first night we slept at Cardiff, and the next morning visited the Castle, the most modern part of which is occasionally inhabited by Lord Bute, to whom it belongs. The ruins of the old keep still remain, and part of the old wall, which is, I suppose, as old as the time of William the Conqueror, as it was there that his son, Robert Duke

of Normandy, was confined by his brother, William Rufus. In
the modern apartments there are some curious old family pictures,
but nothing else very interesting. The next night we slept at
Gloucester, and, from our inn windows, had a fine view of its
beautiful cathedral by moonlight. In the morning we had time
to see the interior of it, and were there during a part of the service, at the commencement of which our little baby was ordered
out by the Dean for talking, which she only meant as an imitation of the clergyman who was reading. She was, however, allowed to stand by the outer door, where she heard the organ and
the chanting of the choristers with great delight. Robert behaved
with the most perfect decorum, and was inexpressibly delighted
with the music and the very splendid interior of the church. The
east window is said to be the finest in England. It is immensely
large, and of the richest style of old stained glass. From Gloucester we proceeded through Cheltenham to Oxford, and had time
on the following morning before the coach started, to look into
New College Chapel, which contains the beautiful window designed by Sir Joshua Reynolds, and which is more than ever valuable, as the original paintings he made for it were burnt a few
years ago in a fire that happened at Belvoir Castle. We also
walked round the delightful garden belonging to this college, and
then took leave, with much regret, of this most delicious of all the
towns I ever saw. We got safe home about four o'clock, after a
journey of two hundred and twenty miles, of rather an anxious
nature to me as you may suppose, with two young children and a
wife within a few weeks of her confinement. The children bore
it extremely well, and were exceedingly good, and I am happy to
say Harriet has not suffered in the least from it. We found the
difference between the posting and the stage coach expense so
so trifling, that we used the former mode as far as Oxford.
I rode all that way on the dickey of the chaise, and often
had one of the children with me, who was handed in and out
through the front window. Little Robert and the baby have
been playing at post-chaises and postillions ever since. * She

* Leslie painted a picture of children playing, for Sir Robert Wigram, in
1847, perhaps from a sketch done from his own little ones at this time. The
picture was repeated, and the repetition is now in the gallery of Thomas Miller
Esq., Preston.

walked very well before we left London, and now talks all day
long, and remarkably plain for her age.　Since my return I have
begun a very large picture from the 'Merry Wives of Windsor,'
containing Falstaff and most of the characters, to the number of
fifteen; but more of this when I write again.　Harriet sends her
love to you, and all, and believe me,

Yours, as ever,

C. R. L.

On Oct. 19th, Leslie's third child, Caroline Anna, was born.

Miss Leslie had some time before this made her first essay as
an authoress, and had entrusted her bantling to her brother's care.
The following letter will show how tenderly and judiciously he
performed his task.

LONDON, Nov. 12th, 1829.

DEAR ELIZA, — I should have written sooner to inform you
of the birth of another daughter, but I wished also to be able to
give you some account of a child of your own, of whose welfare,
I am sorry to say, I have been too negligent since you committed
it to my care.　I can now, however, tell you a little of both of
them.　Harriet was confined on the 19th of last month (my
birthday) with a fine little girl, and both she and it have gone on
extremely well.　And now for *your baby*, who has been a long
time at nurse at Mr. Ebers's, with little advantage, I fear, to its
worldly prospects.　After calling several times in vain, I wrote to
him and so got it away, but with no answer.　I carried it to-day
to Mrs. Hofland, to ask her opinion and advice about it.　She
bears the character of a very amiable woman, and one always
ready to the utmost of her power to serve other authors.　I had
a long conversation with her, and I believe from what she says,
there is little more to be obtained for children's books here than
in America.　She tells me there are many ladies of fortune who,
being fond of seeing themselves in print, write books of that
class and give them away to the publishers, and as their productions sell well, this is of course to the disadvantage of authors
who cannot afford to write for nothing.　Mrs. Hofland got but
ten pounds for her ' Son of a Genius,' the sale of which has pro-

duced a small fortune to the publishers. She thinks you would obtain more by writing for the annuals, and if you have anything unpublished that you can send me a written copy of before it is printed in America — either tales for children or grown people — I will use all the interest I have with the publisher to get you a good price for them; or, if you will attempt a novel and trust me with it, I will do what I can, and *promptly*, *too*, as I am most anxious to retrieve, in some degree, the ground I have lost with you. In one of your letters you wish me to inquire what the booksellers will give for an American novel. You cannot expect such a question to be answered until they see, or have some means of knowing, what the merits of the novel .are. I feel quite safe in assuring you that if you will write *a good one*, I can get you a good price for it.

I am glad you agree with me in distaste for the didactic class of works of the kind. I used to like them, but now that I have grown older and know more of the world, it seems to me to be a great mistake of their well-meaning authors to attempt to deceive mankind into virtue, which I have no doubt, if it has any effect, is only calculated to deceive them into hypocrisy. Truth never did, and never can do harm ; and I feel quite sure that the really moral writers are those who describe characters *as they are*, and not as the authors think *they ought to be*, or ought not to be. I have lately spent a good deal of time at Lord Holland's, painting portraits of himself, Miss Fox and Lady Affleck (Lady Holland's mother). The present Lord Holland is one of the most accomplished and amiable men I ever met with. He is much better acquainted with and more interested in American affairs than any Englishman I have seen who has not been in America. Lady Affleck, who is eighty years of age, was born in New York, and lived there until after her first marriage. The old lady is a staunch American, and talked to me of nothing but America while she was sitting. Lady Holland begged I would introduce a map of New York somewhere in the background of her mother's portrait, which I have done. Lord Holland has dinner parties every day, and they generally consist of the most intelligent people he can collect. Rogers is a very frequent visitor there, and Moore and Sir Walter Scott, whenever they are in London. Lord

Byron used to be much there, and Monk Lewis, whose portrait hangs in one of the rooms. I dined a short time since with Murray, the publisher, and met Moore, who in the evening sang several of his own songs in so delightful a manner, that I never shall wish to hear the same songs again from any one else. Washington Irving was there, and James Smith, one of the authors of the ' Rejected Addresses.' Smith sang several excellent comic songs of his own. 'Irving is in excellent health, and looks almost as young and quite as handsome as ever he did. He is much pleased with Mr. McLane (the Ambassador), and seems to like his own situation of Secretary of Legation very well. I am glad of his having it, as the means of bringing him here ; but I am afraid it will prevent his writing for some time.

I will very soon write to Polly ; in the meantime Harriet joins me in love to you all. C. R. L.

P. S. — I have sent to Longman's some prints of Lady Jane Grey prevailed on to accept the Crown, which I hope will arrive safely.

The following pleasant letter from Peter Powell at Rome, contains a good deal of Art-gossip about the principal members of their old set, and some other painters, as well as some opinions on the subject of Peel's new Police at home and ' paternal despotism ' abroad, which it is amusing to read by the light of facts of 1860.

No 68, VIA SISTINA, ROME,
30th Nov. 1829.

MY DEAR LESLIE, — You think, no doubt, that I shall not leave this Eternal City to all eternity; and I sometimes myself think that there is a spell upon me to prevent my getting back again to old England, as we English nickname it, seeing that in fact it is one of the most modern countries (if we date from its civilisation) in Europe ; and, moreover, the little that it had to boast of as derived from our good old forefathers seems to be rapidly going away, and it may perhaps as well be called new England, or at least, new London, by the time I get to it again.

From what I read occasionally in the newspapers, all the Dog-
berrys, venerable and somniferous in Shakespeare's time and
unchanged up to ours, are now I see to be sent home to sleep in
their own beds, instead of parish watch-boxes; and in their room,
I read, there is to be established an active and virtuous police,
who are to put an end to crimes altogether by punishing people
before they have committed any.

I think Mr. Peel will have his hands full, as well as the prisons
• before long, and I wish him joy of his undertaking.   I have quite
changed my politics since I left home, and should have done the
same with my religion if I had had any.   I am living here under
the most absolute despotism in Europe, and I see the people who
are politically slaves, happier, and more free in fact, than the
people in England with all their noise and newspapers and cant
about liberty.   An English newspaper verily makes me sick.   I
have been now two years in Rome, and there has been but *one*
man executed in that time, and that for murder.   And I have
been to all the theatres, and to all the public spectacles in the
churches and streets, where all the nobility of Rome are collected,
without any fear of being either insulted or robbed — not even
excepting the Theatre of Puppets or Fantoccini here, which is a
most diverting and witty entertainment, and where the admission
to the pit is only twopence.

The bread is always excellent, and is a penny a pound.   I can
dine at the first Trattorias in Rome, including wine, for three
pauls or fifteen pence;* and I have a studio twenty-one feet
square and sixteen feet high, with a bed-room furnished, in one
of the best parts of Rome, for eight dollars a month.

Here are eight months out of the twelve perpetual sunshine,
and an earthquake every now and then gratis; a thing that is not
to be had in England for love or money.

Then I have said nothing about the beauties of the landscapes,
the magnificence of the buildings, the splendid ruins of antiquity
and works of art of all ages to be met with in Italy, the beauty
of the people, and the picturesque costume of the different countries.   In short, it is altogether a delicious country, and if it were

---

* Yet Rome is now cited as the dearest of continental capitals, except
Paris. — ED.

not for a good old mother, two or three brothers and sisters, and
three or four dear good fellows like yourself, for whom I have an
unaccountable prejudice, I believe I should never take the trouble
to visit *old* England again.

These will, however, draw me from this happy region in the
ensuing spring; and, making allowance for seeing a part of Germany in my route, I hope to shake you by the hand, with all my
heart in it, about the end of June.

I thank you very heartily for your last kind letter, which lay,
however, a considerable time at Naples while I was gone to Sicily.
Your sister's epistle was also very gratifying to me, as giving me
good accounts of our good friends on the other side of the Atlantic,
where I should like to take a peep at them, and perhaps may do
some future day. It is but a month's sail in the right season.
What say you to a trip together? Newton, too, should join us.

I see by the papers that Washington Irving is arrived in London, and also in an official capacity as Secretary to the Embassy.
Remember me kindly to him.

I want to read *his* history of Columbus, as well as to see your
and Newton's pictures, which have been painted since my absence.
I hope Newton has found some other equally qualified and candid
friend to look after his *perspective! !*

I was amazingly gratified to hear of Constable's election, and
now I look forward to Newton's being made a full R. A.

Eastlake is just finishing a very beautiful picture, which will be
sent to grace the next Exhibition.

Allan from Edinburgh, I hear, is in Italy, but has not yet
reached Rome. We are all sorry that Turner has not been able
to come out this year as he intended. He made himself very
social, and seemed to enjoy himself, too, amongst us.

And now it is time to say a few words about the good lady
and family at home, all of whom I hope are well.

You gratify me very much by assuring me in your letter that
on my return I shall receive the same kind welcome from you
both, that I was accustomed to meet with before I became such
an absentee; and the same assurance I please myself with in
regard to our valued friends the Dunlops.

Since writing the foregoing, Mr. Allan is arrived here, and

tells me that he saw Newton at Paris, and that he did not seem to be in very good health; I hope, however, that his trip did him good, and that he returned home in good health at any rate.

I have seen the Annual, with your Duke and Duchess reading Don Quixote, which I like very much, though I have no doubt all the good works suffer a great deal by being done in such a pigmy size.

I think these Annuals, though they pay the artist well, perhaps, will tend to deteriorate the art, and spoil all the engravers for larger and better things: indeed the chances are that they will all become prematurely blind.

So Newton says he will not write to me because it is clear I do not care for my old friends in London, or I should not stay so long away from them; nevertheless, as I said before, *but* for my old friends, I do not think I should return to England again. There are plenty of artists here, and several with whom I am intimate enough, but there are none that I revel with so much in talking of art, as with you and Newton.

I wish I could contribute my share of performance as well as talk, and then we should be an invisible trio.

Adieu, my dear Benedict. Kind regards to all friends,

From yours ever,

P. POWELL.

P. S.—Tell Newton that I hope he will have the magnanimity to forego his resolve, and to write to me notwithstanding my demerits, which I am ready to confess do not entitle me to a letter from any of you.

1830.

Pictures of the Year.

PORTRAIT OF DR. SIMS. (Engraved — Private Print.) — PORTRAITS OF MR. AND MRS. KING AND LADY BURRELL. (Painted for Lord Egremont.)

LESLIE was at work in the course of this year upon the ' Dinner at Page's House,' exhibited the next year, and a repetition of

which is now in the Sheepshanks' collection. He had begun the
picture in the autumn of 1829. He was also employed on
'Uncle Toby and the Widow Wadman.'

The painter's second sister, Anne, who had spent some time
with him in this country before his marriage, was now again with
him in England. His elder sister had taken up the craft of
authorship, and her brother was unwearied in his efforts to find a
market for her earliest attempts, as will be seen from the following letter. I may add, that Miss Leslie subsequently had considerable success as a writer of tales and verses, as editress of
American annuals, and last, not least, as authoress of a cookery
book, dealing especially with the dressing of Indian-corn meal,
and found, I believe, very useful during the Irish famine.

LONDON, *May* 20*th*, 1830.

DEAR ELIZA, — You have heard from Anne how little we
have been able to do with your manuscripts. On their arrival,
I lost no time in offering the tale of 'Alphonsine' to Murray,
proposing to make a design for a plate for it gratuitously, thinking it might be an additional inducement for him to take it, as he
had not long since applied to me to illustrate a work I was then
unable to do in consequence of other engagements. He sent me
a very civil note, declining it on the score of its being a translation. The other stories I knew were too juvenile for him. I
then offered 'Alphonsine' to two of the annuals, the 'Gem' and
the 'Amulet,' with the same proposal of making a gratuitous
design. The first declined it on account of its length, and the
other as being a translation. After that, I offered both it and the
tales to Harris (of St. Paul's Churchyard), and to Hurst and
Chance, still proposing to make designs for them for nothing, but
with no better success. Hurst and Chance indeed offered to print
them at your expense, and divide the profits by quarterly settle-
ments. Anne has since attempted to do something with them, of
which she has of course informed you, and I hope the arrangements she is making with Mrs. Hall may turn out to your satisfaction. I like all your tales very much ; still I confess I should
like them better if they had not so much of the didactic cant
that is the fashion now. I am of opinion that the most instruc-

tive of all writings are those that lay open to our view human nature as it really is. But this is too hard a task for the writers of children's books, who find it much easier to sit down and make a nature of their own, in which little monsters of virtue, sense, and fine sentiments, are contrasted with caricatures of folly. I think your characters are more drawn from nature than the generality of them are, but still I think you would be more really instructive if it was not for your determination to instruct. Why might not children's books be written with as much discrimination of real character, as the novels of Le Sage, Fielding, Smollett, and the best of Sir Walter Scott? I anticipate your answer; they would not sell. Then suppose you try a short novel, and take the best models, and nature, for your guide. Do not think of making your characters consistently bad, or consistently good, but draw men and women as they really appear to you. Do not let all the events of a man's or a woman's life turn on one point of their character, as Miss Edgeworth does, for the sake of supporting a theory, but divest yourself of every other intention than that of giving *true pictures of nature.* I would read none of the trash that is now published in the rage for universal improvement, but study, over and over again, the sterling authors of fiction, whose works will last as long as their language, because they are built on the rock — nature.

I find in painting it is necessary to shut my eyes to most that is doing now, and to look only at nature and the best of the old masters. The most original landscape painter I know * says, that when he sits down in the fields to make a sketch, he endeavours to forget that he has ever seen a picture. And I should think an author would do well when he sits down to write a book, to forget, if possible, that he had ever read one. If Scott could have done so, how much that is bad in his writings would have been spared the world! I have left but little room for news. The truth is, I have little to tell. We are all well.

I was unable to complete my picture of Falstaff for the Exhibition, but it is now within a few days of being finished. I shall soon begin another I hope, of equal size, for Lord Grosvenor; but the subject is not determined upon. In one of your letters

* Constable. — ED.

you say Sully wishes to know whether the fancy dresses I paint are really worn by the ladies. No, I make them up from old prints and pictures, and change and alter the forms till I think they look well. This, however, is against my own theory of copying nature, and I think it a bad plan. In future I shall paint the dresses ladies wear, for I am sure nothing can be more splendid. Unbounded extravagance seems the order of the day here with the ladies, and Anne says it is the same now in America.

LONDON, *July 2nd*, 1830.

YOUR story of the 'Travelling Tinman' is printed, and the proof sheets have been sent to me to correct. I have also made a design from it, which is now, I suppose, in the engraver's hands. I chose the subject you suggested, of the two girls discovering the black child in the cart.

Anne, I have no doubt, has given Patty all the news of the family, which is not much. We are all well, and going on as usual.

I have finished my picture of 'Falstaff' and sent it home, and as soon as I have completed the one * I have in hand from 'Tristram Shandy,' I hope to set about another large picture.

1831.

Pictures of the Year.

THE DINNER AT MRS. PAGE'S HOUSE, SUPPOSED TO TAKE PLACE IN THE FIRST ACT OF 'THE MERRY WIVES OF WINDSOR.'

A SCENE FROM TRISTRAM SHANDY. (UNCLE TOBY AND THE WIDOW WADMAN.)

"'I protest, Madam,' said my Uncle Toby, 'I can see nothing whatever in your eye' 'It is not in the white,' said Mrs. Wadman. My uncle looked with might and main into the pupil." (Painted for John Sheepshanks, Esq.; afterwards repeated for Mr. Vernon, afterwards for Mr. Jacob Bell. All three are now in the National Collection at South Kensington.)

A SCENE FROM 'THE TAMING OF THE SHREW.' (Painted for the Earl of Egremont, and engraved: afterwards repeated for John Sheepshanks, Esq., and now in the National Collection. Another small repetition was painted for Joseph Birt, Esq.)

* Uncle Toby and the Widow Wadman.

Petruchio. — " Brav'd in mine own house with a skein of thread!
    Away, thou rag, thou quantity, thou remnant;
    Or I shall so be-mete thee with thy yard,
    As thou shalt think on prating whilst thou liv'st!
    I tell thee, I, that thou hast marr'd her gown."
Tailor. — " Your worship is deceived; the gown is made
    Just as my master had direction:
    Grumio gave order how it should be made."
Grumio. — " I gave him no order; I gave him the stuff."

                                                Act iv.   Scene 3.

ON the 18th of August was born Leslie's second son, Bradford, named after his early friend and first master, Mr. Bradford
of Philadelphia.   Bradford showed a bent for civil engineering;
became a pupil of Mr. Brunel; and is now employed on railway
work in the East Indies.

I have no correspondence for this year but the following letter
from Irving, containing some excellent suggestions for the well-
known picture from the ' Taming of the Shrew,' exhibited this year.

⁂

FROM WASHINGTON IRVING.

LONDON, *Feb.* 23, 1831.

As I understand you intend to finish your picture of Petruchio
while at Petworth, I will give you a hint or two, which I had intended to give on your return to town.   I think the picture one
of the best hits of the kind that you have ever made ; it is worth
while, therefore, in my opinion, to make it a complete one.   The
figures of Grumio and the Haberdasher are deficient in character,
and make that part of the picture weak as to expression, and yet
they may easily be made to tell admirably on the story, and to
heighten the comic character of the whole.   The Haberdasher
might be represented making a cautious attempt to get hold of the
cap, with his eye glancing up at Petruchio, as if confoundly afraid
of getting a sudden thwack on the poll.   This would also tell
upon the character of Petruchio, showing how his domineering
spirit prevailed over the whole dramatis personæ.   I would make
Grumio of a spare form, with a roguish air.   His contest with
the tailor should have a more whimsical expression.   The tailor

himself, though admirably painted, has not, in my opinion, enough of the comic. I find it difficult, however, to convey my notions on paper — especially in the hurry in which I am at present. If I could have ten minutes' chat with you, I think I could act the expression I have in my mind. These hints, however will serve to set you thinking. I want to see this picture a deservedly strong one in all its parts; you will then take the field this spring in uncommon force.

1833.

Pictures Exhibited this Year.

TRISTRAM SHANDY RECOVERING THE MANUSCRIPT HE HAD LOST. (Engraved by Watt: in the possession of Thomas Miller, Esq. Preston; afterwards repeated for John Gibbons, Esq.)

"I had not waited half an hour when the mistress came in to take the papillotes from off her hair, before going to the Maypoles. * * * The toilet stands still for no man, so she jerked off her cap to begin with them as she opened the door, in doing which, one of them fell to the ground. I instantly saw it was my own writing. ' O Seigneur!' cried I, 'you have got all my remarks on your head, madam!' * * * * ' Tenez,' said she. So without any idea of the nature of my suffering, she took them from her curls, and put them gravely, one by one, into my hat," &c.

Vol. vii. Chap. 38.

MOTHER DANCING TO HER CHILD.

MARTHA AND MARY. (Painted for James Dunlop, Esq.: three times repeated.)

" A certain woman, named Martha, received him into her house. And she had a sister called Mary, which also sat at Jesus' feet, and heard his word. But Martha was cumbered about much serving, and came to him, and said, Lord, dost thou not care that my sister hath left me to serve alone? Bid her, therefore, that she help me. And Jesus answered and said unto her, Martha, Martha, thou art careful and troubled about many things: but one thing is needful: and Mary hath chosen that good part which shall not be taken away from her." — St. Luke, chap. x. ver. 38-42.

ON the 18th of July was born the painter's third daughter and fifth child — Mary. This lady possesses very remarkable artistic powers. Unhappily weak eyesight has prevented her from devoting herself to the serious pursuit of painting as a profession, but her copies, sketches, and occasional original compositions show a rare reach of invention and the very highest qualities both as a colourist and a designer. In September Leslie, to the great regret of his many English friends, left England for the United States with a view of entering upon the duties of teacher of drawing at the United States Military School of West Point. He has fully detailed in his Autobiography the expectations with which he took this step, his disappointment, and speedy return to England. Irving was among the friends who, though he formally disclaims any direct recommendation, in effect recommended the step in the following letter.

WASHINGTON, *Jan. 29th*, 1833.

MY DEAR LESLIE, — Your brother has applied to me through a friend to use my influence in persuading you to accept the appointment to the professorship of drawing at West Point. I am unwilling, however, to give advice in any matter that is to change a person's whole plan of life. The advantages of the post have no doubt been sufficiently detailed to you. The situation is one of the most beautiful in the world, and extremely healthy. The pay and quarters would enable you to live in a handsome style. The place being the national military school, assembles men of talents of all kinds. The duties of your professorship would not take up more than two hours a day, leaving you the rest for the prosecution of your art. You would be in the best of situations for the education of your children. You would be in the immediate neighbourhood of my friend Governor Kemble, and of the place where I hope to pass the greater part of my time ; and you are within four hours'. sail of New York, and steamboats pass several times in the course of the day. These are some of the advantages which immediately occur ; your brother can doubtless enumerate others. You yourself will be able to furnish the counter arguments.

The improvements in living, and the resources for living agreeably in the United States, have multiplied wonderfully since I went abroad. I have enjoyed myself delightfully since my return, and am satisfied that I can live as pleasantly here as in any part of the world.

Your appointment is a mark of great respect on the part of the Government, strong interest having been made to procure the situation for various artists resident in the country.

I can only say that it would rejoice my heart to see you on this side of the Atlantic; but I will not take upon myself the responsibility of advising you to come.

I would have given anything to have had you with me on a tour I took last summer and autumn, first to the White Mountains of New Hampshire, and then to the far West, several hundred miles west of the Mississippi, and almost to the Mexican boundaries. I was for two months leading a hunter's life, camping out, sleeping in the open air, and depending upon the chase for provisions. Saw various tribes of Indians; hunted the buffalo, &c., &c., &c. Should you come to the United States it will be very easy to get an opportunity to visit the frontier free of expense, by accompanying some public expedition, and you will witness scenes well worthy of your pencil. I was part of the time with a troop of ninety mounted rangers, clad in the ordinary but varied garments of the frontiers, and our encampments reminded me completely of the descriptions of Robin Hood and his followers. Do scrawl me a line. Let me know how Childe Newton acts the Benedict, and how his charming little wife likes England. Give my kind remembrances to your wife, and believe me ever,

Your affectionate friend,

WASHINGTON IRVING.

His old master Mr. Bradford, his brother, and many other zealous friends did their utmost to procure for him the realisation of the hopes and inducement which led him to leave England, but in vain. Congress seems to have had no special appreciation of the painter, and no particular wish to do anything that should attach him to his native country. Early in the following year he left West Point and the United States, never to return.

1834.

No picture by Leslie was exhibited this year, but he painted about this time, and after his return to this country in May, a portrait of Lady Lilford, for her father, Lord Holland.

Leslie, as usual, spent part of this summer and autumn at Pet-

worth. He writes thence to Constable. The letter is worth
notice for its ample acknowledgment of the obligations under
which Leslie felt himself to Constable in his art. Many will be
of opinion, probably, that whatever might have been the advantage to Leslie of Constable's genuine love of out-door nature, and
his keen and life-long observation of atmospheric effects, the
advantage was counterbalanced by some decided drawbacks, not
the least of them an abuse of pure white, in the attempt to render
the sparkle and brilliance of sunlight. It is no doubt true that
the spotty and splashed look which this use of pure white gave to
most of Constable's pictures, and the raw, cold, and opaque character imparted by the employment of the same pigment in lights
without over glazing, are likely to diminish, and have diminished,
with time. But it seems to me indisputable, that the substitution
of Constable's for Newton's influence and example upon Leslie as
a colourist, was altogether unfavourable to his brilliancy and transparency, if of benefit to the permanence of his work. A comparison of the 'Catherine and Petruchio' with the 'Who can this
be?' and 'Who can this be from?' in the Sheepshanks' collection, will illustrate my meaning.

There is an openness and fulness in Leslie's acknowledgments
very characteristic of the man.

TO JOHN CONSTABLE, R.A.

PETWORTH, *Sept. 5th*, 1834.

MY DEAR CONSTABLE, — I hope you will not put off coming
later than Wednesday or Thursday next, as, soon after that, we
must think of returning to London, and I do think you will really
enjoy the visit.

The Gainsborough which you so truly feel is still on the
ground, and there is a very fine Wilson which perhaps you did
not see. There is a gem of a Bassan also, which came from
London since you were here, and which Lord Egremont allows
me to have in my room. I am afraid you did not quite understand what I meant by *your keen eye.* I am only afraid of it
because I know no fault can escape it. Do not for a moment
imagine I am insensible of my obligations to it. You not only

did me the greatest service in inducing me to enlarge my
' Sancho,' but you entirely composed my ' Sterne and the French
Woman ; ' that is, you composed the light and shadow for me.   I
am not aware that I have painted a picture since I have known
you that has not been in some degree the better for your remarks,
and I constantly feel that if I could please *you* with what I do, I
should be sure to please myself.   But enough of this; you may
think I want compliments, but indeed I do not.

I am glad on every account you are likely to visit Petworth
just now.   I never so much enjoyed being here, and Lord Egremont is so uncommonly well.   Mr. King, his son-in-law, says that
since he has known him he does not remember his being so well.
The weather is delicious.   I trust it will continue as it is during
your visit.

To-day forty people dine here, most of them magistrates, and
the house is as full as it can hold.   Among them is the Duke of
Richmond.   I have just been looking at the table as it is set out
in the carved room, covered with magnificent gold and silver plate.

Callcott has been here, and went to day. * * * *

· Dear Constable,

Yours ever,

C. R. LESLIE.

In the following letter to Irving, now resettled at his home in
New York, Leslie gives an account of his visit to their poor
friend, Newton, in the Lunatic Asylum at Chelsea, where he was
now confined : —

12, PINE APPLE PLACE, EDGEWARE ROAD,
LONDON, *Dec.* 29, 1834.

YOU are often mentioned by others in their letters, but I wish
much to hear from yourself, how you are, what you are doing,
and when there is any chance of your paying another visit to
England.   Mr. Dunlop has sent me the sheets of his ' History
of American Painters.'   I think if it can be made known by a
good review it will have an extensive circulation.   There are
some things in it I regret to see ; but it contains a great deal
which, I think, will interest the public, and would interest in this

country, — but I cannot get either Murray, Bentley, or Longman
to publish it. I find he has made most honourable mention of
me, and that you have helped him to put a good face on the
matter. I read your account of poor Newton with great interest,
and a revival of many pleasant recollections of the days of yore;
but I am sorry for some things Dunlop has inserted of him. I
think some allowance ought to be made for him when last in
America, for it now seems to be the general opinion of his friends
that his malady was gaining on him for some time before it became confirmed. I see him frequently; he always knows me
and often talks as well as ever he did. There is no alteration in
his appearance or manner, except that the latter is more subdued
and quiet. His habits, unlike when in health, are perfectly
regular (but this is, in some measure, the necessary consequence
of his confinement). He goes to bed at ten, rises at eight to walk
in the garden before the other patients are there, for he avoids
their society. He · is not confined to his room, and has every
comfort possible in his situation. He has made more than twenty
sketches of original subjects, all of them good, and some equal to
his very best things. They are from Shakespeare. I believe Dr.
Sutherland does not consider his case as quite hopeless.

I spent six weeks with my wife and children at Petworth in
the summer. The weather was uncommonly fine, and I rambled
more about the neighbourhood than I had ever done before, with
Constable, who was there part of the time. Among other things,
we stumbled on a melancholy looking, remote, stern farm-house,
and while he stopped to make a sketch of the outside, which was
very picturesque, I went in to draw the interior. It was in a dilapidated condition, and the woman who lives there told me it was
known by the name of ' Wicked Hammond's house,' from one of
its former possessors, but beyond the time of her recollection.
There were traditions, however, in the neighbourhood, that this
wicked Hammond was a very bad man, who lived there alone ;
and it was also reported that since his time the house had been
haunted, but this she could not confirm from her own experience,
as neither she nor her husband had ever seen the ghost ; but
that about four months ago, in cleaning out an old well, some
human bones had been found. I asked her if she was sure they

were not the bones of some other animal; but she said the sexton had seen them, and declared that one of them was ' the *arm bone of a Christian.*' I am very busy with a picture of ' Gulliver's Introduction to the Queen of Brobdingnag,' which I think will be my best, as I always do of the last. Columbus is finished, and I hope to have both in the next Exhibition.

1835.

Pictures of the Year.

COLUMBUS AND THE EGG. (Painted for W. Wells, Esq., Redleaf; afterwards purchased by Lord Northwick, and sold at the sale of the Northwick collection in 1859 for 1160 guineas; now in the possession of Joseph Gillott, Esq., Birmingham.)

" Pedro Gonzalez de Mendoza, the Grand Cardinal of Spain, invited Columbus to a banquet, where he assigned him the most honourable place at table. * * * A shallow courtier present, impatient of the honours paid to Columbus, and meanly jealous of him as a foreigner, abruptly asked him whether he thought that in case he had not discovered the Indies, there were not other men who would have been capable of the enterprise. To this Columbus made no immediate reply, but taking an egg, invited the company to make it stand upon one end. Everyone attempted it, but in vain; whereupon he struck it upon the table so as to break the end, and left it standing upon the broken part; illustrating, in this simple manner, that when he had once shown the way to the New World, nothing was easier than to follow it." — *Irving's Life of Columbus.* Book v. Chap. 7.

GULLIVER'S INTRODUCTION TO THE QUEEN OF BROBDINGNAG. (Painted for Lord Egremont.)

" Her Majesty, and those who attended her, were beyond measure delighted with my demeanour. I fell on my knees, and begged the honour of kissing her imperial foot; but this gracious princess held out her little finger towards me (after I was set on a table), which I embraced in both my arms, and put the tip of it with the utmost respect to my lips. * * * She then asked my master whether he were willing to sell me at a good price. He, who apprehended I could not live a month, was ready enough to part with me, and demanded a thousand pieces of gold, which were ordered him on the spot." — *Voyage to Brobdingnag,* Chap. 8.

About this time, too, Leslie painted a family group for Lord Westminster, which was not exhibited.

On the 2nd of July, was born the painter's third son, George Dunlop, — now following his father's profession.

I find the following letters of this year from and to Irving : —

NEW YORK, *March* 8, 1835.

MY DEAR LESLIE, — I have been exceedingly gratified by the receipt of a letter from you, and· to learn that you are going to be so strong in the Exhibition this year. I regret continually that I did not see your Columbus before you sailed. As to your Gulliver, I do not see how you will make the spectators know that the giants are not people of the common size, and Gulliver a pigmy.* The story, luckily, is generally known, and most of the spectators will, in that way, understand the subject.

Your account of poor Newton's situation is rather less gloomy than I had apprehended. It is a great source of enjoyment to him and comfort to his friends, that he is enabled to occupy himself with his pencil. In this way the better part of him, his genius, will not be lost to the world.

Give my kind remembrance to Mrs. Leslie. I write in extreme haste. * ·   *   *   *   *   *   *

•

LONDON, *May* 11*th*, 1835.

MY DEAR IRVING, — I received your letter a short time ago, and hope, now that our correspondence is revived, we shall keep it up until we meet again, — an event I confidently look forward to. You must have heard, very soon after you wrote, of the publication of your ' Tour on the Prairies.' Mr. Rogers, whose opportunities of knowing are the best, says it is very popular with such people as you would like it to be popular with in this country. Murray sent Mrs. Leslie a copy, and we have read it with very great pleasure. I am particularly pleased with the account you give of the Indians, and am glad you have stripped off that theatrical and unnatural character which the poets and romance writers had given them, and have shown (what I always suspected) that they are essentially much more like other people than we have been led to think. I am also delighted at your account of those very respectable little dogs you met with. How I should have enjoyed lounging on the ground with you the day you spent in watching them. As to your·buffalo hunting, &c., I own I prefer reading about it to having been present, not being a

* This is precisely the defect of the picture. — ED.

good horseman, and entertaining (as Leigh Hunt expresses it) "a *distant* respect for a bull." Murray has just sent us your 'Abbotsford and Newstead Abbey,' and we are reading it with great pleasure. I have seen the very honourable mention you have made of me to Dunlop, as it appears in his book, and cannot but think you have said much more for me than I deserve; at any rate you have put the best face on the matter, for had you described me as *I know you know* me to be, there would have been something to put down on the opposite side of the account. Poor Newton has not fared so well; all his faults have been arrayed against him, not by you but by his biographers. I am sorry to say he is no better in mind, though quite well in body, and by no means unhappy, which is the most comfortable thing his friends can now know of him. I have sent my 'Columbus,' and 'Gulliver' to the Exhibition. Wilkie's 'Columbus' is also in the Exhibition, and a very grand picture it is, one of his finest. The figures are nearly as large as life, and look quite so. The boy (Columbus's son) is admirably introduced, and makes a fine contrast with the other figures.

12, PINE APPLE PLACE, EDGEWARE ROAD,
July 8th, 1835.

MY DEAR IRVING, — I write, in great haste, to ask you a question I am desired to do by Charles Heath, who has just called to say he intends publishing an American landscape annual, consisting of views on the Hudson, and he is very desirous of engaging you to furnish the letter-press on your own terms. It is to be on the plan of 'Turner's Annual Tour,' edited by Leitch Ritchie. I have written to Cole, at his request, to furnish the drawings. If you choose to engage in it, I should think you will not find it very troublesome, as you may throw into it so much historical matter relating to Revolutionary scenes. The details of Arnold's treachery, and the capture and death of André, for instance. Pray let me have your answer as soon as possible. Should you decline it, perhaps you may know somebody capable and willing to engage in such a work. I have read your 'Abbotsford and Newstead Abbey' with great interest. Your account of Scott brought tears to my eyes. Nothing can be more beautiful, nor more true than the conclusion, in which you give his character as a man and as a writer. We are all quite well. Mrs. Leslie presented me with another son on the 2nd, and is doing extremely well.

P. S. — Poor Newton, I am sorry to say, is no better.

1836.

Pictures of the Year.

(829) AUTOLYCUS. (Painted for J. Sheepshanks, Esq., and now in the National Collection.)
  "Here's another ballad, Of a fish, that appeared upon the coast, on Wednesday the fourscore of April, forty thousand fathom above water, and sung this ballad about the hard hearts of maids."
                    Winter's Tale, Act. iv. Scene 3.
AN EVENING LANDSCAPE FROM MR. LESLIE'S WINDOW. — A SMALL PICTURE OF AMY ROBSART. (Painted for Mr. Sheepshanks, and engraved. Now in the National Collection.)

THE following letter to Miss Anne Leslie, touches on a point that should still stir the susceptibilities of American patriotism. I am not aware that Mount Vernon has yet been purchased by the nation, in honour of Washington, or that Stuart's full-length portrait of the founder and consolidator of his country's independence yet adorns the place of his birth.

LONDON, *Sept.* 24, 1836.

MY DEAR ANNE, — You will excuse a hasty letter from me just now, as we are in the bustle of packing up for a visit to Petworth. Lord Egremont was in town a few weeks ago and asked us all again, and we set off early to-morrow morning.

I was much gratified by your last letter, giving me an account of your visit to Washington. I once spent a fortnight there when I was with Mr. Bradford, but from what you tell me it must be now greatly improved. Your account of the present state of Mount Vernon is very melancholy. It ought to be preserved, and the picture of Washington by Stuart, which belonged to Mr.

Williams — the finest whole-length of him in existence — should be there.   Mr. McLane, on his return to America, proposed to Congress that Stuart's picture should be purchased for the nation, but the measure was thrown out.

If Henry Carey and a few other public spirited Philadelphians would unite, and raise a subscription for the purchase of it to adorn the Hall of Independence in Philadelphia, they would deserve the thanks of their fellow-citizens both now and hereafter.   The picture belongs to Mr. Lewis, and is still in London, and I believe might be had for seven or eight hundred guineas. It is the common remark of travellers that in America there are no antiquities, — no objects of veneration belonging to times past. Americans themselves feel this, and yet they make little effort to preserve or secure those they might.   To a stranger visiting Philadelphia, how interesting it would be to be shown the houses of Penn and Franklin.   I was glad to find the Hall of Independence preserved, and if it could be filled with the portraits of the most distinguished statesmen and soldiers of the revolution, and among them the picture I have mentioned of Washington, Philadelphia might boast of a monument of the past far exceeding in interest anything to be found in any other part of the Union.

You ask me for an impression of the 'May Day,' and you shall have one soon, when I hope to have something else to send with it.   Eliza had said she thought an engraving from some picture of mine would be acceptable to aunt Hayes, and I therefore sent her one of the only two I had to spare at that time.

1837.

Pictures of the year.

(47) PERDITA.   (Painted for John Sheepshanks, Esq., and now in the National Collection.)   A study for this picture is in the possession of A. J. Heugh, Esq.

> —— "Here's flowers for you;
> Hot lavender, mints, savory, marjoram;
> The marigold, that goes to bed with the sun,
> And with him rises weeping: these are flowers
> Of middle summer, and, I think, they are given
> To men of middle age: You are very welcome!"
>
> *Winter's Tale,* Act iv. Scene 8.

(66) CHARLES II. AND THE LADY BELLENDEN. (Painted for the Earl of Egremont. A small repetition of the picture was painted in 1856.)
"Upon his route through the West of Scotland to meet Cromwell in
the unfortunate field of Worcester, Charles the Second had actually
breakfasted at the Tower of Tillietudlem, an incident which formed,
from that moment, an important era in the life of Lady Margaret, who
seldom afterwards partook of that meal, either at home or abroad, without detailing the whole circumstances of the Royal visit; not forgetting
the salutation which his Majesty conferred on each side of her face,
though she sometimes omitted to notice that he bestowed the same
favour on two buxom serving-wenches who appeared at her back, elevated for the day into the capacity of waiting gentlewomen." — *Old
Mortality*, chap. 2.

LESLIE had this year to deplore the loss of his friend Constable,
for whom it would be hard to say whether he felt more affection
as a man, or more admiration as a landscape-painter. In May,
the Royal Academy was transferred from Somerset House to Mr.
Wilkins's building in Trafalgar Square. The following letter
to Miss Leslie gives an account of the opening of the new building by King William IV., one of the King's last public acts.

TO MISS A. LESLIE.

LONDON, *May 23*, 1837.

YOU will, I dare say, like to have some account of the opening
of the Exhibition in the new building, and I have really not had
time till now to sit down and give it you.

The private views took place on the 28th April, and the King
had sent us word that he would come at one o'clock. As he came
all the way from Windsor for the purpose, he could not be at the
Academy at twelve o'clock as usual. It was therefore arranged
that the general company should not be admitted till three. The
portico of the new building commands a view of the whole length
of Pall Mall to St. James's, and as it is elevated considerably
above the foot-way, most of us were standing there a little before
one, looking anxiously towards the palace, when exactly at the
appointed hour we saw the Royal carriages appear in the distance.
A guard of soldiers, with a band of music, were stationed in front
of the building, and behind them an immense crowd, which ex-

tended on the left to St. Martin's Church, the steps and even the roof of which were covered with people : the bells pealing a merry chime from the steeple. The scene as the King's carriage drew up was altogether very imposing. The old gentleman looked out of spirits ; he has recently lost his favourite daughter, Lady de Lisle, and was in deep mourning, and the Queen was prevented from coming by illness. The King wore neither star nor ribbon, but was dressed in a plain suit of black. The Princess Augusta, the Dukes of Cumberland and Cambridge, and two of the King's sons, and Lady Mary, and Colonel Fox, Lady Errol (another of the King's daughters), Madame d'Este (daughter of the Duke of Sussex), and several lords and ladies in waiting, formed the Royal party. I think they came in eight carriages, all with the Royal arms and liveries. When the King entered the door, Sir Martin Shee presented him the keys of the Academy on a silver plate. They were highly polished, and had arrived that morning from Birmingham, and as it had been found (to the great consternation of the workman), would not fit the locks. The King, however, did not try them, but returned them to the President, saying, " He could not place them in better hands."

His Majesty then went regularly through all the rooms, attended by the President and a lord in waiting, with each a catalogue in their hands, ready to answer any questions, we (i. e., the members of the Council) following at a respectful distance, and taking care (which required some little attention) never to stand with our backs to his Majesty. When he had completed the round of the Exhibition, he asked what o'clock it was, and being told it wanted a quarter to three, he desired Lord Albemarle to make arrangements for the departure. According to etiquette, all the Royal party left the rooms in threes and fours, as their carriages were announced before the King, who was left at last with only the Princess Augusta and a lord and lady in waiting. We were then standing in a row before him, and he addressed us all in a loud tone, and expressed his perfect satisfaction with the Exhibition. He bowed round to us, and we all bowed still lower, and followed him out of the room. When he came out under the portico, the band struck up " God Save the King," and he advanced to the front, bare-headed, and bowed to the people below, who

20

cheered him loudly.   He left the door exactly at three, and in being thus punctual showed his consideration for those who he
knew expected to be admitted at that time.   The rooms were
very soon crowded with the usual visitors ; and about four o'clock
the Duchess of Kent and Princess Victoria came, without any
ceremony, in the midst of the company, having sent us word in
the morning that they intended doing so.   This was never done
before, their visits on all other occasions having been strictly private.   The little Princess has all the charms of health, youth,
and high spirits.   She could have seen little of the Exhibition, as
she was herself, from the moment of her entering the room, the
sole object of attraction, and there were so many people among
the nobility present whom she knew, and every one of whom had
something to say to her.   She heard that Charles Kemble was in
the room, and she desired he might be presented to her, which
gave him an opportunity of making one of his best genteel comedy bows.   She shook hands and chatted with Mr. Rogers.

As the private view, you know, is a show of company and not
of pictures, I have left myself no room to speak of the latter,
but will do so in another letter, and by the first opportunity I
will send you a catalogue.

Turner desires me to tell E*** C**** that he cannot undertake a picture of less size than three feet by four, and that his
price will be 200 guineas for that size.   *   *   *   *

This year, too, was that of Her Majesty's coronation, at which
ceremony Leslie was present.   He gives an account of it to his
sister in the following letter.

LONDON, *July* 24, 1837.

I AM painting Lord and Lady Holland at their house, and
through the kindness of her ladyship I obtained a ticket to see
the coronation from the Earl Marshal's box.   A ticket was also
sent me as a member of the Academy, which I gave to Harriet,
but as they were for different parts of the Abbey and different
entrances, we could not go together.   I was obliged to hire a
Court dress for the occasion, and appeared for the first and last
time of my life with a sword by my side.   I was very near the

altar and the chair in which the Queen was crowned, and when she signed the coronation oath, I could see that she wrote a large bold hand. I intend painting the subject, and Lady Holland obtained for me an order of admission to sketch the decorations in the Abbey before they were removed.

I took Harriet and the four eldest children, and though the crowd was immense, we were protected by two policemen, who kept an open space for us, and placed in the same seat from which I had witnessed the ceremony, where we staid, quite out of the crowd, and as long as we pleased. It is impossible by words to convey to you an idea of the magnificence of the spectacle. Even the appearance of the Abbey with the spectators (before any of the personages engaged in the ceremony came in), was worth getting up at half-past two in the morning, as we did, to witness. We were in the Abbey from five till past four in the afternoon. Refreshments of every kind were to be had there, but I had taken some biscuits in my pocket which satisfied me. The Queen, I am told, had studied her part very diligently, and she went through it extremely well. I don't know why, but the first sight of her in her robes, brought tears into my eyes, and it had this effect on many people; she looked almost like a child. She is very fond of dogs, and has one very favourite little spaniel, who is always on the look out for her return when she has been from home. She had of course been separated from him on that day longer than usual, and when the state coach drove up to the steps of the palace, she heard him barking with joy in the hall, and exclaimed, ' There's Dash !' and was in a hurry to lay aside the sceptre and ball she carried in her hands, and take off the crown and robes, *to go and wash little Dash.* * * * * *

* * * The place where I sat, commanded a view of the peers but not the peeresses, except of the Royal Family, all of whom I was very near. The Duke de Nemours was in the same box with them.

The young Queen visited the Exhibition in August. Here is Leslie's account of the visit.

LONDON, *Aug.* 15, 1837.

*   *   *   *   *   *   *   *   *

Before the pictures were removed from the Exhibition, the little Queen paid it a visit. She did not go in state (that is, with a guard of soldiers), and the policemen and her footmen had great difficulty in keeping the crowd from incommoding her when she alighted at the Academy.

Her mother was with her, and she was attended by the Duchess of Sutherland, the Marchioness of Tavistock, and two young ladies whose names I did not hear. These, with Lord Albemarle, and two young gentlemen, completed her suite. They were all dressed very plainly in mourning, and there was nothing to distinguish the Queen from the other ladies, but a long train, which was not, however, held up. She looked very pretty, and none of the engravings yet published do her anything like justice. Chalon has made a splendid drawing of her, whole length, in the robes of state, and when an engraving of this gets to America, you will know how she looks. Her manner is unaffectedly graceful, and towards her mother she appears the same affectionate little girl we saw at the Academy on the 1st of May, still calling her 'Mamma.' Before leaving the rooms, the President presented each of us to her separately, at her own request, and she afterwards took occasion to address a word or two to each by name. She asked me how many pictures I had there, and if I did not think it a very fine exhibition. The day was very fine, and on her leaving the Academy, her carriage was opened, so that the crowd, which had greatly increased, had a full view of her as she drove away, amidst the most enthusiastic greetings. It is remarkable that the first exhibition of the Academy in the new building, should have been visited by two sovereigns, and two heirs presumptive to the throne (the Duke of Cumberland being the present heir, and the Queen having been the heir when the Academy opened). * * * * * *

In September Leslie was again at Petworth. Lord Egremont

was now in his eighty-fifth year. The globe Leslie speaks of in the following letter to his wife, is the one introduced in his picture of 'Lady Carlisle carrying the Pardon to the Duke of Northumberland in the Tower.'

Sept. 5th, 1837.

DEAREST HARRY!—When I got here yesterday, Lord Egremont and all the family were at Egg Dean fair, so that you may judge how well he is. On his return he would go up-stairs to look at the pictures which were in my room, although I offered to bring them down; and this morning he was up in the top rooms of all after the old globe which I am to introduce into the new picture. He approves of the composition, and I am to go on with it as it is. How much I wish you could be with me! The house is so quiet.

. Heaven bless thee, dearest Harry! I wish it were possible for thee and dear Mary to come here next week, or if you could bring them all. Lord Egremont is so well, and the house is so quiet, and it seems so unnatural for me to be here without thee. * *

1838.

Pictures of the Year.

THE PRINCIPAL CHARACTERS IN THE ' MERRY WIVES OF WINDSOR ' ASSEMBLED AT THE HOUSE OF MR. PAGE. (A scene not in the play, but supposed to take place in the first act) —
———— " There's pippins and cheese to come."
— Sir Hugh Evans.
He had painted the same subject, with variations, in 1831. The picture of 1838 was painted for Mr. Sheepshanks, and is now in the National Collection.

A PORTRAIT OF MRS. BATES. (In the collection of Joshua Bates, Esq. Engraved — private plate.)

OF the year's exhibition, which contained Wilkie's picture of ' The Queen's First Council,' he says, in a letter to his sister Anne, of April 30,

" I have just returned from the Academy, where I think we

shall have an amusing exhibition. There are Queens of all sorts and sizes, as you may suppose, *good, bad,* and *indifferent.* Sully's is not finished, and of course not there; the best are Wilkie's and Chalon's. Wilkie has painted her at her first council, which took place immediately on the news of the death of the King reaching London. There are an immense number of figures, and the peculiarity of the subject, a young girl of eighteen, unattended by any other female, taking her place at the head of a long table and surrounded by all the great dignitaries of the church, state, and law, is very striking. She is dressed very simply, in white (for it is not the etiquette that she should be in mourning till after the funeral of the King), and this adds to her innocent and dove-like appearance. Chalon's drawing of her is, I think, a better likeness than Wilkie's; it is a small whole-length figure, sitting, and in her every-day dress." * * *

This year brought the painter into his first contact with Royalty. He began, in the autumn, his picture of ' The Queen receiving the Sacrament at her Coronation.' He describes in his Autobiography the circumstances to which he owed this honourable but onerous commission. I have known more than one painter who has been similarly honoured, but I fear they would all agree that the honour hardly compensates the anxiety, fret, and loss of time inseparable from having to paint exalted personages, whose days are too much at the bidding of state and ceremonial engagements to allow of their giving a painter either long or regular sittings. Leslie used to employ his enforced leisure on these occasions in copying one of her Majesty's exquisite De Hooghes and a Nicholas Maas. These copies were included in the recent sale of the painter's sketches and studies, and showed that power of catching the spirit and character, and much of the magical atmospheric effect, of the originals, which might have been anticipated from skill like Leslie's united to his feeling and admiration for the works of these wonderful Dutchmen. I print these letters written to his wife from Windsor, as presenting a pretty contrast between the painter's home thoughts and longings and his employment. IIis heart was all the while in the quiet little house in St. John's Wood, thinking of the "old sofa," and

" the door to be cut from Braddy's room," and " what little cheap toy he could bring home for each of the darlings."

CASTLE INN, Dec. 11th, 1838.

DEAREST LOVE ! — The train was heavily loaded to-day, having (besides the weight of my newly-acquired consequence) five coaches and I don't know how many horses. We got to Windsor, however, a very few minutes past ten, and I have established myself in the pleasant bedroom we had together. I had no sittings to-day, nor have I seen her Majesty, who rode out. I was glad to find Lord Melbourne is here, and I sent a message to him to request a sitting to-morrow, and received for answer that he will do so *with pleasure.* The Duchess will also sit, and should I get them both done, I hope to be at home on Thursday. At any rate, I have no doubt of being with you on Friday, *that I may attend the club.** I found at the Castle a letter from Lady Holland waiting for me, full of kind expressions, and the congratulations of Lord Holland and herself. She says they will be away ten days or a fortnight. She has heard from Lord Melbourne and Lady Cowper that the Queen is *extremely pleased with* the picture.

I think the sooner you get the door cut from Braddy's room, the better, but do not have the old sofa removed up-stairs till I return.

The reporter of the ' Court Circular' asked to see me this afternoon, and wanted to know what I wished put in the papers. I told him there was nothing to put in, as the Queen had not been sitting to-day.

I have really nothing more, dear pet, to fill my paper with, and you know I can't write without materials.

Heaven bless thee, and all the rest of thee, from long Bob down to short George. Tell me what little cheap toy I can bring for each of them, — something easily packed.

C. R. L.

P. S. — I shall look anxiously for one of thy nice letters to-morrow.

<hr>

* The Sketching Society. — ED.

I am sorry to say I have a companion in the coffee room. I hope he will go away to-morrow.

WINDSOR, 12th Dec. 1838.

DEAREST HARRY!—I was a little disappointed at no letter from thee to-day, but I suppose thee had nothing to tell me, and plenty to do besides writing. I hoped to be with thee to-morrow, but am sorry to say I cannot. Lord Melbourne sat this morning, like a good prime minister, but was called away, and will sit again to-morrow; and the Duchess of Kent sent word she would prefer sitting to-morrow instead of to-day, and I was obliged to acquiesce. She will have the dress on that she wore. The Queen held a council, and afterwards rode, and I saw her not. Lady Mary Stopford came in, and praised the picture very much, and I thought her a very agreeable person,—and my friend the lighter of fires also looked at it and said, "*that's very like Melbourne*," quite in the style and tone of Peter. I painted till half-past three and then took a turn on the terrace, and now I have the evening before me. I am happy to say the man who was in the coffee room yesterday has gone. The villain sat in my arm chair, the only one of the kind in the room. If I can get the Duchess done in one sitting, I have no doubt of being home on Friday, but if not it will be Saturday; and unless I have something particular to say, I had better not write to thee again, to save the postage, but I do hope for a letter from thee to-morrow. Love and kisses to all, but most to thy dear self, from thy

C. R. L.

At the same date he writes to his sister Anne:—

* * * "MY late letters to you have been chiefly on one subject, the Coronation, a subject now far more important to me than ever. I came here on the 29th of last month by appointment to have a sitting of the Queen, and with little expectation of having more than one. The composition was entirely arranged on the canvas, and the Queen seemed much pleased when she saw it. At the conclusion of the sitting she said she would sit again the next day, and a few minutes after she left the room the Marquis of

Conyngham (Lord Chamberlain) came in, and asked me if the picture was bespoken. He said he knew her Majesty would like to have a picture of mine, and he thought she would prefer this subject to any other. I told him it was begun conditionally for a gentleman who was to have given me an answer a month ago whether or not he would take it. As this gentleman had been in town, but had not called to see the picture, and to let me know his decision at the time he had himself appointed, I considered it now to be at my own disposal, and that of course I should feel very highly honoured should her Majesty wish to possess it. The next morning Lord Torrington, with Lady Tavistock and some of the maids of honour, came to look at it, and said they were sure, from the way in which the Queen spoke of it at dinner the day before, she intended to have it, which I soon heard was the case.

"I have been here ever since with the exception of a day or two in town (I perform the journey in an hour by the railroad), and the Queen has sat five times. She is now so far satisfied with the likeness that she does not wish me to touch it again. She sat not only for the face, but for as much as is seen of the figure, and for the hands with the coronation ring on her finger. Her hands, by the bye, are very pretty, the backs dimpled, and the fingers delicately shaped. She was particular also in having her hair dressed exactly as she wore it at the ceremony every time she sat. She has suggested an alteration in the composition of the picture, and I suppose she thinks it like the scene, for she asked me where I sat, and said, 'I suppose you made a sketch on the spot.'

"The Duchess of Kent and Lord Melbourne are now sitting to me, and last week I had sittings of Lord Conyngham and Lady Fanny Cowper (a very beautiful girl and one of the Queen's train-bearers), who was here for a few days on a visit to her Majesty. Every day lunch is sent to me, which, as it is always very plentiful and good, I generally make my dinner. The best of wine is sent in a beautiful little decanter with a V. R. and the crown engraved on it, and the tablecloth and napkins have the royal arms and other insignia on them as a pattern.

"I have two very good friends at the Castle, one of the pages, and a little man who lights the fires. The Queen's pages are not little boys in green, but tall and *stout gentlemen* from forty to fifty years of age. My friend (Mr. Batchelor) was a page in the time of George III. and was then twenty years old. George IV. died in his arms, he says, in a room adjoining the one I am painting in. Mr. Batchelor comes into the room whenever there is nobody there, and admires the picture to my heart's content. My other friend, the fire-lighter, is extremely like Peter Powell, only a size larger. He also greatly admires the picture; he confesses he knows nothing about the robes, and can't say whether they are like or not, but he pronounces the Queen's likeness excellent."   *   *   *

1839

Pictures of the Year.

* " Who Can This Be? " —* " Who Can This be From? " —* Head of Sancho Panza. (Engraved). —* Head of Dulcinea. (Engraved. All painted for John Sheepshanks, Esq;, and now in the National Collection.)

Portrait of Dr. Howley, Archbishop of Canterbury. (Painted for Mrs. Howley, and engraved.)

Small Portrait of the Duchess of Sutherland in her Coronation Robes, and of the Marquis of Stafford. (Painted for Sir H. G. Moon.)

Leslie was this year much employed on the Coronation Picture. During his evenings he was busy with the pen, putting together his Life of Constable, which was a work of love and duty with him. Mr. Forster of Pall Mall, who conducted the sale of the pictures and sketches, which remained in Constable's possession at the time of his death in 1837, has told me of the affectionate pains and interest with which Leslie superintended and aided in the preparations and arrangements for the sale. To use Mr. Forster's expressive words, " he seemed to treat the pictures as affectionately as if they had been his friend's children." And this was his real feeling. But Leslie was one of those men who thought no amount of trouble or labour too great to encounter for a friend. He was the usual negotiator of Irving's literary

* See Introductory Essay.

bargains, and laboured in the same way as cheerfully for his sister.

It is mainly, if not entirely, to his strenuous efforts that we owe the subscription to purchase Constable's picture of 'The Cornfield,' for the National Gallery; and Leslie's correspondence touching that purchase makes up a goodly bundle of MS.

His affectionate regard for all Constable's children was redoubled after their father's death.

TO MISS A. LESLIE.

" March 18, 1839.

" WE are all as usual, and I have been constantly working on my picture for the Queen, every day or two putting a new face in it, here and there, as I can get them to sit. It will not be possible for me to have it ready for the Exhibition, as some of the most important personages will not be ready till after Easter. The picture is now at Buckingham Palace, and I had sittings from the Queen and the Duchess of Kent, and her Majesty is to sit again this week (I hope, for her sake, for the last time). She is extremely obliging, and puts me in high spirits about the picture by liking it very much.

" Ask Edward Carey if he would publish a book of my writing, and with my name. It would be <i>The Life of an Artist</i>, filled with the most interesting letters on all matters relating to art."

" June 16, 1839.

*   *   *   *   *   *

" My picture is at present at Cambridge House, where I am painting the Duke of Cambridge, Princess Augusta, and Miss Kerr (lady in waiting to the Princess). On Monday I take it to Clarence House, to paint the Princess Augusta (the Queen's aunt), and then I shall have finished the Royal Family. I have now thirty two portraits in the picture. It is very amusing to me being at the houses of those Royal personages, and seeing how they live among themselves — much more so than seeing them at drawing-rooms and levees, though not so splendid."

* * * "In a day or two I shall send the little picture I have painted for E. Carey, and I shall request him to hand you the price of it (25 guineas), which I must beg you to accept from me. I could not get permission to copy the sketch of Lady Fanny Cowper for him, but I will paint some pretty face (a lady) as a companion to the one I now send; and if it does not meet with his approbation, he may return it, or perhaps somebody else may take a fancy to it in America.

"Some time ago Wilkie told me that a friend of his in New Orleans had purchased of Earle your copy of 'Katharine and Petruchio' as an original picture, and never doubted its being so, until he saw the engraving from Lord Egremont's picture. He then wrote to Wilkie to ascertain the truth ; of course I have set the matter right, but I am very sorry such a deception should be practised.

"The Queen is, I believe, satisfied with my picture ; but I did not see her Majesty when I took it to Windsor.

"There is no probability that a knighthood will be offered to me, and therefore it is needless to say I should assuredly decline it if offered. But I do not, like the fox in the fable, call the grapes sour that are above my reach ; on the contrary, I think titles very good things, but then they should be accompanied by proportionate wealth. In our humble way of living, ' Sir Charles,' and 'My Lady' would be ridiculous. Were the case even otherwise, and I could keep my carriage (which I think a titled person should do), as long as such men as Chalon, Turner, and Mulready are undistinguished except by the addition of R.A. to their names, I may certainly be content with that honour.

"I have been introduced to Joseph Bonaparte (at his request, by Captain Morgan, who brought him to England), and I am much pleased with his fine, benevolent, and intelligent head, and his simple, natural manners. Strange to say, something in his expression (not features) reminds me of Lord Egremont. His features and the shape of his head (I should think) are like Napoleon's." * * *

1840.

Pictures of the Year.

(Exhibited.) PORTRAIT OF THE RIGHT HON. CHARLES CHRISTOPHER BARON COTTENHAM, LORD HIGH CHANCELLOR. (Painted for W. Russell, Esq., and engraved.)
(Not exhibited.) CHILD IN A GARDEN, WITH HIS LITTLE HORSE AND CART. (A portrait of George, the painter's youngest son.)
GRISELDA. (Both in the National Collection.)

LESLIE was hard at work this year on his picture of 'Fairlop Fair.' He loved suburban fairs, and had been a great haunter of them in his student-days, with Newton, Powell, Willis, and Irving. All his studies for this picture were from the life, and his portfolios were full of gipsy sketches, made for it.

Much as Leslie loved Constable, and anxious as he was to do honour to his memory in his Life of him, he found the pen a more fatiguing tool than the pencil, and complains a good deal in his correspondence about the weariness of pen and ink and paper.

"*April* 27, 1840.

* * * " The truth is, all my leisure moments have of late been so entirely engrossed in putting together the memoir I have undertaken to write of Constable, that I have scarcely been able to take up a pen for any other purpose. If I live to get through it, I will never write anything of the kind again. * * * Tell Sully I have seen the present he sent to Mr. Rogers of the Queen's portrait. We dined with the old gentleman lately. Moore, the poet, and his wife and son were there, and a large party, to whom the picture was shown. Mr. Rogers remarked how singular it was that he should receive the portrait of the Queen of England from America, and painted by an American.*

" I undeceived him, however, as to the last circumstance. I fear you will think the practice I have lately had in writing, has not improved my hand; but the truth is, I am thoroughly tired of pen, ink, and paper.

* Mr. Sully was an Englishman.

" Tell Eliza I think it is very kind of her that she ever writes
to me now she is an authoress."

The following letter is of interest for its estimate of books and
men : —

LONDON, *July* 18*th*, 1840.

DEAR ELIZA, — For once I will answer a letter on the day of
receiving it. I wish I could always do so, it would save me
from many perplexities. Yours of the 15th June has this moment reached me, and I am much gratified by the good account
you give of yourself, and the very delightful one of Tom's
family. * * *
There is not a man in the world I respect more than I do my
only brother. Having such a brother, how can *you* call Uncle
Toby "an old goose." To my mind Uncle Toby is the most perfect specimen of a Christian gentleman that ever existed, for I
don't like to doubt that he has existed. Sir Charles Grandison
is not to be compared to him. Mr. Shandy, an admirably drawn
character also, is cleverer than Uncle Toby, but " My Uncle " is
the wisest man. But you ladies always prefer scamps if they
have talent, to good men who are not so brilliant ; Lord Byron
was a prodigious favourite with the ladies. And you really seem
to think I could go to Paris to see the arrival of the remains of
Bonaparte ; I would not walk across the street for it. He was
certainly a man of genius, but an entirely selfish person. Had I
remained in America, I would have made a pilgrimage to the
tomb of Washington, whom even the profligate Byron could not
help eulogising —

            " And left the name of Washington
            To show the world there was but one."

(I quote from memory.) And on consideration I admire you for
the constancy of your attachment to Napoleon, for I recollect
when we were children we used to make you very angry by saying that " *Bonaparte was Betsy's beau.*" After all, I must say
ladies are always admirers of genius in men, and not being men,
they do not know how bad bad men are. Lady Byron thought

she could reform her Lord, poor simpleton! Bonaparte's heart-less conduct to Josephine ought to damn him with the sex; but no, he was a brilliant and successful soldier! Yet, I think it would not be difficult to prove that Washington displayed more military talent in contending with the well disciplined soldiers of England, so badly supported as he was by the Congress, and with an army of raw recruits who left him every few months to return to their farms. It is a mistake to suppose that there was much national enthusiasm among the American private soldiers. It was their leaders only that felt it. While I was at West Point, I read the life of Washington, and could not help contrasting him with Bonaparte, who began his career at the head of the best soldiers then in the world, made so for him by the revolutionary generals who had preceded him. His great triumphs were obtained over Germans and Italians, but he never faced the English, as Washington did, till Waterloo. But from these great heroes I must digress to myself.

I am very busy with a picture of Fairlop Fair, and am painting landscape a good deal out of doors, in most delicious weather — the most delightful of all employments to an artist. Harriet and the children are all well. My Reminiscences go on; but I never proposed to Edward Carey to publish them. I shall leave them as a legacy to my children, and never meant anything else. It was the memoirs of my friend Constable I spoke about, which, with the materials I have, I do not hesitate to say I shall make the most interesting life of an artist that has ever appeared.

I received six hundred guineas for the Queen's picture. This was the price fixed by myself, and which I had previously named to the gentleman I was to paint it for, before she expressed a wish to have it. I did not think it right to ask the Queen more. Never was sovereign who spent royal money in a way more creditable to the spender than she does, and this is great praise. In a former letter you spoke of coming to England; I hope this is true.

Yours ever,

C. R. L.

Here is a pleasant picture of a painter's holiday : —

MY DEAR ANNE, — I owe you a letter, and may not soon
have a better opportunity of paying the debt than at this place,
where I have been idling for the last week. Harriet has been
here longer with the four eldest children, and now we are all together in a little cottage on the cliff, which commands a fine
view of the sea and harbour. A month or six weeks here will,
I trust, do all the children a great deal of good, and they all now
look much the better for being here. Robert, who has grown
nearly as tall as I am, and still retains his fondness for everything marine, handles the oar very well, and we often indulge him
with a boat, though never without a boatman with him. He is
also learning to swim. I tried at first to teach him, but being an
indifferent swimmer myself, he did not get on. He has had one
lesson from a boatman, and with one or two more, I dare say he
will swim pretty well. You know the Isle of Thanet is a very fine
farming country. When I first came the corn-fields were in all
their glory, and the harvest was going on. Nothing can be more
beautiful than many of the villages in the neighbourhood. On
the 23rd, the time for which we have hired this little cottage will
expire, and we shall then return to town. I shall have been
here a fortnight, and the rest of the party six weeks., I shall
then, I hope, soon complete my picture of 'Fairlop Fair,' for
which I have been making some sketches even here, as there
are abundance of donkeys here, and still more at Ramsgate, and
there is a family of gipsies encamped in a lane not far from us.

1841.

Pictures of the Year.

(*Exhibited.*)

LE BOURGEOIS GENTILHOMME.

M. Jourdain.	—— " Tout beau.
	Holà! Ho! Doucement!
	Diantre soit la coquine!
Nicole.	Vous me dites de pousser.
M. Jourdain.	Oui — Mais tu me pousses en tierce avant que de
	pousser en quarte, et tu n'a pas la patience que je
	pare." Act ii. Scene 3.

(Painted for J. Sheepshanks, Esq., and in the National Collection, and repeated twice; once for Lord Holland; the second repetition is in the possession of Joseph Gillott, Esq.)
FAIRLOP FAIR. (Painted for the Duke of Norfolk.)
THE LIBRARY AT HOLLAND HOUSE, WITH PORTRAITS. (Painted for Lord Holland and engraved.)

(*Not exhibited.*)

LUCRETIA. — A STUDY FOR THE QUEEN IN HER CORONATION ROBES. (Both in the National Collection.) — THE FIRST LESSON,* from a design by Raffaelle. (Painted first for Mr. Rogers, and now in the possession of Thos. Miller, Esq.; subsequently twice repeated * and engraved.) — THE QUEEN IN HER CORONATION ROBES. (In the National Collection.)

LESLIE was hard at work this year on ' The Christening of the Princess Royal.'

If, as one of the earlier passages in the following letter to his sister says, " he was trying to grow rich," the latter part shows some of the motives he had for it. Separated as he now was for life from his brothers and sisters at Philadelphia, his heart clave to them as closely as ever.

LONDON, *July* 15, 1841.

MY DEAR ANNE, — I am very many letters in debt to you, but never have I had so little time to myself as this spring and summer. I have, for the last two months, been painting every day from home on the picture of the ' Christening,' and, anxious to make the most of the long days, I am occupied from nine in the morning till seven or eight in the evening, and after that I have generally notes on business to answer, which take up all the evening. To tell you the truth, I am trying to grow rich.

I have now a few words to say on a subject of great importance to you and to me. I have long, dear Anne, regretted that you should be under the necessity of receiving that assistance from Henry Carey which it is my duty, as it will in future be my pleasure, to give you, and which, if my health is spared me, and my time not interrupted, I trust I shall be able to continue. I have sent fifty pounds to Henry for your use; and wish to know what your expenses per annum will be at a boarding-house, as I suppose it will not be so convenient to Henry and Patty that you

* A third repetition painted on the etching was sold at the sale of Leslie's sketches and studies.

should continue to live with them after Virginia's marriage, who I learn will remain with her husband in their house.   -

Mr. Dickens, on starting for America in December of this year, carried to Irving this letter from his old friend, touching on Time's changes, since those merry struggling days of Buckingham Court.

12, PINE APPLE PLACE, EDGEWARE ROAD,
Dec. 31*st*, 1841.

MY DEAR IRVING, — Mr. Dickens tells me you urged him to become acquainted with me, for which I now send you, by him, my thanks, and every good wish of this wishing season. I have long wanted to write to you : but of what can I write? My present circle of friends are most of them unknown to you. Of all our old cronies in by-gone days, Peter Powell is the only one left, and he is living at Clapham, and I see him less frequently than I wish. But he is the same merry, amusing, light-hearted, discontented little Radical that you remember him. My wife, who sends her best regards and good wishes to you, is (I think) very little altered in appearance since you saw her. She looks more like the sister than the mother of her elder children. Robert is now six feet high, and I am anxiously looking out for some employment for him for life ; no very easy matter to find. I am growing grey, and am still forming better plans and resolutions for the future than I can adhere to. This has been a sad year for the Arts. The loss of Wilkie and Chantrey seem, with our present prospects, not likely to be soon supplied. Chantrey's death was not unexpected, as he had been for some time evidently declining. But the death of dear Wilkie was entirely so. Had he remained in England, it is believed we should still have had him with us, and probably for many years. A few days ago, I saw the last oil picture he touched. It is a small whole-length portrait of Mehemet Ali ; somewhat sketchy, but beautifully painted. The head full of life and character, and with that sort of expression which carries the conviction of its being a likeness. It is dated the 11th of May, and he died the 1st of June. I well know how you must have felt on hearing the sad news. At a meeting of his friends for the purpose of devising the best method of doing honour to his memory, and at which Sir Robert Peel presided, Lord Mahon spoke of the great pleasure he had enjoyed in Wilkie's society and yours, when he met you together in Spain. My chief object in writing is to induce you to do the same.   Yours ever truly,

C. R. LESLIE.

WASHINGTON IRVING, ESQ.,
  New York.

1842.

Pictures of the Year.

SCENE FROM TWELFTH NIGHT.
> *Sir Toby.* — " Accost, Sir Andrew, Accost! "
> *Sir Andrew.* — " What's that ? "
> *Sir Toby.* — " My niece's chambermaid."
> *Sir Andrew.* — " Good Mistress Accost, I desire better acquaintance."
> Act. i. Scene 3.
> Painted for Thomas Baring, Esq., but repeated for Edwin Bullock, Esq., Handsworth, near Birmingham.)

SCENE FROM HENRY THE EIGHTH.
> (Painted for John Sheepshanks, Esq., and now in the National Collection. Repetition of diploma picture.)
> *Queen Kath.* — " Take thy lute, wench: my soul grows sad with troubles: Sing, and disperse them, if thou canst: leave working."
> Act iii. Scene 1.

THE CHRISTENING OF THE PRINCESS ROYAL was still in progress.

LESLIE'S ' Life of Constable' was published this year. Dickens returned from America, where he had seen the members of Leslie's family; and Robert Leslie, whose passion was for the sea and a sailor's life, sailed for New York in September with his father's old friend, Captain Morgan. Robert Leslie's pictures of nautical incidents are distinguished by great originality and truth. Indeed, I believe they are the only truthful pictures ever painted from sailor-life aboard ship. It is a matter of regret that he has now abandoned the profession of a painter. This year, too, Washington Irving was once more in London.

Leslie writes to his sister (Feb. 8, 1842) —

* * *. " My picture of the ' Christening ' is not yet finished. I am chiefly waiting for the Queen Dowager, who has been at the point of death. But as she is recovered, and is now in London, I hope soon to have a sitting.

" You will be pleased to hear that poor Miss Wilkie, in the deep affliction she suffered from the death of her brother, first derived amusement from one of your books. She was staying with Mr. and Mrs. Collins, who are great admirers of all your writings, and I think it was ' Mrs. Washington Potts ' which, when they read it aloud, first drew a smile from Miss Wilkie.

, " I have lately painted a small picture from ' Twelfth Night,' of three figures — ' *Accost, Sir Andrew, accost !* ' "!

He writes to Miss Anne Leslie, (May 11, 1842) —

" Washington Irving is now in London, and looking uncommonly well. He is in the greatest possible demand, and I consider •myself lucky in having seen him three times. To-day he has promised to call here to see my picture of the ' Christening.' Yesterday we met him at Murray's at dinner. Tom Moore was there, and Lockhart. Moore sang half-a-dozen of his own melodies as delightfully as ever. One, of which the air is extremely beautiful, ' *Come o'er the sea, maiden to me,*' he encored himself in, and sang it better the second time than the first. The ladies were in raptures."

And on July 30, 1842, he tells the same sister —

" I have advanced very far in a large picture from the ' Vicar of Wakefield.' The ' Fudge ' scene. It has fifteen figures. ' The Christening ' goes on slowly. I will send you a copy of the ' Life of Constable ' when it is ready ; and as I get that off my hands I hope to be a better correspondent."

.

1843.

Pictures of the Year.

PORTRAIT OF BENJAMIN TRAVERS, ESQ., F.R.S.

THE QUEEN RECEIVING THE SACRAMENT (the concluding part of the ceremony of Her Majesty's Coronation) on the 28th June, 1838.

"The picture represents Her Majesty habited in the Dalmatic Mantle (the Coronation Robe), having taken off the Crown on approaching the altar, and wearing no jewels. The peers and peeresses, who had worn their coronets from the moment in which the Queen was crowned, have now put them off. The Sacrament is administered by the Archbishop of Canterbury, assisted by the Rev. Lord John Thynne, in the absence of the Dean of Westminster. On the farthest side of the altar is the Lord Chamberlain (the Marquis of Conyngham) and the Bishop of London. The Sword of State is borne by Viscount Melbourne, near whom are the Duke of Wellington and the Duke of Sutherland. The Crown is held by the Lord Great Chamberlain (Lord Willoughby D'Eresby), next to whom is the Earl Marshall (the late Duke of Norfolk). Under the lower canopy are seated the ladies of the Royal Family. Nearest Her Majesty is the late Princess Augusta, attended by Lady Mary Pelham; the Princess Augusta of Cambridge, attended by the Hon. Miss Kerr; the Princess Hohenloe and the Duchess of Kent, attended by Lady Flora Hastings and Viscount Morpeth. The other ladies and gentlemen in attendance under the canopy, are the Ladies Caroline Campbell and Caroline Legge, and Viscounts Villiers and Emlen. Immediately behind the Queen are the Mistress of the Robes (the Duchess of Sutherland) and Lady Barham (Lady in Waiting). In the foreground are five of the eight young ladies who bore the Queen's train, namely, the Ladies Caroline Lennox, Adelaide Paget, Fanny Cowper, Wilhelmina Stanhope, and Mary Grimston. Beyond the Coronation chair are the Duke de Nemours and Prince George of Cambridge, and behind it are the Dukes of Sussex and Cambridge, the Duke of Coburgh, Prince Ernest of Phillipstahl, the late Duke of Argyll, and two Pages of Honour (the Marquis of Stafford and Lord Mount Charles)."

SCENE FROM "THE VICAR OF WAKEFIELD."

"Virtue, my dear Lady Blarney, virtue is worth any price; but where is that to be found? Fudge!"   Chap. 11.
(Now in the Collection of Thomas Miller, Esq., Preston.)

PORTRAIT OF HENRY ANGELO, ESQ.

SCENE FROM MOLIÈRE.

M. Purgon. J'ai à vous dire que je vous abandonne à votre mauvaise constitution, à l'intemperie de vos entrailles, à la corruption de votre sang, à l'acreté de votre bile, et à la féculence de vos humeurs.

Toinette. C'est fort bièn fait.

Argan. Mon Dieu!
M. Purgon. Et je veux qu'avant qu'il soit quatre jours vous deveniez
dans un état incurable.
Argan. Ah! miséricorde!
Le Malade Imaginaire, Act iii. Scene 6.
(Painted for John Sheepshanks, Esq., and now in the National Col-
lection.

THIS year Leslie made his first attempt at fresco, in the garden-
house of Buckingham Palace, as he details in this letter to his
sister.

" LONDON, *July* 28, 1843.

" I have been very busy painting a *fresco*, a first attempt, in a
little pavilion in the gardens of Buckingham Palace. I leave
home every morning at eight or nine, and do not return till seven
in the evening. I am now writing before breakfast. I was
asked to do this by the Prince, and there are seven other artists
engaged in the same way — Maclise, Landseer, Sir Charles Ross,
Stanfield, Uwins, Etty, and Eastlake.

" Two or three of us are generally there together, and the
Queen and Prince visit us daily, and sometimes twice a day, and
take a great interest in what is going on. I hope to finish in a
day or two. The subjects are all from Milton's ' Comus,' and
mine is *Comus offering the cup to the lady.*"

TO MISS ANNE LESLIE.

August 18, 1843.

I HAVE sent by Captain Morgan a few engravings — an
archbishop and a judge * for you — as you are a portrait painter.
The archbishop is not handsome, but I think you will like his
expression. He is one of the most agreeable and amiable men I
ever met with.

The window in the picture of the archbishop is that of his
library at Lambeth Palace. I like to paint people in their own
houses, and with their own rooms for the background; and I
think you may find it both a popular and useful mode of painting
portraits when you can do so.

* Archbishop Howley, and Lord Chancellor Cottenham.

1844.

Pictures of the Year.

SCENE FROM COMUS.
"Hence, with thy brew'd enchantments, foul deceiver."
(Now in the collection of John Naylor, Esq., Leighton Hall.)

SANCHO PANZA IN THE APARTMENT OF THE DUCHESS.
Don Quixote, Part ii. Chap. 33.
(Painted for Robert Vernon, Esq., and now in the National * Collection. A repetition of the Petworth picture. Not exhibited.)

LUCY PERCY (Lady Carlisle) BRINGING THE PARDON TO HER FATHER THE EARL OF NORTHUMBERLAND IN THE TOWER. (Painted for Lord Leconfield, and now at Petworth.)

PORTRAIT OF MISS BURDETT COUTTS.

CHRIST AND HIS DISCIPLES AT CAPERNAUM.
1. "At the same time came the disciples unto Jesus, saying, Who is the greatest in the kingdom of heaven?
2. "And Jesus called a little child unto him, and set him in the midst of them,
3. "And said, Verily I say unto you, Except ye be converted, and become as little children, ye shall not enter into the kingdom of heaven."   *Matthew* xviii. 1–3.
(Painted for J. Lennox, Esq., New York.)

THIS year Leslie was one of the hanging committee at the Academy. That harassing and thankless office discharged, he gave himself, for the first time since his visit to Paris in 1817, the pleasure of a continental tour. In company with Mrs. Leslie, her sister-in-law, Mrs. Samuel Stone, and Mr. Dunlop's niece, Miss Gamble, he visited Belgium, from Ostend, by Bruges, Ghent, Brussels, Mechlin, Liège, Aix-la-Chapelle, and Cologne; thence to Bonn, and by the Rhine to Mayence; thence down the river to Dusseldorf, and through Utrecht to Amsterdam, Rotterdam, and Antwerp, where the party took steam for London.

His letters to his children, his sisters, and his friends the Chalons, give his impressions of the tour, which to Leslie, with his especial love of Flemish and Dutch art, was replete with instruction and interest.

* See my Introductory Essay. — ED.

MY DEAR HARRIET, — Your mamma and I have greatly
enjoyed our excursion so far, much more even than we expected;
and could we be sure that you are all well and happy at home,
we should be perfectly happy. Your mamma is so delighted
with the solemn music and splendid ceremonies in the churches
here, that I am almost afraid she will turn Roman Catholic. Indeed, though there are many things trifling, and some things that
appear to us ridiculous, yet there is so much that is truly solemn
and devotional, so much to delight the eye and ear, and the priests
and people appear so sincere in their manner, that I am sure nobody who has any sense of religion at all can help being deeply
affected in their churches. I could spend the whole day listening
tó the music, which is the grandest I ever heard. We are particularly fortunate in being here in this month, which is devoted to
services in honour of the Virgin; and in all the churches the
image is placed over the principal altar, and over her canopies,
sometimes fantastical, but often very superb. She is dressed in
the most costly materials, and has a crown of silver on her head,
and so has the infant in her arms, who holds a long silver cross,
the lower end of which is a spear which pierces the head of a
green dragon under the feet of the Virgin. Over the Virgin's
head is a large halo of silver stars. How much dear little Polly
would be delighted with all this! At Bruges, during one part of
the service, the image of the Virgin was carried round the church
in a procession of priests in the richest dresses, with boys in
white swinging censers of incense up in the air, while the music
and chanting were most impressive. The organ is accompanied
by other instruments. Some of the priests play on enormous
brass trombones, the notes of which are of the deepest bass, while
in the organ-loft there are fiddles and violoncellos. I never heard
anything at the opera that seemed to me so fine.

We have had delightful weather though cool, but that is the
better for walking about. Yesterday afternoon we drove three
miles out of Brussels in an open carriage to Laeken, the palace
of Leopold. As he is at present there we could only see the
outside, which is very handsome. The gates in front are magnif-

icent, and reminded us of the gates at Hampton Court. Near it is a small palace that was the residence of the present King of Holland when he was Prince of Orange. His father, when King of this country, used to walk from Laeken every day to Brussels quite unattended. It is said that one day he helped up an old woman who was coming to market, and had fallen from her horse or donkey. She did not know who he was, but on his giving her some money, it was so much more than she supposed anybody less than a king could give, that she guessed who he was.

We have not yet seen many first-rate pictures, and it will be some time before we do, as we propose going to Cologne and up the Rhine to Frankfort before we visit Holland and Antwerp. Those places will be last, but I am sure not least with me. But I will now give my pen to your mamma.

In a letter to Robert from Bruges, after giving an account of the voyage, in compliment to his son's passion for the sea, he goes on to say —

" Everything is new, strange, and amusing, though the appearance of many things in the country, in the villages we have passed through, and in this place, remind me of the Dutch and Flemish pictures. Your mamma and I are constantly reminded by the looks, and even the dress of the little chubby children in the streets, of the children in Jan Steen's pictures."

FRANKFORT, May 22nd, 1844.

DEAR JOHN AND ALFRED CHALON, — I must indulge myself in writing to you, though I am far from sure my letter will be worth the postage. When I left home I did not suppose I should have reached this place, but the facilities of travelling and the pleasant weather have enticed us on. We turn back, however, to-morrow, and hope to be in London the beginning of June.

The scenery of the Rhine has not disappointed me. The rocks, castles, and towns are very picturesque, but I must say, the vineyards are by no means ornamental.

It is all very well for a poet to speak of,

" The vine-clad steeps ———; "

but to the eye, at the distance from which they are seen from the steam-boat, those parts of the hills that are accessible to cultivation, look as if covered by *enormous threadbare carpets*, a pale green pattern on a drab ground. Besides this, there are innumerable low walls, built in rows, one above the other, like steps, to keep the earth from slipping down. I have no doubt but that the scenery was far more beautiful before the vine was introduced.

We were delighted with the towns we have seen in Belgium; Bruges, Ghent, Brussels, Mechlin, and Liege. Antwerp we expect to see on our way back.

We were particularly fortunate in being in Belgium this month, in which there are some peculiar services performed in the churches in honour of the Virgin. In consequence of this, we have seen much that was magnificent mixed up with a good deal that seemed to us childish and theatrical; but the music was sublime.

At Cologne we were greatly interested in what we saw going on at the Cathedral. It has never been more than half finished, and the King of Prussia has determined to complete it. For this purpose, four hundred workmen are constantly employed, and it is supposed that it will be many years before it is finished.

It seems that the original plan, as far as it is indicated, will be closely adhered to. The style of ornament, which is exceedingly rich, is exactly followed in what is already done of the new part. In the interior, I saw something that looked like a large square band-box, suspended against the wall, at a great height, in which an artist of Frankfort, of the name of Steinle, was at work, painting a figure of a large earthenware angel in fresco, — one of a series filling the spaces above some lofty arches of this form. The figures that were finished, were well composed and graceful, but wretchedly coloured.

At Bonn, in the hall of the college in which Prince Albert was educated, we saw three large frescoes by a pupil of Cornelius, — very poor imitations of Raphael.

To-day we have seen some oil pictures by Lessing, Overbeck, and others, of which I like Lessing's the best. In the Museum where these are, are some modern landscapes, and a large sea piece (a storm), — detestable. But to make amends for these, the same collection contains some fine works of the early Flemish masters, particularly a series of very small pictures by Van Eyck, of the history of John the Baptist, which, though hard in their outlines, and quaint in the costume, are perfectly exquisite in colour, and as fresh, and bright, and rich, as if painted but yesterday.

There was also a small Jan Steen, which, in comparison with the modern German pictures, looked like silver compared with mud.

Our intention is to call at Amsterdam and the Hague on our return, where I expect to be much delighted.

I am, my dear friends,

Yours ever truly,

C. R. Leslie.

The autumn was spent by the painter in London, after leaving his family at Bembridge, in the Isle of Wight. His friend Captain Morgan took them round in his ship, the 'Victoria,' to Portsmouth. He writes to his sister, Miss Leslie, from on board the ship.

(*Aug.* 20,)

"I wrote Patty some account of our trip on the Continent, which we greatly enjoyed. We saw a great deal in a short time, and I am now quite satisfied to remain in England for the rest of my life. As I grow older, I feel less disposed to encounter the fatigue of travelling. I may possibly, when I can afford it, take a peep at Paris again; but I do not think I shall ever get so far as Italy, that country which everybody says every artist should see."

(*Aug.* 29, 1844.)

"Will you tell Edward Carey, in answer to his inquiry, that the price of 'Comus'* is 250 guineas without a frame. Should it go to America, I would rather send it with no frame, as the picture I took with me, of 'Martha and Mary,' was injured by an ornament of the frame becoming loose, and I have seen a

* The picture is now in the collection of John Naylor, Esq. — Ed.

picture of Wilkie's very much injured in the same way. The price I have named is not more than *half* the price I should ask for a picture of the size of ' Comus,' painted under other circumstances than that was. Being for a fresco, it is painted in a bolder manner, and more calculated for distance than if I had painted it with no such purpose. I am unable to get Mr. Lenox's picture done in time for the Captain, but hope very soon to send it."

1845.

Pictures of the Year.

The Heiress. (Painted for E. Bicknell, Esq.)
Scene from Molière.
    Trissotin. — Sonnet à la Princesse Uranie sur sa Fièvre.
        Votre prudence est endormie,
        De traiter magnifiquement,
        Et de loger superbement,
        Votre plus cruelle ennemie.
    Bélise. — Ah! le joli début!
    Armande. —   Quil a le tour galant!
    Philaminte. — Lui seul, des vers aisés possède le talent.
                Les Femmes Savantes, Acte iii. Scéne 2.
(Painted for John Sheepshanks, Esq., and now in the National Collection.)

1846.

Pictures of the Year.

Scene from " Roderick Random."
    At length the important.hour arrived, and the will was produced in the midst of the expectants, who formed a group whose looks and gestures would have been very entertaining to an unconcerned spectator. But the reader can scarce conceive the astonishment and mortification that appeared, when an attorney pronounced aloud the young squire sole heir of all his grandfather's estate, personal and real. My uncle, who had listened with great attention, sucking the head of his cudgel all the while, accompanied these words of the attorney with a stare and a *whew* that alarmed the whole assembly. The oldest and pertest of my female competitors, who had always been very officious about my grandfather's person, inquired with a faltering accent, and visage as yellow as an orange, if there were no legacies? and was answered " None at all; " upon which she fainted away. The rest, whose expectations (perhaps) were not so sanguine, supported

their disappointment with more resolution, though not without giving evident marks of indignation, and grief at least as genuine as that which appeared in them at the old gentleman's death. My conductor, after having
kicked with his heel for some time against the wainscot, began, " So, there's
no legacy, friend. Ha! here's an old succubus. But somebody's soul
howls for it, d—n me." — Chap. IV. (Painted for John Gibbons, Esq.
A smaller repetition was painted for Thomas Miller, Esq., Preston, in
1856.)
MOTHER AND CHILD. (Painted for John Gibbons, Esq., engraved by J. H.
Robson, A.R.A. Repetition painted for James Lenox, Esq., New York.)
PORTRAIT OF CHARLES DICKENS, ESQ., in the character of Captain Bobadil.
(Engraved.)
      " A gentleman! Odso, I am not within."
            Every Man in his Humour, Act i. Scene 5.

THE correspondence of this year is of purely family matters,
and exhibits Leslie now, as always, in the character of the most
affectionate, generous, and thoughtful of brothers. The delicate
health of his sister, Mrs. Carey, was a source of great anxiety to
him, and his letters are filled with suggestions and advice as to
her case. His second sister, Anne, too, had just lost the situation
of mistress of drawing, which she held at Rutger's Institute, in
New York ; and her brother was ready with the help of his
counsel and his purse. The only passage bearing immediately
on the painter's work occurs in the following letter. The picture
referred to is now at Petworth.

                                        (*Oct.* 7, 1846.)
"THE picture I have just finished is from a true story in the
reign of James I. The Earl of Northumberland was imprisoned
in the Tower for fifteen years, on suspicion of being concerned in
the Gunpowder Plot. He spent his time in scientific pursuits,
with some of the most learned men of the time, who constantly
visited him, and Sir Walter Raleigh, who was at the same time a
prisoner. His youngest daughter, Lady Lucy Percy, had married the Earl of Carlisle, a man her father greatly disliked, and
to make her peace with him, her husband, who was one of
James's favourites, procured his pardon. The picture represents
the lady bringing the pardon to her father, while engaged with his
literary friends in study. It was begun many years ago for Lord
Egremont, who was descended, by the female line, from the Earls

of Northumberland, but I laid it aside at his lordship's death, and I have now just finished it at the request of Colonel Wyndham, the present possessor of Petworth."

Washington Irving was in London in August this year, but unluckily Leslie and he missed seeing each other, owing to Leslie's absence from town for a few days with his family, on a trip round to Portsmouth in the liner commanded by his friend, Captain Morgan.

"12, PINE APPLE PLACE, EDGEWARE ROAD,
"<i>Aug.</i> 20<i>th</i>, 1846.

"I WISH," he writes to Irving, "it would please the American government and yourself that you should be minister here. You will not suspect me of meaning a compliment when I say what you must know very well yourself, that no other man would be anything like so popular in England. I had been looking for you every day since May, when you said you should probably be here, and it is very provoking to have missed you at last. I was to have let *Father Luke* know of your arrival, and we were to have dined with him. Are you in such a hurry that you can't come back to London for a few days? I wish you could, and could spend them here; for we can give you a bed, and nothing would give us greater pleasure."

1847.

Pictures of the Year.

MARTHA AND MARY. (A repetition of the picture painted for Mr. Dunlop in 1833. Now in the collection of Edwin Bullock, Esq., Handsworth, near Birmingham.)

THE PHARISEE AND THE PUBLICAN.

" And the publican, standing afar off, would not lift up so much as his eyes unto heaven, but smote upon his breast, saying, God be merciful to me, a sinner." — LUKE, xviii. 13.

(Painted for James Lenox, Esq., New York.)

CHILDREN PLAYING AT COACH AND HORSES. Not exhibited. (Painted for Sir Robert Wigram. Repeated for Thos. Miller, Esq.) — THE LADY IN COMUS, (in the possession of John Heugh, Esq.) — PORTRAIT OF CAPTAIN E. E. MORGAN.

THE following passage from a letter of this year, is interesting

for its reference to his son Robert's picture, which will be remembered by many of my readers in the Exhibition of this year,
as fully bearing out all Leslie says of it. There was an individuality and truthfulness in Robert Leslie's pictures from sea-
faring life which gave them a special value, and justify my regret
that he should have abandoned the profession of a painter. The
letter shows, too, how full of commissions Leslie's hands were at
this time. Every picture he painted was eagerly bought, and had
the painter received one-half of the prices which have subsequently been realised by his pictures, in the changes of hand
undergone by so many of the galleries collected by the new class
of patrons — the enriched manufacturers — he would have died a
very wealthy man. As it was, he was so slow and scrupulous,
even to fastidiousness, in his work, and so moderate in his prices,
that, popular as he was, his income, when at its highest, was but
a modest one. From his letters there always peeps a rigid spirit
of economy, in all that relates to pleasure or luxury. It is
noticeable in the little details of the visit he paid to Paris this
year, in company with his daughters Harriet and Mary.

" LONDON, April 16, 1847.

" ROBERT's last work is a picture of figures, the grouping, &c.,
entirely his own, and nothing can be better than the manner in
which he has told the story of a ship's crew coming aft in a body
to complain to the captain relative to their allowance of biscuit.
They are all the truest sailors that ever were painted, and entirely
free from anything vulgar, and the effect of the whole is true and
sunny. I hope it will attract notice in the Exhibition.

" I have sent three pictures to the R. A.: a repetition of the
'Martha and Mary,' but varied, about the size of Colonel Perkins's picture; a picture of four children playing at coach-and-
horses, painted for the Vice-Chancellor, Sir James Wigram; and
a picture of the parable of the 'Pharisee and the Publican,'
which is for Mr. Lenox, and I therefore hope you will see it.
The pictures I am engaged to paint are, one for Mr. Bates, one
for Mr. Niewenhuys, one for Mr. Labouchère, M. P., one for
Lord Charles Townshend, one for Mr. John Harris (a stranger
to me), one for Mr. Gibbons (who has already five of my pic-

tures), one for a Mr. Vaughan, one for Mr. Sheepshanks, one
for Mr. Bicknell, two small ones for Sam Stone (who has bought
a picture of mine and two of Robert's), one for Mr. Colls, one for
Mr. Bullock, the owner of the 'Martha and Mary' (lately
painted), and one for Lady Chantrey (the widow of Sir Francis).

I mean to take care of my health, live regular, and not work
too hard; but my late attack * told me in very plain terms that I
am growing old, and I try to make up my mind more and more
every day to be thankful for prolongation of life, and contented to
die whenever it may please God, knowing that *that* time, whenever it comes, *must* be the *best time for me*."

He tells his sister (May 31, 1847) —
* * * " You will be glad to hear that Robert has sold his
picture from 'Two Years before the Mast' to Mr. Gibbons, the
possessor of my ' Roderick Random,' for one hundred guineas."

*

12, PINE APPLE PLACE, EDGEWARE ROAD,
May 31, 1847.

MY DEAR IRVING, — I have thought of making my next picture the interview between Columbus and the Queen of Portugal,
described in the fourth chapter of the fifth book of your ' Life of
Columbus,' and if you could kindly give me any hints to help me
in the composition, I shall feel greatly obliged. Can you tell me
why the Queen was at a monastery, and not with her husband —
what was her age, and from what history I can get particulars
that will be useful? In short, any information you will take the
trouble to send me, will be very acceptable.

At the same time, tell me how you are, and when will your
' Life of Washington' appear, and when there is a chance of our
seeing you here again.

WASHINGTON IRVING, ESQ.,
         New York.

He writes to his wife from Paris —

---

* At the beginning of the year he had been confined to his room for three
weeks by palpitation of the heart. — ED.

" HOTEL DES TUILERIES,
   " RUE DE RIVOLI, A PARIS,
      " *Sept.* 22*nd*, 1847.

" DEAREST HARRY, — It seems almost a sin for me to be enjoying the delights with which we are surrounded without you. But I hope we may be here some day together. Little Polly is regularly admitted a student in the Louvre. How amused you would be to see her sitting, in all her uprightness, on a high stool, with her sketch-book in her hand, and her water-colours beside her, before a most beautiful Terburgh, drawing, and rubbing out, and not finding it possible to please herself, *as usual.* Yesterday afternoon, we went to Franconi's, an immense place for horse-riding, where the performances are in the open air, and in the day time, the audience sitting under cover. We there saw a tournament performed, which would have delighted dearest George beyond measure.

   *   *   *   *   *   *   *   *

" On Sunday we heard mass in the church of St. Roch ; the music very fine. We then went to Versailles along a most beautiful road, from which we had a splendid view of Paris. We dined at Versailles, and on our return, the girls being tired went to bed, and I strolled out, ' a here-a and there-a.' Seeing a dim light through the window of one of the old churches, I went in, and heard some most exquisite music. There were no lights in the church, except on the altar, which was covered with candles, and the decorations all white. The priests were also in white, and two women were singing, with a priest who sang the bass.

" I was so sorry Harriet was not with me, but, as we expect to remain over next Sunday, I can take her. The girls are charmed with the beautiful gardens, and the shops in the Palais Royal, and the air is as pure, and fresh, and mild, as in the Isle of Wight ; even the filth of the town, which is considerable, scarcely affects it. But, there are so many large squares, wide streets, and public gardens, that we are very little annoyed with smells. We live next door to the King, and enjoy his garden much more than he does himself. He is now at the Tuileries, but we have seen nothing of him."

22

· " *Sept. 23rd*, 1847.

" I DON'T know when I have felt so well as since I have been in Paris, though I eat and drink things that I always avoid at home. But the air is so delicious, and the amusements so many, and, above all things, the Louvre is such a happiness to me, that it seems impossible for me to be otherwise than well here.

" The weather to-day is perfect, neither too hot nor cold ; exactly the kind to walk about in. We have had but one rainy day since we have been in France, and that did not keep us at home, for there are so many arcades, and the Palais Royal, the most amusing of places, has all the side walks covered. We breakfast and dine there.

" We have not yet been to a theatre, excepting Franconi's Hippodrome ; but I think we must go to one or two. The difficulty is to choose among so many.

" I think we shall leave Paris about the middle of next week, perhaps sooner. The expense of the trip I shall not regret ; it has done, and seems to be doing, us all so much good.

" As for the pictures in the Louvre, tell Mr. Beales, I am the most impressed with the two great ones by Paul Veronese. He pleases me more than Rubens, though Rubens is very great here. The ' Marriage at Cana ' is glorious, and in an admirable state of preservation. It is filled with the gayest and brightest colours, yet all in exquisite harmony. The other, the subject of which is ' Mary Magdalene washing the Feet of our Saviour,' is, I think, in its general effect, the grandest of the two. It is more solemn — indeed, there is nothing in the Louvre of Titian so impressive in effect. There are two other pictures, by Paolo, very fine. One is injured, by the sky having turned black ; the other, the subject of which is ' Esther before Ahasuerus,' is inimitable, but it is hung too high. I never saw fainting so well expressed as in the Esther. The De Hooghe, of which the sketch hangs in our bed-room, is here. It is fine, but I prefer the Queen's and Sir Robert Peel's De Hooghes. Tell Bob, the Ruysdael, of which he made a little sketch, is here. His sketch is very like it in effect. Nicolas Poussin does not appear to great advantage in his own country. There are very much finer pictures, by him, in our National Gallery, than in the Louvre."

TO MISS ANNE LESLIE.

"*Nov.* 22, 1847.

" In September I spent a most delightful fortnight in Paris with Harriet (the younger), and Mary. We had the finest of weather (though some days rather 'cold), and enjoyed it to the full; and I think it did me great good. In a dozen letters I could not describe all our enjoyments and amusements there. Harriet will write to you and tell you something about it, as she has more time than I. I must, however, tell you that, on our way back, we spent a beautiful Sunday morning at Amiens, and heard High Mass in the cathedral there, which surpasses everything, in architectural beauty, I saw in Belgium. The sun was shining bright through the lofty windows, and the whole looked so light, so elegant, and so sublime, as to seem scarcely the work of human hands. I could fancy that a company of angels had been sent down to build it, and that the exquisite music we were hearing, proceeded from a party they had left behind them.

" 24*th Nov.* — Since I wrote this letter I have been elected Professor of Painting to the Royal Academy, by a unanimous vote.

" My business will be to deliver six lectures annually, which will be rather an amusement than a trouble, and for which I shall receive £60 — £10 for each lecture."

1848.

Pictures of the Year.

(157) LADY JANE GREY.

" Most gentle, most unfortunate,
Crowned but to die; who in her chamber sate,
Musing with Plato, though the horn was blown,
And every ear and every heart was won,
And all in green array were chasing down the sun."—*Rogers.*
(In the possession of Thomas Miller, Esq., Preston.)

(162) THE SHELL.

" His countenance soon
Brightened with joy; for murmurings from within
Were heard, sonorous cadences! whereby,
To his belief, the monitor expressed
Mysterious union with his native sea."— *Wordsworth.*
(Painted for John Gibbons, Esq.)

THE references to France, revolution, and the Napoleon dynasty, with the remarks on the Exhibition as compared with the exhibitions of Leslie's younger days, make the following letter to Miss Anne Leslie, worth inserting. Never was a man by disposition less of a " laudator temporis acti " than Leslie. He appreciated all new manifestations of excellence in his art, to a degree very rare among old Academicians, and he was the first and most generous among those of his own standing to recognise the merit which gave value to the early works of the young Pre-Raphaelite school.

" *June* 16th, 1848.

" WE are not much afraid of a revolution here; though the times are very critical, and the misery the French have spread all over their own country, and indeed over the continent, will in some degree affect England and America. France is infinitely worse off than under the worst of her former governments, and must suffer a great deal more before things come right with her.

" I dined yesterday at Holland House, where was Guizot. He speaks English very well, and as I sat near him, I heard all he said. His countenance, though intelligent, is not an inviting one. He looks hard and severe. He has not laid aside his decorations, but wore a red ribbon and one or two orders. The last time I dined at Lord Holland's, Jerome Bonaparte and his son were there. The son is extremely like Napoleon, and perfectly conscious of it. Jerome is not, neither is he like Joseph, who had more the look of the Emperor. If there was now a Bonaparte with the talents of Napoleon, he might have some chance with the French ; but I have not heard that any of them possess more than ordinary abilities."

"*July* 26, 1848.

"It is the fashion to say that every exhibition is better than the last, a fashion I cannot fall into. I never expect to see again such as I have seen, when we had Lawrence, Owen, Jackson, Wilkie, and Constable. Turner sent nothing this year, and talked of never exhibiting again. I hope, however, he will, and often, for we can ill afford to lose him.

"I have sent to Tom and to Eliza impressions of an engraving from a picture I painted of the library at Holland House. I forgot whether you were ever in the house when you came here. The present Lord Holland has made many alterations, and some very great improvements there, but he has not yet touched the library, and I hope he will not. I heard that he talked of reconverting it into a picture gallery, but I hope he will not, for it will not make a good one without an expenditure that would almost build a gallery.

"I have nearly finished my picture from Don Quixote, and shall immediately begin one from Henry VIII., from which play I am to paint a pair."

"2, Abercorn Place, St. John's Wood,
"*Nov.* 22, 1848.

"My Dear Irving,—I received your letter by Mr. Putnam (whom, however, I have not seen, as he had not time to call on me), and have sent to him a pen sketch of ' Diedrich,' the slightness of which you must excuse, as I am much engaged, and am obliged to spare my eyes all I can, for they are failing me. I am entirely out of practice in little things of this kind, and have no doubt you will be able to have something done much more to your mind in America. If so, pray throw it away without scruple.

"I sent you a letter a short time ago by the hands of '*the Dusty*,' containing a letter I found in the ' London Magazine' of General Washington's, which seems to be genuine, and which I thought you might not have seen. It shows that the General had a sense of humour, and I believe no man of very great mind was ever without it. Let me know whether you received it."

1849.

Pictures of the Year.

(Exhibited.) SCENE FROM HENRY VIII.
    Wolsey. — " Here I'll make my royal choice."
    King. — " You have found him, Cardinal."
                              Act i. Scene 4.
    (Painted for I. K. Brunel, Esq., and sold at the sale of his gallery this
year for £960.)
(141) SCENE FROM DON QUIXOTE. — (Second part, Chapters 31 and 32.)
    The Duke's chaplain, after attacking Don Quixote for his devotion to
knight errantry, and Sancho for his belief in his master, reprimands the
Duke for encouraging their fancies, and leaves the company in a passion.
(Painted for Joshua Bates, Esq.)
(Not exhibited.) THE NECKLACE. (In the National Collection.) Repetition
— an oval with a locket — in the possession of Richard Newsham, Esq.—
SOPHIA WESTERN. (Repeated.) — LADY WITH SCARLET GERANIUM IN
HER HAND. (Painted for C. Constable, Esq.) — CAPTAIN AND MRS. MOR-
GAN*AND CHILDREN. (Painted for Captain E. E. Morgan, New York.)

HIS brother, Captain Leslie, had lost his wife. Leslie writes
to his sister on the occasion : —

                                " *March 27th*, 1849.

"I HAVE been so incessantly occupied with my lectures at the
Academy, in addition to my regular occupations, that I have been
unable to write to you. The sad intelligence your last letter contained, came on us quite by surprise. I had heard lately from Captain Morgan, that dear Tom and his family were quite well. I feel
a strong repugnance always to writing letters of condolence, and
have determined, therefore, for the present not to write to Tom ;
as, if I could see him, I should not speak to him on the subject
of his great loss, unless he spoke of it first to me. Give my
love and best wishes to him when you see him. I always look
on death as a calamity only to the survivor, for I am sure that
God takes us all whenever it is best for us. I shall exhibit two
pictures this season : a large one from ' Don Quixote,' painted for
Mr. Bates, and a small one, with many figures, from ' Henry
VIII.,' painted for Braddy's master, Mr. Brunel. Robert has

painted two views from the Isle of Jersey, which he visited last summer. The last is his best picture, and I think he regularly improves. I am now painting a scene from 'Tom Jones,' near the close of the story. Tom is showing Sophia Western her own face in a looking-glass as a pledge for his good behaviour after marriage. I have sent two small pictures lately to Mr. Lenox, and shall soon send him another. By Captain Lord I will send you my last lectures. I wrote four new ones, and all are printed in the 'Athenæum.'"

"*Dec.* 27, 1849.

"I AM busy with a small picture from Shakespeare — the dying scene of Katherine of Arragon. It is for Mr. Brunel, and is a companion to the one I painted for him last year of 'Henry VIII. and Anne Boleyn.' It is nearly finished, and I shall then begin a large one of Falstaff acting the part of the King.

"Have you read Macaulay's History? It is as entertaining as a novel; but no doubt the truth is greatly distorted by his political and other opinions. What will the Philadelphians say to his character of William Penn? I have no doubt he has done him great injustice."

1850.

Pictures of the Year.

BEATRICE.
 "Look where Beatrice, like a lapwing, runs close to the ground."
 Much Ado about Nothing, Act iii. Scene 1.
 (Painted for John Gibbons, Esq., Regent's Park, and twice repeated.)
(124 TOM JONES SHOWING TO SOPHIA WESTERN HERSELF, AS HER BEST SECURITY FOR HIS GOOD BEHAVIOUR.
 "If I am to judge," said she, "of the future by the past, my image will no more remain in your heart when I am out of your sight, than it will on this glass when I am out of the room."
 History of a Foundling, Book xviii. c. 12.
 (A repetition of the picture of 1849, painted for John Harris, Esq., Prince's Gate, London.)
(135) SCENE FROM HENRY VIII.
 Katherine. — "Sir, I most humbly pray you to deliver
 This to my lord the King,

In which I have commended to his goodness
The model of our chaste loves, his young daughter,
Beseeching him to give her virtuous breeding,
*   *   *   *   *   and a little
To love her for her mother's sake, that loved him
Heaven knows how dearly. My next poor petition
Is, that his noble Grace would have some pity
Upon my wretched women, that so long
Have followed both my fortunes faithfully.
*   *   *   *   *   *   *   *
The last is, for my men. They are the poorest,
But poverty never could draw them from me.
*   *   *   *   And, good my lord,
As you wish Christian peace to souls departed,
Stand these poor people's friend, and urge the King
To do me this last right."

Capucius.   " By heaven, I will;
Or let me lose the fashion of a man!' "

Act iv. Scene 2.

(Painted for Isambard K. Brunel, Esq., F.R.S., and sold at the sale of
his pictures this year for 800*l.** Repeated smaller, and in the possession
of John Naylor, Esq., Leighton Hall, near Welshpool.)

THIS year Miss Anne Leslie visited her brother in London,
and Leslie lost his brother-in-law, and old schoolfellow, Mr. De
Charms. He writes on the occasion to Miss Leslie.

(*Sept. 30th*, 1850.)

" I REMEMBER him about 1804 one of the head boys, and one
of the very best in Dr. Rogers's school. How little likelihood
was there at that time of our future course of life as it has
happened — that we should some twenty years afterwards have
married sisters in this country ! De Charms was respected as a
boy by all the boys in the school, and I am sure he was loved
by Dr. Rogers, and he has passed through life respected and
esteemed by those who knew him. * * I feel sure that in every
relation of life he invariably did that which he considered it his
duty to do. Still, after all, we are very imperfect judges even of
those we live most with. Our real characters are known only to
God ; we do not even know them ourselves."

* This was the amount of Mr. Brunel's commission for this picture, and its
companion from the same play, which realised 950*l.* At the same sale, Sir
Edwin Landseer's ' Titania and Bottom,' for which he received 450*l.* from Mr.
Brunel, was sold for 2800*l.* — ED.

1851.

Pictures of the Year.

(Exhibited.) A Study.

(140) Falstaff personating the King.

> *Hostess.* — " O, the father, how he holds his countenance! "
>
> *Falstaff.* — * * * " Harry, I do not only marvel where thou spend-est thy time, but also how thou art accompanied; for though the camo-mile, the more it is trodden on, the faster it grows; yet youth, the more it is wasted, the sooner it wears. That thou art my son, I have partly thy mother's word, partly my own opinion; but chiefly a villainous trick of thine eye, and a foolish hanging of thy nether lip, that doth warrant me. If then thou be son to me, here lies the point — Why, being son to me, art thou so pointed at? "
>
>   *First Part of King Henry IV.*, Act ii. Scene 4.

(Painted for John Harris, Esq., Prince's Gate.)

(Not exhibited.) A Group of the Duke of Northumberland's Tenants at Stanwick. (Painted for the Duke.)

TO MISS ANNE LESLIE.

May 18th, 1851.

I am very busy with a large picture from ' The Rape of the Lock ' for Mr. Gibbons, and am indeed overwhelmed with com-missions. I wish I· could transfer some of them to Robert; but he must bide his time. He has wonderfully improved within the last year, and I have no fear of his ultimate success. He has taken a house near us, in Northwick Terrace, and he, Jane, and the baby, are all very well ; the last of the three generally comes to see us once a day, and is most engaging. I have also been from home. The Duke of Northumberland, whom I have known for some years, having met him at Mr. Rogers's when he was Lord Prudhoe, asked me to make some sketches for him of some of his old servants at Stanwick, in the north of Yorkshire, where he spends most of his time, and I passed ten days there with him and the Duchess. You know how pleasant he can be, and I found him always the same. The Duchess, too, is very agreeable. You, perhaps, know that she is a daughter of the Marquis of Westminster. I painted her when she was a child, in the family picture of her grandfather, the late Marquis."

TO MISS LESLIE.

May 18th, 1851.

I AM ashamed to think how long a time I have suffered to pass without writing to you, and I have only the old *bad* excuse to offer of dislike to letter writing, even to those for whom I have the greatest affection, with the somewhat better apology of increasing weakness of my eyes, which makes it important to me to save them as much as I can for painting. I now must not read or write by candlelight, and the little time I can spare in the day for letters is consumed very much by notes, which I *must* write, and often on business with which I have little concern. I have nothing of consequence to tell you of ourselves ; we are going on as usual. I am very busy with a large picture from ' The Rape of the Lock ; ' and if I have my health and strength for a few years longer, I shall be able to save some money for my family, as I have pictures engaged at my own prices for ten years to come. The increase of the private patronage of Art in this country is surprising. Almost every day I hear of some man of fortune, whose name is unknown to me, who is forming a collection of the works of living painters ; and they are all either men in business, or who have made fortunes in business and retired. Nothing can more strikingly display the resources and wealth of this· country than the gigantic scheme that has been so successfully carried out, and with such wonderful rapidity, in Hyde Park. The influx of visitors to London has not yet, however, been so great as was expected. It will, no doubt, increase, but I do not think there is any danger of any one of the evils that have been predicted from the concourse of foreigners or country visitors in London. Famine, pestilence, and revolution, were the foremost of these ; but, for the present, the only effect on the state of the metropolis produced by the Great Exhibition is that the shops, the theatres, and other places of amusement have been, in a degree, deserted for it.

1852.

Pictures of the Year.

(Exhibited.) JULIET.

> " What if it be a poison, which the friar
> Subtly hath minister'd to have me dead;
> Lest in this marriage he should be dishonour'd
> Because he married me before to Romeo?
> I fear, it is; and yet, methinks it should not,
> For he hath still been tried a holy man:
> I will not entertain so base a thought." .

Romeo and Juliet, Act iv. Scene 8.

(Twice repeated; one repetition is in the possession of Richard Newsham, Esq.,

(Not exhibited.) GIRL HOLDING A DOVE. (In the collection of Thomas Miller, Esq., Preston.) — GIRL READING. (In the possession of Edwin Bullock, Esq., Handsworth, near Birmingham. Repeated.)

TO W. IRVING.

ABERCORN PLACE, ST. JOHN'S WOOD,
LONDON, *Jan. 18th*, 1852.

WHY do you never write to me? I have not heard whether you received a copy of a note written by Gen. Washington, which I found in an old magazine, or a sketch I sent by Mr. Putnam (at your request) of Diedrich Knickerbocker. I hear frequently of you, and that you are well and happy in your beautiful retreat. I shall never cease regretting that I could not have visited you, as you kindly proposed, when you were at Madrid. But it was literally out of my power, and I doubt now if I shall ever see Spain, or even Italy, which of all places in the world I most wish to visit.

TO MISS ANNE LESLIE.

May 9, 1852.

THIS spring I have been more than usually engaged, being on the Council of the Academy, and having to assist in arranging the Exhibition. I really expected to be quite knocked up by this, but have got through it better than I hoped. It is not a good Exhibition, many of the principal artists, among them E. Landseer, having nothing there. I did not get my large picture from the 'Rape of the Lock' ready, and have only sent a small one of 'Juliet.'

HAMPTON, *Aug.* 29, 1852.

I AM quietly out of town, and enjoying myself very greatly at this beautiful place. We are about a mile from Hampton Court, where George and I go every morning. He is copying pictures in the palace, and I have my 'Rape of the Lock' there, where I am painting the background, perhaps in the very room where the scene of my picture occurred.

The weather is perfection, and we stay till the end of September.

TO W. IRVING.

HAMPTON, *Aug.* 29, 1852.

SINCE I received your letter of the 25th May, I have had no time to answer it till now, for I am subject to many such interruptions as you complain of, and I dare not use my eyes at night. I think often of you, and long for your 'Life of Washington,' which I trust I may soon see, though you say nothing about it. I was much interested by your account of your "happy home" at Sunnyside, with all your habits and occupations there ; and I will tell you how I am living just now at this beautiful place. We have taken a house from the beginning of this month to the end of September, close to Garrick's Villa, which you may remember as beautifully situated on the river about a mile above Hampton Court. The weather has been delightful ever since we have been here, and promises to continue so.

I am painting a large picture from 'The Rape of the Lock,' containing fourteen or fifteen figures. I have taken the moment in which Sir Plume is desiring the Baron to return the lock Belinda is in the foreground crying, and surrounded by ladies, and the group of gentlemen further in the picture. As the background represents a room in the palace, I am finishing the picture there. I can paint at the palace for two or three hours each morning, uninterrupted by visitors, and on Friday, when it is closed to the public, the whole day.

I generally go from here in a boat, and my two girls, who spend much of their time on the water, row me back about one o'clock. We dine early and spend the afternoon either on the water, or in the Palace gardens, or Bushy Park, and sometimes at Richmond, and *to me* there cannot be a more luxurious life, with such perfect weather as we are enjoying. My eldest son is in Devonshire with his wife and two children. My second son, Bradford, is working for Mr. Brunel at a railway bridge at Chepstow, and the rest of us are here. We were a little uneasy lately respecting the English and American fisheries, but I hope all such disputes between the two countries will be got over without a war.

1853.

Leslie exhibited no pictures at the Royal Academy this year.
(Not exhibited.) SLENDER, WITH THE ASSISTANCE OF SHALLOW, COURTING ANNE PAGE. (Repetition of his early picture of 1825. Repeated smaller, and in the possession of Thomas Miller, Esq.)

TO MISS A. LESLIE.

Oct. 20, 1853.

I am painting a large picture from Mr. Lenox's subject of Our Saviour calling the Little Child, with alterations, and I hope improvements.

He sent me an admirable Daguerreotype of his picture, which is of the greatest use to me.

1854.

Pictures of the Year.

Exhibited.) A PRESENT. —(Painted for W. C. Sole, Esq.) PORTRAIT OF MRS. W. S. SOLE.

SCENE FROM "THE RAPE OF THE LOCK."

Sir Plume demands the restoration of the lock.

" (Sir Plume of amber snuff box justly vain,
And the nice conduct of a clouded cane)
With earnest eyes, and round unthinking face,
He first the snuff box open'd, then the case.

*   *   *   *   *   *

It grieves me much (replied the Peer again)
Who speaks so well, should ever speak in vain;
But by this lock, this sacred lock, I swear
(Which never more shall join its parted hair;
Which never more its honours shall renew,
Clipp'd from the lovely head where late it grew);
That while my nostrils draw the vital air,
This hand, which won it, shall for ever wear.
He spoke, and speaking, in proud triúmph spread
The long-contended honoúrs of her head."

(Not exhibited.) PORTRAIT OF JOHN EVERETT MILLAIS, ESQ., A.R.A.—
VIEW OF THE THAMES AT HAMPTON — MOONLIGHT.
(Both sold at the painter's sale.)

TO W. IRVING.

May 13th, 1854.

OF the old set of our mutual friends here, I do not know that
any are remaining but Peter Powell, Buskin (J. Russell), and
Mr. Rogers. Peter is wonderful for his age, and still performs
in private. He is coming here on the 1st of June *to a dance.*
Buskin is still trying to get a good theatrical engagement, but
does not succeed. He reads Shakespeare to schools, and gets
something thereby. But Mr. Rogers is truly wonderful. *He is
ninety-one*, and is not aware of any disorder or ailing whatever.
His memory fails him a little, but he is still pleasant, and has
company every morning to breakfast, and often to dinner and tea.
He has not attempted to use his legs since the accident he met
with a few years ago, by which he broke his thigh bone, but he
drives out every day in his carriage and often calls on us. Miss
Rogers is not so well in health as her brother, but her memory is
still unimpaired. They visit each other daily, and she often
breakfasts and takes tea with him. I am better than I have been
for the last few years, thanks to Mr. Travers and the care he has
taught me to take of myself.

When you can find time pray write to me. I very much want a 'Life of Washington.' When shall I have yours?

1855.

Pictures of the Year.

(Exhibited.) SANCHO PANZA AND DON PEDRO REZIO.

" Then," quoth Sancho, " that great dish that stands fuming there before me, methinks 'tis an olla podrida, and by reason of the diversities of things it hath in it, I cannot but meet with something that will do me good."

" Absit," quoth the physician, " Far be such an ill thought from us There is nothing that worse nourisheth than an olla podrida, fit only for your prebends and rectors of colleges, or your country marriages. Let your Governor's tables be without them. And the reason is, because always, and wheresoever, and by whomsoever, your simple medicines are in more request than your compounds; because in simples there can be no error, in compounds there are many, altering the quantity of things of which they are composed. But what I know is fit for the Governor to eat at present, to preserve his health and to corroborate it, is some hundred of little hollow wafers, and a pretty slice or two of quince marmalade, that may settle his stomach, and help his digestion."

When Sancho heard this, he leaned himself to the back of his chair, and by fits now and then looked at the physician, and with a grave voice asked him his name, and where he had studied.

                                   Don Quixote, Part ii. Chap. 47.

(Painted for Lady Chantry.)

(Not exhibited.) OLIVIA, TWELFTH NIGHT. (Repeated.) — THE LATE DUKE OF WELLINGTON LOOKING AT A BUST OF WASHINGTON. (Painted for Miss Burdett Coutts; repetition painted for the Hon. Abbott Lawrence of Boston, U. S.) — THE LATE DUKE AND PRESENT DUCHESS OF WELLINGTON ON THE STAIRCASE OF BUCKINGHAM PALACE. (Painted for Miss Burdett Coutts.)

IN this year Leslie published the substance of his Academy Lectures, with additions, under the title of 'A Handbook for Young Painters.' The composition and revision of it had occupied the latter part of 1854.

1856.

Pictures of the Year.

(Exhibited.) (144) HERMIONE. (Painted for I. K. Brunel, Esq., F.R.S. Repeated.)

(Not exhibited.) A repetition, with alterations, from "THE RAPE OF THE LOCK." (Painted for Edwin Bullock, Esq., Handsworth, near Birmingham.) — THE OPERA BOX. (Painted for E. Bullock, Esq.)

TO MISS LESLIE.

February 10th, 1856.

The infirmities of age are now coming upon me, and I am obliged to be very careful of myself. Still I was able to go to Paris for about ten days in November last. The improvements there since Louis Napoleon has made himself emperor, are truly wonderful. Whatever may be his moral character, it certainly seems greatly for the good of France that he is on the throne; where it may be hoped he will long remain. I hope we shall now be at peace with Russia, and I hope we shall not get into a war with America. But political affairs have of late years so entirely baffled all calculation, that it is impossible to guess to-day what may happen to-morrow.

•

1857.

Picture of the Year.

SIR ROGER DE COVERLEY IN CHURCH.

" As Sir Roger is landlord to the whole congregation, he keeps them in very good order, and will suffer nobody to sleep in it besides himself; for, if by chance he has been surprised into a short nap at sermon, upon recovering out of it he stands up and looks about him, and if he sees anybody else nodding either wakes them himself, or sends his servants to them." — *Spectator*, No. 112.

(Painted for Thomas Miller, Esq., Preston.)

THESE later years furnish nothing to record of the painter but constant work, and affectionate interchange of recollections with the American branches of his family. Early in 1857 his daughter Caroline was married to Mr. Fletcher, under the fairest auspices, soon belied, alas, by her premature death, in March, 1859.

Here is the last glimpse of the painter which his correspondence gives us. It is a sunny one; and leaves such an image of the man as best fits his life and tastes, — surrounded by his family,

rambling in the chestnut shades of Bushey Park, feeding the
deer that came fearlessly to his kindly hand, painting the background of his "Jeanie Deans" in the green avenues of Hampton Court Garden, and copying from his beloved Cartoons.

TO MISS LESLIE.

HAMPTON COURT, *July 19th,* 1857.

WE have been here (that is, my wife, and I, and Mary), for
the last seven weeks, and expect to remain two weeks longer.
Harriet, Mr. and Mrs. Fletcher, and George, are now here with
us. I came to paint from nature, the background to a picture I
am engaged on, of 'Jeanie Deans' interview with Queen Charlotte.' We have had so far a very fine summer, sometimes
rather too warm, and nothing can be more lovely than this place.
We are in a small house, the back windows of which look into
Bushey Park, and the deer come to the windows and feed out
of our hands. We are very close to the Palace, the gardens of
which are, to my mind, the most beautiful I ever saw. Besides
the background of my picture, which I am painting from one of
the stately avenues of trees in the park, I am copying one of
Raphael's Cartoons in the Palace — 'The Miraculous Draught
of Fishes.'

Nothing can be more delightful than this sort of occupation;
and if I had myself only to consider, I should be perfectly happy.
But I am sorry to say, Caroline is still very delicate, and has .
been so since her marriage. She has the best of husbands, and
has no earthly want but health. We think, however, that she has
gained strength since she has been here, and when the rest of us
return to town, she and Mr. Fletcher will probably go somewhere
to the sea-side, and Harriet with them.

George is a very good boy, and is getting on very well as a
painter. He sold a little picture lately to Mr. Monckton Milnes,
who has taken a good deal of notice of him, asking him to dine,
&c., and he is going in a few days to Bristol, to copy a picture
for an American gentleman.

Robert still lives in Devonshire, and was very well when we
last heard from him. Braddy is married, and has a very nice

little girl. He is working very hard with Mr. Brunel, who seems to appreciate his abilities, which are not small. Such is our history to the present time.

For two years after this, Leslie's pictures adorned the walls of the Royal Academy exhibition-rooms. The trace of declining powers was upon them, but they had still his unfailing grace and sweetness of sentiment. His lees were better than the first runnings of many a more ambitious painter.

1858.

Pictures of the Year.

CHRIST REBUKING HIS DISCIPLES BY CALLING THE LITTLE CHILD.
                                                                    St. Mark ix. 33–35.
A repetition, but larger than the first picture of the same subject, and with alterations. (Painted for Henry Vaughan, Esq.)
LADY IN WHITE HOOD. (A Study for the Queen Caroline in the "Jeanie Deans" picture. Painted for J. Birt, Esq., now in the possession of John Naylor, Esq.)

1859.

Pictures of the Year.

HOTSPUR AND LADY PERCY.
          Lady. — " What is it carries you away? "
          Hotspur. — " Why, my horse, my love, my horse."
                                        First Part of Henry IV., Act ii. Scene 3.
          (Painted for Joseph Miller, Esq., Virginia, U. S.)
(211.) JEANIE DEANS AND QUEEN CAROLINE.
          " Tear followed tear down Jeanie's cheeks, as, her features glowing and quivering with emotion, she pleaded her sister's cause with a pathos which was at once simple and solemn."
                                        Heart of Midlothian, vol. ii. ch. 21.
          (Painted for J. Birt, Esq., now in the collection of John Naylor, Esq.)

THE day after the Academy opened its doors, while the public were still crowding round these two pictures, — one remarking, perhaps, " Leslie is falling off," to which a more thoughtful spectator might have responded, by pointing out the good taste, beauty and sentiment which still reigned through even these less vigorous works — the painter lay dead and cold amid the unutterable grief of the wife who had lived a life of unclouded happiness with him for three and thirty years, and the children who had been so near his heart, and who had loved in him the most thoughtful, self-sacrificing, and tenderest of fathers.

He only survived his much loved daughter Caroline by two months.

His illness was not of long duration. He was first sensible of it during a visit to Petworth, to which he had repaired for change of scene and distraction of mind after the first shock of his daughter's death. He went thence to Worthing, but finding himself worse returned home, when, notwithstanding the utmost attention from his friends, Dr. Williams, Sir Benjamin Brodie, and Mr. Partridge, he gradually sank, and died tranquilly on the 5th of May. The disease was pronounced to be one of the liver. His love of art, his son George informs me, seemed to grow stronger as he approached his end. He expressed to his family his delight at finding his illness did not affect his eye for colour. He had several of his favourite pictures placed so that he could see them from his bed; and his son remarks, he never saw him enjoy anything more keenly than he did some of his friend Mr. Thurston Thompson's photographs from the cartoons of Raffaele.

Leslie had long looked death in the face, and met its approach with the calm faith in God and Christ which is apparent in all I find expressed of his sentiments upon religion. These are not unimportant elements in forming our judgment of a man. I do not know that I can more appropriately close this selection from Leslie's letters, than by the following extracts bearing upon this matter.

(From a letter to his wife.)

" Cadge * and I went this morning to the Foundling. The day is lovely, and the little pets there looked lovely. While sitting in church, a thought passed in my mind which might suggest a sermon, though, I dare say, it has occurred to many others, and may have been used by preachers, though I have not heard

* His daughter Caroline.

it. I thought, what must be the impression on any person of matured mind who, for the first time in his life, should read the sayings of our Saviour. We are accustomed to them from our infancy, and having first heard them read at a time when we are quite incapable of understanding their weight and value, it is hardly possible for us to be impressed by them as those must have been who lived when he lived. His answer, for instance, when the woman taken in adultery was brought before him; when the tribute money was shown to him; when the rich man asked what he should do to go to Heaven; and when the disciples disputed who should be greatest in Heaven. Then the Sermon on the Mount, the Lord's Prayer, the parables, and his last affecting discourse to his disciples. If we could imagine ourselves (for a moment) to be the persons who first heard such things said, how truly should we feel that ' never man spake like this man;' and how well should we understand what the two disciples felt, when they said, ' Did not our hearts burn within us while, he spoke!' But familiarity with these precious sayings from our infancy, prevents their ever making the vivid impression on us, which they must have made when uttered, and therefore I believe it is that God permits different estimates of Christ's character to exist in the world, that our attention may be constantly drawn to it by discussion. For my own part, nothing can alter my conviction, that if ever Divine truth was uttered in this world it was by his lips."

(On a slip of paper attached to his will.)

" I trust I may die as I now am, in the entire belief of the Christian religion, as I understand it from the books of the New Testament, that is, as a direct revelation of the will and goodness of God towards this world, by Jesus Christ, the Saviour and Judge of the world. In full reliance on the special providence of God, I feel sure that whenever, and by whatever means, I die, will be the best for me; and I trust this belief will always make me patient and submissive to the will of God, feeling sure that there is no *real evil but sin*, from which I pray God to deliver all of us now and hereafter."

APPENDIX.

LIST OF THE PRINCIPAL PICTURES PAINTED, AND OF ALL THE PICTURES EXHIBITED BY C. R. LESLIE, R.A.

Those marked * were exhibited at the Royal Academy at the date prefixed.

1812. EARLY PORTRAITS. (See Correspondence.)

1813.* MURDER. — Macbeth; Act 2nd, Scene 1st.

1814.* SAUL AND THE WITCH OF ENDOR.

    * PORTRAIT OF MR. J. H. PAYNE, in the character of Norval.

1815. PORTRAIT OF A LADY. (Miss Maxwell ?)

1816.* DEATH OF RUTLAND; 3rd Part of Henry VI., Act 1st, Scene 3rd.

1817. PORTRAITS OF AMERICAN FRIENDS; painted in Paris. (See Correspondence.)

1818. GIRL WITH A DEAD BIRD.

1819.* PORTRAIT OF A LADY.

    * SIR ROGER DE COVERLEY GOING TO CHURCH; painted for James Dunlop, Esq. Engraved, and in the possession of John Naylor, Esq., Leighton Hall, near Welshpool.

    The same subject repeated for the Marquis of Lansdowne.

1820.* LONDONERS GIPSYING.

    PORTRAIT OF WASHINGTON IRVING.

1821.* MAY DAY IN THE TIME OF QUEEN ELIZABETH. Engraved by Watt.

    FINISHED STUDY OF THE SAME; painted for Alaric Watts.

    REBECCA IN PRISON — IVANHOE; painted for the Marquis of Lansdowne.

    (About this time Mr. Leslie painted portraits of Mrs. Fry and Samuel Gurney, and a picture of a child in a Cardinal's dress.)

1822.* THE RIVALS; painted for Sir Matthew W. Ridley, Bart. Engraved. Small Study of same in the possession of Edwin Bullock, Esq.

1823. (See Correspondence.)

1824.* SANCHO PANZA IN THE APARTMENT OF THE DUCHESS; painted for the Earl of Egremont. Engraved. Repeated for Mr. Vernon. Repeated smaller and purchased by Samuel Rogers, Esq.

A repetition painted for Leslie's sister in America, now in the possession of John Farnworth, Esq.

PORTRAIT OF SIR WALTER SCOTT, repeated and engraved.

1825.* SLENDER, SHALLOW, AND ANNE PAGE; painted for Sir Willoughby Gordon. Engraved.

* SIR HENRY WOTTON PRESENTING THE COUNTESS SABRINA WITH A VALUABLE JEWEL ON THE EVE OF HIS DEPARTURE FROM VENICE; painted and engraved for Major's edition of " Walton's Lives."

* SIX ILLUSTRATIONS TO THE WAVERLEY NOVELS. Engraved.

1826.* DON QUIXOTE IN THE SIERRA MORENA, DECEIVED BY THE CURATE, BARBER, AND DOROTHEA; painted for the Earl of Essex. Engraved. Small Study for the picture in the Sheepshanks' collection.

QUEEN KATHERINE AND HER MAID. Diploma picture.

1827.* LADY JANE GREY PREVAILED ON TO ACCEPT THE CROWN; painted for the Duke of Bedford. Engraved.

* STUDY FOR THE HEAD OF DON QUIXOTE.

* STUDY FOR THE HEAD OF SANCHO PANZA.

1828. " THE BRIDE."

PORTRAIT OF MISS STEPHENS; painted for the Earl of Essex.

LADY IN A DUTCH DRESS, WITH A SCREEN IN HER HAND.

1829.* SIR ROGER DE COVERLEY AND THE GIPSIES. Engraved.

1830. PORTRAITS OF MRS. KING AND LADY BURRELL; painted for the Earl of Egremont.

PORTRAIT OF DOCTOR SIMS.

PORTRAITS OF MR. AND MRS. DILLWYN AND FAMILY; painted for John Dillwyn, Esq., near Swansea.

THE INFANT PRINCES IN THE TOWER; painted for Mr. Rogers; now in the possession of Joseph Gillott, Esq.

1831.* THE DINNER AT MR. PAGE'S HOUSE.

" MERRY WIVES OF WINDSOR." (Repeated in 1838.)

1831.* UNCLE TOBY AND THE WIDOW WADMAN; painted for John Sheepshanks, Esq. Afterwards repeated for Mr. Vernon; also for Mr. Jacob Bell. All three pictures are now in the National Collection at Kensington.

1832.* SCENE FROM THE "TAMING OF THE SHREW;" painted for the Earl of Egremont. Engraved. Repeated for John Sheepshanks, Esq. Now in the National Collection, Kensington.

A small repetition painted for Joseph Birt, Esq.

1833.* TRISTRAM SHANDY RECOVERING THE LOST MANUSCRIPT; in the possession of Thomas Miller, Esq. Repeated for John Gibbons, Esq.

* MOTHER DANCING TO HER CHILD.

* MARTHA AND MARY; painted for James Dunlop, Esq.

1834.

PORTRAIT OF LADY LILFORD; painted for Lord Holland about this time.

1835.* COLUMBUS AND THE EGG; painted for W. Wells, Esq., sold at Lord Northwick's sale, now in the possession of Joseph Gillott, Esq., Edgbaston.

* GULLIVER'S INTRODUCTION TO THE QUEEN OF BROBDINGNAG; painted for the Earl of Egremont.

(THE FAMILY OF THE MARQUIS OF WESTMINSTER; painted for the Marquis of Westminster, about this time.)

1836.* AUTOLYCUS; painted for J. Sheepshanks, Esq., now in the National Collection.

A SMALL PICTURE OF AMY ROBSART; in the National Collection.

LANDSCAPE, EVENING; view from Mr. Leslie's window.

1837.* PERDITA. — Winter's Tale. Painted for John Sheepshanks, Esq. Now in the National Collection.

STUDY in the possession of J. Heugh, Esq.

Repetition of THE INFANT PRINCES IN THE TOWER; in the Sheepshanks' Collection.

* CHARLES THE SECOND AND LADY BELLENDEN. — Old Mortality. Painted for the Earl of Egremont. A small repetition of this picture painted in 1856.

1838.* THE DINNER AT MR. PAGE'S HOUSE. — Merry Wives of Windsor. Painted for John Sheepshanks, Esq. Now in the National Collection.

THE QUEEN RECEIVING THE SACRAMENT AFTER THE CORONATION. — June 28th, 1838; commenced in 1838:

1838.*   exhibited, 1843.   Engraved by S. Cousens, R. A.   Painted
for her Majesty.
PORTRAIT OF MRS. BATES.

1839.*   " WHO CAN THIS BE ? " and

  *   " WHO CAN THIS BE FROM ? "   Painted for John Sheepshanks, Esq.   Now in the National Collection.

  *   SANCHO PANZA.   Painted for J. Sheepshanks, Esq.   In the
National Collection.

  *   DULCINEA.   Painted for J. Sheepshanks, Esq.   In the Na-
tional Collection.
PORTRAIT OF DR. HOWLEY, Archbishop of Canterbury.
Engraved.
SMALL WHOLE-LENGTH PORTRAIT OF THE DUCHESS OF
SUTHERLAND IN THE CORONATION ROBES.
THE MARQUIS OF STAFFORD.   Both belonging to Sir F. G.
Moon.

1840.*   PORTRAIT OF BARON COTTENHAM, LORD HIGH CHANCEL-
LOR.   Painted for William Russell, Esq.   Engraved.
CHILD IN A GARDEN WITH HIS LITTLE HORSE AND CART.
  .   In the National Collection.
GRISELDA.   In the National Collection.

1841.*   SCENE FROM " LE BOURGEOIS GENTILHOMME."   In the
National Collection.
A repetition, painted for Lord Holland.
A repetition, in the possession of Joseph Gillott, Esq.
LUCRETIA.   In the National Collection.
FAIRLOP FAIR.   Painted for the Duke of Norfolk.
THE QUEEN IN THE CORONATION ROBES.   In the National
Collection.

  *   THE LIBRARY AT HOLLAND HOUSE, with Portraits.
Painted for Lord Holland.   Engraved.
THE FIRST LESSON, from a Design by Raffaelle.   Painted
for S. Rogers, Esq., in the possession of Thomas Miller,
Esq., Preston.
There are three repetitions of this picture.

1842.*   SCENE FROM " TWELFTH NIGHT ; "   Act I.   Scene 3.
Painted for Thomas Baring, Esq., M. P.
A repetition of this, painted in 1850, is in the possession of
Edwin Bullock, Esq.

  *   QUEEN KATHERINE AND HER MAID.   Now in the National
Collection.   Repetition of Diploma picture.
Commenced a picture of THE CHRISTENING OF THE PRIN-
CESS ROYAL.   Painted for Her Majesty.

1843.* PORTRAIT OF BENJAMIN TRAVERS, ESQ., F. R. S.

* SCENE FROM THE "VICAR OF WAKEFIELD," Chapter XI. Now in the collection of Thomas Miller, Esq.

* PORTRAIT OF HENRY ANGELO, ESQ.

* "LA MALADE IMAGINAIRE;" Act III. Scene 6. Now in the National Collection.

CHRIST AND HIS DISCIPLES AT CAPERNAUM; Matthew, Chapter XVIII., verse 2. Painted for James Lenox, Esq., of New York.

1844.* SCENE FROM "COMUS;" in the collection of John Naylor, Esq. Afterwards painted in fresco in the Pavilion, in Buckingham Palace Gardens, for Her Majesty.

* SANCHO PANZA IN THE APARTMENT OF THE DUCHESS. Repetition of Petworth picture. Painted for Robert Vernon, Esq. Now in the National Collection.

LADY CARLISLE CARRYING THE PARDON TO THE DUKE OF NORTHUMBERLAND IN THE TOWER. Painted for Lord Leconfield.

PORTRAIT OF MISS BURDETT COUTTS.

1845.* THE HEIRESS. Painted for E. Bicknell, Esq.

* SCENE FROM "LES FEMMES SAVANTES," Act III. Scene 2. Painted for John Sheepshanks, Esq. Now in the National Collection.

GIRL IN A COBLENTZ CAP, WITH LILIES OF THE VALLEY IN HER HAND. Painted for Robert Burton, Esq., New York.

1846.* READING THE WILL.— Roderick Random. Painted for John Gibbons, Esq.

Small Repetition, painted for Thomas Miller, Esq., in 1856.

* MOTHER AND CHILD. Painted for John Gibbons, Esq. Engraved by J. H. Robinson, Esq., R.A.

Repetition, painted for James Lenox, Esq., of New York.

* PORTRAIT OF CHARLES DICKENS, ESQ., in the character of Bobadil. Engraved.

1847.* MARTHA AND MARY. Repetition of the picture of 1833. Painted for James Lenox, Esq., New York.

Repeated for Edwin Bullock, Esq., Handsworth, near Birmingham.

* THE PHARISEE AND THE PUBLICAN. Painted for James Lenox, Esq., New York.

* CHILDREN AT PLAY. Painted for Sir Robert Wigram.

THE LADY, IN "COMUS;" in the possession of John Heugh, Esq.

1847.* THE LOCKET (oval). Painted for Richard Newsham, Esq.
Repetition, in the possession of Thomas Miller, Esq.
PORTRAIT OF CAPT. E. E. MORGAN.

1848.* LADY JANE GREY READING PLATO. In the possession of
Thomas Miller, Esq.

* THE SHELL. Painted for John Gibbons, Esq.

1849.* SCENE FROM HENRY VIII.— Act I. Scene 4. Painted for
Isambard Kingdom Brunel, Esq., F. R. S.

* SCENE FROM DON QUIXOTE :— THE DUKE'S CHAPLAIN
ENRAGED, LEAVING THE TABLE. Painted for Joshua
Bates, Esq.

THE NECKLACE. In the National Collection.

SOPHIA WESTERN. Repeated.

LADY WITH SCARLET GERANIUM IN HER HAND. Painted
for C. Constable, Esq.

CAPT. AND MRS. MORGAN AND CHILDREN. Painted for
Capt. E. E. Morgan, New York.

1850.* BEATRICE IN THE GARDEN. Painted for John Gibbons,
Esq. Repeated.

*. SOPHIA WESTERN AND TOM JONES — Book XVIII. Chap.
XII. In the possession of John Harris, Esq., Princes
Gate.

* SCENE FROM HENRY VIII.; QUEEN KATHERINE.—Act IV.
Scene 2. Painted for I. K. Brunel, Esq.
Repeated smaller ; in the possession of John Naylor, Esq.

ROBINSON CRUSOE READING THE BIBLE ; in the possession
of James Dugdale, Esq. Engraved.

1851.* A STUDY.

* FALSTAFF PERSONATING THE KING. — 1st Part of Henry
IV. Act II. Scene 4. Painted for John Harris, Esq.,
Princes Gate.

A GROUP OF THE DUKE OF NORTHUMBERLAND'S TEN-
ANTS. Painted for the Duke of Northumberland, at Stanwick.

1852.* JULIET. Repeated twice ; one painted for Richard Newsham,
Esq.

GIRL HOLDING A DOVE. In the collection of Thomas
Miller, Esq.

GIRL READING. In the possession of Edwin Bullock, Esq.,
Handsworth, near Birmingham. Repeated.

1853. SLENDER, WITH THE ASSISTANCE OF SHALLOW, COURTING
ANNE PAGE. Repeated smaller ; in the possession of
Thomas Miller, Esq.

1854.* A PRESENT; painted for W. C. Sole, Esq. Repetition.

* PORTRAIT OF MRS. W. C. SOLE.

PORTRAIT OF JOHN EVERETT MILLAIS, ESQ., A. R. A.

* SCENE FROM THE RAPE OF THE LOCK; painted for John Gibbons, Esq.

1854. VIEW ON THE THAMES AT HAMPTON.

1855.* SANCHO PANZA AND DON PEDRO REZIO; Don Quixote, Part II., chap. 47; painted for Lady Chantrey.

OLIVIA; Twelfth Night. Repeated.

PORTRAIT OF THE LATE DUKE OF WELLINGTON, LOOKING AT A BUST OF WASHINGTON; painted for Miss Burdett Coutts.

Repetition; painted for the Hon. Abbott Lawrence, of Boston, U. S.

THE LATE DUKE AND PRESENT DUCHESS OF WELLINGTON, ON THE STAIRCASE OF BUCKINGHAM PALACE; painted for Miss Burdett Coutts.

1856.* HERMIONE; Winter's Tale; painted for I. K. Brunel. Repeated.

A Repetition, with alterations, of the Scene from the Rape of the Lock; painted for Edwin Bullock, Esq.

THE OPERA BOX; painted for Edwin Bullock, Esq.

1857.* SIR ROGER DE COVERLEY IN CHURCH; Spectator, No. 112; painted for Thomas Miller, Esq., Preston.

1858.* CHRIST AND HIS DISCIPLES AT CAPERNAUM; Matt. xviii. 2. Larger than the first picture of the same subject, and with alterations; painted for Henry Vaughan, Esq.

STUDY FOR QUEEN CAROLINE; painted for Joseph Birt, Esq.; in the possession of John Naylor, Esq.

1859.* JEANIE DEANS' INTERVIEW WITH QUEEN CAROLINE; painted for Jacob Birt, Esq.; in the possession of John Naylor, Esq.

* HOTSPUR AND LADY PERCY; painted for Joseph Miller, Esq., Virginia, U. S.

(*Of uncertain date.*)

LITTLE GIRL, WITH HER DOLL, AND A TAZZA OF FLOWERS; in the collection of Joseph Gillott, Esq.

GREEK MAIDEN HOLDING A LYRE (Moonlight). Engraved by Finden. In the collection of E. Bicknell, Esq.

THE END.